TOUCHED BY THE DEVIL

BOYS OF PRESTON PREP

ANGEL LAWSON

SAMANTHA RUE

To all the angst-bois and bad ass bitches that inspired us to write this book.
Never stop.

PROLOGUE

Sebastian

There's something ironic about how the uber-wealthy go to tiny, back wood, hick towns for vacation. God forbid we go to one of the five-star resorts that line pristine beaches, or the comforts of a modernized summer home in the mountains. Nope, every year the Wilcox family makes the trek to the little town of Briar Cliffs to stay in our hundred-year-old, musty cabin, overlooking the river that my father has been coming to since he was born, and *his* father came to since he was born. Apparently, it's family tradition to bore the hell out of the Wilcox men, which is just a dangerous fucking move.

It makes us restless, and if history has proven anything, it's that there's nothing worse than a restless Wilcox.

Makes no damn sense. Even my dad hates it; he holes up in the makeshift office, drowning himself in work. When Mom actually decides to get sober enough to leave the house, it's only to spend time with the other summer wives, who she doesn't even like. Gossiping and trying to show each other up isn't her scene. Being locked in the cabin with my absent father isn't her scene, either. I pace around like a lion in a cage, trying to find something to do with my hands, going crazy with the ripple of unspent energy sparking beneath my skin. And Heston. Well, Heston is the worst of all. Putting him in any contained area with me and our mom is a recipe for disaster. This has never been a quality family bonding experience, is what I'm saying.

It's my sense of restless, energy-rippling boredom that ejects me from the cabin one summer night on the hunt for weed, pussy, and maybe a fight. Three things a determined seventeen-year-old can find pretty easily, even here.

"Yo, Wilcox."

I look up and see my friends Reid and Mitchell walking down the cracked sidewalk. I jerk a nod in greeting. "Thing One, Thing Two. What's going on?"

"In the Briar Cliffs?" Reid asks, bumping his fist with mine. "Jack and shit."

"Except," Mitchell says quickly, "we heard there's a party down at the dock. Wanna come?"

"Let me check my schedule," I joke, pulling out my phone, which predictably has no service. I've had shit-all to do for weeks now but work on my tan and try to charm the pants off a few girls. "Yep, looks like I'm free."

We head off, passing the antique shops and pharmacy, taking the turn to the dirt road that heads down to the water. I know this place like the back of my hand, every nook and cranny. The steep cliffs overlooking the river. The seedy liquor stores. The mom and pop shops. The suburbs ten minutes north of here. Parents feel secure in letting their kids roam free around the Briar Cliffs from a young age—the wisdom being that there's not much trouble to get into, and whatever trouble we do find, they'd done it all before.

Reid reaches inside his jacket and pulls out a silver flask. It's pretentious and a little douchey, but when offered, I take a swig. The liquid burns like fire down the back of my throat, then warms my belly. I hand the flask back over and ask, "Is this a townie party or summer people?"

There's a distinct difference between the two. Summer people, like myself, have the kind of parties you write home about. Great booze, big boats, and freaky bitches dying to be the center of some rich boy's attention. Townie parties, though. Those are thrown hastily together on a wish and a prayer. The booze is cheap swill, the boats aren't safe for occupancy, and the girls...

The girls are dicey as fuck.

Not always a bug, sometimes a feature.

"Probably a mix," Mitchell says, taking a drink and then wiping his mouth with the back of his hand. "I got a text from Karen telling me to come."

Karen is a local girl who works down at the marina. She's a sexy ginger that Mitchell had the pleasure of hooking up with last weekend on one of the docked boats. I spent last weekend bareknuckling it with some douche from Rockport and won two-hundred bucks, a loose molar, and a bag of weed. For the Briar Cliffs, that's a pretty great night.

We reach the top of a rise, and down below is the public dock. During the day, little kids jump and dive off the end, and families picnic on the beach. At night, it's an infestation of older kids and a few college students. This is the place to be if you're looking for some trouble. I head down the hill toward the crowd that's already gathering.

"Hey, Bass," a girl calls out. I look over and see Madison, a girl who's spent summers here almost as long as I have. Mostly I see her tits pressed tight against the fabric of her tube top.

"Hey, Mads, how are you?"

She walks over, gait a little wobbly. She's already drunk. "Fine, fine, fuckin' peachy."

I slide my arm around her waist, peering down her top. "You sure look fine."

"So do you." Her hand presses against my abs, feeling the muscle. Madison has never been shy, but we've only hooked up once. "I've been wondering something..."

"Yeah?" I lick my lips, thinking I might be ready to raise that number to two. "What's that?"

"Where has your brother been this summer?"

And scene.

I drop my arm but try to keep the easy expression on my face. "Heston didn't come down with the family," I say, trying not to grit my teeth over his name. "Busy getting ready for college."

"Oh," she pouts, "too bad."

"Yeah." I reach out to Reid and swipe the flask from his hands, taking another too-long swig. "Too, fucking, bad."

It should make it better, not having him here. Not having to listen to the way he talks to our mom. Not needing to jump in and push back against the way he spits at and ridicules her. Not spending weeks on end, tense and mindlessly pissed off, wishing him away.

Instead, I just keep feeling all the spaces he *should* be. I keep coiling for fights that never come, bracing for snide remarks and hateful glares, always ready but never spent. It's like the fighter's equivalent of blue balls.

"Hey!" he complains, rightfully.

I swallow it down and shove it back at him. "Sorry." I reach into my back pocket and pull out a small bag of weed, tossing it to him. "Take it."

He nods appreciatively. "Come on, let's light up."

But I've already started skimming the crowd, looking for something, someone, a *reason* to blow off a little steam. It doesn't take long when I spot a few kids that I'd beefed with a week ago over a parking spot following my last fight. They'd parked too close to my car—my sweet Jasmine—and these motherfuckers showed her no respect. Downright rude, really.

The biggest guy leans against the boat house, cat-calling a group of clearly uninterested girls nearby. They all shift uncomfortably when he says, "Come on, sweet thing! Don't be like that."

My hackles rise in a familiar way, shoulders going tight, face smoothing out.

"Meet you in a few," I say to Reid, and start toward the dock. I sweep past the huddle of girls—townies, I gather, from the accents and clothes. Back home, I'm used to conservative uniforms at school and trendy outfits at parties. But these girls have an edgy grittiness that Preston Prep girls can't buy. Frayed cut-off shorts.

Worn boots. Stony expressions. I make eye contact with a pair of hard, hazel eyes and dart my gaze down to her lips. They're pressed in a tight line. Whatever she sees in me, she's not impressed.

Well, sweetheart, I think, *justwait until I'm done with these fuckwits.*

"Sugar," the big guy pushes off the wall, leering at her, "you know, you'd be a lot prettier if you smiled every once in a while."

Hazel eyes scowls and cuts her eyes at him, jaw setting. She's wearing a loose flannel shirt, which should be universal code for unsexy. Unfortunately, it just makes us really wonder what's hiding underneath. Which is exactly what's got this dumbass up her grill.

She bites back, "You'd be a lot prettier if you fucked off and died, Derek," and the other guys all laugh.

Derek presses a hand to his chest, feigning hurt. "Come on, Sug, I bet I could make you smile for once." He moves closer and the group of girls parts like the Red Sea, giving him berth. The only one still holding her ground is the girl he's harassing. She's tiny, yet her stature implies she's tough as nails. Long black hair hangs over her shoulder, the tips dyed blue. "We've fought this thing between us for too long. Stop playing frigid princess and let me warm you up."

"Sure, I can probably find some lighter fluid," she says, all faux-casually, looking around. "Setting you on fire could get me down-right toasty."

I snort, but he takes a step forward, and something wavers in her eye. A flicker of fear. A hard swallow bobbing her throat. I dart between them and look up at the stupid oaf.

"Looks like this girl isn't interested in what you're selling, *Derek*," I say, looking behind me to shoot her a grin. I get nothing back but hard glare. *Okay, then.* "Why don't you move along."

The oaf laughs. He's got a couple of inches on me, and he's big, but it's not the lean mass that I have. I'm fast. Quick. And I already feel the building hum of anticipation in my knuckles, ready to slam into something hard and meaty. Beating his ass would be a plea-sure. "Why don't *you* move along, pretty boy. This isn't about you."

I grin. "First, thanks for the compliment. I really am pretty.

Second, I've seen how you treat other people's things, and it's not great, Derek, it's not great." He tilts his head, assessing me for a minute, like he's trying to place me. "Third—and not to sound egotistical or anything—but *everything* is about me."

Derek narrows his eyes at me and a twisted grin tugs at the corners of his mouth. A moment later he lifts his two meaty paws and shoves them at my chest, pushing me back. The girl I'm defending skirts out of my way, but I keep my eyes on this asshole. He hardly moved me, but he's just given me the opening I need to justify ruining him.

"Thanks," I say, grinning. "This was getting boring." I jerk my elbow back and slam my fist right into his jaw. I barely feel the pain in my knuckles, just the momentum of my arm propelling them forward. I follow through on the punch and then slam a second fist right into his gut. He growls like a beast and swings, but I jump back fast enough that he misses. He tries to barrel into me next, hoping to take me down to the ground, but it's easy to step out of his path and bury a fist into his kidney.

"Oh, so close!" I taunt, seeing some of his boys gathering in my periphery. Fucking classic. Can't take someone one-on-one, just keep adding dudes to the pile. Fine by me. "Everyone can get a turn," I assure them, swiping one of Derek's flying fists.

"Stop!" a girl cries from the growing crowd. "Stop fighting!"

I play for a second like I'm deeply considering it. "Nah. Not until this piece of shit learns a little respect." But Derek's had time to recover. He doesn't lunge at me, taking in my stance—fists up, legs loose and quick. Instead, he shakes out his shoulders and braces himself, mirroring me. The sight of it pulls a laugh from me, high-pitched and crazed. "Now we're talkin'."

No more of this clumsy rage-driven shit. It's too easy.

His fist flies forward, but I duck it. I'm not counting on his left fist following it, but it's a messy, badly-coordinated punch. This guy is no south paw. His knuckles barely graze my cheek. Even though he's not here, I can hear my brother's voice in my head, vicious and taunting.

You're such a little bitch, Bass. Look at you, gonna get your ass beat by this loser? Typical. Can't even handle a drunk townie. Fuck, you're embarrassing. This is the only thing you're good at, and you can't even win.

It makes my focus narrow tightly in on him, filling my head with a violent red and something so chaotic that I can't pin it down long enough to understand it. I just know it makes me want to pound this fucker's face in.

I reach back and slam my fist forward, getting in a solid hook that rocks Derek backward. I don't stop. I plan to keep burying my fist into his face until it's bloody and limp. A flash of movement comes from the side, and I know one of his boys is coming to help him. I react on pure instinct, jerking back and slamming a tight fist into the face coming at me.

The sound is almost sickening—the sharp crack, the loud gasp, the soft sound of a small body hitting the ground.

It takes me so long to realize that it's *not* one of Derek's boys that I'm already turned back to the oaf, fist raised. But I freeze, doing a bewildered double-take.

Because that was not a hard jaw.

That was not a man.

The body on the ground has long dark hair, with blue tips. A girl, the girl I've been *defending.*

My fist drops to my side.

"Fuck," I say, and the crowd shifts, her friends shuffling forward with palms covering their mouths, watching her lifeless body.

I had to have killed her or something. She's not moving, and I don't punch like a little bitch. I follow through. That had been a hard hit—a devastating hit—to someone smaller than me. To someone who's not used to it. To someone with soft skin and a delicate neck. I move forward in horror, looking down at her limp body, but notice instantly that her eyes are open. Unfocused. Squinting, like she's confused.

"Hey," I try, bending down to touch her arm. "I'm sorr—"

Her hazel eyes finally go into focus, landing on mine. She opens her mouth, dragging in a big inhale, and releases it in a bone-chilling scream.

I jerk back first, and then everyone else does. The scream—it doesn't stop. It keeps building and climbing, but it doesn't die. Even when she drags in another breath, it's just to feed that blood-curdling shriek pouring from the pit of her chest.

I look around nervously, but the crowd is frantically dispersing. This is too loud, too much attention. The cops will come. People will ask questions. We'll all be fucked.

Thick with terror and a pain that goes far beyond the punch I'd landed. I stare at her for another for a moment, and then I do the only thing a Wilcox can in a situation like this.

I run.

1

"Nice ink." Dr. McCord glances at my chest. I'm not sure which one she's talking about. The collar I've been working on for the last year, or the Devil's mark that I got two months ago. Either way, I know she's checking out my chest, and I fight the urge to puff up and pull out a pick-up line. I mean, who isn't into older, sexy, smart women?

But I'm guessing trying to bang your cougar of a doctor is probably not the best display of good decision-making skills—something I've been trying to build.

Well.

Halfheartedly, anyway.

"Thanks," I reply, trying to sound aloof. I glance around the room, my eyes landing on the fake ficus in the corner. Although it's the third of January, it's still decorated cheerily for Christmas, little shiny bulbs hanging from the thin branches.

"How was the end of first semester?" she asks. "Everything go okay?"

Well, Doc, let's see. I joined a secret society, got a tattoo, committed no less than five crimes, received and gave oral in the Stairway to Hell, pulled an epic prank on my school, got in a few fights, burned my brother, got burned by my brother, made a few new friends, and oh right, recovered from this concussion. My second one in six months. Hence, the visit.

"Pretty okay," I reply blandly. "Chill."

She pulls out her little light and flashes it in my eyes. "How have the headaches been?"

"Better, I guess." I shift on the table, making the paper sheet crinkle. "Nothing I can't handle."

She gives me a stern glance over her glasses. "You have had a series of concussions, Sebastian. It's not about what you can handle. It's about making sure that your condition is improving."

"I'm improving," I say, just wanting her off my back.

"How?"

She wants details. "No more dizziness, no puking. My light sensitivity is..." Shit. Total shit. "...a lot better. I've stopped fi— playing lacrosse and altered my conditioning." I peek up at her to make sure she didn't catch the slip. I haven't been in a fight or played lacrosse in two months. She just doesn't strictly know about the fights.

"How's your vision?" She's taking notes on a sheet of paper. I lean forward, curious, but she shifts away.

"Twenty-twenty." I flash her my best panty-melting grin.

Ah, she's a tough one. She barely reacts. "Uh huh. Any school issues? Memory loss? Irritability?"

Memory loss? I fucking wish. That'd make my life easier. But even with a head injury, I'm not lucky enough to have the one symptom that'd actually help.

"Doc." I level her with a look. "I'm fine. Seriously. I'm following all the rules. I've never felt better, because I'm in peak physical condition." I drag my lip through my teeth, eyes roaming down her tight doctor body. "If you don't believe me, you can check me over again."

She gives me another look, this one full of disbelief, but puts the pen and paper away. Crossing her arms, she says, "Although I'm not sure I'm buying that you've completely slowed down, I do think you're recovering nicely."

My eyebrows lift. "Does that mean I have the go-ahead on lacrosse?"

A line forms between her eyes and matches the one set between her lips. "I think you need to take it easy for one more month—"

"Another month!" I start.

"—*then* we'll test again, and if everything looks nice and healed, I'll release you to the team." I make no attempt to hide my annoyance and she continues, "I know you don't realize it, Sebastian, but your brain health is very important. Even though you don't care about bashing your head in all the time, the rest of us want to make sure you have a happy, healthy, productive life."

I wonder who's included in the 'us' she's talking about here. My dad? Eh. My mom? Yeah, she'd probably care if she could, but she can't. Heston? I choke back a laugh. He's the reason I'm in this situation in the first place. The truth is, the only people who truly give a shit are the woman standing in front of me right now, and a handful of Devils.

"Thanks for the vote of encouragement, Doc," I say, reaching for my shirt. "I'll give it one more month." Despite being a huge fucking bummer, this isn't technically a huge problem. I've been working more and more down at the garage on Jasmine anyway, and the Devils take up some of my time. As long as I get back on the field by the first of February, it'll be fine.

It has to be fine.

≈

"How's she doing today?" I ask, casting a wary glance at the ceiling, toward Mom's room on the second floor. I can't hear anything, which is always a good sign.

Liesel, our head of housekeeping, follows my gaze. "Well, your brother was here earlier."

I shift my shoulders, popping the joint. "Fuck."

"It wasn't as bad as all that," she assures me in her thick accent.

"He didn't even go up to see her. Lucky. Nasty piece of work, he is. Always picking on the poor woman." Liesel shakes her head disapprovingly. She's in her fifties now, but still has the same stern face I remember when I was kid. She's the complete opposite of my mom. Liesel's got pure steel running through her veins. She comes to work every day in sharp, structured blazers, and doesn't stick around long enough to know just how far beyond 'picking' Heston likes to take things.

I mutter, "Tell me about it."

"It might help if you stuck around this year," she tells me, yet again, shaking a finger in my face. "Mothers need their children."

I can hardly contain my laugh. "Yeah, sure." Maybe Mom needs *me*, but Heston? What a riot. "Can't, though. I'm going back today."

Liesel throws her hands in the air, muttering something sharply German under her breath as she walks away.

If she knew the deal, she'd probably understand. I don't live at Preston because I want to. I live there because it's the only way I can give my mom some measure of peace.

You'd think our property—a converted golf club of eight total buildings—would be sprawling enough to keep Heston and her from ever needing to be in the same room. He could take the pool house. He could have lived in the cottage at the back of property and had himself a grand old fucking time. He could have even probably scored the entire length of the main house's basement, which has two kitchens, four bathrooms, a pool, and enough space to comfortably entertain both the swim and football teams.

But no, not Heston. His top priority when it comes to accommodations is having someone close enough to torment. I almost feel bad for the people he's going to college with—a new, exciting spread of victims for him to play with. Almost. I'm currently too engaged with worrying about his current victims to give it much thought.

My mom's rooms are separate from my dad's, and for as long as I was old enough to notice, always have been. It's a sweet setup consisting of its own living space, but I can't stand the way she holes up in there.

When I climb the massive staircase and walk my way to the heavy double doors, I take a moment to prepare myself.

She's not dressed, but that's no surprise. The blinds are still closed and it's smoky, the stale scent of cigarettes hanging thick in the air. She's sitting in the chaise in her silk robe, trying to gather her hair up. Putting herself together. Trying to make it seem not so bad.

"Sebastian!" Her attempt at a smile is watery, ruined by the tracks running down her cheeks. "I was hoping you'd come see me before you left. It is today, isn't it?"

"Yeah," I say, pathetically touched that she managed to keep track of time. "I'm about to head out."

She covertly wipes her cheeks, trying another bright smile. It hurts to watch, these moments where she tries to pull herself together like a brave little toaster. "I'm glad, because I—I got you something. It's here, see? Open it, see?"

I gingerly hold the envelope she thrusts in my hand, but can't focus on anything but her wet eyes. "Mom, why are you crying?"

She flaps a hand. "Oh, you know how I get. It's not important." She pushes at the envelope, imploring, "Open it!"

"It *is* important," I argue, but know better than to push by now. She probably spends half of her life crying. Depressive episodes like hers don't come with a *reason*. That doesn't mean I'll stop asking.

Sighing, I tear open the envelope, revealing a gift card to the local pet supply store. I know instantly why, and it's more of a gesture than anything. I probably have enough money in my bank account to buy the pet supply store—like, the entire business.

She meets my smile with her own—this one a touch more organic. "You be sure to feed those poor little kitties, now. Make sure they're getting enough. Don't skimp!"

"I won't," I promise, leaning down to kiss her cheek. "The cats are going to be just fine."

"And send me some pictures!" she demands, eyes going bright at her own suggestion.

My mother frets like no other. The second I made an offhanded comment about the feral cat colony at school, she was fretting. She probably never stopped. That's the thing about my mom. She can't take care of anything—can barely take care of herself—but goddamn. She tries so fucking hard. A ceaseless thread throughout my life is the question of how someone with so big a heart managed to create a complete fucking sociopath like Heston. Sometimes I think he just left his soul with her, doubled it up, made it too big to handle all these harsh things in life. Sometimes I blame him for it—her sickness—and I know it's not fair.

He only deserves the blame for making it worse.

It hurts to leave her, but in a way, it's also a relief. This is the deal. If I live at school, Heston will leave her alone. He won't talk to her. He won't even look at her. He won't poison her thoughts with his toxic tongue, driving her deeper and deeper into the darkness.

As I pull out the drive, I just remember her brave little toaster smile and tell myself it's better this way.

⁓

I UNLOAD Jasmine and carry my bags back to the dorm, and it's not so bad. A stark contrast to the rest of my family, I've never been a huge fan of manors and mansions and estates, anyway.

That being said, I did manage to upgrade rooms to a single— Hamilton Bates's old suite—which allows me some extra amenities, like a separate living area.

"Hey, man," Carlton says, sticking his head in the open door. "How was the doctor?"

Fucking Devils and their phone tree. How sad is it that a secret band of eleven fuck-ups, criminals, and sad sacks are a better family to me than my own flesh and blood?

Very.

"Fine. I didn't get the all clear yet, but I should before the season starts."

He nods, seeming satisfied with this. And then he looks around. "Christ, dude. This place is looking rough."

"What?" I turn to the room, scratching idly at my jaw. "Nah, it's not rough. It's just—"

"Messy," he finishes. "Yet somehow also weirdly empty. How do you even do that?"

I flip him off. "It's a bachelor pad. Don't be jealous you're still sharing a double with Ben."

"You need a couch. And a rug. And possibly an industrial-strength vacuum cleaner. How the fuck does the resident let you keep it like this? I get chewed out for a messy closet."

I flash him a grin. "Money, power, influence—"

"The fact that he's super gay and you have *that* face."

I shrug, not bothering to deny it. I'm cute as fuck, so sue me. But Carlton does have a point. There are empty pizza boxes on the floor —no table yet—and socks strewn everywhere. It doesn't look like someone lives here, so much as someone's been... *squatting*. I rub the back of my neck, looking over the room. "I guess I'm not really here much."

I don't need to say why.

Liesel used to say that my mom has the downs, but I have the ups.

It feels like I can't stay still. Being down this long because of the concussion has been a first. I don't have anything to ease this elec-tric, turbulent thing flowing through my veins. The second I step through this threshold, I get the itch to leave, find something to do. I'm not the kind of person who sits in his room, fucking around. I go out, I fuck, I fight, I find something to get into. These days, that list keeps growing shorter and shorter.

Carlton must sense this, because he suddenly says, "So there's this meet-up tonight. Under the Peach Street bridge. Midnight."

I perk instantly at this, my frustration melting away. "Oh yeah? You taking the 'Vette?" I'd helped Carlton find this sweet '68 Corvette that needed a lot of work but is on its way to glory.

"I probably won't race it, not until I upgrade the engine, but I'm going to show it." He leans against the door. "You should bring the Shelby."

Jasmine. My Ford Shelby. God, she's the most beautiful thing in my life. I do like showing off my girl. "Yeah, okay. We'll have to get around Buster." The ancient campus security guard is notorious for being slow and tired but can still put a wrench in any good plan. "How about we just meet down there."

"Good idea." He holds up a fist for me to bump before wandering off down the hall.

Carlton's the one who got me into the car meet-ups. They're a mixture of street racing, burnouts, and car show. He found out about them through his side hustle—selling weed and pills—because it's a good place to push product. He invited me down because I was idle. Bored. Angry. Fucking *painfully* restless. Unable to fight due to the last concussion, I had to pull back on my workouts, and other than a few hook-ups here and there, I've had fuck-all going on.

The meet-ups are pretty last minute, passed through word of mouth around the community. Carlton's usually the first to know, since everyone wants him there with his merchandise. It's not at all unlike fighting. The whole set up is illegal and a complete, sloppy rush. Once the crowd converges, the roads are blocked, and mayhem explodes. It's a massive adrenaline rush, and it's not the same. It's not physical enough to even come close to the fighting. But sometimes, when my hands are on the wheel and the smell of rubber burns my lungs, I can almost feel this dark, angry thing burning itself out of me.

But the best part, by far, is that my brother has no fucking clue this world even exists. It's the one thing in my life he hasn't tainted yet.

If I have anything to do with it, he never will.

2

"ARE you sure you have everything packed?"

I lug the suitcase down the front steps and try to hide the impatient, antsy thing crawling under my skin. It keeps screaming *'go, go, go'*. It's a miracle I don't just fucking evaporate from the force of it. "I don't need much," I say to my mom, trying to paint my impatience as upbeat optimism. "We wear uniforms every day."

The house behind us looks as cluttered and toppling as I always feel. I won't miss it. 'Safe as houses' people always say. Those people have obviously never seen this shit shack. It's squat and old. Drafty. All at once too loud and too quiet. Sometimes it feels like the faintest wind could knock it down, reduce it to rubble. I've spent the last eight years bracing for it, bones aching, muscles protesting, just wishing for one moment where I can finally relax.

The truth is that I want to bring as little as I can from this place. It's a ridiculous fear, this worry that the hostility and constant, pressing unease might infect wherever it is I'm going, like an offensive smell. But I want to start Preston Prep fresh, with as little baggage—literal and figurative—as possible. I'd applied for the scholarship on a whim, thinking there was no chance I'd get it this late in the year. Even my own family thought trying was foolish. Why would a small-town girl like Sugar Voss want to go to a snobby, rich-kid school like Preston?

To get away from *him*.

The screen door opens with an abrasive whine, ominously heavy footsteps following in its wake. I ignore it—*him*—and walk toward my car to open the passenger door. The springs creak even worse than the screened door, and a piece of rusted paint comes off in my hand. But it's drivable, and it's the only thing left in this house owned by my father. Aside from my camera, it's the only thing from this place I'm determined to take with me.

"Time to leave already?" he asks, voice deceptively casual. "Figured you'd back out, you're such a chicken-shit."

"Now, Doug," my mom says, her tone exasperated. "Sugar's going to be just fine. She had perfect scores on her entrance exam, and she wants to go." In a lower voice, she pleads, "Please don't. Not today."

I can almost hear the impatience in her own voice, too. It'll be easier for her when I leave. She won't have to put up anymore token protests. She won't have to deal with my burns or cuts or bruises. She'll be able to care about me from a distance, where I won't cause trouble between them. It'll be a nice life for her. Doug doesn't treat her the way he treats me.

I push back the seat and reach for my bag, shoving it through the small gap. Even though I can't see him, I can feel him, *sense* him. Always have. It's not the house that makes this place unbearable. It's *this*. The persistent wait. The knowledge that it's coming and there's nothing I can do to stop it. Not that I haven't tried. There was a time I put in an effort—struggled to tiptoe around, make myself small and convenient and whatever version of well-behaved was 'in' that week. I used to think I had some control.

I used to be an idiot.

My stomach balls tight. I fight against the seat and suitcase, flustered by the sound of his footsteps getting closer.

I feel his breath on my neck.

My skin crawls. *Crawls.* Every instinct in my body surges toward flight, but I know better than that now, learned long ago that it's worse when I run from it. His breath washes across the skin of my neck like hot acid. "Here," he says, voice deceptively even, "let me do that."

I hope you fucking die. "I've got it."

"Do you?" He takes the suitcase from me and slides it in the space. Because I knew it was coming—it always does—I'm already rigid and cringing when his hand clamps around the base of my neck, digging in hard. From the outside, it probably looks normal. But his hand squeezes, and if it were on the other side of my neck, he'd be strangling me. It *hurts.* But worse than the hurt is the way being touched makes me feel. I gnash my teeth to bite back my scream, body thrumming with something uncontrollable.

It didn't used to be like this. Before this summer, Doug used to have to put in the effort of hitting me to get this kind of reaction. Oh, and he was good at it, too. The more tolerance I built to his blows, the worse it got. He ramped it up so well.

Now—after what happened that night on the docks—this is all it takes.

One. Fucking. Touch.

I should run. Fight. Twist away. But he knows I won't, and so do I. Because it's taking everything in me to just breathe. I can't contain my shudder when he hisses in my ear, "I know you're running away because you think you're better than us, but you'll be back. Crawling on your hands and knees after how those rich brats will treat you. You're nothing, you hear me? You're trash. No one wants you."

He finishes by giving me a teeth-rattling shake. Tears spring to my eyes and my jaw clamps shut, but I keep quiet and still. Even though my neck is screaming in protest, this is nothing. He's done worse. So much worse. I've spent the last eight years wishing Doug away and it never happened. Not once. Catching my breath, I jerk back, elbowing him hard in the ribs.

"You little fucking bitch," he spits, but it gives me room to slide in the front seat and slam the door. Taking one last look at my mother, I crank the engine and peel out of the driveway as fast as I can. The tires squeal, and I stop caring about how it looks to the neighbors.

The smaller he grows in my rearview mirror, the more it feels like a layer of my skin is left behind with him. I draw in a breath and release it in a scream that no one can hear, hands clutched tight around my steering wheel. This scream isn't the like the other ones. There's no fear here. There's no pain. This scream is pure fucking promise.

It's the last time—I say it in my head like a prayer—the *last* time my step-father will ever hurt me. For the first time in years, this scream ends in a grin. I don't need to look in the mirror to know it's maniacal and slightly crazed-looking.

Preston Prep may be the home of the devils, but I'm not scared.

I've already survived hell.

MOST OF THE drive is a slow unwinding. I feel freer than I have since before my dad died, like I can do anything, go anywhere, be whoever I want. It'd be naïve to call it happiness, but I feel optimistic enough to call it relief.

As if the fates are trying to take me up on the challenge, the Mustang sputters and wheezes a slow, painful death, three miles from campus.

So close, but so far.

Shit, shit, shit!

I manage to get my car pulled into the parking lot of a small diner and sit there for a moment, thinking. Unwilling to let this ruin my good day, I go through my usual series of troubleshooting steps. Pumping the gas. Letting it rest. Putting it into neutral. But all attempts at getting it back running are ultimately futile.

"Seriously?" I growl at the goddess who's probably listening and laughing at me right now. "You couldn't give me one fucking break?"

Thunking my forehead on the steering wheel, I sigh and look

out the driver's side window. Past the diner is another parking lot. Up by the road are stacks of tires. A garage. Halle-fucking-lujah.

~

"So, uh... thanks for picking me up." I tuck my limbs in close, fingers laced together in my lap. "Kind of a shitty way to meet, but obviously I don't know anyone else at Preston, and since you'd given me your number when we were assigned as roommates—"

"Hey, don't sweat it," Georgia says, tucking a piece of long red hair behind her ear. "I've been sitting around all day, bored out of my mind, waiting for everyone to get back. It was good to have something to do."

She pulled up in a light blue convertible. It's January, so the top is up. The smell of leather is still strong, making me think the car is pretty new. Of course, every car seems new compared to my big rusted pile of metal and sorrow. I knew the kids at Preston Prep had money, but when Georgia drives under the archway leading to the academy, I'm pretty sure that the Mustang breaking down may have been more of a blessing than a curse. It would have stuck out like a sore thumb in this place.

"Have you... been at Preston long?" I ask in a feeble attempt at small-talk. This girl and I have fuck-all in common. She looks sweet and put-together. Normal. Easy. Her clothes are nice and feminine, and she's wearing jewelry—delicate golden necklace, silver hoop earrings. Her fingernails are painted pink. Back home in The Cliffs, we make fun of girls like her.

I'm wearing some ratty jeans and an old band tee, hidden beneath a denim jacket that people around here would probably refer to as 'vintage chic'. I just refer to it as 'the only jacket my mom had in the back of her closet'. The only thing close to jewelry I own are the pair of dog tags hanging around my neck. My nails are chipped and bitten down, cuticles rough. Here at Preston, girls like her probably make fun of girls like me.

"Since middle school," she says. "Before that, I was at the primary school, which isn't technically the same school but it's not much different. Uh, a few years ago I spent a semester abroad, too. But, basically, I've been in this same circle of hell my whole damn life."

She screeches into a parking spot between a BMW and a Tesla and pops the trunk. I get out and walk around to the back of the car, grabbing my suitcase. I'm pulling out the handle when I notice a shiny, royal blue muscle car across the lot. It's a Ford, way nicer than mine, and I can't help but think I've seen it before. "Is that a play on the whole Devil thing, or is this place really a hellhole?"

She laughs and points me toward a brick walkway. "A little of both, I guess. I don't hate it here, but I've got a better group of friends now. For a while there, things were rocky."

I give her a look out of the corner of my eye, doubtful. Nothing about the way Georgia holds herself signals a lack of confidence. If anything, she looks like she belongs here. Even the other few students milling around barely spare her a glance.

Me, on the other hand...

"You're going to want to cover that up tomorrow," Georgia says, pointing to my wrist. "Visible tats are against Preston's code of dress. Totally lame."

I look down at the tattoo on my wrist. It's just a small thing—something I'd gotten to honor my dad. Two raven wings and a date. It'd been last year, back when the thought of being touched was distasteful, but not quite this fucking horrible, heart-stopping thing it's become. A part of me always feared this would happen—that the skin-crawling whirr of anxiety that came from being touched would someday graduate to a Full-Blown Issue.

Well.

Here it fucking is.

I'd done a lot stupider things than the tattoo back then, but none as permanent. I don't regret it, but the dark ink on my wrist serves as more than one reminder.

Firstly, there's no one left to protect me. No one is going to stand between me and the Dougs of this world. I'm all I've got, so I better be real fucking good at it.

Secondly, there's no making this *thing*—the way I feel when people touch me—any better. I tried. I did the work, I played at being normal, and it just got made worse. It's easier now, just accepting it for what it is, seeing it as a part of me, as much as the color of my hair or the freckle on my collarbone. Everyone has problems. We're supposed to be able to cope with them, but sometimes we just can't. Sometimes we have to learn to avoid. It's not cowardice. It's just survival.

We cross the campus, and there's no doubt that, even in the dead of winter, it's beautiful here. The Briar Cliffs have their own beauty, but it's not timeless. You need to be awake to watch the sunrise over the river, but if you are, it's real pretty. Quiet. Tranquil. Sometimes, going to the cliffs at six in the morning with nothing but my camera and a big cup of coffee was the only thing that got me through. All of that pretty tranquility only lasts for a blink before time steals it away, the Cliffs morphing back into gloom and bad odors.

But that's what the camera was for.

Here, even at noon, it's like something out of a movie. I have a clear view of the bell tower, something I've only seen online or in the brochure that came in the mail. Thinking it might be a good place to snap some shots, I nod at the tower, wondering, "Can you go up in that?"

A small, secretive smile lurks on her lips. "Technically, yes, but like everything else in this place, it's not that easy. That tower belongs to the Devils and no one goes up but them." She cuts her eyes at me. "Or an invited guest."

Whatever the hell that means.

"The Devils?" My suitcase has been rolling behind me, thumping on the uneven bricks, but stops suddenly. I look back and see that the wheel's stuck. I wiggle to get it out and her hand reaches out, grazing mine.

I flinch away.

"I think it's wedged between those bricks..." She meets my gaze and I do everything I can to keep my expression neutral. The wheel gives, popping out of the crevice, and she grins. "See?"

She holds out the handle and slowly I reach down and grip the side of the bar. This is easier back home. Most people already avoided me, anyway. And the ones who don't? Well, let's just say the Briar Cliff motto has a lot to do with minding your own damn business and not asking too many questions. It's a whole culture. This girl is looking at me like she's dying to know why my face is white as a sheet.

"Thanks." My heartbeat pounds in my ears, lungs feeling constricted. I search for something, *anything*, to redirect. I shouldn't be surprised. This ridiculous plan to masquerade as someone whole and normal was always a feeble hope. "So, uh, the Devils? What's that all about."

"Oh, right," she says as though nothing has happened. Outwardly, nothing has. It's just me, being a freak. I take a deep breath with every footstep. "It used to be a douchey group of guys that ruled this place with a special brand of bullying."

"Basic assholes," I say.

"Pretty much." She leads us in the direction of two large, red brick buildings. There's one on each side of a grassy courtyard. "They actually got disbanded last year. Total drama." She rolls her eyes. "But a few months ago, there was this like, reemergence. Seems like maybe they're back."

I have no idea what she's talking about, but I do make a solid note to myself that I don't want anything to do with any of that. I'm here to get away from bullying assholes, not dive back into it.

"So anyway," she continues, leading us up to one of the buildings. 'Hayden Hall' is carved over the dorm. "Don't go into the tower unless you're invited *and* only if you want to."

"Got it."

She lifts her arms wide. "Welcome to the dorms. Girls live in Hayden. Boys in Cresswell."

I look up at the building that will be my home for the next six months and take a deep breath. I don't know anyone here, and no one knows me. Exactly how I want it.

～

Sleep should come easy to me, knowing *he* isn't just down the hall. But even though I don't feel the deep thrum of building panic, it's still difficult. The room is unfamiliar. The lights from outside play against the wall in a way I'm not used to. The sounds of Georgia's breaths and sleep-shifting is a constant reminder that I'm not alone in here.

It's stupid. Georgia really seems okay, even though she's a little physical for my tastes. Her hands are constantly moving, touching her hair or face, reaching for things—me. In just a few short months, I've become a master of standing just outside of the contact zone. It's tiring, I think, staring up at the white ceiling. My hand is clenched around the shaft of the knife under my pillow, the way a kid would cling to a blanket, getting used to other people's movements. At home, even with Doug invading my space all the time, he was familiar. Dangerous, but familiar.

The devil I knew.

When morning comes, I dress, pausing only when Georgia rolls over in her bed, yanking her pillow over her head. It's easy to sneak out the door.

My goal is to get where I need to, either early or late. The less people around the better. I need to build a system here, a solid routine that reduces the likelihood of contact as much as humanly possible. From the quick tour Georgia gave me the night before, I locate the dining hall easily. I grab a coffee and a bagel, swiping my meal card through the little slot. The green light blinks, approving it—approving *me*. There's this hum of background anxiety that people will realize I'm not supposed to be here, that it was all a mistake. I mean, who gives a scholarship to a girl mid-way through the year, and especially Cliff trash like me?

You're nothing, you hear me? You're trash. No one wants you.

Well, the Adams Scholarship did.

Getting out of the Briar Cliffs had long been a dream of mine, one that seemed desperately out of reach until college at the very least. But I'd subscribed to a newsletter that lists available scholarships to private schools and prestigious camps, and buried in with the rest, I saw one for Preston Prep that hadn't yet been awarded this year. I applied on a whim, meeting the criteria for low income, academic excellence, and—with the help of a portfolio thrown hastily together on the public library's scanner—creative potential. My tragic background probably lent a helping hand, too. What I was, most of all, was desperate to get out of my house and just... *away*. It could have been a shack on the side of the highway, and it would have been enough for me. If I hadn't been accepted here, I probably would have run away eventually. I'd have just gotten into the Mustang and went as far as it could take me. I'd been shocked when the email came, announcing I'd won.

Three weeks later, here I am, standing among the ancient oaks, historic buildings, and a dining hall that looks straight out of Harry Potter, trying to figure out how to fit into a world with rich kids, secret societies, and world class facilities.

I go out the exit just as the entrance door swings open, and a group of guys walks in. Perfect timing, as planned. They're a blur of red and black. Letter jackets, names and awards stitched on the back, shouting greetings at the workers, banging trays along the serving line. They jostle against one another, and there's no hostility in it, but my ever-present unease stills simmers under the surface.

I walk out the front door and head toward the parking lot, prepared to walk the three miles to the garage to check on my car. I need the time and cool, fresh air, to think about how I'm going to pay for getting my car fixed. I have eight-hundred dollars in my bank account, which is all that's left from my summer job. Everything on a classic car like the Mustang is expensive, always costing more than is strictly necessary for the piece of junk it is. I know once the mechanic gets under the roof, he'll find even more problems. A smart person would sell it for scraps and buy something reliable and dependable. But there's no way I can do it.

Halfway there, the deep rumble of a muffler echoes off the pavement. I turn and see a burst of shiny bright blue as it streaks past, the leaves on the street and my hair blowing from the gust of wind it creates. I catch sight of the license plate before it vanishes down the road.

JAS-MIN.

By the time I see the glowing diner sign up ahead, I'm thinking I may have a plan. If the repairs cost more than what I have, maybe they'll let me put it on a payment plan. I can get a job after school and pay in increments. It's not like I'll need it much since I'm living on campus. They can hold onto it until I can pay in full.

I take a deep breath and cross the street, walking up to the garage. Even though it's Sunday, one bay is open, and the sound of fast, hard music carries into the parking lot. Merle, the manager, told me he'd be here by ten and it's only 9:30. I consider the fact he's here already to be a stroke of rare luck and head through the open door.

The Mustang is up on one of the lifts, but the first person I see is bent over the hood of a different car—the blue Ford. Jas-min.

He must hear my footsteps because he emits a hard sigh and says, "Not open yet." In a lower mutter he probably doesn't expect me to hear, he adds, "So fuck off."

His jeans are faded, pale blue, frayed at the cuffs that hang over the tops of his black Converse. I don't know who this guy is, but it's definitely not sixty-year-old Merle, in his army green jumpsuit. I see his hand reach into the toolbox, knuckles red, streaked in grease. My hair-trigger fight or flight response tickles at my sore neck and I take a step back, deciding to wait outside. I need some air, anyway.

My foot catches on something, and the sound of metal clanging to the ground bursts through the garage. The mechanic tenses, and then jolts up, taking care not to hit his head on the roof of the hood. It's his hair that I see first; fine, almost white, pushed messily above his forehead. But it's his eyes that squeeze all the air from my lungs. They're intense, piercing, and horrifyingly familiar. Even if I hadn't already met him once, I'd still know those eyes anywhere.

They're the impending promise of chaos.

Nothing makes him less terrifying, not even the surprised part of his lips. My hand goes to my jaw and I will my feet to move. That's the problem with my body. It never cooperates anymore.

His fault, my brain hisses.

"Damn, girl, you startled me," he says, running his greasy hand down his thigh. "You're looking for Merle, right? He doesn't usually get in until a little later on Sunday. But I guess…" I don't miss the way his eyes rove over my body, nor the way his demeanor has grown suddenly friendly. "Maybe I can help."

"No," I say, voice flat and hard, hand curling around the knife in my bag. "I think I've had enough of what you call help."

His eyebrow lifts, accentuating the scar slicing down toward his eye. His gaze sweeps from my head to my toes once more, and every hair on my body stands on end. I force my legs to move and take a few steps back.

"…not to sound egotistical or anything—but everything is about me."

The memory of his voice, that whole night, barrels down on me like a runaway train that only gains speed when he steps toward me.

"Stop!" I shout, pulling my knife from my bag and thrusting it toward him. "Come one step closer and I swear to god I'll cut your fucking balls off."

His face goes slack before screwing up angrily. "What the fuck's your problem? I was just—" His eyes narrow, and I see the wheels turning, tension drawing into his pretty face. His grip tightens on the wrench in his hand, eyes sparking in recognition. He breathes a low, "Aw, fuck."

He knows. He *remembers*. My jaw twinges in memory, too. It was three weeks before I could eat solids again, and it still aches sometimes, like a phantom blow. It's not like I can't take a punch. Eight years with Doug taught me everything I needed to know in that regard. It was the randomness of it. The lack of expectation. The knowledge that Doug could be anyone, anywhere, at any time.

I'm never safe.

Not from people like *them*.

"Look," he begins, holding his hands up defensively. "That night at the Briar Cliffs, I never meant—"

"Shut up." The only thing that'd make it worse is an apology. 'Sorry' is bullshit. I've heard enough of those in my life to know. "Tell Merle I'll be back about the Mustang later."

His eyes dart to the car on the lift, and he looks at it much like he just looked at me. I use the distraction to make a hasty retreat, running out of the enclosed garage and back into the cold winter air. I'd done everything I could to get away from the abusive asshole back home.

There's no way I'm dealing with another one here.

3

Sebastian

With the barest thread of control, I manage not to lose my shit until she's off the property. I don't know at first just what I'll do—as usual—but I can feel it swelling inside of me and bucking to break free. The instant she's gone, I reach back and hurl my arm forward, flinging the wrench across the room. It smashes noisily into the workbench, landing with precision, scattering tools all over the floor. It's meager and dissatisfying. It's not the feel of my fist meeting bone, a flame licking up my spine and exploding from my muscles. I thrust my hand into the box and pick up another, throwing it at the same spot, and then another. I lose track of what gets thrown, unable to see past the thing burning inside of me, pummeling the fuck out of the wall.

It barely leeches the blind fury from the pit of my chest.

No matter how many direct hits I make, I can't get that girl's expression out of my mind. It was like she'd seen a ghost. No, worse, a *monster*.

I'm the one who saw a ghost. How else could I possibly fucking explain that girl from the Briar Cliffs—my dirty secret, the worst thing I've ever done—just waltzing right into this garage. It took me longer than it should have to recognize her. The blue tips of her hair were gone, and everything about her looked tired and harsh—especially her eyes. They're what made me connect the dots. Those big hazel eyes. The fear was the same today as it was then.

She's terrified of me.

At least this time she didn't scream.

Jesus Christ.

I shove my hands in my hair, and it takes me longer now than it used to, gathering up all this fury and packing it away. It was easier when I could just beat the fuck out of someone and lay it all on them. There's probably a name for it somewhere, in some boring, overly-technical textbook. Fucked-Up Pretty Boy Syndrome. If it had an illustration, it'd just be wild, Pollock-esque scribbles. The caption would read 'prognosis: terminal.'

I try breathing. Everyone tells me do that when I get like this. 'Just breathe, Bass'. Most useless fucking thing ever. My lungs are not the problem here. Still, I do it, air whistling through my gnashed teeth.

My eyes dart to the Mustang up on the lift, the one she said was hers. I noticed it when I got in this morning, mostly due to the fact I was surprised someone had been able to get it here in the first place. It was obviously held together by dirt, rust, hope, and a prayer. The paint is completely gone in places, and lot of the ornamental details are gone. It's a complete junker—a total piece of shit. A beater. A lemon.

A challenge.

Breathing doesn't help, but *that* does. I look at the body and let my brain start racking up a list. Plenty could probably be salvaged, with a shitload of work. But that's not even to speak of whatever's going on under the hood. And the interior, which is probably grotty, too.

Now that my adrenaline has waned, I look back over at the tool bench, biting back a groan. Fucking hell, Merle is going to kill me.

He already barely tolerates me coming here in the first place. I'd charmed the old man—as much as the crusty, old bastard can even *be* charmed—into letting me rent a bay to work on Jasmine whenever I want. There's a particular kind of affinity that runs through gear-heads, a common thread. Merle must have sensed it in me the first time I came in here with Jasmine. It's best in the mornings and at night, when it's quiet and there aren't any customers here. Those are *my* times. That's why I was so annoyed at a customer just walking up when I still had twenty minutes of blissful peace left.

Having something to do with my hands helps. A project to focus on. A physical, tangible objective. The only issue is that I've put so much work into my Jasmine that she's in top shape. More and more, I've been snagging wayward tasks from Merle, desperate to keep myself occupied for just a little longer. This place has been my only goddamn saving grace these last few shitty months.

And now *she's* a part of it.

That realization is depressing as hell and sparks the rage still smoldering in my chest. Without thinking, I give into the impulse to pick up one last wrench and throw it as hard as possible across the room. It hits the exit light over the door and the plastic casing cracks, shattering to the ground.

"What in the ass-licking hell is going on here?"

My eyes drop down to where Merle is standing in his green coveralls, eyebrows ominously low, coffee in one hand, paper bag in the other. The broken sign flickers a frantic 'EX' over his head.

I thrust a hand in my hair. "Fuck."

The only thing worse than this hot thing burning in my chest is the shame—the dark cloud of remorse—that always follows an outburst like this.

It leaves me feeling sick and vaguely scared of myself in that way I used to be when coming out of a fight, slamming rudely back to reality with cut-up knuckles and bloody faces. It's why I started picking them. Hard to feel ashamed about beating the shit out of someone who deserves it. Even harder to feel scared about hurting someone when they signed on, knowing full well the consequences.

"Boy, I don't know what brought on this tantrum," he nods to the broom leaning against the wall, "but you have until noon to unfuck yourself and get it back together. Understand?"

Fuck you, old man. Screw this. Go to hell. I swallow it all back. If Merle kicks me out of here, what will I have? No fighting, no work outs, no cars? I'll go fucking guano. "Yes, sir," I grind out. "Sorry, sir."

I walk over and grab the broom, stepping over the tools scattered all over the floor. Merle steps out of my way and heads into his office, muttering about me the whole way.

Before starting, I take one last look at the Mustang and wonder exactly what it is about this girl, her mere presence, that apparently brings out the worst in me. I know one thing for sure—if I'm going for self-preservation, the only thing I can do is stay the hell away from her.

I HANG the last tool on the peg board just as the clock over the office door rolls to noon. Merle has spent the last hour checking out the Mustang. Jotting notes on a clipboard and shaking his head. It's pretty obvious that whatever needs to be done to the car, it's extensive. Unsurprisingly. I don't know much about the girl, but she's from the Briar Cliffs. She drives a car like this because she *has* to, not because she wants to.

"How bad is it?" I ask when he slams the hood.

He gives me a look that says my outburst has been forgiven, but not forgotten. "Aside from the body work, the transmission barely qualifies to be called one, and the engine needs a complete rebuild. But, excluding those, I can probably get it running for about a grand." He walks toward the office, head shaking. "You ready to tell me what happened this morning?"

I shake my head. "I promise, it won't happen again."

A car pulls into the parking lot, and we both look out the open garage bay door. I recognize the car immediately as Georgia's. What surprises me is who climbs out of the passenger seat.

The hazel-eyed girl.

Motherfucker.

I glower as I watch her raise a hand, shielding her eyes from the sun. "I'm going to go unpack those boxes in the storeroom that came in yesterday."

Merle's eyebrow raises. "You're *what*?"

I don't answer, just stalk into the back. The storeroom has a glass window with closed blinds. I stand in the dark and peer through the slat. The girl walks into the garage, eyes darting around, and from the tense set of her face, it's obvious that she's looking, *bracing*, for me. Her shoulders ease when I don't turn up.

I take a moment to get a proper look at her. When I first saw her in the garage, I'd been interested. She's got a nice, small, compact body, but her demeanor is so fucking big, you could almost miss it. Narrow waist, big eyes. Full lips, set in a scowl. Smooth-looking, porcelain skin, contrasted with her dark hair, blowing chaotically in a passing breeze, fluttering around her like an ink cloud. Her chin is always up, those hazel eyes staring down her nose at everything. She looks exactly like the kind of girl you'd expect to threaten to cut your balls off.

The good thing is that she doesn't seem to want to see me again either. The bad news is that, if she's riding around with Georgia, there's no way she isn't a student at Preston Prep. And like, how the hell did she even pull that off?

"Well?" I hear her ask, her arms wrapped around her middle like a shield. It's an insecure gesture, but her face is full of severity. "Can you fix it?"

"Oh, I can fix anything," Merle says, "but with a car like that, it's going to cost. Finding parts isn't easy, and it's pretty clear there hasn't been regular maintenance on it." Merle starts listing off the vehicle's problems, running down a pretty broad list. With each word her jaw tightens and that look of exhaustion in her eyes grows. "It won't be road-ready for less than a thousand."

"Shit," she mutters, rubbing her forehead. "Fucking shit!"

"I knocked off a few of the bigger projects—the things that can hold off for a bit." He looks at her sympathetically. "Do you have a dad I can talk to? A parent?"

One of her cheeks lifts with an incredulous lip-curl. "The car is *my* responsibility." She plants a hand on each hip, thinking. "Look, I have some of the money. Well, most of it. But I'm going to need a little time to get the rest. Do you have a payment plan?"

I listen as Merle explains that he doesn't work like that. This garage runs on cash or credit alone. It's pretty clear, as I predicted, that she doesn't have access to either. The defeat in her expression doesn't match the tough exterior. The combat boots and torn jeans are a staple among the Briar Cliff girls for a reason. They're not the soft, pampered type like Preston kids. They work because they have to. But this chick stands like she's bracing for a hit, feet always planted in a wide stance.

It makes me uncomfortable. This girl has the look of someone who's used to getting piled on, and despite our grab-bag of differences, that's something I can relate to. I idly wonder if it'd make her feel better, knowing that karma's already shanked me in the back.

From my hiding spot, I watch her tell Merle she'll figure out by tomorrow how to get the car off the property. A moment later, her and Georgia peel out of the parking lot.

When I'm sure they're gone, I slink back out of the supply room and approach the Mustang. It's ugly and beat to hell, but in a weird way, that's almost its best feature. This lady was a sweet-ass ride back in her day, but no doubt about it, she's seen some real shit. This isn't some fancy little show-car. This girl has *lived*. I unlatch the hood and lift it up, assessing the engine.

"Close the hood, Bass. I need to take it off the lift and put it out back. She says she's coming back tomorrow, but we'll see." I let go of the hood and it slams shut, sending a shiver of rust to the ground. He echoes my thoughts, "It's too bad. Was probably a real beauty back in the day."

I nod in agreement and stare pensively at the car. Something twisted and complex squirms inside me at the thought of her rotting away in some junk yard.

"What if—" I start, then stop. I take a breath, both aching to commit and all at once wary of doing so. "What if I work on it. For free."

He looks at me like I just offered to stick my dick into an electrical outlet. "Why the heck would you do that?"

Because I'm bored. Because Jasmine is out of flaws to silence this black, sick thing roiling inside of me. Because I can't stand the thought of casting aside something so broken and sad. Because it has a brave little toaster smile. Because the girl who owns this car sort of resembles it.

I answer, "I'm renting the bay, so I'll put it there. My car is in good shape. I could use a new project."

Merle gives me a curious glance. "You got a crush on this girl or something?"

"No," I say firmly, then give him a patented Wilcox grin. "You think she looks like my type?"

"I think a dumbass like you would be lucky for a girl like that to give you a second glance." He throws up his hands. "You rent the bay, you can do whatever you want to with it."

"Okay," I say, but quickly add, "will you tell her you worked something out? Just say you got a deal or something, but it may take longer. I don't know. I just don't want her to know it's me."

"So, you *do* like her." When I narrow my eyes, he shakes his head. For some reason, I can't ever seem to impress this guy. Merle isn't afraid of me and he doesn't buy into my bullshit. "What's with the secret, then? Why can't she know you're her fairy godfather?"

"Because if she finds out, she won't accept it."

His laugh sounds as old and rusted as the Mustang looks. "So. It's like that. Should've known. Guys like you always go for the complicated ones." He waves me off and heads back to the office. "I'll come up with something. She's not really in the position to complain."

Merle is right. It is complicated, but not in the way he thinks.

It'd be easy to say that I fucked up—that I hurt her—and it'd be true. I could call this penance, a clearing of conscience. That'd look pretty good.

But I look at that sad, broken car and think that, even despite all the work it needs, it'd probably be the easiest thing to fix in either of our lives right now. It's a cop out, more than anything.

～

I CAN'T DENY how calming it is to settle into the focus of planning. The body is shit, but it's least urgent. Most important is the engine. What's beneath this hood is Frankenstein's monster. I kick around under there for a good hour, just marveling at the weirdness happening. Non-original parts for cars decades newer than this beast, hoses held together with clamps and electrical tape, a radiator cap that used to belong to a Gatorade bottle—it just keeps getting fuckier and fuckier.

"No one respected you, did they?" I ask the car.

It doesn't answer back.

Before long, I confirm Merle's initial assessment. The alternator is toast. But if it weren't, the solenoid's going to kick the bucket any day now, and the ignition switch is dry-rotted and falling apart. In conclusion, there are probably a dozen different forces conspiring to make this car *not* start.

Whoever worked on this lady before me was happy just putting any old thing in her, but I'm never satisfied with anything but original. Ridiculously, I decide to rebuild the alternator and starter myself.

Merle pulls a face. "Don't be a fuckin' idiot, boy. Buy one for a few hundred, slap it in there, and call it a day."

"Nah," I argue, dipping back beneath the hood to take off the belt. "There isn't much left in here that's original."

"This isn't a show car. It's a beater. It's just gotta get her from point A to point B." This is where Merle and I butt heads. He's pragmatic, all about the practicality. To him, a car is transportation. It should be dependable and secure. I'm guessing forty years in this

37

business, dealing with hard-up customers who need to just get to work will do that to you.

Dependable and secure is important, but so is character. "I get it, I do," I assure, walking around him to get a wrench. "But why not? Come on, Merle, like...." I gesture to the car. "*Come on.*"

He just shakes his head. "It's your life."

Only sometimes, I think.

4

"What did he say?" Georgia asks when I walk back into the room. I'd stepped into the hallway to take the call from the garage, which I was fully expecting to come with a new slew of charges. I know what kind of condition my car is in. It doesn't make it any easier to let it go.

Now, I'm standing here, staring at my phone in complete bafflement. "He... changed his mind?"

Georgia's forehead creases. "About the car needing work?" Her voice is dripping with enough doubt that someone else would probably find it insulting. It just makes my chest bounce with a laugh, because it's not like she's wrong.

"About the cost," I elaborate, dropping into the desk chair. "He said he'd work on it for a reduced price, so long as I'm cool with leaving it there for a few weeks. And something about finding a junk yard with older parts that are less expensive? I don't know, but apparently I can afford it now."

Georgia's face lights up. "Sugar, that's awesome! I know you were worried. That must be such a weight off your shoulders."

She has no idea.

Georgia isn't like the girls from back home. I barely know her, but she's such an expressive person—so damn genuine all the time —that it's hard to dislike her. She wears every emotion right on her sleeve, right down to the disappointment she'd shown when I turned down her offer to lend me the amount of repair costs I couldn't cover with my own savings. I've never known someone willing to lend a stranger a few hundred dollars, no questions asked.

There's just no way she could possibly understand my financial situation. I've ridden in her car, seen the inside of her closet, the rings on her fingers. Her phone is the latest model, as is her laptop and smart watch. It's not like I begrudge her or anything. I knew what I'd be getting into by coming to a school like Preston, and it's not as though she can help coming from wealth. But the economic divide here is palpable. Students here probably blow a thousand bucks without a second thought.

But even though she can't really relate, she isn't wrong. Feeling a little more weightless, I give the chair an indulgent spin. "At least I don't have to worry about it right away. I could really use some time to settle in before looking for a job." I pick up a shoebox and start sifting through my rolls of film, sorting them by importance. Back home, I'd send these off to be developed the next town over, but Preston Prep has its own arts wing, complete with dark rooms and the necessary materials. "I wonder what made him change his mind?"

Georgia gives me that sunny smile, saying, "Maybe he's just a nice guy," and it's all I can do to not bark a laugh in her face. Kindness without strings or motive? Yikes, that's some sheltered rich kid bullshit.

More diplomatically, I mutter, "I have a hard time believing that, considering the caliber of asshole he has working for him."

It's just my luck that the second I'd begun to really relax—to think I was safe—that I run into the one guy who's ever come close to hurting me as badly as Doug. The worst part is the feeling of terror. The panic. The sense that I can't protect myself. The power-lessness.

"Asshole?" Georgia frowns at this. "Did something happen?"

I never told Georgia about my first visit to the garage. She just offered to drive me back there, and after walking six miles that morning, I gladly took her up on it. I drop the box of film onto the desk, sighing down at it. "You know, it's just the most random fucking thing. Last summer I had this *run-in* with a guy back home. He was vacationing there for the summer, and we were at the same party, and then..." I trail off. Now that I'm saying it aloud, I think it might be too much to dump on a stranger who's already seen me at a pretty low point. I'm still burning from the humiliation of her seeing the fingertipbruises Doug had left on my neck yesterday. Luckily, she assumed it was a hickey.

But her eyebrows pull in and she asks, "What happened?"

Reluctantly, I explain, "So... this other guy was messing with me— the son to one of my stepfather's friends—and all of a sudden, this guy jumps in the middle of it, picking a fight with him." That's an under-statement, but I'm not sure how to describe it. The way he smiled so amicably, showing his teeth, even though his eyes were hard and frightening. The way his whole demeanor seemed to buzz and crackle like a live wire. The curve of his shoulders, twitching and impatient.

He wasn't just picking a fight.

He was an addict looking for a fix.

I'd know it anywhere. I've seen it in Doug a thousand times— that gleam in his eyes that taught me how much control I didn't have. That I could be good, quiet, as unobtrusive as possible, and that it would never matter. When Doug got that look, he wanted something to hit.

"He pretended like he was jumping in to defend me or some-thing, but it was obvious he just wanted to get into it. Had a real smart-ass mouth on him, too." I tug at my sleeves, covering my wrist and the tattoo. "Anyway, look. The thing is, I don't like fights. Shit's hard enough, you know?" She doesn't. She can't possibly know. But she offers a nod anyway. "I just fucking hate them. And this guy—

this total *bully*—stepped in, making an already unbearable situation even worse. So I just..."

"You just *what*?" I look up and realize all Georgia needs is a bowl of popcorn. She's into my drama like I'm describing a CW show.

"I jumped in to stop it." I reach up to touch my jaw, still feeling a phantom twinge. "And the guy fucking decked me. *Hard.*"

It fractured my jaw, hurt for weeks, and still aches sometimes. But the worst part wasn't the blow. It was the fear. It was the *touch*. I'd been shoving all this vicious terror into the back of my chest for years, piling it up, unknowingly molding it into something lawless and beastlike, but I'd done it. I'd kept it contained. Hidden. Confined.

Until that night.

One savage touch from him, and now I can't even handle something as simple as a handshake without falling apart. That's the real crime—something Georgia probably couldn't understand. How could she, when even I don't?

Georgia shifts to a sitting position, wrapping her arms around a pillow. "Wait. You're saying this same guy works at *the garage*?"

I jerk a shoulder in a tense shrug. "Apparently. I walked in, and there he was. It took him a minute to recognize me, but he figured it out." It didn't take me long at all. I knew it the second his face emerged from under that car hood. Handsome—pretty, almost. The Devil in sheep's clothing. He was exactly the same as I remember, buzzing and crackling, wired and unpredictable. I think I probably even knew it was him before I ever saw his face, the way my body reacted, beyond my control. My teeth clench in frustration at the memory. "Fucking asshole."

"That sounds pretty terrible." Georgia's tone is sympathetic but somehow stilted. She looks a shade paler, so I figure maybe she's not used to hearing about stuff like this. "But, you know, maybe there was something else going on with him. Or maybe he has his own problems that he's dealing with."

I gape at her, beginning to suspect that Georgia is painfully naïve and too optimistic for her own good. Must be a nice world she lives in, where people do kind things for the sake of it and bullies just need, like... what? Understanding?

Give me a break.

"Even if that were the case, that doesn't mean his problems have to be my problems." I clench my jaw. "Either way, I'm going to do everything I can to stay the hell away from him. The last thing I need in my life is another toxic, aggro dude who can't control his temper."

I glance back up at Georgia, worried I've revealed too much, but she's busy staring down at her hand, twisting her ring around her finger. Like the car, I don't expect this girl to understand where I'm coming from, but now that I'm starting a new life, I'm thinking my old routine of hiding and denying is for the birds. Starting over here, I'm going a different way, establishing my boundaries early. Firmly.

Rule number one: Keep your hands to yourself.

Rule number two: No assholes.

As the afternoon passes, the dormitory fills up with returning students. Georgia, I find, is a pretty popular person, and why shouldn't she be? She's pretty and nice and normal. She has a lot of friends popping by to say hello.

Half of me is fascinated by these people—girls mostly—coming in and out, lying on the same bed, touching one another's things, fingers always moving and pressing and brushing and stroking. There's an intimacy in the movements that I've never experienced or wanted. I feel like I'm watching a nature documentary, expecting them to turn into primates picking bugs off of one another.

The other half of me is simmering with impotent fury. I knew this was coming, intellectually. Sharing a space with someone, being at their whims, comes with a certain amount of compromise. Why shouldn't she have people over? This is her home, too. It makes me want to get up and pace around, shove my fingers into my hair and *pull*. I just want them all to get the fuck out. As much as

I try to fight it, the space feels even less like my own than it already had, which wasn't much to begin with. Skin itching from having so many people in such a tight space, I keep cracking my knuckles, trying so hard to school my expression into something easy and blank that I'm pretty sure I just end up looking like a psycho.

It's hard to miss the looks—curious and wary. I've spent months fighting the escape of this wild, nervous thing inside of me, but I've never perfected the act of normalcy. I focus my energy on organizing my desk, just to give my hands something to do, feeling like an animal. Trapped. Cagey. Observed.

I wonder what Georgia would say if she knew that bully who just 'has his own problems' was the catalyst to the way my lungs feel shrunken and flooded.

A girl name Caroline comes in, dressed in black and red flannel pajama bottoms and a T-shirt. She has on thick glasses and gives me a quick smile when we're introduced.

"What happened to Zadie?" she asks, claiming the end of Georgia's bed. "I thought you two got along okay."

To be honest, I'd wondered myself, but thought it was rude to ask. I like Caroline already.

"She moved in with Daphne when her roommate changed schools," Georgia says. She's facing the closet and changing out of her shirt and into a tank top. When she bends over, I see the top curve of a tattoo sticking out of her shorts, right above her butt cheek, but I can't make out the design. "She didn't like that I had 'guys over all the time'." She uses air quotes and rolls her eyes, then looks at me. "For the record, it was only like two—well, maybe three—guys, and I specifically picked a weekend she wasn't here. I made sure they didn't touch her stuff or bother her at all."

My face screws up in response. Guys, here, in my space? I bite back a strained groan at the thought. But then I remember Georgia so sweetly offering to give me three hundred dollars, just like that, and I think... okay. *Fuck.*

Maybe if I just keep to the boundary stuff. "Just... maybe not when I'm here?" I try to compromise. "If you give me some notice, I'll find somewhere to hole up, so no wires get crossed."

Georgia looks pleasantly surprised at this, so maybe I hadn't hidden my distaste so well. "Really? That'd be awesome! And hey, I'll do the same in return. If you ever want the room to—"

"Yeah, no," I scoff, head shaking. "I'm good. Dating is not in the cards for me this year."

Caroline snorts. "I'm not sure what Georgia is talking about counts as *dating*—"

"Hey!" Georgia shouts, but then just rolls her eyes. "Fine, you have a point. But there's nothing wrong with playing the field until you find that perfect guy to settle on."

The girls catch up and eventually begin talking about people I don't know. Some girl named Vandy just finished some kind of program. Her boyfriend, Reyn, gave her a personalized portrait of her cat for Christmas. Some couple named Emory and Aubrey are still a thing, and rumor has it he's giving her his Devil ring for Valentine's Day. I finish organizing my desk and glance back when things go abruptly quiet. They're talking in lower voices now, leaned in close, expressions serious. Whatever it's about, it's not for me to hear.

I feel weirdly relieved to see it. All of the openness and expression was starting to freak me out. Secrets, privacy, boundaries... those are comfortingly familiar.

"I think I'm going to go walk around campus before it gets dark," I say, wanting to give them some space. Honestly, I could use some myself. It's been a long twenty-four hours. I grab my coat and camera, and wave when Caroline offers that it was nice to meet me.

It's late afternoon, but being the dead of winter, it feels later. The leafless trees stand guard over the old buildings and I snap a couple photos here and there, trying to capture the odd sense of Preston's somberness.

In an effort to avoid other people on campus, I step off the main sidewalk onto a well-worn path. I know there's a lake on the back of the property, I'm just not sure how to get there. The trail cuts behind the buildings, one I recognize as the dining hall. Along with the whir of ventilation, it has that smell—heavy, stale grease—the dumpster pushed up against the brisk wall. A thick grove of trees runs behind the building and I eye it, wondering if I have enough time to explore before it gets dark. I'm about to march on into the grove when I see movement across the grass. The shape is dark and small, a creature hiding in the thick stalks. I tip toe over and duck down to see a black cat, paws out, ready to pounce. Before I can react, another cat slinks forward, a few feet away, deftly climbing up an old tree trunk. This one is white with orange patches.

"Hey guys, what's happening?" I say to them both. My voice disturbs the hunter, and he jumps away, closer to the trunk, eyeing me distrustfully. They're skinny—not exactly scrawny, though. They remind me of the cats that hang out on the dock back home. Not quite feral, because they rely on the people nearby to feed them, but also not completely tame. The orange and white one watches me carefully and I'm not sure, but her belly looks swollen —probably pregnant. I drop down to a less threatening level, bringing the camera up to snap a few shots. "You guys like it back here away from everyone, too, huh?"

They hug the trunk and just stare back at me, a perfect exercise in contrasts. They're good subjects, nice and still, and I don't regret spending a whole roll of film on them. The black one has big yellow eyes, but the white and orange cat's eyes are a gorgeous emerald green. I sit with them for a while, but neither will come very close.

Well I can't say anything about that. I don't want anyone touching me either. Sure, I have to rely on other people, family and some friends, but I know better than most that any of those people can turn at any moment.

The dark one is more interested in hunting and it's getting dark. I can tell I'm keeping it from a potentially fulfilling meal. I stand and spot a third cat, this one an ashen gray, sitting at the edge of the tree line. "I should probably go, but maybe I can bring you guys some treats. How about that?"

They stare at me like I've lost my mind. I probably have. Coming to this school was a crazy, desperate decision, one that has already had consequences. Here I am, stuck without a car, and the very source of the thing I'd been so determined to run from is right here, in the very town I ran *to*.

But school starts tomorrow, and so what? Maybe I hadn't run from something so much as ran toward something else. That's what I'm really here for; a good education.

I head back down the path and glance back, feeling the eyes of the cats watching me. It's strange, but for the first time since arriving at Preston Prep, I don't feel so alone.

5

I WAIT until the main hall is thick with students before cutting through the crowd toward the science wing where the juniors have their lockers.

The first person I see is Sydney, hair in a side ponytail, lips bright red, skirt barely covering her ass despite the cold. It was never talked about or agreed upon, it was just one of those automatic things. The Devils have decided to stick together. As a result, we've all avoided Sydney like the plague after she fucked with Reyn and Vandy last fall at homecoming. Trying to sink her talons into him and almost destroying what he had going on with his girl? Uncool.

I zig zag around her, hoping that maybe she won't see me.

"Hey Basssssss."

"Fucking hell," I mutter, looking back and giving her a scowl. The girl couldn't take a hint if it were anvil-shaped and dropped from the heavens above. She doesn't even look put out about my glare, just smiles back at me, wiggling her fingers in a wave.

Worst hookup decision ever.

Suddenly, a hand clenches around my wrist, yanking me into the lockers. I dramatically rub my shoulder, swinging my scowl around. "Ow."

"Whatever," Vandy scoffs. "You and I both know that didn't hurt."

All the twisted-up stress and anxiety instantly melts away. "V! You're back!" I sling an arm around her shoulder. "How was it? Was Dr. Drew there?"

She frowns and holds her finger to her lips. "Keep it down, asshole!"

"Oh, right." No one is supposed to know Vandy spent Christmas break in rehab. "How was your, uh, *holiday*?"

"Good." And even if her pretty blue eyes go a little tight at the mention, her tone sounds like maybe she means it. "Honestly, not as bad as I was expecting. No kumbaya, minimal number of share circles, really good food, and..."

I quirk an eyebrow down at her. "And?"

Her cheeks flush in that way Vandy has. Even though she's a Devil now, and one of the most popular Juniors in school, a part of her will probably always be Emory's bashful little sister. "I don't know. I just feel better. Good, you know? Like I can handle it now."

"You couldn't before?" I frown, even though I know addiction can be a beast. Vandy's just always kept things so close to the vest. You'd never know she was struggling with a nasty painkiller addiction.

Just then, a heavy hand lands on my arm and it's peeled off of Vandy's shoulder. Reynolds McAllister pulls his girl close and glares. "Wilcox."

"McAllister," I reply, mocking his authoritative tone. Military school did a number on this kid. But I'd probably be lacking a sense of humor too, if roles were reversed. I wouldn't trust a guy like me around her either. Vandy is a catch, but she's not my type, and it's really hard to see her as anything but a sisterly-type.

"We'll catch up at lunch," I say, catching sight of the flame of red hair that I'm looking for. "Save me a seat."

I duck away, just in time to avoid watching V and Reyn suck

face. God, they're so cute together, it makes me want to take a picture and then vomit all over it.

Fine, I may be a little bit jealous of the fact they're happy and getting sex on the reg. From the glow those two put out, it's got to be some good banging, too. Lucky fuckers.

I slide up to Georgia just as she begins spinning the dial on her lock. She looks up and smirks. "Ah, Bass. I've been waiting for you to show up."

I sink into a lean against the lockers. "Were you aware?"

"That you're the unluckiest bastard I've ever met?" The lock clicks, and she opens the door.

I reach out to sweep her hair away from her neck, grin turning mischievous in that way girls always like. "I don't know about that. You picked me to be your Stairway to Hell hook-up, didn't you? Doesn't seem unlucky to me."

Used to be, I could flirt with Georgia and she'd get all flustered. Oh, and it was a fucking delight, too. She's got this pale, freckled skin that goes the brightest shade of pink. It's a shame that I never got a look at her tits.

Now, she just rolls her eyes, completely unfazed by me. "Bass, we talked about this. It was good, but—"

"You're just not that into me. We're better as friends. Blah blah blah." I move my hand in a talking motion. It's not like I'm pining over Georgia. It was just oral, for god's sake. She's a great girl, totally stacked, excellent kisser, cute as a fucking button. But her and I would be a recipe for disaster. Sometimes she gets this look in her eyes—something hungry and rabid—and I think that possibly we're a little too alike. Plus, I have a type.

Sweet, bashful girls like Vandy are great, and cute girls with hidden depths like Georgia are awesome. But at the end of the day, this is what I want: Some pretty little bitchy number sitting in the passenger seat of my Shelby, like some kind of trophy. It's a painful cliché, terribly shallow, but eh. The heart wants what the heart wants, and the dick's not much different.

"I know. I agree. It was a one-time deal," I assure her. "But, back to *my* problems—"

"You mean your dirtiest, most shameful secret, showing up right here on campus?"

I cut my eyes down the hall, feeling my face darken. "Yes, that one. When did you know?"

"When she told me about the asshole at the garage and how she originally met him. It was after we got back to the dorms." She pulls out her books, sliding me a knowing look. "This was, of course, following an interesting phone call from the mechanic, who's apparently offered to work on the car at a *very* reduced price. Know anything about that, slugger?"

I frown. "*Don't.*" If Georgia had felt the weight of the hit, seen her laying there motionless on the ground, heard her screams...

No.

Hitting that girl isn't a joke.

"Listen, Bass," she says, slamming the door and spinning the lock with a quick twist. She levels me with a look. "I don't know what you're doing with the car, but take my advice here. There's a vibe going on, and it's screaming 'leave her alone.' Sugar seems like a troubled girl, and if I'm reading things right? The last thing she needs is to deal with you any more than necessary."

I clench my jaw, knowing that she's right, but also knowing that I'm going to fix that damn car. I'm already balls deep in the thing. It might be her car, but a part of it, in some way, is already mine, too. "Wait," I say, doing a double-take, "I'm sorry, did you say her name is *Sugar*?"

What kind of fucking name is *Sugar*? More importantly, who names a girl like *that* Sugar? Do her parents even know her?

Sugar and spice and everything that wants to cut my fucking balls off.

Georgia presses a hand against my stomach and winks. "Good thing you don't have a sweet tooth, right?"

She's gone before I have a chance to respond.

The bell rings and there's no time to worry about it further. I have Dr. Ross next, and the last thing I need is to start the semester off on her bad side. I turn the other direction and stroll into her class with plenty of time to spare. I nod to Reyn, whose long legs are taking up half the aisle. I tap on Afton's desk as I pass. She blesses me with a half-smile and her shirt is unbuttoned one less than is strictly approved by dress code. *Thank you, Miss Cross.* She has no use for high school dick, but she's still a team player.

I lift my head toward my desk—last row, second to last seat— when my step falters.

Unlucky bastard, indeed.

The girl, Sugar, is occupying the seat right in front of mine. She's dressed like every other girl in this damned place; black and red plaid skirt, crisp white shirt, and regulation white knee socks. It's the shoes that stop me cold. Black lace-up boots with scuffed toes. My eyes flick up to her face and while her expression is stone, I see the flush of red on her cheeks.

Dr. Ross clears her throat. "Is there a reason you're standing in the middle of the room with your mouth hanging open, Mr. Wilcox?"

"No ma'am." I flash her a grin. "Just taking in all my classmates after a long winter break." I pass Elana, grazing a knuckle over her jaw. "Hey girl, love the new scarf. Aubrey, you're looking good." I glance to the back, toward Reyn, who watches me through narrow eyes. "Reynolds, you're looking extra glowy this morning. I see the holidays treated you well."

"Wilcox," he grinds out, "I swear to god—"

I'm doing everything I can to slow the inevitable, but Dr. Ross is not one to be trifled with. One more second and she'll toss me in detention for the rest of the year.

"Mr. Wilcox..." Her voice conveys her annoyance, yet I still don't stop.

"And you, Dr. Ross." I peer at her, hand over my heart. "Is that a new brooch? It really matches your eyes. Mr. Dr. Ross is quite the gift giver, I see." With that, I slide into my seat, hoping everyone is distracted and annoyed enough that the hostile vibes rolling off Sugar aren't discernable.

The final bell rings and Dr. Ross jumps right into the lesson. I get out my notebook and pencil, flipping it open to a clean page. The rest of the class settles in, the muscle memory kicking in after a few weeks off. On the best of days, I struggle with staying attentive, but today it's outright impossible. I lean back, stretching one leg forward, and flip my pencil through my fingers. Sugar makes a sound—this soft, yet somehow hard breath—and jerks to the side to yank her backpack closer to her desk, all protective and tense. What does she think I'm going to do, grab it and run off? *No, Sugar, that's my boy Reyn back there.* He'd steal the shirt right off your back, if given half a chance. But thievery isn't my vice.

I knew the girl, *Sugar*, was small. That had been entirely too evident when I decked her. But she seems even smaller now that she's sitting right in front of me, so close. Slim, narrow shoulders that almost curve inward, petite little ears with tiny hoops slipped through them. I stare at the long, dark hair in front of me, wondering when she got rid of the blue tips, wondering why she moved here, trying to figure out how in the hell this little townie from the Briar Cliffs—my biggest sin—showed up at Preston Prep.

I'm not the one who doesn't belong here. This turf is as close to mine as any other.

She shifts, making the ends of her hair drag along the top of my desk. I slide my pencil forward and cave to the desire—no, *compulsion*—to run the tip of it through the inky black fringe. Mesmerized, I slowly run the pencil from one end to the other, watching the little strands fall like a silky, dark, sweet-smelling curtain—

Whip!

"WHAT THE HELL?!"

Still holding my pencil, I look up into Sugar's face—her blood-red, pinched, and totally pissed-the-fuck-off face. She's looming in the aisle, having thrown herself violently out of her seat. Her eyes are an inferno, chest heaving in these sharp little jerks that make zero sense to me. It's like she's having a problem breathing. There's this vein on her neck that I'm pretty sure I can see throbbing.

I sit here, stunned speechless as I look back at her.

Please don't scream.

"Miss Voss," Dr. Ross says, standing wide-eyed at the front of the room. "Calm yourself right now."

"This guy touched me!" Sugar spits, thrusting an accusatory finger at me. I don't miss the way it trembles. "He grabbed my hair!"

I gape, my baffled gaze pinging between her fiery eyes and Dr. Ross. "I did not!"

Dr. Ross looks more concerned than pissed. She takes a step toward Sugar, who reacts by grabbing her backpack and promptly sprinting for the door. It closes with a sharp click behind her when she flies from the room without a second look.

The whole class is stunned silent, although a few people are definitely looking at me. Aubrey, Elana, and Afton, for sure. I shrug, all '*hell if I know*', and Afton narrows her eyes.

"I'll go find her," Afton offers, standing quickly.

"Take her to the infirmary."

"Yes, ma'am." Afton grabs her own bag and walks out of the room. This time, every guy watches her go.

I exhale and sink into my seat, tapping my pencil on the desk. I'm thinking that, this time at least, I'm wrong. Maybe everything isn't about me. Whatever is going on with that girl, it has to be something else. I mean, that shit was straight up coconuts, wasn't it?

For some reason, I look back at Reyn for confirmation of this.

He looks just as confused.

I shift my gaze to the front of the room and realize Dr. Ross is staring at me. "Mr. Wilcox."

I straighten in my seat, pulling a polite expression over my features. "Yes, ma'am?"

She peers over her glasses at me. "I don't know what you did to that girl, but make sure you apologize."

"Yes, ma'am."

"And prepare for two days of detention for interrupting my class."

Annoyance flickers in my chest. Two days? What the fucking *fuck*? I don't argue back. I know she'll make it five in a heartbeat. Maybe longer. I bite back the anger and nod. "Yes, ma'am."

6

KEEP YOUR HANDS TO YOURSELF.

There's one rule.

One.

Keep your goddamn, motherfucking hands to yourself. It can't be that hard. Kindergartners grasp this shit the first week of school.

That's what I keep saying to myself as I roam the hallways of this massive, godforsaken place trying to find the bathroom. I'd bolted from the room like a complete lunatic, running down two different halls before I came to my senses and realized I'm completely turned around. The halls are eerily quiet, void of the nonstop disruption at my old public school. Finally, I see a small marker on the door that says 'women' and duck inside. A quick look around makes it obvious that the higher quality of private school education extends to bathroom accommodations, too.

I mean, not one broken sink or mirror in sight, and *every* stall has a door.

Walking over to the sink, I drop my bag on the floor and stare at my face in the mirror. My nose and eyes are red, the tell-tale sign of

55

my ultimate weakness. My hair is windswept from running down the hall, so my ears are exposed, showing off the little hoop earrings Georgia had insisted I wear. The uniform is still straight and pressed, and looking at myself, I can barely recognize the person staring back.

This isn't the girl from the Cliffs, with her dark eye makeup and ratty jeans. This isn't the person who walked through the docks with a fuck-you shield wrapped around her. This isn't even the person I was a couple days ago, elbowing Doug and escaping the consequences.

Who are you? I mentally ask. Who is this person who looks like a schoolgirl and acts like a mental patient? This isn't me. It's jarring and disorienting, like at some point I've been knocked unconscious, and this whole experience is some very vivid dream playing out in my head.

Though, were that the case, my brain certainly wouldn't put that asshole here.

Seeing him in the doorway had been startling. And not just his presence, his appearance as well. The two other times I'd seen him, he'd been dressed so casually, like any other high school shitheel. But today he looked like the other boys, dressed in his uniform coat with his red and black tie slightly askew. A wolf in sheep's clothing. He looked both out of place and perfectly at ease.

I should have known he'd be a student here. Why wouldn't he be? Only rich kids migrate to the Briar Cliffs in the summer, and this place is full of them.

It was bad enough seeing him, but then he had to make an utter ass out of himself as he made his entrance. Seriously, what an egotistical jack-off. Not just abusive, but an idiot as well. All easy smiles and swagger, the kind of guy who thinks he's untouchable. Clearly, no respect for boundaries, the way he was touching everyone and everything. He even mouthed off to the teacher, who looks scary as hell.

I take a deep breath and take the earrings out. This won't do—playing at being like any of the other girls here. I don't want to be like them. Look at Georgia, so trusting and optimistic. If that's 'nor-mal', then I don't want it.

Grabbing a paper towel, I run it under the sink water. I've just wiped off my face when the bathroom door opens. A gorgeous girl from Dr. Ross's class walks in. She's tall and thin, with perfect hair and a calculating expression on her face.

"Oh," she says. "There you are. How the hell did you get all the way to the tech hall?"

I blink. "Me?"

She rolls her eyes and approaches the sink, checking herself out in the mirror. "Aren't you the one who just ran like a bat out of hell from class?"

I lean back against the sink. "Yeah, that'd be me." I give her a sidelong look. "On a scale of one to ten, how crazy did I look?"

"That's relative." She digs through her backpack and pulls out a makeup bag, unzips it and with sharp, glossy nails, extracts her lip gloss. "I'm Afton, by the way. And let me tell you, everyone here may look all nice and put together, but that's what money is for—to cover everything in a shiny wrapper, bow and all, so it looks fully functional. The matching uniforms don't hurt, either." She swipes on a thick coat of pale red. "But crazy, along with dark secrets and deviant behavior, is pretty standard around here, and the first day at Preston isn't easy. I think you're fine."

I exhale, feeling slightly better, although I'm still not sure why this girl is talking to me. "Well, at least I fit in," I laugh sarcastically. "What an impression to make, huh?"

"So, what'd he do?" she asks, snapping back on the cap. She drops it in the bag and pulls out a hairbrush.

"Who?"

"Sebastian," she clarifies. "He messed with you?"

Sebastian. Wilcox. A name to match the face. The anger wells up in me again when I bite out, "He was messing with my hair." And then I have to pause, because that sounds... totally fucking pathetic. Who wigs out like that just because someone touched their hair? Afton flicks her gaze to me and I can see the doubt there.

"Look, I know it doesn't sound like a big deal, but I just... I really don't like people touching me."

I prepare for the inevitable. Questions. Skepticism. That look that says I'm a huge drama queen for having the gall to value my personal space to the degree of having random classroom outbursts.

But she just says, "Fair enough," and runs the brush through her hair, creating perfectly shiny waves. Who *is* this girl? "I'm sure he didn't mean anything by it. He's not a bad guy."

I snort. "That hasn't been my experience with him."

"You know Bass?" she asks, finally turning to me, eyebrows drawn. "What, from before?"

I pause, considering her. "You got any eyeliner in that thing?" I point to her makeup bag, and she looks surprised, but pushes it down the counter.

I choose her darkest liner and lean in close to the mirror to apply it. "We crossed paths last summer. He got in a fight with this guy at a party, and when I tried to break it up, he punched me." I can see in the reflection that her gaze darts to my jaw, despite the fact I haven't mentioned *where* he punched me. "It was a whole thing."

She asks, "Like, an accident?" and I pause, nostrils flaring.

"Sure," I say, moving to my other eye. "An accident—like a drunk driver hitting a car of random people is an accident." I smudge the liner a bit before putting it back in her bag, sliding it down the counter to her. "Thanks," I say, feeling a little more like myself.

Afton assesses herself one last time, then places her brush in her bag and slowly zips it up. She turns away from the mirror and looks at me. "Sebastian Wilcox is a hotheaded, temperamental, impulsive, sweet-talking charmer."

I don't know about *charm*, but, "Sounds about right."

"But, he's not a bad guy. His older brother, Heston? *He's* a bad guy. Some of the other people around here? Total shitheads. But Bass isn't one of them."

I stop just shy of rolling my eyes at her. "No offense, but I sort of have this whole philosophy. When people show me who they are, I believe them the first time." I put Georgia's earrings into my pocket, real careful-like, so I don't lose them. "He showed me who he is. Volatile, violent, selfish, dangerous... probably an abusive piece of shit."

"He's not...!" she starts, but instantly stops, her lips forming a tight line. "Bass is actually a good guy. He's loyal and funny and incredibly hot." She gives me a hard look, "And you can *never* tell him I said that."

"I won't," I reply, wanting to argue with all of that, but not bothering. This girl obviously likes that shitbag—I won't be changing any minds here—and I'm not trying to beef with one of Preston's resident Scary Girls.

"Here's the thing," she says. "Bass is going through a lot right now. It's not my drama to talk about, but just be aware that you've only been introduced to his worst shade. I'm not saying you should be best friends with the guy or anything, but there are a lot of people around here way more dangerous than Sebastian Wilcox. I'd suggest that you ignore him, but he's like a fly to honey, and if I'm not mistaken your name *is* Sugar, right?"

"Yeah," I reply, eyes narrowing, "but what the hell does that mean?"

She picks up her leather bag and slings it over her shoulder. "Well, just look at you. You're different and pretty and look like you could shove that boot up someone's ass. And I suspect that hitting you that night bothers him way more than he'd ever admit. The guys around here like to have control, and it sounds like he completely lost it that night. It's probably driving him crazy, which would explain whatever happened in class today." Her phone vibrates and she looks down, revealing a ghost of a smile. "I need to take this, but sit with us at lunch today, okay? Georgia will be there."

I take a moment to consider this. "Will *he* be there?"

"Most likely." She heads to the door, hair swinging behind her. "Oh, I'm Afton by the way."

"Nice to meet you, Afton," I say, although I'm not really sure what just happened. The offer of lunch is phrased like an invitation, but I get the feeling most people don't turn this girl down, which is possibly why she left before I could agree. Even though I don't decline, I don't plan on taking her up on it, either. Afton may be the Queen Bee of this school, but I don't intend on being in anyone's hive.

~

THE REST of my morning goes by without incident and is pleasantly Sebastian Wilcox-free. Well, for the most part. I have a study period before lunch and am assigned to go to the library to catch up on a long-term project. That's where I inadvertently sit next to what I can only assume is the school gossip, which results in me learning more about everyone than I really want to.

I choose a seat, but I'm more distracted with how to feel about pulling out my laptop than who I'm sitting by. Part of me wants to feel embarrassed at the way it looks. The screen casing is held together by duct tape, a long, jagged fracture going down the corner, that I've tried to cover with stickers. There are three keys missing, and it doesn't quite close right. A bigger part of me thinks, *fuck it*, and dumps it unceremoniously onto the smooth tabletop, mentally daring anyone to look my way. It's an ancient, loud machine that whirs like a beast when I boot it up.

It's not long before the two girls sitting on a couch across from the table capture my attention. Their heads are titled together conspiratorially. "Three weeks? He probably knocked her up and she left town to deal with it."

"I heard rehab."

"That tracks," the girl with dark hair says. Her skirt barely covers her thighs. "Kicking a three-year habit is hard, especially when your delinquent boyfriend can just steal whatever you want."

I stare at my computer, listening. How can I not? Afton had said this place was full of deviants. Sounds like she was right about that.

"So what's the sitch, Syd. You still going to make a play for Reyn, or what?" the other girl asks. I sneak a peek at the folder sitting on

60

the table in front of her. The name 'Fiona' is handwritten in blocky letters.

"Hell no." The Syd girl snorts. "He's obviously the kind of guy who only goes for pity fucks. Not my speed." She presses her pen to her bottom lip. "I've got my eye on someone else now."

Fiona grins. "Oh yeah? Who?"

"An old conquest. He would've been mine by now if I hadn't been distracted by Reyn coming back." She crosses and uncrosses her legs. "Bass and I go way back. I think it may be time to rekindle that spark, know what I mean?"

Sebastian. Here we go again. I shouldn't be surprised he'd be into a girl like the one in front of me. Everything about her reeks trouble. Even if he's not looking for it, I get the feeling it follows him around like a magnet.

"I hear about him and Carlton going to the car shows all the time, now that he can't fight anymore. I found a hookup who can send me the time and location of the next one. I'm hoping once he's hopped up on adrenaline, he'll be ready to give this another shot."

"It's a solid plan," her friend says. The lunch bell rings before I can hear anything else, and I return my battered laptop to my bag and head into the hall. The swarm of students goes in one direction, toward the dining hall. I fall behind the current, tucking my limbs in close, putting on my best fuck-you-glare to discourage any closeness. When I finally get into the line, I surreptitiously search the large room. It doesn't take long to find it. Right in the center of it all, I catch sight of Afton's straight posture and Georgia's red hair. Weaving his way to their table is the tuft of blond hair that's haunted my nightmares for months. My pulse quickens at the mere sight of him, and nope, there's no chance I'm sitting with these people, no matter how popular or connected they are. I didn't come here to climb a ladder, anyway. I came for an education and a ticket out of the Cliffs.

I grab one of the to-go boxes at the end of the counter and quickly swipe my card. I then cut along the backside of the room, away from the tables, and duck out the side door.

The sun is out, which makes it warm enough that my lack of

coat isn't an issue. I make my way back behind the dining hall, back to where I'd seen the cats the night before. I don't see any as I approach, but I take a seat on the tree stump and open my lunch. There's a turkey sandwich with lettuce and cheese, a bag of chips, and an orange. I peel the orange and then pull apart the meat in the sandwich, hoping to lure the cats into the open.

It doesn't take long before I see the mama cat peek her orange nose out from behind a bush. Moments later, the black one slinks from the tree line. There's no sign of the gray one, but I carry over a few pieces of meat and leave them on the ground. They watch me suspiciously as I go back to the stump.

What these cats don't realize is that I'm a very patient person. I have nowhere to be and nothing to do but eat my orange and try to get them used to me. The black cat emerges first, nose twitching as he sniffs the turkey a few feet away. He makes a wide arc around, both coming closer and farther away at the same time.

Quietly, carefully, I take out my camera.

The black cat eats the turkey as the mama looks on, skeptical but clearly wanting. I capture a series of shots of her sitting near the bush, her round belly making the sharpness of her shoulders seem even more striking.

I'm swinging my camera around to get a look at the black one when someone else fills my lens. Sebastian Wilcox stands about twenty feet away, hands shoved in his pockets, aloof expression on his face.

Startled, it takes a moment of fumbling to be sure I don't drop my camera. If I do, I'm beyond fucked. The only reason this place wanted me was because of my photos. Without a camera, I'm....

You're trash. You're nothing.

I swing my hot gaze to his, fuming. It doesn't matter that he looks surprised to see me, one leg still outstretched as if he'd frozen in place. I still go tense and still at the thought of him seeking me out.

I lurch upright and grab my bag, clutching it close, dipping my hand inside to find my knife. Startled by my movements, the cats both run away.

No—not running away.

Running *toward* Sebastian. Even the gray one darts out of the woods, making a beeline for him.

"For the record," he starts, holding up his hands. "I did not follow you out here."

I glare at him, both speechless and furious.

"But I am starting to wonder if maybe *you're* following *me*," he says, shoving his hand into the small side pocket of his backpack. He pulls out something metal and round. "Because I have a standing lunch date with these three sexy beasts."

I gawk—yeah, *gawk*—as he pulls the tab on the can and the scent of tuna wafts through the air. The orange and black cat circle nearby, but the gray one goes right up to him and rubs all over the legs of his dark pants, tail winding around his ankle. He squats and rests the can on the ground before opening a second, and then a third. He shoves one toward the mama cat, who tentatively comes closer, but still not quite within reach. The black cat pushes her out of the way.

"Don't be a dick," he says, talking directly to the cats. "Abby is eating for a multitude—she is legion—so don't be greedy," he admonishes the black one. "I mean, you're the one who knocked her up, after all."

Wait. "You named them?" I blurt, even though I should be using the distraction to make my escape.

He glances up, giving me a view of his clear blue eyes. He looks me over, and it's not like before. This is not an eye-fucking. It's full of uncertainty and pique. I get the feeling he's putting me through a test.

I must pass.

He lifts a shoulder in a loose shrug. "Sure. Gave them rightful Devil names. That's Abbadon," he points to the orange and white cat, "Hades," the black cat, "and Lucy—you know, for Lucifer." He runs his finger over her ear, and I notice the small half-moon. "I managed to trap Lucy last year, get her fixed and tagged. She'd already had a couple of litters and the animal rescue was able to re-home them." He frowns down at Hades. "But the other two are skittish, I've been working to get him close enough to catch. I almost got them used to me before Christmas break, but I had to leave, so now we're back to square one."

It's the most I've heard him speak, and although I hear what he's saying, I'm mostly watching him. His movements, his expression, the way he jerks his head, flicking his hair from his eyes. I keep waiting for something to make him explode, holding the hilt of the knife, just in case. But out here, focused on the cats, scratching under Lucy's chin, his whole demeanor is deceptively chill.

It doesn't put me at ease, and I don't try to hide my sneer. "So, what, you're like some kind of cat savior?"

He gives me a weird look, something in his eyes shuttering. "I don't know about that. Sometimes I need to get away from shit—take a walk. I came back here one day and found these guys."

He stands and both Abby and I take a few steps back, keeping a wary eye on him. If he notices, he doesn't say so, but he does pick up his backpack and look over at me. "Dr. Ross told me to apologize for what happened in class. You'll learn pretty quick that she's not the teacher you want to fuck around with. She's savage."

"Well, I guess it takes one to know one."

His jaw tics and his eyes go tight for a moment, like he's biting something back. "I can assure you that what happened in class today won't happen again. Consider it a momentary lapse in judgment."

I tighten my hand around the handle of my knife, still hidden in my bag. "I suspect you have a lot of those, don't you?"

"I may struggle with impulsivity a bit." His tongue darts out, wetting his bottom lip. "Although some people find that to be one of my more endearing traits."

"I'd love to meet one of those people."

"You really would," he says matter-of-factly. His eyes drop to my bag and he gestures with a nod. "Word to the wise; if you get caught with a fixed blade like that on campus, it'll be a whole situation."

I grind out, "I'll take my chances."

"Suit yourself, Sugar Voss." I don't like the way he smiles when he says it—all sly and dark-eyed, like we're sharing a secret.

I'm saved from answering when, from across campus, the sound of a bell tolling marks the time. Afternoon classes are about to begin. I grab my boxed lunch and keep an eye on Sebastian as he collects the now-empty cans, tossing them into the dumpster. The cats dart back into the tree line and I keep a wide berth, walking in the grass, never once letting go of my knife. When I round the side of the building, I take off, practically feeling the weight of his stare as he lopes out behind me.

Maybe Sebastian was following me. Maybe he wasn't. It doesn't matter.

I won't let myself get caught alone with him—or his shitty attempts at apologies—again.

7

———————

SIXTH PERIOD SPANISH sucks a fat one. Not just because Señor Tressel insists on talking about his boyfriend the whole time—that happens every day—but because I keep running all these encounters with Sugar Voss over in my mind and shit's just not adding up here.

Something about that girl isn't right.

She doesn't like me, which is...

You know, it's fine.

Totally fucking fine.

I punched her in the face. Of course, she doesn't like me. But it's not like I did it on purpose. It's not like I picked her out of a crowd and decided to lay the girl out. It's not like I'm walking around looking for girls to wail on. *Fuck.* That's completely antithetical to my whole scene. No, let's be fair here; she jumped in the middle of a fight. Who does that and doesn't expect a little collateral damage? Someone needs to tell Sugar Voss that if you play stupid games, you win stupid prizes.

I half-listen to Señor Tressel conjugate verbs and just keep

66

thinking. In fact, I stew in this bullshit, because here I've been haunted by punching that girl, and it wasn't really my fault. A normal person would have understood that. They would have given me credit for feeling bad about it when they're responsible, too. They would have forgiven me. But Sugar Voss is walking around my turf, acting like I'm some kind of monster, and it's fucking ridiculous.

So ridiculous that it pisses me off.

I grab my notebook, shove it in my backpack and stand.

"Por favor, señor Wilcox, a donde vas?"

"El bano," I mutter, charging across the room, not giving a rat's ass where he thinks I'm going. I barge into the hallway, annoyance building with each step. What gives her the right to judge me, anyway? She doesn't know me. More importantly, who is this girl to imply that people don't find me endearing? *Excuse you*, but I'm endearing as fuck. People *adore* my ass. I'm rich, devastatingly handsome, ripped—like seriously ripped, thank you very much—and fun as hell. I save kittens. I rescue girls from creeps. I help little old ladies across the road. I'm practically a goddamn saint.

And who is Sugar Voss? Some self-righteous rando who can't take a punch and freaks out all the time?

The plan evolves in a rush and I dart from room to room, peering into each of the windows. I'll show Sugar Voss how endearing I am. I'll prove to her that she's the one with the problem here.

I skid to a stop outside American Lit and press my nose to the window. Third row, four seats back. That's who I'm looking for. I yank open the door and step inside. Mrs. Baxter cuts her lecture short and smiles when she sees me. "Sebastian, isn't this a surprise?"

"Afternoon, Mrs. Baxter," I say, pouring on the charm. It doesn't take much. She loves me. Because I'm loveable as hell. Says I remind her of Gatsby come to life. "I hate to interrupt you, but Vandy needs to go to the counseling office."

She looks across the room and I follow her gaze. Vandy's forehead creases and her eyes narrow. I smile back pleasantly and shrug. Butter could not even fucking begin to melt.

"Should she take her things?" Mrs. Baxter asks.

"Probably," I say, flashing her smile. "They didn't say how long it'd take."

I wait by the door as Vandy gathers her books and backpack. She moves slow, her gait awkward from that car accident Reyn got them into when they were kids. Normally, this kind of speed would make me crazy. Too slow and stilted, but V's been through a lot of shit and she's tough as nails. I respect the hell out of her.

I also need her help.

Holding the door for her, she passes me and walks into the hall-way. Before the door is even shut, she asks, "Okay, what are you up to?"

"What?" I take the books she's holding, tucking them under an arm. "Why am I up to something? It's completely feasible that I came to get you for pressing counseling office business."

She rolls her eyes. "No, it isn't."

I hadn't really thought this out, but I figure being honest is the best way to go with Vandy. She lives with Emory and dates Reyn. Her bullshit detector has to be spot on.

"I need you to help me with something."

"What kind of something?" Suspicion lurks in her eyes. "Is this a Devil thing?"

"No, it's personal." I run a hand through my hair, sweeping it back from my forehead. "It's a girl."

The doubt vanishes instantly, replaced by a wide-eyed, joyous expression. "Oh my god, a girl? As in one you *like*? Who is it? Does she go here?" She buries a playful shove into my shoulder. "It's about time you had a real girlfriend."

I throw up a hand. "Woah, V, you're getting way ahead of yourself. This is not about that." I grimace, casting a look down each side of the hallway. "Come on, you know I don't do girl-friends."

She rolls her eyes but looks weirdly disappointed. "Of course you don't. Neither does Emory."

"Yeah, no," I assure. "I'm not pussy-whipped like your brother. His problem is that he often has too many girlfriends."

She makes a face at that. "Then what is so important that you need me to help you in the middle of class?"

"The thing is, there's been this huge misunderstanding." I pace back and forth. "I need to clear it up."

"Well," Vandy says, all long and drawn out, eyes casting around. "Where is she?"

I stop. "Huh." I follow Vandy's gaze around, like somehow Sugar is going to suddenly appear. "I dunno. I mean...shit. I really didn't think this through."

The final bell rings, and the hallway floods with students. I'm about to give up, and I should, because there's no reason for me to be obsessing over this. I mean, who cares if some girl from the Briar Cliffs hates me? Why should she matter? But then I see a flash of red hair and say, "Come with me. Please?"

Vandy sighs. "Yeah, let me text Reyn. He was going to the weight room with Emory anyway."

Students file out of the academic buildings and head in a variety of directions; toward the gym for basketball, the natatorium for swim, the parking lot to head home, or back to the dorms for residents. I take the most direct path toward Hayden and have to keep slowing my pace for Vandy.

"How's the concussion?" she asks, once she's finished her text.

"Better." I instinctively touch the back of my neck. "Another month of rest and then I should be cleared for lacrosse."

"And you've stayed away from the fights?"

"Yes, *mom*." If the Devils were divided into positions, Vandy would definitely fall under the role of Den Mother. "I'm sticking to car stuff now."

She frowns. "Do you think that's any safer? I've seen the videos. It looks pretty dangerous."

"It's only dangerous if you're bad at it." I flash her a grin. "Fortunately, I'm an amazing driver."

She gives me a look that's full of steel and warning. "So was Reyn."

Ouch. Walked into that one, didn't I. "It's not really the same," I tell her, and although I want to make a comment about their accident having involved a *deer*—which isn't likely to happen at a rowdy meet-up—it'll just open her up to a million other possibilities. Instead, I pull ahead of her when we reach Hayden, putting in the code and opening the door.

"Where, exactly, are we going?" she asks, once we're inside.

"Georgia's room."

It's four flights to the senior hall. About halfway there, I realize this might have been a bad idea. Vandy and stairs aren't the best mix. She's almost a whole flight behind me and I double back, chest twinging at the grimace on her face.

She must see the look I give her, because she snaps, "I'm fine. I've just been out of PT because of the—" she snaps her mouth closed, but eventually mutters, "—holiday."

Ah, right. Three weeks in rehab means she hasn't been getting her physical therapy. Fuck. Knowing Vandy, if I offered to help, she'd probably bite my head off. Instead, I stick at her side, going her pace, trying to act more patient than I feel.

Once we're on the fourth floor, I lead us to the familiar room. After the Stairway to Hell rite, Georgia and I hooked up a few more times. Nothing serious, just some oral here and there. Despite being one of the horniest people I know, Georgia's got some weird hang-ups about sex, but I wasn't about to complain. She's hot, funny, and was completely down for no commitments.

When we reach her room, I bang on the door, sparing a red-faced Vandy a covert glance. A moment later, Georgia opens it, her expression turning to confusion when she sees the two of us together.

"Hey, what's going—"

"Is your roommate here?" I ask, pushing into the room. Sugar's sitting on the bed, legs crossed, an ancient laptop open on her thighs. Even from here, I can tell it's a real junker, a lot like her car. It's covered in stickers that are peeling at the edges, and I'm pretty sure her screen is being held together by duct tape.

The instant she sees me her entire body goes rigid. "Oh, hell no." She spits, "Get out!"

"*Bass*," Georgia says in warning.

"I know. I know." She told me to back off, but Sugar's the one in my territory. Her car is at my garage. She's sitting in my class. She's feeding my cats. She's living with my ex-oral buddy. She's everywhere, looking at me like I'm some class-A jackoff. Like I'm an asshole. Like I'm a monster.

Suddenly, the thought comes to me, and I realize exactly why I can't fucking breathe until she hears me out.

She's looking at me like I'm *Heston*.

I grab Vandy by the shoulders and direct her over to Sugar. I don't miss the look exchanged between her and Georgia.

"Please tell her," I say to Vandy, "that people like my impulsivity. They find it endearing, actually."

V gives me a look that could kill, then turns to Sugar, sticking out her hand. "Hi, I'm Vandy."

Sugar, back ramrod straight, stares at her hand and doesn't take it. She bites out a slow, "I'm Sugar."

"Oh, I like that name! Very unique," V says with a smile. "You just transferred here?"

Sugar's eyes dart to me and then back to Vandy. "Yeah, it's my first day."

"How was—"

I cover my mouth with my fist and cough. "Ahem."

Neither look my way.

"How was it?" Vandy repeats.

Sugar's eyes are still all tight and narrowed, but she tensely offers, "Okay, I guess. A lot different from my school back home." I don't miss the way her gaze jumps to her bag, like she's calculating the distance between her and that knife she probably has hidden in there. "But I wanted different, so I can't really complain."

"I can't imagine," Vandy says, shifting her weight in a way that says that climb up the stairs hasn't been kind to her. "I've basically gone here my whole life—"

"Are you shitting me?" I explode, anger bubbling to the surface.

"Vandy! I brought you here for a reason! Not to make friends with the new girl!"

She whips around to glower at me. "*What* has gotten into you today?"

A hand rests on my shoulder and I jerk around. Georgia glares at me. "Bass, dude, you need to go."

"I'll go when Vandy tells her." I thrust my hand in my hair. What's wrong with these girls? Why won't they back me up?

"You'll go now," Georgia says. "Or I'll call Reyn and tell him you're acting like a dick to V."

"I'm not acting like a—" I look at V, whose lips form a thin line. She doesn't exactly look hurt but I'm not seeing any Team Bass vibes from her. *Unbelievable.* These are my friends—my Devils—my girls. I'd take a bullet for them. If someone were messing with Vandy or Georgia, I don't even care. Concussion or not, I'd be throwing fists. But here I am, getting fuck-all.

I throw up my hands. "Fine. Whatever. I don't need to justify myself to any of you." I cut my eyes at Sugar. Her expression makes it clear that I'm exactly who she's been expecting me to be. "Fucking women."

I storm out of the room, slamming the door behind me, knowing one thing for sure; I don't need approval from any of them.

∾

AN HOUR LATER, I'm at the garage, blowing off some steam by pulling out the Mustang's radiator hose. I spit a curse at a hose clamp and rip it away, the skin of my knuckles scraping harshly against a bolt.

"Motherfucker." I hiss, watching as the blood runs down the back of my hand. I sag in defeat. This car has not been kind to me today. It's almost like it knows I was a dick before and now it's punishing me by proxy. "I'm not the bad guy here," I growl at the engine.

Even I don't believe it.

I still don't believe it ten minutes later when Reyn's Jeep and Emory's truck pull into the parking lot. "Aw, shit."

Merle's in the back, finishing up his bookkeeping for the day, which is good, because from the looks on Emory and Reyn's faces when they step out of their respective cars, whatever's coming next isn't going to be pretty.

Vandy climbs out of Emory's truck, and she looks almost as pissed as they do, except her glare is trained on her boyfriend and brother. "You two, so help me god—"

Reyn walks right up to me and jabs a finger sharply into my chest. "You're lucky you have a concussion, or I'd beat the *shit* out of you." And from the look in his eyes, I know he means it. "Do you know how much pain she's in from you dragging her up four flights of stairs? Tell me, Wilcox, what do you do when you're in pain? Huh? *Tell me!*" He shoves me back, face wild with anger, and I can't do anything but gawk back at him. "Do you take a little something to make it go away? I know you do, you piece of—"

"Reynolds!" Vandy's voice is some crazy amalgam of fury and hurt, and *fuck*.

Fucking shit. V's in recovery. If she's in pain, she can't take *anything*. "I didn't realize—I didn't know."

Reyn spits, "You didn't fucking care!"

Emory grabs Reyn by the shoulder and jerks him back. But if I thought he might be on my side here, I'm dead wrong. He looks me in the eye and grinds out, "What the fuck were you thinking, dragging her out of class like that? Taking her all the way up Hayden?"

"I wasn't," I admit, my anger all burned out. It's replaced with something heavy and slow-moving, and when I meet Vandy's gaze, it burns almost as badly. "V, I didn't mean—I'm sorry. I wasn't thinking."

"I know," Vandy says, eyes tracking Reyn as he leans against Sugar's Mustang, arms folded, still seething.

Sagging, I ask, "Are you okay? How bad is it?" and it makes her eyes flash hot.

"Oh my god, the three of you! The problem was not the fucking stairs." She looks like she wants to tear her hair out. "So what if I hurt a little? I can handle it, I'm fine. The *real* problem here is how you acted in that room. What the hell, Bass?"

Reyn jerks his chin in my direction. "He's having some kind of beef with that new girl."

"I'm not having beef!" There's a sting in my knuckle when I squeeze the wrench in my hand, but I barely notice the trickle of blood. "She's the one with a problem here! I was just trying to show her that I'm not an asshole."

Vandy tilts her head, visibly confused. "By acting like an asshole?"

"By introducing her to someone who knows I'm not an asshole." Only now, I'm not so sure that's the case.

Vandy turns to her brother and boyfriend, sighing. "Guys, can you give us a minute?"

"Why should I?" *Christ.* Reynolds McAllister sulks like no other.

Her face goes sharp. "Because I can fight my own battles. I didn't need the two of you racing over here like two yipping guard dogs." Apparently unable to argue with her, they both slink off back toward their cars, eyes still watching. Vandy turns back to me. "What's going on, for real?"

"Look, you remember at the beginning of the year, right? When we made the video?" I don't need to say which video. The first initiation rite into the Devils was for everyone to spill their deepest, darkest secret, all while being filmed. It was a sort of mutually assured destruction; can't become a Devil until you've shown your demons. "Remember the girl I accidentally—"

"No way," V says, eyes wide with disbelief.

Jaw tightening, I nod, sweeping my hand in gesture. "She just shows up here—everywhere—and she's treating me like I'm some sort of creep, like I meant to hurt her or something, and it's bullshit, you know? She's the one who jumped in the middle. She's the one who followed me here. I didn't even fucking—"

Vandy says, "Stop!" and I realize that I've started pacing again, that hot angry thing returning to my chest.

I'm about to lose it again.

The way Reyn and Emory are both tense, poised to spring, tells me it's obvious to them, too.

"I'm cool." I take a deep breath. "I'm chill."

Vandy asks the same question that's going through my head. "Why are you letting her get to you like this? You hurt her, Sebastian. She's entitled to her feelings. Just leave it be."

"It's not that easy!"

She rolls her eyes. "Come on, you can't handle one person not liking you?"

"It's not about that," I argue, and it isn't. I shouldn't care. I know this. I try to explain, "I know the kind of person I could have turned out to be. Can you imagine Heston, but with the physicality to back it up?"

She blanches. "That could never be you."

"Exactly," I say, flinging the wrench into the toolbox. "It can *never* be me."

She looks like she's starting to understand. "Well, this isn't the way. Either she gets to know you, or she doesn't. You can't force her."

I realize, "You forgave Reyn, right?" and fling a hand toward him, blood flying. "You blamed him for the accident, but you forgave him. How did he do it?"

Her eyes follow my hand, and she snatches it up, gaping at the wound. "What did you do to your—oh for Pete's sake." She turns to yell, "Em, bring me the first aid kit from the glove box?"

"It's fine," I insist, but she just holds it between us, eyebrows puckered.

"I never blamed Reyn for the accident," she reveals in an even tone, looking into my eyes. "I blamed him for putting us in the position to have one. There's a difference."

I feel my face go slack, because *huh*. Is that the problem? Could Sugar be madder about me picking the fight than the fact I hit her?

It doesn't quite feel so easy.

Emory returns with the first aid kit, Reyn in tow, and they both look on with narrowed eyes as Vandy cleans my bloody knuckles. I don't hold it against them—it's not fair. I hurt her, and here she is fixing me up.

Just when I thought I couldn't feel any lower.

"I'm sorry," I tell her.

She curves a shrewd eyebrow down at my hand. "For...?"

Girls always do this *thing* where an apology has to come with an itemized bill. It's annoying as fuck, but I suppose I get it. How can you truly be sorry if you don't know what you did?

I know exactly what I did. "For using you like my yipping guard dog."

She sends me a sad smile. "You're forgiven."

Before they leave, Reyn turns to me. Even though Vandy's forgiveness seems to have softened his anger toward me a little—he does have a little experience with needing her forgiveness, after all —he still gives me a sharp look. "You know, Bass, speaking from experience? At some point you're going to have to stop saying what a good guy you are and actually become one."

He and Emory lead Vandy away, and *fucking ouch*.

I would have rather he beat the shit out of me.

8

Sugar

I learn a few things during the first week at Preston Prep, the least of which being my darkroom chemical and procedure training. Private school education is definitely superior to public. I'm already behind, which means working my ass off if I want to keep up with the rest of my class. I discover that, despite our differences, the kids are the same here as anywhere else—just *more*. More rewards. More opportunity. More privileges. More expensive drama. They drop brand names and exotic locations like they're nothing, and I grow convinced half these people haven't even met their parents since middle school ended.

If it weren't for the photography club, I'd feel entirely adrift.

"Micha, this is stunning," Mr. Lee says, exhibiting one of the member's photos.

We're in what I'm told is the newly renovated Hollis Bates Creative Arts building. We're a mere group of seven, so the massive presentation room makes us seem like a particularly sparse bunch. We'd all moved our seats to a huddle at the front of the room, and it's...

Well, it's nice.

There's a lot of space to stretch out without fear of being touched. The younger girl sitting next to me—Michaela—keeps offering me the open bag of M&Ms she's been eating from, arm extended in the space between our seats. She gives me a sweet grin when I finally relent, popping a handful in my mouth. I reluctantly return it.

The photo Mr. Lee is examining up front belongs to her twin brother. It's a bold, colorful shot of a dancer in motion, her hair swirling fluidly around her face.

"You really captured the movement here," he's telling Micha. "I enjoy the use of color."

Micha himself is a study in bold color, from his bright green eye shadow to his neon purple shoes. He straightens in his chair, asking, "Is there going to be a Creative Corner feature this week?"

Michaela makes an exasperated noise, muttering, "Glory hound."

"There will!" Mr. Lee pauses and turns to me, explaining for my benefit, "We have a little student exhibition space in the lobby of the arts wing. Every week we like to pick some creative works to display from various mediums—"

Michaela pipes in, "That is, when the illustrators and creative writing people aren't hogging it all up."

The general, bitter mutters of agreement are a tip-off that this must be an ongoing feud in the arts wing. Another thing I've learned about Preston kids is that they're scarily competitive.

Mr. Lee adds, "This week we have *three* spots!" Everyone oohs and ahhs. Another thing I've learned. People here get excited over the most minor shit. At my old school, this kind of collective reaction would be reserved for the promise of an edible free lunch. "I'll announce my picks at the end of the meeting," he tells Micha. "Okay, who's next. Ah, Sugar Voss! Let's see what you're made of, shall we?"

Fighting a grimace, I carefully pull the photo from my bag. It'd taken me five tries to properly develop it, still unfamiliar with the process. Mr. Lee clips it up and stands back, finger on his chin as he examines it.

It's the mama cat—Abbadon—from that day I'd been feeding them. Her eyes are wide, gaze sharp, and it's not that she isn't a pretty cat, because she is. But I'd chosen it because she has these little scars around her cheek and a dirty nose. She looks like alley cat royalty. A creature who's both won and lost. She's looking out of frame at Hades, stealing her turkey, and I know it's lame. Using a cat as a subject has to be like the Wonderwall of photography. But aside from possibly Georgia, I'm not comfortable enough with anyone here to just start snapping off photos of them. I don't know the good places to catch a landscape. I'm not even sure if I'm *allowed* to go to that lake, yet.

"Well," Me. Lee begins, and I prepare myself for a lukewarm compliment. "This is definitely nabbing a creative corner slot."

"Really?" I blurt incredulously. He can't be serious.

But he nods, gesturing to the photo. "The lighting is striking, the way it plays off the eyes, and the use of black and white was a good choice. You've captured something really emotive here. It conveys such a strong sense of longing." He turns to me, eyebrow raised. "It's very somber, Sugar."

"I agree." Micha leans forward to meet my eyes. "It's really going to balance mine out up there in the creative corner."

I'm too stunned and embarrassed to do much more than smile tightly back at him. Emotive, somber longing? For a moment, I miss my old school, where pictures of cats are pictures of cats, and no one ever looks beneath the surface.

After the meeting—Micha had scored a spot, as had his sister—the twins and I stand around the lobby of the building, waiting for our photos to be mounted. I don't actually give a shit. In fact, after the whole emotive-somber thing, I'm beginning to think I'd prefer not being credited at all.

They're bickering over whose photo is better and it's giving me a headache. The back of my teeth start aching, that phantom jaw-twinge acting up, and I rap a knuckle against a placard to get their attention.

"I'm sure you'll both do this Hollis Bates artist-person justice."

Micha snaps his mouth closed to look at me. "Oh, Hollis Bates isn't an artist. She's just super gay."

Michaela explains, "Her dad doesn't know the difference."

He puts a hand to his chest. "Bless his heart. But if he wants to donate a chunk of his fortune so we can have a nicer building, I'm not going to complain."

It isn't until Mr. Lee mounts the frames and I see their names that it hits me. "Adams?" I ask them. "Like the Adams scholarship?"

Neither looks surprised. As we exit the building, the sister offers, "Our parents set that up. They're really into philanthropy. You got it, right?"

I shift uncomfortably. The thought of charity was a lot less mortifying when it was a faceless entity. "Uh, yeah."

"I know what you're thinking," Micha says, randomly high-fiving a passing freshman. "Like this is some twisted Miss Havisham situation where our parents realized our sad, underappreciated photography club needed members, so they decided to bring in a ringer."

Me? A ringer? I give him a skeptical look.

He raises one perfectly shaped eyebrow. "Yeah, you're the ringer. Your portfolio was the shit, gorg."

I want to respond that he's delusional, but I see Sebastian walking toward us and clam up.

Sebastian has managed to keep his hands to himself these last few days. There haven't been any more inappropriate incidents in Dr. Ross's class or anywhere else.

That doesn't mean I'm not keeping an eye on him. To the contrary. Sebastian Wilcox has triggered something inside of me—an intensely heightened awareness. I'm on constant alert, wondering and watching him all the time. I feel like if I let down my guard, for even a minute, he'll strike.

The problem with Dr. Ross's class is that I can't actually watch him. He still sits behind me, completely out of view. I have to rely on my other senses, honing sharply into his every movement. It's almost like back home with my step-father, Doug. The instant

Sebastian sits in his seat, my brain fills in the gaps of what I can't see. There's the sound of him unzipping his backpack, the scrape of his notebook when he tosses it on his desk. The echoing click-clack of his mechanical pencil. The slide of his shoe as it moves along the tile floor and stretches out, invading the space beside my desk. My back straightens when he moves, silently tracking the way his limbs reach out for anything he can touch, feel, grab onto. Days have passed and he hasn't messed with me again. Really, he barely glances at me. I've erected a force-field and it's nearly like he's *abiding* by it.

There are other sounds that pass through the barrier. Like when he sighs or mutters under his breath. Sometimes he curses, other times he's working out his assignment, documenting each step along the way. The strangest thing is the reverberation of his laugh. If we're positioned just right, I can feel it in my own chest. It's weird to feel someone on the inside, when I won't allow them to touch the outside.

At least he doesn't seem to be approaching us, eyes fixed to his phone.

That is, not until Micha calls out, "H-hey, Bass." His sister perfectly mirrors his expression; the dreamy smile and smitten eyes.

I don't hide my own expression of horror when he looks up, stopping to regard them. There's no mistaking what's going down. The twins are crushing on this asshole something fierce. I'm literally walking with the Sebastian Wilcox freshman fanclub. He brightens under the attention like a flower to sunlight, blue eyes sparking. It makes me want to barf.

His eyes only flick to mine for the barest moment before he thankfully ignores me, sending them a roguish grin. "Why, Michaela Adams," he greets, taking her hand and pressing a kiss to her knuckles. God, she looks like she's about to actually swoon. "You're looking lovely today. And Micha." Micha's already got his hand out, and I swear there might be drool happening. Sebastian doesn't miss a beat, taking his hand and pressing the same quick, chaste kiss into Micha's knuckles. "As always, the second prettiest guy at Preston." He flashes Michaela a sparkling smile. "I'm the first, of course."

He's already strutting past us when Micha pushes a casual, too-late 'psssh' through his lips. "I'm so prettier than you."

Sebastian just throws up a two-fingered salute, disappearing into the arts building.

Michaela lets out a squeal. "Oh my god, he kissed my hand!"

Micha gushes, "And *mine*! Why do I have to be a freshman?"

"Yeah, it's the freshman thing standing in your way, and not the fact that he likes girls."

He flicks a hand at her. "Whatever, I'm more of a girl than you."

"Fair." She nods, apparently unable to argue with this. "And no way you're prettier than him."

He just nods back. "Also fair."

I can't take it anymore. "Oh, come on." I stop in my tracks, lifting a hand toward where he disappeared. "The guy's a total jerk! Plus, that hair? *Really?*"

"Sebastian's not a jerk," Michaela says, and she's not even arguing with me or anything. She says this like she's informing me that the sky is blue—like I've missed out on something important and fundamental.

"He's really nice," Micha agrees, head tilting, "unlike his brother, who is undeniably the worst. And what's wrong with his hair?"

Michaela twirls one of her braids, eyes glossing over. "It looks so soft."

"He's always pushing it out of his face." He does that thing where he rakes it back, forehead-to-crown, like some kind of shampoo model. "Which means it annoys him, but he keeps it because he's a vain fuckwit."

They both give me confused looks, and I can tell that it doesn't matter. What is *with* this place? Is there something in the water that makes everyone think Sebastian Wilcox is god's gift to men and women alike?

Maybe it's not everyone else, my brain unhelpfully supplies. *Maybe it's you.*

No.

No fucking way. Anyone who can be like him, buzzing with tense fury one day and this flirtatious and charming the next, can't be anything but bad news.

~

I'm surprised that Georgia seems determined to be friends with me, despite the difference in our backgrounds. It's pretty obvious that I'm the one with the hang up over our economic differences. I'll just add it to the pile.

Eventually, I allow Georgia and Vandy to talk me into sitting with them at lunch. Afton is there, along with a few other girls. One is Caroline, the girl who stopped by our dorm room on my first day. There are boys, too, but I stick to the opposite side of the table, away from their loud, deep voices and erratic movements. One boy is Vandy's brother, and the other's her boyfriend, Reyn.

Without really wanting to, I watch the couple, fascinated by how they touch one another. It's constant—arms brushing, finger-tips grazing, sharing food. Once, when I look under the table for my dropped fork, I see his hand skating up her thigh, under the hem of her skirt.

When I straighten back up, I glance away, hoping no one can see the pink of my cheeks. I'm not a prude—far from it. Christ, I'm a river rat, born and bred. Skinny dipping is in our blood. But the sight of his fingers gliding up her thigh—slow, intentional, painfully intimate—right in the middle of a public lunch bustle makes something inside of me squirm.

My eyes land on a familiar head of blond hair a few tables away. He sits with other boys who are as loud and brash as he is. In that moment, our eyes meet. His are stone cold and aloof, passing over me like I'm no one. *Nothing.* I'm only worried about the heat on my face. Does he notice? Can he tell that my skin feels like it's on fire? If he does, he doesn't reveal it, turning back to his friends. I want to say that I forget him, ignore him, but I don't. Even here in the dull roar of the dining hall, I find myself tracking him—his hands, his

83

movements. He's constantly gesturing, touching, hands curling into fists and releasing, so easily. Hands that can break. Hands that can hurt. My skin itches, just watching how easy it is for him. He's wild and carefree. Impulsive and unrestrained.

He's the opposite of everything I am.

"So, Sugar, you in for Friday night?" Georgia asks, drawing my attention back to the table.

"In for…" I raise an eyebrow, hoping no one notices my distraction. Or the source of it. One look at Vandy proves she's too engrossed in Reyn to notice anything else. Maybe because of where and what his hands are doing at the moment. *Shit.* Now my face is red again. Who does that at the lunch table?

"The guys are all into these 'car shows'," she says, using finger quotes. "I don't know why they call them that."

"Because," Afton chimes in. I didn't even know she was listening. "Basically, it's a bunch of guys showing off their cars and driving like maniacs. It may as well be a dick-measuring contest."

This is what rich kids do? I'm somehow both curious and completely uninterested.

"Uh," I tap the edge of my fork on my tray. "I should probably catch up on some of my homework. I'm a little behind." Understatement. Freshmen like the twins are probably learning shit that I would have been taught this year, had I gone back to my old school. Things here move so fast that it makes my head spin.

"Aw, come on," Georgia pleads. "Didn't you say you came here for the new experiences?"

I chew the inside of my cheek. "Partly."

"Well, this is one of them!" She looks around, prompting other nods of encouragement. "Sneaking out of the dorms, heading off campus, participating in borderline illegal behavior." She lists them off like it's a badge of honor. "It's fun, seriously. Total Preston rite of passage."

It doesn't *sound* particularly fun. Honestly, it sounds exactly like the kind of dumb shit the kids back home would do. But my new roommate looks at me expectantly and it feels wrong saying no to someone making an effort to include me.

I mean, how bad can it be?

∼

THE THICK STENCH of sulfur and the sound of squealing tires meet us as we get to the overpass. Down below, on the state highway, a barricade of cars has blocked the road in both directions, headlights illuminating the area. The harsh scent of chemicals—spray paint, I realize—hits me. On the other side of the street is a kid in a black sweatshirt, hood up over his head, tagging a cement pillar.

"So this is what rich kids do on a Friday night, huh?" I lean over the rail, looking into the street below. Georgia is on one side of me, Caroline the other. Vandy and a few other people from the lunch table are milling around. There are other kids, but they're the kind who don't seem like they go to Preston. They're more like kids from home. For the first time in my life, I feel weirdly split between two worlds, even though neither of them are actually mine.

"I'm sure some kids are partying tonight. I think Miranda Bradshaw is having people over," Georgia says with disinterest. "Things have kind of been weird around Preston since homecoming."

"What do you mean?" I have to shout the question since one of the drivers below decided to open their trunk, revealing a massive stereo system. Rap music bounces off the cement, deep bass reverberating through my chest.

"There was a huge prank at the dance," Caroline says, "that basically revealed that this secret society that'd been kicked off campus for inappropriate behavior was back in action. The school flipped out because it's a direct violation of policy, and it made the administration look like total dumbasses. They've been cracking down on parties and stuff."

"You don't think they'll find out *this* is happening?" I ask, watching as two cars pull into the middle of the circle.

Georgia shrugs, chomping on a piece of gum. "Most of these kids are from North Ridge or farther away. It's kind of underground. Not exactly on their radar."

"How did you even find out about it?"

85

She nods toward the circle and I see a familiar blue muscle car. The driver leans out the window gesturing wildly with his hands. My reaction is visceral, low in my stomach. Deep in my throat.

"We used to go to Bass's fights, but after the concussions he got a new hobby," Caroline says. "The fights weren't exactly the healthiest thing—" she and Georgia share a meaningful look, "—so we're being supportive."

They talk about him like a brother. Like someone they care about. Like someone they don't want to get hurt. It's baffling. He doesn't even really run in their circles during school. Sebastian seems to have his own circle of friends, his own lunch table, his own extracurriculars. What is it that binds them all together?

Down below, I see his blonde hair duck back in the car and hear the rumble of the Ford's engine as he revs it up. Georgia grins, "Say what you want about Bass, but he's always up for some crazy fun."

Because he's crazy, I want to say, unable to keep my eyes off of him or his vehicle. The Shelby gleams, shiny like a sapphire in the other cars' lights. From above, I have a perfect view of the white racing stripes that arc over the top of the car. The energy in the crowd shifts and everyone huddles together down below or gets a spot on the bridge. Someone lights a bundle of fireworks, sending smoke and sparks into the air. The back lights on Sebastian's car pulse red and the sound of the engine is commingled with the squeal of tires. A moment later he's in motion, peeling away from the others and spinning terrifyingly fast.

I honestly have no idea what I'm watching, other than a boy who obviously has a death wish. But he's not the only one. Like the fireworks, the crowd hovers too close, and the Ford drifts nearer, spins closer, with every turn. Through the window, I see his hands gripping the wheel, never once losing control. My heart pounds, terrified of watching a tragedy unfold, and my hands clench around the railing. Just when I think he's lost it completely, the back tires getting precariously close to the crowd, he straightens out, shifting in gear and speeding down the road.

All he's left is the scent of burnt rubber and my heart in my throat.

"Holy shit," Georgia cries. "That was crazy! Right?"

I can't find my voice to answer, but yeah, that was crazy as fuck. He's deranged. Full-speed chaos. I find myself straining to hear the sound of a crash in the distance, evidence that trouble had finally caught up to him, but that doesn't come. What I do hear, over the music and crowd, is the whine of a siren. "Is that…" I start, looking down the road, away from where Sebastian had just gone.

"Fuck," Georgia mutters.

"Police!"

The cry comes from the crowd and the whole place erupts into chaos. "Run!" Georgia yells, half-laughing. "Get to the car!"

I follow the girls, unsure of how to get back to the alley where we parked. We're fine on the bridge—momentarily—but then the crowd runs up the embankment from the street below. It's hard to hear with all the shouting and the squeal of the cars racing down the street, all muted under the pounding of my heart. I didn't come all this way to get locked up for watching bullshit car theatrics. I keep an eye peeled for Georgia's red hair and see her duck in the slit of a cut chain-link fence. I race toward her, but suddenly there are too many people, bodies everywhere, crushing, and pushing against me. Touching. Grabbing.

You're nothing.

I freeze, body going stiff, lungs constricting with panic.

"Sugar! Come on," she says, thrusting her hand to me. I stare at it, unmoving, blood pumping in my ears. She wiggles her fingers. "Sugar!"

I shake my head and take a step back, crashing into a body.

"Watch it!" I spin and see male hands coming toward me, palms out. It's pure hindbrain instinct, bracing for a hit, flinching back.

I lurch away, looking for a way out—*away from* all these hands and bodies—running blind until the flickering blue lights push me off the road. I need a place to catch my breath, to hide, and finally duck behind a sign in front of a church. I nestle against the brick, tucked between thick shrubs, and put my head between my legs, panting shallow breaths. Fuck. What a time for one of these.

I only distantly register the police cruiser rolling by quietly, lights swirling off the front of the church. I take a few moments to gulp down air and calm this wild panic gripping my chest.

You're fine, I keep telling myself. *No one touched you—not really.*

The relief at this is an old friend.

The disappointment? That's new.

Before long, the taillights vanish around the corner and I start to feel the crushing weight of fatigue that always follows a panic attack. I stay there for a little while longer, though. Long enough that the dampness in the air turns to sprinkles, wetting my hair and shoulders.

Groaning in frustration, I stand and dust off my hands, looking around.

Now I really have no idea where I am. I reach for my phone and search for Georgia's number. But just as I'm about to press 'call', a car rolls out of the shadows behind the church. Its window slowly rolls down.

Sebastian Wilcox rests his forearm on the window and looks at me with those piercing blue eyes. "Need a ride?"

You *have to* be shitting me.

9

I HAVE this thing about picking scabs.

Always drove my mom nuts. Every scar I've gotten could have been a lot smaller if I hadn't picked at the healing wound so much, unthinkingly, like a compulsion. There's a huge scab on my knuckle right now, and I've been fiddling with it all night, exposing the raw pink skin beneath.

There's another scab standing out there in what's rapidly becoming a full-on rain shower, looking into my window with a stony expression.

Guess I can't help but pick at that one, too.

"Come on," I say, patting the seat beside me. "Promise I won't bite." She turns and marches away, arms wrapping around her middle. Rolling my eyes, I coast alongside her. "The sky's about to drop and it's cold as balls out here. We're both going to the same place, it doesn't have to be—"

"Fuck off!" she snaps, strides lengthening.

I know I should, but probably the only thing worse than

subjecting her to my presence is leaving her on the side of a rainy highway on a cold night.

"Nah," I answer. "What are you gonna do? Walk all the way back in the rain? Stop being stubborn."

Her hair swishes heavily behind her and I can only barely make out the shape of her face, but there's no mistaking the tightness of that jaw. She's like a goddamn cinderblock wall. No getting through that.

"Come on!" Exasperated, I smirk, offering, "You can bring your knife."

She stops.

I press down on the brake a little too late, surprised that even worked, but it still takes a long, suspended moment until I hear the passenger door click open. The pair of dog tags swinging around her neck enter before she does.

She's got the knife, alright. She's not even holding it blade up. She's holding it like she's in the middle of stabbing someone already. *Jesus Christ*. Maybe I should have left her on the side of the road after all.

She turns to me only halfway, damp hair veiling her pale cheeks. "Touch me and I'll bury this in your fucking throat."

And people think I have issues with violence.

"Noted." I try a smile, but it doesn't penetrate. If anything, it just makes her lip curl more. Fortunately, when I step on the gas and start down the road, she seems to relax—minutely. At least she kind of chills on the whole knife-wielding thing, resting it in her lap in favor of gathering her hair up into one of those sloppy buns girls are so good at. As soon as she's done, she picks the knife back up, tapping it anxiously on her knee.

Sugar leans into the door, body inched as far away from me as possible. Never mind the console between us that houses the gearshift and other instruments, she's acting like I could fly at her at any moment. I'd have to resort to gymnastics to even get to the passenger seat, but her breath fogs up the window and her hand clutches the handle of her knife like she's plotting her escape.

She's shivering.

"I'm taking the long way back to campus," I tell her, getting on the loop that runs around town. "Just to avoid cops."

She nods, her hand smoothing the frayed threads loose around the holes in her jeans. There's one up near her upper thigh, showing a pale strip of flesh, then another down at the knee. I drag my eyes away from the movement, looking back at the dark road.

"I'm going to turn on the heat," I warn, keeping my movements slow, measured, as I reach for the knob. This is like riding with a skittish, slightly deranged kitten. When she doesn't react beyond mashing herself a little closer to the door, I turn on the stereo too, hoping to cut some of the awkward silence. Being around people who hate me isn't something I'm used to, particularly with girls.

She pulls this angry-gawking expression at my sound system. "I *like* this song," she says, all accusingly, like I plotted to ruin it for her and now she's pissed off about it. Like how dare I have the *nerve* to listen to the same music as her?

"Hey, so do I. Guess we have something in common, huh?" I give her a smile that just makes her sneer back. "Could knock me over with a feather."

She lifts her chin, flashing a vicious, sharp smile. "A feather wasn't quite what I had in mind."

Now it's my turn to gawk. Goddamn, this girl is a spitfire. Scary as hell. Quick to step up. Slow to back down. Almost as good-looking as I am. I shoot a glance at the pretty little bitchy number currently occupying my passenger seat, and it's like lightning.

Oh, I'm in for this.

I'm *all in*.

It takes a few minutes, but her shivering eventually stops. She doesn't necessarily chill, but she at least doesn't look ready to fling herself out the window. *Progress.*

"What were you doing behind that church?" she abruptly asks, her voice more even than I've heard it so far.

Surprised at the question—both the content and lack of attitude—I spare her a quick glance. "Hiding out," I reply, lounging back in my seat, wrist draped casually over the wheel as I deftly shift gears. I know I can't impress her, but this sudden impulse to show off for her isn't something I'm built to oppose. "I heard the sirens and knew I should get off the streets. Cops busting up car shows is more of a 'when', not an 'if'." I switch lanes, engine revving loudly as I fly past a truck. "I always have a backup plan set." Fully prepared to have my balls threatened again, I ask, "Uh, what about you?"

I'd seen her crouched behind the church for a long while, wondering if I should make myself known. I might have, if not for the fact she had her head buried in her knees, shoulders hitching with loud breaths. I figure she was crying. Nothing worse than a crying girl—except maybe one with a knife.

Fucking hell, Merle had me pegged.

"I guess I was hiding, too." Her fingers twist at the frayed thread and she sounds more tired than anything else. I can work with that. "I was running after Georgia and Caroline, but..."

I glance over and see her tight jaw. "But...?"

"We got separated and then there were too many people, and this asshole bumped into me." It all comes out in a rush, like it's been bottled in her chest. "I just had to get out of there."

My brain holds onto these little nuggets of information, like pieces of a puzzle. It may be the concussions, or the fact I'm an idiot, but a bigger picture is slowly starting to take form. "So what you're saying is that I'm not the only guy you don't want touching you."

She cuts me a look and my balls shrink up a little. "No, you're not."

My instinct is to reach across the seats and tuck the strand of hair hanging by her cheek over her ear. It's strong—a compulsion —*pick pick pick*. Part of it is my usual impulse to touch, plus my tendency toward oppositional defiance, but there's something else, too. There's pain written all over her face, and it's weird, but I don't like it. There's some moronic urge brewing to take it all away, to make her feel better—good. Huh. Maybe this is what it's like when you suddenly realize you're into someone. That feeling is what keeps me from crossing the line.

Well, that and the fact I don't want to be stabbed to death.

Would really stain Jasmine's leather seats.

I rest my hand on the gear shift instead, letting the Shelby eat up the road, "So, where'd you get that Mustang? That thing must have been a sweet piece back when."

After a tense beat, she offers, "It was my dad's."

It's killing me not to tell her about the rebuild. I'm almost done with the alternator, and the hoses just came in yesterday, and I can get started on the transmission soon. I've been driving Merle crazy by chattering over it all week.

"Oh, that's cool." I'm wondering what kind of dad gives a girl a broken-down, unreliable car that's barely holding together. "My dad would never give me something like that."

She tugs at that thread and stares out the side window. "'Give' is probably the wrong word. 'Left' is more accurate."

Fuck. Her dad is gone. Bailed? Dead? I'm dying to know, but I sure as hell don't want to ask. "Well, it's cool that he had and kept something like it. It's awesome. My dad *hates* this car. Can't figure out why I don't want something flashy and new, that's all smooth and quiet." I run my hand over the dash, feeling the vibration as it barrels down the road. "Smooth and quiet is the most boring shit. I like feeling every bump and turn in this. It's different—more authentic. The engine? The way it hums? Fuck, it's like a heartbeat. You don't just drive a car like this, you live it."

I glance over and see Sugar watching me, her dark eyebrows furrowed and her lips puckered in a not-so-unappealing pout. I clamp my mouth shut because, *Jesus*, she did not ask for that info dump, but she surprises me by asking, "Your dad bought you this car even though he hates it?"

"Oh, hell no," I laugh, "I bought my sweet Jasmine here with my own money."

She snorts and shakes her head. "Sure."

"What?"

"A car like this is super expensive. He may not have specifically paid for it, but I'm sure your parents helped in some way. Trust fund? Savings account?"

A flicker of irritability rolls up my spine. "I'm not going to say my parents don't take care of me, Sugar, but they didn't pay a dime toward this car. I earned it myself. I built her from the frame up with nothing but my own sweat and blood. Learned how to maintain it, upgrade it, all on my own. She's completely mine, in every sense of the word."

She gives me a look that tells me just how much she doubts this. "So you have a job?"

"'Job' is a bit of a stretch," I admit, swallowing back the tinge of shame. Why should I be ashamed, anyway? I was good at what I did. "I won it. Fighting." I chance a look to gauge her reaction to that, and find her big hazel eyes glaring right back at me. I'm quick to explain, "But I'm not doing that anymore. I stopped fighting."

The road is dark, and I can't read her expression, but she says, "Caroline mentioned you had a concussion." It's not phrased as a question, but I can hear it anyway. Is this curiosity? It's not much, but it's something.

I see our exit coming up and turn on the blinker. "I've had a few, but yeah, the last one really fucked me up." My hands grip the steering wheel, thinking about that fight. How I'd lost control and let him get the best of me. It's not like I couldn't have beaten him. "My family and the doctor all think it's from lacrosse, so I've been benched until I get cleared. I really want to play my final season. The team counts on me, so I've stayed out of the ring."

"And now you race cars?" She grips the knife and slices easily through the frayed thread on her jeans. "Not sure that's less dangerous."

I shrug. "What can I say. I'm a Devil through and through. Vices are kind of our thing." The Preston gates are up ahead. I turn in the driveway and find a parking spot in the back, away from the other cars. I cut the engine.

Reaching for the door, I watch her chew out a slow, stilted, "So... the ride. Thanks. I guess."

"No problem." I stare out the window, hands gripping the steering wheel, and I can't. I can't just leave it alone. *Pick pick pick.* "Wait. I need to fucking—I mean, I want to..."

She pauses, looking at me with those big round eyes, doubt and wariness lurking in every corner. "Yeah?"

Taking a breath, I start, "Look, Sugar. I'm sorry about that night in the Briar Cliffs. The truth is, just being at that place sets me on edge, and I saw that asshole messing with you and it lit the fuse. That punch was meant for him, not you. Swear."

"Yeah, I know," she says tonelessly, unlatching the door. It opens with a heavy creak.

I tap the steering wheel, feeling jittery. "So, uh, apology accepted?" God knows why, but this is suddenly very important to me.

"Sure," she says, but it doesn't sound like she means it. She gets out of the car and slams the door.

Sure.

Sure?

Fucking 'sure'?

I scramble out of the driver's seat and run to catch up with her short, choppy strides across the lot.

"That's *it*?" I call after her. "I mean, not trying to be a d-bag here, but I can count on one hand the number of times I've apologized to someone. I think that deserves a little more than some vague-ass 'sure'. It was an accident, you *know* it was an accident, and here you've turned it into this crazy fucking *thing*, so I think I'm entitled to a little more than 'sure'."

She comes to a stop, whipping around. *Oh, fuck.* There's the wrath. I see it vibrating across her compact little body, fists all clenching. And because I actually am a d-bag, when she crosses her arms over her chest, I check out her tits. For science. Gotta know if this attraction thing is legit, don't I?

"Are you fucking serious right now? You get into my business, start a fight, hit *me*, fracturing my jaw, and are banking on that half-assed apology to make you entitled to something?" She laughs, but it's not the fun kind. It's pure ice. "Here's the thing, Wilcox. You think you're special, but you aren't. I know guys like you. All you do is roll over everything and everyone in your path. Grabbing, jabbing, punching, kicking, *driving*. You hurt, and then you blame it on something else. A bad day. A misunderstanding. Being *set on edge*." She presses a fingertip to her temple like it's a gun, eyes alight. "You think being reckless like that is actually charming. I see it in that smug-ass smile of yours, which you get away with because you're so fucking pretty, people let it slide." She scoffs, eyes dragging up and down my body like she's looking at pond scum. "Well, I call bullshit on that. I'm not letting it slide, and I'm not swayed by your sharp jawline and soft-looking hair. I'm not swayed by you at all, because there's one rule in my life—keep your goddamn hands to yourself—which is something that's clearly beyond your capabilities."

Her words land like a blow—harder than the one that gave me this concussion—not because she's wrong. Of course she's right, and I have absolutely no idea how to react to that. I can't chase after her. I can't smile or grin, or flirt my way out of it, or do any of the things that I'd normally do to win someone over, because now I'm starting to get it. Something about this girl is *broken*, and whatever that thing is, I can't fix it. Not the way I normally would—not the way I'd own a fight, or win another girl over, or repair a car—with my hands.

Or can I?

"And if I don't want to?" I ask.

She glares at me, flustered. "What?"

"Play by your rules?" I take a step forward, holding my hands up and wiggling my fingers. "These hands do a lot more than hurt, Sugar. They can make a girl feel really good, too. Hell, they can make me feel pretty damn good if I'm in a jam."

Her cheeks turn an incredible shade of red and the spark reignites in her eyes. "You're disgusting."

"Am I? Because I think I just heard you call me pretty." I lick my bottom lip, thinking *yeah*. Yeah, I'm so fucking into this. "You're not so repulsed by me after all."

"You're wrong. I hate guys like you."

"Yeah? Then why are your cheeks all flushed?" I look down at her chest. "And you're breathing heavy, and you didn't have to get in the car with me, but you did, because even if you hate me, there's something about me that keeps bringing you back."

"That's not true," she says, but there's something about the way she says it. The frown that creases her brow. The way her eyes flicker with worry.

She's doubting herself, and she doesn't like it.

We're inches apart now, and she still hasn't run. She looks up at me with those bitter, angry eyes but here's the thing. I don't think all that hurt is about me. It has to be about something else —*someone else*—and I'm pretty fucking sure I can make her associate me with something else.

I bend and go for it, crashing my mouth to hers. I feel her body go stiff even as her lips grow pliant against mine.

She doesn't stab me, and for some reason, I'm surprised.

For Sugar Voss, that's gotta be the equivalent of a marriage proposal.

My kiss isn't gentle or kind, but I never have been. The tip of her nose is cold, bumping against my cheek as a I pull a hard, sucking kiss from her full lips. Her mouth is hot against mine and when I lick against the seam of her lips, they obediently part, granting me access to the slick warmth inside. Without really expecting her to, I make a sound when she surges back, licking angrily against my tongue.

Oh, fuck yeah.

Now it's a fight—a struggle between us—two dominating forces caught in a battle. Kissing, fighting? *This*, I know. From the way she's kissing me back, all breathless and defiant, a bitten-off grunt in the back of her throat, so does she. I'm getting so into it that I don't even give a second thought to lifting my hands, pressing them against the small of her back and crushing her body to mine, all hard and soft and—

She jerks back and shoves her hands against my chest, sending me stumbling back. I'm still so lost in the fog of that kiss that I don't see her knee before I feel it—*oh fuck, no no no*—driving right into my crotch.

"Oof," I groan, hands clutching my balls as I buckle and fall to my knees. The ground is wet and cold when I tip over onto my side, eyes squeezed shut against the pain. So degrading, the way I quiver down here in the grass. I look up and see her puffy, pink lips twisted into a mean grin.

"Rule number one, asshole." She gives her a knife a twirl before dropping it into her bag. "Keep your hands to yourself."

~

I STROLL into the main building the next day, hoping no one can tell that I spent two hours with an ice pack on my junk. It may have been a little over dramatic, but I was nursing a bruised ego as much as my balls. I've been in dozens of fights, have lightning-fast reflexes, can control a speeding car, but somehow, I managed to let a girl named *Sugar* get the best of me. Shit's demoralizing.

It didn't help that the kiss was fucking amazing.

So amazing, that I'm actually thinking a knee to the balls was worth it.

"Hey, Bass," Sydney says, falling in step as I walk toward my locker. "Saw you at the car show last night. Sucks that the cops showed up. I was hoping we could hang out afterwards."

I cut my eyes over at her. She's in her cheer get-up, basketball season being in full swing. "Yeah, too bad, but that's part of the deal. The cops always show."

I stop at the locker and she presses her hand against my chest, gazing slyly back at me. *Ugh.* "Well, next time we should have a backup plan. We can arrange to meet later."

This girl either can't take a hint—or won't. One of the two. I open my mouth to tell her it's not going to happen again—ever— but over her glittery hair bow I see Reyn open his locker door. He pauses for a second, then pulls out a black envelope. *Fuck.* Apparently, I got Devil business brewing in the locker behind me. Not something Sydney can see.

"Yeah, we'll figure something out." I rest my hand on my locker handle. "I've got to get to class. You know what a hard-ass Dr. Ross is about tardies."

Her eyes get all annoyingly bright. "Right! We'll definitely figure something out." She drags her fingers down my chest. "Have a good day."

I wait until she walks off before opening my locker door. The envelope is taped to the inside. But there's something else sitting on top of my books.

A fucking clear plastic baggie filled with ice. Propped against it is a handwritten note: *Next time I hope you remember rule number 1.*

So that's how it's gonna be, huh?

I look around to see if anyone is watching—if *she's* watching—but I don't see Sugar in the hallway. I grab both the envelope and the bag of ice, slamming the door. On the way to class, I think of all the things I can do to retaliate. My instinct is to dump the ice on her head, but that one would land me in a shit-ton of trouble. She obviously wants me to react. Probably hoping I'll lose it, just to affirm that she's been right all along about me being an impulsive, violent d-bag. What Sugar doesn't realize is that I've spent every second of my life on this pale blue dot alongside the most abusive, bullying, asshole brother she could probably imagine.

Oh, yeah. I can play the long game, sweetie.

She's already in her seat when I walk into class, eyes focused forward and ignoring me. This is how it's been since the day she blew up that first day and stormed out of class. Full avoidance. But it's bullshit. I know she's aware of me. She's too stiff all the time. Too measured in her movement. I'm living in this girl's head, no doubt about it.

I slide into my seat and rest the bag of ice on my desk, opening the zipper and taking out a piece. I lean forward, forearms propped on my desk, and get right up close to her ear, giving it a loud *crunch*. Her shoulders rise in response.

"Mr. Wilcox," Dr. Ross says, frowning at the bag of ice. "What are you doing? You know there's no food or drink in this classroom."

"I apologize," I say grinning sheepishly. "This isn't food or drink. I suffered a painful injury last night and I've been icing it ever since."

Dr. Ross narrows her eyes. "Keep the bag *closed*."

"Yes, ma'am."

It's Friday, which means Dr. Ross spends at least half the class reviewing notes on the Promethean board. Once she turns off the lights and settles into her rhythm, I lean up on my elbow and whisper, "Are you sure you don't want some of this ice? Because you seemed pretty hot last night when your tongue was in my mouth."

Her shoulders tense, pen freezing in her hand.

"You can pretend like you don't want me to touch you, Sugar Voss, but I think you're fooling yourself." I lean forward and run my finger along her neck. "If you think my tongue in your mouth felt good, wait until I use it somewhere else."

Her reaction is swift, in a heartbeat she's out of her desk and has the bag of ice in her hands.

"Ms. Voss!" Dr. Ross shouts, but it's too late. She's opened the zipper and dumps the melting, ice cold water on my head.

"Holy sh—" I yell, the freezing water running down my face and neck. I lurch up, hands out, catching some of the ice. Sugar's got her top two buttons undone, and it only feels natural to take a handful of ice, pluck the shirt away from her collar and drop it down in there.

She gasps and stumbles back.

"Oh, shit!" someone laughs. "He didn't!" It's followed by an eruption of gasps, laughter, and rising pandemonium.

Dr. Ross yells, "Sebastian!" and I gesture to where Sugar is fanning out her shirt, face pinched.

"She started it! You saw her! She dumped that on my head!"

Sugar whips around to the teacher, hotly arguing, "He touched my neck and—"

"I don't want to hear it!" Dr. Ross looks like she's about to have a coronary. "Out! Both of you, get out of my room!" I don't even need to look at her face to see how pissed off she is—or how much trouble I'm in. "Now!"

Whatever the fallout, I'm thinking it was worth it. Because if Sugar Voss thinks this is going to work—that striking back is going to put me off her scent—then hot damn.

This girl really doesn't know me at all.

10

THE THING about going so long without touch is that it gets easy. It's just the lack of something. It didn't take long for me to forget what was even so great about it. I almost stopped feeling like I was missing out on anything at all. It was a good place to be in. Real nice.

And then Sebastian Wilcox fucking kissed me.

Red-faced and furious, I storm out of Dr. Ross's room. Cold ice is trapped in my bra and pooling at my waist. I yank my shirt out of my skirt and let the ice cubes fall to the floor with a clatter. Two pieces land at the toes of a pair of black boots.

"Are you happy?" I snap, glaring up at Sebastian. He's pulled the hem of his own shirt out of his pants and I watch him swipe the edge of it over his face. All it does is give me a peek of his ripped abdomen. *Jesus wept.* This fucking guy. "Now we're both in trouble."

He drops his shirt, narrowed eyes staring back at me. "You started it when you tried to neuter me last night."

"Which you started when you—" I swallow back the word. *Kiss.* When he fucking kissed me. When he completely bulldozed over all my hard work at not *wanting*. I bite out a hard, "You know what you did."

He gives me a crooked, knowing grin. "I know you liked it."

I gnash my teeth and start down the hall. The last thing we need is to get into it outside Dr. Ross's room and get in even more trouble. He follows me. Of course he does. This kid is like a bad rash. A handsome, six-packed, chiseled-jawed rash. "Spoiler Alert, Wilcox: If a girl knees you in the crotch, she's probably not that into your kiss."

"Or," he says, sidling up to me, "she's so into it that she panics and freaks out. You're obviously scared someone might find out you're not such an ice princess after all."

I jerk to a stop, looking behind me and seeing a maintenance room. I try the door and find it unlocked. Thinking of nothing but my inability to afford getting into further trouble, I grab a handful of Sebastian's backpack and drag him roughly in there behind me. It's dark and quiet, and I instantly regret it. Trapping myself in an enclosed space with a violent, abusive, entitled prick?

Not one of my best ideas.

He rests his hand on a shelf and grins down at me. "Wanted me alone, eh?"

"Yeah," I say, discreetly pulling my knife from my bag. "I did."

He sees the gleam of the metal but doesn't seem to care. "If you think this whole scary girl vibe is a turn off, I've got real bad news."

"And if you think your whole bad boy vibe is a turn on, then I've got news for you, too." I give him a scathing look. "Not that it's even remotely authentic. I've broken in pairs of shoes tougher than you, Wilcox."

He leans close, smirking, to whisper, "You can break me in, Sugar Voss. Take as long as you want."

I scowl back at him but know he can hear the desperation in my voice. "Why won't you just leave me alone?"

His eyes dart to my mouth and linger there, even as he shrugs. "I don't know, but I can't."

I rear back, heart hammering at the possibility he might lean in. "*Won't*."

He grins. "That, too."

"Well, you'd best start trying." I feel my nostrils flare angrily, but whatever he sees in the fire of my gaze just makes his smile even cockier. "The other girls around here might tolerate your bullshit, but I sure as shit won't. What happened between us last night was nothing. Do you understand? This is not a mixed signal. I'm not into this!"

He tilts his head, those blue eyes inspecting me closely. "Yes, you are."

I gawk at him. "Are you deaf? Deficient? Did someone drop you on your head as a small child? I'm holding a knife to your crotch!"

"I'm observant," he says, gaze roving over my face, neck. "I can see your pulse in your throat. It's going like a hummingbird. Your pupils are all dilated, and you keep looking at my mouth. Sure, you've got that knife to my balls, but your heart's not quite in it." He leans in but stops just before our lips can touch. My head is already mashed against the shelf behind me. I can't get away. His hair is wet, his white shirt splotchy with damp spots. I can feel his warm exhalation when his lips part. "You're so fucking hot for this, Sugar."

He's right.

Of course, he's right. But he doesn't understand, and he probably never would. It's not about him—not really. It's more about the knowledge that I can't have it with anyone at all. It's that shiny, feel-good thing, just out of reach. It's that I stayed awake until four in the morning replaying that kiss over and over, remembering how it felt to really *feel* someone else. Their lips, their tongue, their breath. The way it felt to inhale someone. To want them. To be wanted *by* them.

Of-fucking-course I want it.

But, "Even if I was into dating someone right now," I grind out, "it sure as hell wouldn't be you."

His eyebrow arches. "I don't think what's going on here is about dating. Which is good, because I don't date anyway."

I'm afraid to know what he *does* do with girls, because I don't need it. The kiss will probably fuel my libido for the next six months. The way I'm reacting to whatever he's putting off right now might not really be about him, specifically, but my body doesn't actually give a damn.

I swallow back that desire—that fiery, tempting want—and tell him what he needs to hear. What *I* need to hear. "There's nothing going on here, and there never will be, so whatever game you're playing, you can count me out."

I duck beneath his arm and push past him, bolting back into the hallway. I know that leaving Sebastian Wilcox and all his trouble behind is easier said than done, but one thing is clear. That look on his face as I left the maintenance room—eyebrows scrunched low, frown sharp—was disappointment. I doubt he has much experience with it. But me?

That sinking feeling in my stomach at the thought of never having a kiss like that again is more than familiar.

~

"Hail to the Devil!"

"Hail to the Devils!"

The crowd chants around me, arms raised while the cheer squad shakes their gold and black pom-poms. Someone dressed in a Devil's mascot outfit strides up and down the floor, thrusting his pitchfork into the air with each chant. Sweaty basketball players run up and down the court, their sneakers squeaking on the court. The only 'school spirit' back home in the Briar Cliffs is the fifth of vodka kids used to sneak behind the Applied Math trailer. Unless you had a family member playing or were dating someone on the team, people didn't show up to cheer.

That's not the case at Preston. Devil pride runs deep here.

I try my best not to get twitchy in the crowd. That's really when this wild, anxious thing trapped in my chest is at its worst. To be truly aware here would take more energy than I have. I can't keep attuned to all the arms, all the hands, all the bodies.

I have no control.

It's not like it's any better when I'm by myself. Doug has

always preferred to corner me when we're alone. At twelve, when my mom worked the late shift. At thirteen, when the busses stopped running to our street and I had to sit trapped in a car with him every day before school. At fourteen, when my grandma died and my mom had to go away for a few days to tie up her nursing home affairs. My moments alone with Doug are the source of my worst nightmares. His punishments always hurt, but that's when the big stuff happened; broken bones, rabid beltings, burns that stung for days after. It used to be hard to believe he ever really held back when my mom was around, but the scars are a constant reminder.

No. Life with my step-dad conditioned me to fear the small, quiet moments.

A single night around Sebastian Wilcox conditioned me to fear the busy, loud ones.

Vandy leans over Georgia to say, "Reyn's having some people come over tonight after the game. You guys want to come?"

Georgia's eyebrows shoot up. "Is his dad going to be there?"

"Um," Vandy says, her forehead creasing, "I think so. He's been around a lot more since," her eyes dart at mine, "*everything* in the fall. But he's pretty laid back, you know?"

Georgia nods excitedly. "Count me in!" She looks at me and asks, "Want to go?"

I give her a weird look, because I'm beginning to realize Preston kids have this *thing* where they just invite me to other people's parties. Back home, that shit would never fly. Aside from various happenings at the docks, if you showed up uninvited to someone's party, you'd probably get your ass kicked.

A slew of excuses gather on the tip of my tongue, but Vandy jumps in and says, "His new place is awesome. There's a heated pool, a hot tub, and a game room downstairs. Come with us? Please?" She clasps her hand together beneath her chin, her big blue eyes beseeching.

If there's one thing I've learned, it's that no one says no to Vandy Hall. At first, she just seemed spoiled, but being under the weight of that adorable pout makes me realize why. Telling her no would be like swatting a puppy with a rolled-up newspaper. I sigh. "Yeah, sure."

Georgia lurches upright, startling me. "Let's go get our swimsuits and I'll drive us over."

"Oh, wait," I say, but she's already jumped up and is headed down the stands. I race to catch up with her, squeezing past the group of guys who sit at our lunch table. I suppose they'll be at the party, too. Emory, Reyn, Ben, Carlton, and Tyson seem to go everywhere together. I'm at the end of the row when a pair of long legs blocks my way.

Oh, right.

And this jerkoff, too.

Sebastian's sprawled back on the bleacher, taking up too much space for one person. He gazes up at me with a cocky grin that makes me want to plant my boot in his face.

"Move," I demand through gritted teeth.

"Say please," he demands, "and I'll let you pass."

"Sebastian, I swear to god. Get out of my fucking way."

"Why should I?" His eyes sweep down my body. "I kind of like the view."

"Dude," Emory says, shoving him in the arm. "You may like the view but she's blocking the court. Let her go."

Emory's not really coming to my aid or anything here, but I appreciate it anyway. "See? You're bothering everyone. Not just me."

He pushes himself to his feet, close enough that our bodies are nearly flush. He leans down and says, "Don't worry, I'll get that 'please' out of you eventually."

I fight down a shudder at the feel of his breath washing over my ear and shove my hands into his shoulders—*hard*. He stumbles, and then falls, landing clumsily into the group of guys surrounding him.

"What the fuck, Wilcox!" Ben shouts, jostling him away. The other guys gripe at him too, and I take the distraction as an opportunity to get away, rushing down the steps to meet up with Georgia.

"Were you saying something before we got separated?" she asks, walking out into the lobby.

"Oh, right," I stammer, still flustered by the altercation with Sebastian. That guy just won't give up. "I don't have a bathing suit."

She grins. "Don't worry, Sugar, I've got you covered."

❧

As it turns out, Georgia doesn't.

Have me covered, that is.

Oh, she has bathing suits—bikinis exclusively—and none of them provide much coverage at all.

"I don't know about this," I say, looking at myself in the mirror. We're in the small changing room off the pool at Reyn's house. "I'm the biggest river rat you'll ever meet, and this is more skin than I've shown in my entire life." Even when the girls at the cliffs went swimming, we mostly just did it in our underwear.

"It's hot," Georgia says, tying the string of her bikini at the hip. "You look incredible."

I look like a fucking joke, with my dark makeup and battered dog tags setting starkly against the bright, happy turquoise string-thing.

I cut my eyes at her. "Yeah, I'm not super into looking hot or incredible." I tug at the top, making sure my tits are secure. One false move...

I'm not insecure about my body. It's nothing special, but I'm thin and curvy in the right places. I know I could look good if I wanted to. Which, I don't.

It's the scars that are a problem.

I always had passable cover stories, back home. A cooking accident. A bad cliff dive. A track mishap. A fall off my bike. They were believable in their gradual deliveries. An incident here, an incident there... not super suspicious, and if it ever was?

Well, river rats don't ask questions.

Vomiting out all of those cover stories at once is a different beast. Transparent. Not even remotely believable. Might as well say I ran into a door. I'd probably need to pass around a spreadsheet just to keep up with it all, anyway. Georgia hasn't even seen the

107

worst of it yet, hidden behind my long hair, and already I see her eyes tracking the strange dots on my thighs, the slash on my ribs, the discolored skin around my collarbone.

Georgia, by contrast, has the most perfect, smooth, glowing skin. Girls at Preston are like that, all clean and flawless and pure. Kind of makes me hate them, if I'm being honest.

Vandy walks out of the bathroom just then, sporting a colorful two-piece. My eyes are instantly drawn to the first flaw I see—a spot of black ink tattooed on her inner thigh. Then they're drawn to the second, a wicked scar that wraps from her stomach to her back. It makes the slash on my ribs look like the result of a minor scratch.

I freeze—just for a split second—long enough for her to notice me gawking. Her eyebrows raise.

"Uh, sorry," I say, flustered. I'd heard she'd been in a bad accident, the one that left her with that limp. "I didn't mean to stare, I was just—" *I was just wrong,* I don't say.

She runs her hand over it. "It's pretty startling the first time you see it. I used to hide it. A year ago, you wouldn't have caught me dead in a two-piece, but now…"

"Now what?" I ask, trying to follow.

"Now that she and Reyn are boning all the time, she's a little less insecure," Georgia pipes in, securing the other tie. "That's what having a boyfriend who worships the ground you walk on can do for a girl."

"It's not just Reyn," Vandy says, eyes rolling, "although that's a part of it. I'm just in a better place now. I mean, everyone knows about the accident, so why bother hiding it? And Reyn… well, yeah, he makes me feel pretty damn sexy." She gathers her hair up to tie it back. "Plus, the scars on Reyn's back are pretty bad, and he's still—"

"Your boyfriend has bad scars on his back?"

She goes still, eyes jumping to mine. "Uh, yeah?"

"Are people weird and nosy about it?" I wonder, elaborating, "Like, I mean, your group of friends."

Vandy's expression turns shuttered and hard. When she speaks, her voice is as cold as her eyes. "Not until just now."

I feel my head jerk back in surprise. Holy shit, the sweet little spoiled girl has some serious claws. "I didn't mean anything by it. Just curious."

Georgia awkwardly jumps in, "I think most everyone's already seen them by now. It's not a big deal."

This doesn't make his girlfriend look any less like she wants to kick me out, so I think *fuck it*. If these are the people I'm going to be spending my year with, then maybe Reyn and Vandy have it right. Best to just put it out there and get it over with. I follow Vandy's lead and pull my hair up into a ponytail, exposing my back.

Then I turn to put my clothes away, shoving them roughly into my bag.

When I turn back, Vandy's just staring at me, mouth parted. It only lasts a moment before she smoothly recovers. "I was just saying that... you know, people don't actually care. Reyn's scars don't detract from his looks at all." Her smile is small and sad and vaguely apologetic.

Georgia latches onto this with gusto. "They really, really, *really* don't." She sighs, then makes an apologetic face at her friend. "Sorry. You know I think you and Reyn are end game, but your boy is super hot. Me? I'm still looking for my knight in shining armor. Something tells me he's not going to go to Preston, but I keep trying anyway."

"Well," I say, shifting uncomfortably. I think Vandy just told me I'm still pretty or something. "I'm not looking for my knight or any kind of end game. I just want to graduate and move on with my life. Guys are not on my radar right now."

Vandy and Georgia stare at me, look at one another, then burst out laughing.

"What?"

Georgia asks, "What exactly is going on with you and Sebastian?"

My lips pull back in a sneer. "Hatred and resentment? He's an egotistical creep, who for some reason enjoys bothering me."

"I see the way you look at him," Vandy argues, and I gape at her.

"Like I want to stab him in the dick?"

She chews her lip pensively for a moment. "Yeah, actually. But there's just a vibe."

Georgia agrees, "For someone like Bass, the line between fighting and fucking is pretty thin. I'm not saying the girls around here are pushovers, but he probably isn't used to one who fights back." Georgia says. "Like that ice! Oh my god. Leaving that in his locker was inspired."

"Wait, you're the one who put that in his locker?" Vandy asks. "Reyn told me about it."

"Well, Georgia knew his combination," I say defensively. "And he deserved it."

"See? That's what I mean." Georgia points at me. "He's good-looking, popular, and comes from a wealthy and influential family. He's fun but loyal. And fuck, that boy gives the best head. A Preston girl will do anything for that combination, but he's made it perfectly clear that he's not into Preston girls."

"Whoa, whoa, back up." I hold up my hand. "Did you say he's *good at head*? You two hooked up?"

She shrugs. "Yeah, a few times. No sex. Just fun. It started as a..." She glances at Vandy, whose expression is blank. "Well, it was like a dare, I guess. But he's not what I'm looking for and it's pretty obvious I'm not what he's looking for."

A flicker of emotion burns in my chest at this admission. I like Georgia and have no reason not to trust her. She's been really helpful to me since I arrived. If she says that she and Sebastian hooked up and everything is cool between them, it gives me pause. But that's not all I'm feeling. There's a burning ember of something else. Jealousy.

Not about her being with Sebastian. We all had lives before I came here. No, I'm jealous with the ease that she talks about it all. If only it was that simple to cave to someone like that. Just hook up with no trepidation. To let them see you at your most vulnerable. To let them touch you like that, want you, like it's no big thing. There's no way I could do it.

Especially with Sebastian Wilcox.

"Well," Georgia says, grabbing a towel off a stack on the counter,

"I'm not saying you need to cut Bass a break, but if you think fighting with him is going to make him back off, you're wrong. Sebastian Wilcox lives for a battle. The more you push back, the more he's going to keep coming for you."

A heavy rap bangs on the door and Vandy opens it. Reyn stands on the other side, eyes glued to his girl. "Jesus, Baby V, you trying to kill me with that thing?" She grins shyly and walks out. A moment later his hand splays across her scar like a shield, and he kisses her temple.

"Disgusting, aren't they?" Georgia and I follow them, towels over our shoulders. Cold winter air blasts against my exposed skin, and as much as I'm dreading facing all these people, freezing my tits off isn't a better option. I head toward the pool, which is currently filled with everyone who hangs out at the lunch table, but realize Georgia is hanging back.

"Are you coming?" I ask, dipping my toes in the heated pool. *Ahhhh.* Rich people know what they're about.

Georgia scans the pool deck, her gaze pausing by the patio. A tall man stands in the doorway to the house, handsome with strangely familiar features. Distractedly, she says, "I'm going to head into the house for a minute. Grab some water. You go ahead."

She walks away before I can protest, and I search the pool for someone to talk to. Reyn and Vandy are caught in a lip-lock on the steps. I can see Aubrey and Emory over in the hot tub. Tyson treads water in the deep-end with a girl I don't recognize. I think I heard he has a girlfriend that goes to school somewhere else. Caroline, Elana, Carlton, and Ben are batting a volleyball back and forth. Faced with the decision of hanging out with a bunch of couples or playing a sport, I make the quick decision to wade back to the edge and go hide back in the changing room.

"Leaving so soon?"

Sebastian is standing by the edge of the pool in nothing but red swim trunks that are two inches too short and a size too small. I have to take a moment to gawk angrily at him, because seriously? I'd gotten a glimpse of his abdomen that day in the hall, but Jesus Christ.

Sweet mother of all fuckery.

How is this fair?

He's *ripped*, from the lean muscles of his shoulders and arms, to the hard planes of his chest, down to the ladder of abs and the cut V between his hips. Beyond that, I'm struck by the tattoo spanning both collarbones that declares, '*Only the Strong Survive*'. He's also branded by a pitchfork logo. The same one that Georgia has below her neck. The same one that Vandy has on her inner thigh. This school pride thing is beginning to look more cult-like every day, and it'd almost have to be, because in no universe is someone who looks *this perfect* anything but evil.

Seeing him like this, in the flesh, combined with the way he's looking at me—all dark-eyed and smirking—sends a ripple down my spine. I feel like I should chant some Latin or burn some sage or something. A sharp retort stalls on my tongue, because he's already moving, jumping into the water and sending a wave of water crashing over me and everyone else.

"Bass! You asshole!" Elena shouts. Her hair is piled on top of her head and it's obvious she didn't plan on getting it wet.

"Sorry, babe." He gives her a wink, and she shakes her head in annoyance. "See?" he says, swimming over to me. "You're not the only one I piss off."

"So, she's kneed you in the balls before too?"

"No, that's an honor only you have. Well... and Vandy once. But I don't count it. It was an accident, and unlike other people who shall remain nameless—" His eyes dart all over the place, caught in a struggle between looking at my mouth, my chest, and my eyes. "—I can tell the difference." A cool gust of wind blows across the pool deck and I duck down, seeking warmth under water. His eyes track the motion before meeting mine. "So you're still special, Sugar Voss."

God, and now he's doing this stare thing—head dipped slightly down, gazing at me through his wet lashes. He's too close. Too handsome. Too everything. I take a deep breath and submerge myself just to get away from the sudden intensity, pushing off the bottom and swimming across the pool toward the others. Sebastian follows, but not me specifically, instead snatching the volleyball from Ben.

"Dude!" Ben cries, lunging for him. Ben's big—a football player, if I'm not mistaken—and he grabs Bass around the waist, dragging him under. They wrestle like two giant octopuses, arms and legs everywhere, a whirl of slippery motion until Bass emerges, spiking the ball to Carlton.

"Is it always like this?" I ask Caroline, who's moved to the side of the pool.

"Immature and a touch homoerotic?" She scoffs. "Always. I swear to god all they do is grope one another. They need to get laid."

A wave of water sloshes toward us and Elana squeals as Bass dunks her under water.

Emory abandons the hot tub to cannonball into the deep-end, and Aubrey jumps in the pool after him. Even Reyn and Vandy come up for air to join in. The entire pool is a free-for-all and all the closeness, unrestrained delight, and jostling bodies make me twitchy and over-stimulated. I start to swim away but a pair of strong hands suddenly grab me by the waist.

"Aww, Sugar, trying to get away? I don't think so. Not in that sexy little bikini."

Panic engulfs me and I twist around, fighting frantically against Sebastian. It's almost a relief now that it's happened. Just like back home, when I'd spend days on edge, waiting for Doug's next outburst, punch, kick, *punishment*. Yes, it was awful, but the waiting was worse.

This is it. This is when Sebastian finally traps me, hurts me, and it'll be my fault for not being more careful—for looking at that nice body and wolfish grin and intense blue eyes, and being stupid enough to let my guard down for one second.

Gasping for air, I shove wildly at his fingers, shaking hands trying desperately to pry them away.

Whatever he sees in my face startles him into letting go. "Hey, hey, chill," he says, raising his hands. "I wasn't going to do anything, I was just horsing around."

I'm too lost in the motion of rubbing my hips—the place where his hands were—and trying not to hyperventilate. It doesn't hurt, and it feels strange, like something is missing. His hands on me should have hurt. I'm still stuck in that in-between of waiting and knowing that it's finally coming.

Why doesn't it hurt?

When I finally start coming back to the moment, I realize that his hands might be gone, but he's got me cornered on the step where Reyn and Vandy were making out just moments before. The water fight in the pool is still going strong just a few feet away, but the air vanishes around us, like we're caught in a bubble.

Sebastian's looking back at me with an odd expression, brow furrowed and lips pressed into a tight line. "You good?"

No. "Fuck off."

He does not, in fact, fuck off. "It's the rule, right?" I lean warily back against the step, but he just moves forward, placing a hand against the step, bracing me in. "No hands?"

"You really want to get cut, don't you?"

"Well, I sort of figure you couldn't fit a knife in those seven inches of fabric masquerading as swimwear."

I snarl, "Try me," but it just makes his head tilt.

His eyes wander back and forth between my own, really slow and methodical, scrutinizing. "Jesus, you're beautiful. You know that?"

I lift my chin in response. "Leave me alone."

"You really don't like it when I touch you, do you?" He asks this less like he's worried—like he cares—and more like I'm some interesting bug he's just found.

I shake my head. "No."

"But you did like it when I kissed you." It's not a question. They should be the same thing—touching and kissing—but they aren't, and he knows it. I know it.

He lifts a hand to gently—carefully, without touching—pluck the dog tags hanging from my neck. They look smaller in his fist than they ever have my own and the sight of it, of him holding this huge part of me, makes my stomach clench nervously. "Tell me you don't want me to kiss you again, Sugar."

I swallow, my eyes focused on his fist, closing around the dogtags.

The words won't come.

He gives the chain a gentle tug. "Tell me you're not into whatever's going on between us."

"I'm not," I say, but it's weak and he's so close, making it hard not to fall under the sway of all his smooth, hard skin and that strong jaw. Beneath the water my fingers twitch, wanting to touch his tattoos, to feel the ink beneath the pads of my fingertips. He bends, tensing his arm, forcing the warm pool water to surge against my chest. Even though I'm wet and it's cold outside, my skin feels like it's on fire. My nipples peak, and I start feeling it again, that desire building in the pit of my stomach.

God, I fucking hate it. I don't want a guy like Sebastian. I don't want to feel *this* for someone who's mean and reckless. Someone I'm afraid of. Someone I could never really be close to. Am I broken? Is this another scar that a childhood under Doug's boot has left on me?

"I don't want this," I repeat.

"Something tells me that's not the truth, Sugar Voss. Something tells me you want me as much as I want you." And then he does it. It's such an odd relief—so much like the one I'd felt when he touched me, and I knew the pain was coming. Only this time, it isn't pain. He bends, brushing his lips across mine, and it's like a nuclear explosion against my nerves. Bright. Hot. Chaos.

He's so slow and tentative at first, probably worried that I may knee him in the balls again. But I don't. I kiss him back, melting under the warmth of his lips, yielding to the tug of the chain against my neck as he draws me near. It's all the encouragement he needs to deepen the kiss, a shocking dichotomy of hard and soft. His teeth tug against my bottom lip and I open for him, feeling his tongue sweep inside.

It's even better than the kiss before. I'm less shocked now, able to fully experience the wash of his breath, the texture of his tongue, the taste of him, the heat. Fuck, it's intoxicating. I just want to sink into him, get lost in the wave of sudden sensation and touch.

The others are completely forgotten, and all I can think about—all I can feel—is this boy claiming my mouth with his own. He keeps his hands away from my skin, but there's this wayward itch of want simmering in the pit of my stomach. I don't recognize it instantly, I just know it's a dangerous thing, whatever's missing from this. The thing I suddenly want.

It hits me like a ton of bricks.

I *want* him to touch me.

I yank myself away from the kiss, scrambling back up the step.

His chest is heaving, forehead creasing in response. "Don't," he says, his hand reaching out to grab my wrist. "Don't walk away from me again." He presses up against me, and I can feel how much he wants me. His cock is hard and pressing against his shorts. My stomach erupts into butterflies, even as I break from his grip, heart hammering like a wild thing against my ribcage.

"I said no," I tell him, taking a few steps back.

His jaw goes sharp and tense. "Jesus Christ, Sugar, way to be a fucking cock-tease."

I've felt a lot of anger in my life, so much of it always boiling under the surface. I've lived anger, breathed it, swallowed it, slept within the storm of it. It was a powerless, impotent anger I could never act on. It was the kind of anger that changes a person, molds them into someone hard and inert.

But I've never felt as angry as I do this moment, being accused of leading on a person I've said nothing but no to.

My reaction is all instinct. I raise my hand and send it flying, landing a hard, stinging slap across his cheek. His head whips to the side and—oh my fucking *god*—it feels so good. Like my chest was filled with fire and I'm finally exhaling, taking my very first breath, singing something with the power of it.

Sebastian staggers back and gives his head a soft shake. His eyes are unfocused, and his brow is pinched, and I get this red-hot impulse to lash out again. To *hurt*.

Before I can, Carlton is there, screaming. "What the hell are you doing?!"

I rise quickly out of the water, heart pounding in my chest. "I said no."

Caroline's watching us all the way down the pool, waving her arms, eyes wide. "He has a concussion! You can't hit him!"

I can, though.

I can hit. I can hurt. This isn't impotent anger. Sebastian isn't my step-father. I can strike out here, where everyone is soft and nice and so goddamn comfortable.

Can't I?

From the looks everyone's giving me, perhaps not.

Sebastian says, "Stop," and digs his fingers into his eyes. And then, louder, "Stop! It's fine. Just surprised me a bit. My fault."

Tyson asks, "Bass, what the fuck did you do to her?"

I don't stay to hear the answer. I run toward the changing room and I don't look back, not wanting to know what these people think about me. He deserved it. I know he deserved it. He had to have deserved it. The only thing more terrifying than the in-between of waiting for pain and being hurt is the knowledge that I'm just as capable of delivering it.

11

"DAMN IT," I mutter, fighting with a bolt inside the Mustang's engine. I've spent most of my non-school time this week at the salvage yard and searching online for parts. So much of this fucking engine is a rusted, corroded mess, which is not to even mention the remains of a rat nest—although, thankfully no rats. Taking this thing apart has been a fucking nightmare and a half, and sometimes I wonder why I'm bothering.

It's not like she'll appreciate it, especially if she knew it was coming from me. The satisfaction I'd get from restoring it would last the amount of time it'd take for her to drive it out of the shop. The project itself has been a distraction, but also a gigantic pain in my ass. I'm spending most of my free time here, either sweating or freezing my balls off, absolutely no in-between, and on days like today, nothing ever goes right, it's just failure after failure.

"Fuck!" I grit my teeth and pull at the wrench, straining my muscles. Finally, with the help of some lube and sheer strength, the bolt gives, spinning off. I grab the tiny piece of warped metal and fling it across the room at the trash can. "Stubborn motherfucker."

My phone buzzes then and I grab it with one greasy hand while the other pats for my pack of cigarettes.

It's a text from Georgia.

G: Leaving PP with Sugar. She's coming to the garage.

Just fucking great.

S: Thanks

I grab a rag and wipe my hands, easing away from the car. After that scene last night, I have no doubt she'll throw a fit if she finds out I'm the one working on the car. Jesus, that girl is a mess. I've never chased a tail this hard before and got back nothing but soreness and disappointment.

I thought about her all night. It was hard not to, what with the slap still ringing in my ears. It's part of the reason I got to the garage so fucking early on a Saturday morning, annoyed at myself for digging her so hard. *That* shouldn't be a surprise to anyone. Sebastian Wilcox is hot for a girl who wants to cut his balls off? A girl who recoils at the mere thought of me touching her? A girl who has made it unilaterally clear she's not into him? Sounds perfectly on brand. I mean, why go for one of the girls at school ready and willing? Nah, that'd just be *too easy*. A hard-on for a girl who hates me sounds perfectly sane.

Ten minutes later, the crunch of gravel announces Georgia's arrival.

Bracing myself for impact, I lean back against one of the toolboxes and light my cigarette. Which version of Sugar will come through that door today? Pissed off? Moody? Sad? Timid? Hot for me? Cold for me?

I hear her footsteps echo off the concrete walls and a moment later, her tiny figure is in the doorway.

She stares at me blank-faced for a beat, and then lets out this deep, "Oh." The disappointment is evident in her tone.

I flick the ashes from my cigarette. "Good morning to you, too, Sunshine."

Her face puckers disdainfully. "Is Merle here? I realized I left something in the car when I dropped it off."

"He won't be here for a few hours."

Her eyes ping around everywhere; the ground, the bay, the cracked 'Exit' sign, her own scuffed boots. After a moment, she decides, "I can come back later."

I rake my hair back, sighing. "That's ridiculous. Your car is in the bay. Go ahead and check it out if you want." She gives me another one of those blank looks and I gesture to the 'Stang. "Go on. I'm not going to touch you."

She looks skeptical and vaguely annoyed, but she passes me anyway, keeping a wide berth. Her sweet scent still carries over to me. That damn smell was the first thing that hit me when I got in Jasmine after driving her home from the car show. It's been in my head ever since.

Sugar opens the passenger door and leans inside, giving me a real nice view of the curves of her ass. I get this crystal-clear vision of me steeping up behind her and putting my hands there, skating them to her hips, pulling her back into my hard dick.

I wince and turn away, rubbing my forehead. My concussion probably couldn't afford that shit. I don't look back until I hear the door close. "Find everything okay?"

"Yeah, I actually left my license in the car." She tucks it in her back pocket. "Would've been a shit show the other night if the cops picked me up and I didn't have it."

"Nah," I say, "you were with me. I wasn't going to let you get arrested."

She rolls her eyes and walks around to the front of the car. She bends and peers inside. "Any idea what he's doing in there?"

"Hmmm," I say, pretending like I'm not completely aware of every single thing going down under that hood. I keep my distance as I approach, staying on the other side as I prop my elbows on the body and study the interior. "The carburetor is shot. The engine needs a lot of work. Spark plugs, timing chain, hole in the oil pan..." I glance over and see her paled face staring back at me. I assure, "It sounds like a lot but it's really not a big deal. Basic stuff."

"That's way too much. That's not all vital, right?" She wraps a hand around her slender neck, giving it a kneading squeeze. "What's the bare minimum he can do to make it drivable?"

"Eh, let the old man have his fun," I say, pushing off the car to take a better peek inside. "A car like this isn't a job, it's a privilege."

I don't miss the way her eyes track my cigarette as I bring it to my lips. "Getting people to do free work for me isn't okay, Sebastian. I'm not a charity case."

"Of course, you're not. But seriously, a car like this doesn't fall into a mechanic's lap that often. Believe it or not, this is Merle's idea of fun. Gives him an excuse to go to the scrap yard to bicker and trade with the old guy who runs the place." I lean back on my heels, and this time, I don't miss the way her eyes follow my cigarette when I gesture to the office. "Really, you're doing him a favor."

She still looks unsure, and I'm not sure if I'm reading her right —fuck, as if I ever have—but I take my pack of cigarettes and broadcast my throw with a couple bobs. She catches it aggressively, hard like a punch, and raises an eyebrow.

I nod at the pack. "Go ahead."

Mistake.

Holy shit, what a mistake.

She plucks one from the pack and puts it between her plush lips, igniting it with the lighter I'd had tucked in the cellophane. Then she sucks a long, dragging inhale from it, eyes sliding closed for a suspended moment. She lets out a slow, "Fuck," when she exhales, lips pursing. Transfixed, I watch as she leans back against a cluttered workbench, dark eyes inspecting the cigarette's ember. "I haven't had one of these in months." She says it softly, like she's talking more to herself than me.

Even still, when she goes to toss the pack back, I shake my head. "Keep it. Only place to do it on campus is out by the dumpsters, though. Out back, where the cats are." Instantly, I'm reminded of the photo I saw a few days ago hanging in the lobby of the arts building. I'd notice Abbadon anywhere, so I'd stopped and inspected the name of the student who'd taken it. *Sugar Voss.* Fuck, the picture was *good*, too. It was moody and sharp-edged, just like the subject.

Just like the girl who'd captured it, too.

She doesn't pocket the cigarettes, however. She just holds my gaze and places them neatly on the bench behind her.

Well, now that my dick is hard from watching her suck on that cigarette, I should be expecting some sort of harm on my person. I take the strategy of distraction, running my hand over the Mustang's back panel. I touch the spot where a decal used to be. "I don't know what you or your dad did to this car, but it sure looks like it lived a full life."

The cigarette must have leeched more tension from her than I realized, because that comment actually brings out the hint of a smile as her eyes rove over the chipped paint. "My dad loved this car. My grandfather brought it home when he was fifteen—not even old enough to get a license. It was in rough shape back then, and they spent the whole year getting it road ready. He took it to college where he joined ROTC. That's when it began its life journey all over the world."

I rest a hip on the car and ask, "Where all was he stationed?"

Her eyes shift heavenward, face pensive. "Germany, California, a two-year stint in Australia, then Hawaii."

"That doesn't sound too rough. A government-paid trip to a tropical island? Sign me up."

"You'd probably make a good soldier," she says without a trace of irony. "You're definitely not afraid of anything."

I assess the tiny girl in front of me. She's small enough for me to pick up and toss over my shoulder, which I would have already done with any other girl. But not Sugar. We've already had two altercations. One more and we may both end up in trouble. But not being able to just go for it—to just have her? It's driving me fucking crazy. My chest has been constricted since she walked in the room, my mind consumed with the thought of her. My dick's on high alert every time I see her, the way her eyes laser-focus that 'fuck you' energy everywhere they look. But after last night, I keep my distance. She's wrong about that.

I'm scared shitless of her.

"All that change in climate must have been rough on this girl," I say, touching a rusted spot near the wheel well. "That's a lot of humidity."

"Yeah," she says, staring at either my hand or the rust. I don't know which. "He wasn't around a lot to take care of it and then…" Her voice gets small for a second, but she recovers, looking right at me, voice and stature both defiantly firm. "And then it became mine."

There's definitely something missing from the story, but it's obvious she's not ready to tell it—at the very least, not ready to tell *me*. I hold her eyes anyway, wanting her to know that I hear her. See her. And holy fuck do I want to touch her.

But most of all, I realize, I just want to know her.

"Look," she says, watching the ember of her cigarette as she flicks some ashes away, "about last night… I shouldn't have done that."

"Which part?" I ask, "Kissing me back or slapping the fuck out of me?"

Her eyes raise slowly to meet my gaze. She answers simply, "Yes."

Now it's my turn to grin. "Eh, I probably deserved it."

"Probably?" she says, voice incredulous. "You absolutely deserved it! Where do you get off saying I'm a—" She snaps her mouth shut, jaw going sharp. "It doesn't matter. I'm tired of being fucked with and you just won't stop, but violence isn't ever an answer."

"Well," I argue, "*sometimes* violence is an answer."

She points her cigarette at me. "And that's why you and I will never get along."

I squint, wiggling my hand. "I think it's probably more that you keep acting like you want to stab me."

She flashes me a sharp, insincere smile. "Who says it's an act?"

"I thought violence wasn't an answer?"

"What can I say," she says, lifting a shoulder in a way that makes me want to trace the outline of her collarbone. "You have a way of asking the right questions."

I tuck my hands in my pockets before they get me in more trouble. Unfortunately, I can't shut my mouth. "So was that supposed to be, like, an apology?"

She scoffs at my being unimpressed. "As much as you apologized for hitting me."

"Good, then we're even. Two hits. Two sorry excuses for apologies."

One of her cheeks lifts up in a sneer. "We're not even. Not even remotely."

And I just decide that I'm fed up with it all. I've done shittier things than hitting Sugar by accident, but never has a simple mistake managed to make me feel like this. I toss my cigarette away and say, "You know what? Fine. Take a shot."

All that tension returns to her frame when I step up to her, arms out. "What?"

"Hit me," I explain. "Go as hard as you can. I won't fight back." I saw the way she looked before, back in the pool. That spark in her eye when she hit me. The way her body stayed coiled afterward, like she wanted to keep hitting. I know that feeling like the back of my hand. Pulling back—pulling *away*—from that instinct is like the worst form of blue balls. It sticks with you, fuses to your spine like a parasite.

She inches back, forehead wrinkling. "I'm not going to hit you."

"You already have. Twice. Neither of them were exactly accidental," I point out, feeling my voice grow cold, but not caring, "but if we're still not even, then let's just get this over with, right? Go ahead and hit me."

I have no idea how someone can simultaneously shrink back and rear up, but that's exactly what she does. She's such an exercise in contradictions that it makes my head spin. "You have a concussion," she says.

"Fuck the concussion!" I snap, feeling even more annoyed when she flinches at my tone. "No one's ever made me feel like a shitty human being before. If this will make us even—if this will make you stop hating me for something I never meant to do—then it's worth it to me. So do it."

Instead, she gives me a dubious look. "What, you actually feel guilty?"

I gape at her. "Of course, I feel guilty! I was trying to protect you, and I fucked you up instead. I'm not the monster you seem to think I am."

"Then why do you keep doing this?" she demands, gesturing frantically between us. "Why won't you just leave me alone?"

"They're two different things," I insist. "I'm chasing your tail because I'm into you, Sugar. Any other girl would be able to take that, but you—"

I can see the shutters slamming over her features, face going hard and blank. "Any other girl? Like I'm some kind of freak because I don't want you touching me?" And, oh, she's pissed. But there's something else there, too. Something vulnerable. Something hurt. An insecurity.

My groan turns into a growl as I roughly push my hair back. "I just meant, because of what happened that night. I've never hit a girl before. Yes, that makes you a special case."

At least some of that stony sharpness eases. "You think if you hadn't hit me, I'd be into this." She says this real casual-like, just a passing observation. "You're wrong."

"Maybe." I shrug, looking down into her eyes. "But I'll never really know. Not until you make this even. So, take a shot." I plant my feet and brace for the impact. Sugar's a small girl. Her punch probably won't jostle me much, but who knows. I've underestimated lesser people before. "And don't tuck your thumb. Girls always tuck their thumbs. Last thing I need is you blaming me for breaking it on my face."

For a second, she actually looks like she's going to do it. She really does make a fist, shoulders squared, chin raised defiantly, and *fuck me*. She's hot as hell, even like that—even when she wants to hurt me.

Slowly, she deflates. "I'm not going to punch you, Sebastian."

I deflate, too. "Why the hell not? I've got it coming. No one could blame you."

She pushes off the bench and walks to the Mustang, running a hand over the edge of the hood. "The girls all came to our room last night." She spares me a quick glance to elaborate, "Vandy, Afton, Caroline, Elana… the other one, Vandy's brother's girl—"

"Aubrey."

She nods. "They were mad at me for hitting you, but they seemed kind of pissed off at you, too."

I have no fucking idea where this is going. "Sounds about right."

She crosses her arm, eyes fixed on the toes of her scuffed boots. "They really care about you. Even when you're being a complete bastard, they still want to protect you. I don't really get it."

"Neither do I," I say honestly.

"I think maybe…" She makes a face, like whatever's about to come out of her mouth has a sour taste. "I think you must have some kind of redeeming qualities, to get so many good people on your side like that. God knows what they are."

I'll be damned. That almost sounded like a compliment.

"Well," I reason, "I am *very* pretty."

"That's the thing." She gives me a baffled look. "I don't think any of them even want to fuck you."

Sighing, I say, "I know. The curse of platonic female friendships. They won't even show me their tits. Kind of makes you wonder what the point is."

Sugar must sense that I don't mean it, because she gives me an exasperated look. "They seem to think you're someone worth standing up for. Maybe you could show me a little of why that is sometime."

I blink in surprise. "Provided you'd actually let me? I really could."

She stares at me, jaw working around her response. "To be clear, this is me letting you off the hook for hitting me—*not* all the other shit."

I raise an eyebrow. "So what is this, like a ceasefire?"

Her eyes narrow threateningly. "Only because you have some very convincing friends."

"Noted." Look at that. Team Bass finally coming in clutch. I'm going to have to buy my girls something shiny. I offer her my hand. "Truce?"

But she just stares at it, inching back half a step. "Sure."

Jesus Christ, this 'sure' shit again. "Sugar," I start, leveling her with a look. "Basic rules of engagement here. Shake on a truce."

Her gaze flits back and forth between my eyes and my hand, shoulders rising tightly. She's suddenly radiating tension, and even though it's cold in here, I can still see a fine sheen of sweat glistening on her forehead.

She lets out a gusty, frustrated exhale. "I can't."

I drop my hand. "You can't."

"Yeah, I fucking can't, okay?" She says it all belligerently, looking like she's waiting for me fight her on this.

I don't.

Instead, I reach for her, ignoring her flinch, and carefully pluck that pair of dog tags from her chest. I close them in a fist and give it two pointed shakes.

They fall noisily against her when I let them go. "Good?"

She looks down at them for a long moment, then at me, face blank. Her responding, "Good," sounds rough and wrung out, but she exits the shop without brandishing her knife even once.

Progress.

Never let it be said that Sebastian Wilcox doesn't take any opportunity by the balls.

The following Wednesday, I park myself in the lobby of the arts building and wait. I lean against the wall adjacent to the 'Creative Corner'—painfully lame—and twirl a flower between my forefinger and thumb. Just a few minutes earlier, I'd gently rescued a few of the better-looking white jasmines from the Martha Preston community garden.

I've never been one for any of Preston's creative programs myself, but I know our school has a good department. Well-staffed and well-funded, especially since the Bates family donated more than enough for the new creative arts building. Maybe Hamilton can come out as gay and get us a new lacrosse field.

I know basically nothing about the photography club, except that Sugar is apparently a member. Personally, I never saw the draw. Anyone can point their phone at something and snap a picture. Who needs a club for that? Then again, I *am* here, putting my precious balls on the line, once again. That has to say some serious shit about artistic merit.

When they start spilling out of the room, I see the Adams twins first. Micha and Michaela notice me at the same time—perfectly in sync—and both start fumbling their folders.

"Uh, hey, Bass!" Michaela gives me a dreamy smile and her brother's not much better.

"Michaela." I smile back, deciding—fuck it—and extend a flower to each of them. "Micha."

They look like they're about to faint.

God, freshmen are so easy.

"Great. The fuck are you doing here?" Sugar's standing behind them, eyeing me resentfully.

I level the same smile at her I'd given the twins. She doesn't even twitch. "Wooing the shit out of you," I answer, giving her the rest of the flowers.

She looks at them, and then at me, and then tosses them aside.

I press a hand to my chest. "Ouch."

She's already marching away. "Go away, Sebastian."

I block the door. "I'm not done wooing you yet. There were going to be chocolates and candles and possibly even a shiny new knife to threaten my manhood with."

She glares at me, that vein in her temple already starting to bulge. "What the hell, Wilcox? I thought we had a truce."

"We do," I say, frowning. "You said I should show you sometime. In the real world, giving someone flowers is widely regarded as a nice gesture. I didn't do it to give you a hard time."

She raises a hostile eyebrow. "And you didn't bring me flowers to woo me, either."

I roll my eyes. "Fine, you're right. I wanted to ask a favor."

"A favor?!" She gapes at me for a long moment before laughing harshly. "Oh, you're really something else."

"Not a favor," I hastily backtrack. "More of like a... business transaction."

She folds her arms, already looking sick of me. "A business transaction. Is this a sex thing?"

"Only if you want it to be." At her total lack of amusement, I point to the photo hanging in the corner. "I want that picture of Abby." I'd asked Mr. Lee, but he said it wasn't up to him. Students owned their own photos. I rush to clarify, "Not for free. I'm happy to pay. What would it be, like a hundred? Two hundred?"

She just stares at me blankly.

"Three?"

Nothing.

"Four?"

Still, nada.

I sigh, pulling my wallet from my pocket and peeking inside the billfold. "Well, if it's anything over six, I'll need to come back."

"Six hundred dollars," she says, voice flat, "for a picture of a cat."

I scratch the back of my neck, wincing. "Is that, like... too little? I don't know, I've never bought a photo before. Just tell me a price, I guarantee you I can pay it." My mom's always asking for photos of the cats, and sometimes I'll send a snapshot here and there, but this? Fuck, that picture is amazing. It'd be the perfect gift.

She smiles, but it's not happy. It's all sharp edges and bitterness. "So this is your angle now, huh? You're just going to buy me off."

"Wait, what?" I look around in the hopes that someone can tell me what just happened, but the twins and everyone else have already left, exiting from the south hall. "I'm not buying you off, I just wanted—"

"I'm not selling you a damn thing, Sebastian."

I'd argue, but I know that look on her face. She's insulted and pissed off, and there's no getting through that. I don't really understand. I'd treated all my girls, The Playthings, to matching bracelets and a nice dinner for sticking up for me. They fucking loved it.

Girls always like it when you give them things. It wasn't buying anything off, it's just how I show my appreciation.

But this is different, I guess. Even if it's a transaction, it's pure money. Maybe that's weird for someone with Sugar's background. I fold my wallet and tuck it back into my pocket. See? I can learn from bad experiences, too.

"Well, you're full of disappointment today. But fine."

"Is that all?" Her gaze keeps pinging to the door behind me, so I slide away from it, extending an arm in invitation.

"By all means."

She looks even more suspicious, either at my easy acceptance or that I'm letting her go. She sweeps past, filling my nostrils with her clean, girly scent, and is gone before I can even think of any parting words.

That's the thing about Sugar Voss. Anyone else would have had their pants charmed off, but she's going to make me fight tooth and nail for her.

Luckily, that's something I happen to be good at.

12

"Sugar!" my mom says when I pick up the phone. I'm walking behind the dining hall with a bag of cat treats that I picked up at the store earlier. Actually, answering had been a fluke and now I pause, face screwed up as I hear her ask, "Why haven't you been answering? Is everything okay? How's school?"

Funny how she's so worried about me all of a sudden. "School is... fine," I reply haltingly. "I've just been really busy."

She knows this is bullshit. She's fully aware I've been ducking her. But if there's one thing my mom excels at, it's the art of ignoring a problem. She slips easily into the conversation she's probably pretending we're having. Cordial. Normal. "Are you homesick yet?"

I swallow down a mean laugh. *Yeah, right.* "There's not a lot of time here to worry about things," I answer diplomatically.

"That's good, I suppose." I hear water from the sink run and check my watch. Ah, yes. It's five. Doug likes to eat at 5:45, *sharp.* The thought makes me shudder, just knowing that there's this sudden connection to him, over the phone, through my mom. As if just talking to someone in the same house could make him manifest. She goes on, "I wanted to let you know that I scheduled the ceremony for the twenty-third of February."

It takes me a long, confused moment to even understand what the fuck she's talking about. We haven't even spoken since the day after I arrived at Preston, but she's acting like she's picking up a conversation we had yesterday. Then it clicks.

Ah, right. The ceremony. Every year my mother likes to go to the cemetery and lay flowers at my dad's headstone to commemorate his death. It's depressing and fucking tedious, like reliving his funeral over and over again. Just thinking about it brings the hot prick of tears to my eyes. I'd actually forgotten all about it.

I clear my throat. "What day is that?" I ask, seeing the cats creep out from the woods. They're a little more used to me now and know I bring food. I sit on the tree stump and tear off the top of the bag.

"Um." She rummages around. "A Thursday?"

I exhale in relief. "It may be a little hard for me to get away that day. You know with classes. Plus, they like to give tests on Fridays."

"Well if it's a problem I'll talk to the dean. It's important that you be there." She pauses. "Your father would have wanted it."

Now I really do laugh. My father would have wanted a lot. He probably would have wanted my mom to marry someone who didn't beat the shit out of me, for starters. Just, like, baseline standards here. He would have wanted me to live in a house where I felt safe. Mostly, my father would have wanted to still be here. He wouldn't have wanted to have been killed in action during his tour in Afghanistan.

And I like to think that he would have wanted me happy, not dwelling over his death nine years later. But this isn't about what my father would have wanted. Not really. This is about her.

The fucked-up thing is that I don't hate my mom. Even after all the years of Doug, her watching him hurt me and doing nothing to stop it, I mostly just feel sad for her. When she'd cry with me after a beating, petting my hair, icing my bruises, cleaning up the blood, she'd just beg me to stop goading him so much. Even then, the only emotion I could muster toward her was a bland kind of apathy.

Doug had eaten up all my resentment. I didn't have any left for her.

This memorial is the same as it's been since she married him. She probably doesn't realize that I know. The ceremony is a flimsy veneer of unity between mother and daughter, as if we still share something pure and sacred—something Doug can never touch.

It's a lie.

"No," I decide, feeling exhausted down to my marrow. "Don't call. I'll work it out."

I have Preston. I have a new life with new people, something with promise at the end of this dark, shitty tunnel known as my life. My mom has Doug and nothing else. I'll give her this.

But I won't give her anything else.

I hang up without saying goodbye.

Numbly, I take out a handful of treats and toss them a few feet away, waiting for the cats to come forward. They still won't let me touch them. They allow Sebastian to touch them, but not me. It doesn't seem fair.

Fuck.

Nothing seems fair.

Lucy comes first, nibbling on a treat, even getting close enough to sniff at my fingers. Having saved myself a shitload of money on the car repair costs, I spring for the good treats that are greasy and smell like bacon. It does the trick and Hades inches closer, snagging a treat from my outstretched hand before bolting back. I toss a few treats further away for Abby, who is still the most timid. Her pregnant belly is so round that she waddles a bit already.

It's quiet out here with the cats. Tranquil. Briefly, I wish that I'd taken that pack of cigarettes from Sebastian. Georgia's been weird all day—withdrawn and uncharacteristically somber. I'm not looking forward to going back to the room. I don't know her well enough to pry, and I know her a little too well to ignore it.

But the sun is rapidly sinking behind the horizon, so I secure the bag of treats in my backpack and push myself to my feet. The cats seem sad to see me—or at least the food—go.

Usually, I dread when Georgia has company. She has a lot of

friends and they're not just the casual acquaintance type of people. They're around all the time and they can be a little intense. This particular group of Preston kids is just a little too tight-knit and I can't help but feel like an awkward outsider when they all get together. Especially when it's the entire strictly-female half of the group cornering me about slapping the shit out of their buddy.

That had sure been something. Annoying, sort of infuriating, a little intimidating. But they'd all been pretty understanding when I explained the situation. It didn't matter. They still defended him— they always would. Mostly I was just baffled and a little jealous. How does a guy like Sebastian inspire that kind of loyalty?

So yeah, I get a little twitchy when Georgia has people over, but when I sneak into the room and see Emory and Aubrey, I just feel relieved.

I keep the door cracked at first, watching, listening, trying to get a read on the vibe. They're all in her bed—weird, but okay—Emory on one side of Georgia and Aubrey on the other, sort of like... cuddling.

See? A little too close to be normal.

The tip of Georgia's nose is glowing red, as is the ridge of her eyes, clear evidence that she's been crying. But she's smiling now at something Emory said, smacking his shoulder with a loose hand.

"You do not!"

Emory argues, "Do too!"

Georgia rolls her eyes. "If you do, then you put it out there your-self. Because you're a freak."

Aubrey says, "Hell yeah, he is," and high-fives Emory over Georgia.

"I doubt anyone's even seen it," Georgia adds. "No one wants to see your sex tape, Em."

He feigns insult. "How dare you, everyone wants to see my sex tape. It's very artistic, you know. I could probably make money on the internet."

"You're right." Georgia hums. "I'd pay to *not* see it."

Aubrey throws her head back, laughing, and Georgia laughs along. I feel some of the tension draining from my shoulders, knowing she's being taken care of with these people. I'd like to be the kind of friend who could do this—the person who comforts and makes someone laugh—but I'm not.

I'm the kind of friend who gets surprised with a violence intervention.

As I linger, wondering if I should enter or leave, the laughter dies down and everything grows quiet.

Emory's voice is low and soft, but still has this threatening edge that makes me stiffen. "Tell us who recorded it, G."

But Georgia doesn't answer—not for a long, tense beat. When she does, it's only to say, "It's been almost three years. It doesn't matter." She repeats, "It doesn't matter," like she's willing herself to believe it.

It doesn't feel right, eavesdropping on this strange, sad, angry moment. They all pull apart when I open the door.

"Oh, hey, Sugar!" Aubrey greets when I enter, dumping my bag on my bed. "We're taking this poor creature to the Nerd later. She's having a rough day and we're in full-on 'fuck calories' mode. Want to join?"

It's not even awkward and stilted, like she's asking just to be polite.

But before I can decide, I notice a box on the foot of my bed. "What's this?" I ask, frowning down at it.

"Oh, I dunno," Georgia replies, messily pulling her hair up. "It was just by the door when I got here."

The box is plain cardboard and about the size of a brick. My name is printed on the top, but there's no address. It's not technically mail. I sit on the bed and run my nail under the tape, watching Georgia pull on her shoes in my periphery. She looks a lot better than she had this morning, a motionless lump beneath her blankets, telling me that she was skipping classes today.

When I have the box open, I stare blankly at the contents.

"What is it?" Georgia asks, all three of them leaning over with curiosity. I hold it up for them and Georgia frowns. "Is that a button or something?"

"Sort of," I say, weighing the circular object in my hand. It's metal and plastic, bearing the Mustang logo in a bright, vivid blue. Unless I'm mistaken, it fits in the center of the steering wheel, covering the horn. "I think it's for my car."

Georgia's head tilts. "Oh. Did you order it?"

"No. I really didn't." I don't have the money for something like this, but I know who does.

From the way the three of them glance at one another, they all do, too.

I've been feeling awkward about Sebastian ever since I talked to him about my dad and the Mustang—ever since he cornered me in the arts building—and now he's made it worse. I close the box and stand. "Hey, the Nerd... that's the diner by the garage, right?"

Emory nods. "Yeah, it's a short walk."

I pocket the emblem, asking, "Could I catch a ride over with you?"

Georgia pulls on a sweater with an apprehensive expression. "What are you going to do?"

"I'm just going to return it," I assure her. "He shouldn't have fucking—it isn't his business. I can't accept it."

Aubrey gestures to my pocket. "I'm sure it was just a nice gesture. I doubt he meant anything by it." The delicate, silver bracelet on Aubrey's wrist glints in the light of the lamp. It's the exact same bracelet the other girls have started wearing. A gift from Sebastian, according to Georgia. They're obviously used to this sort of behavior.

There's no fucking way.

He's not going to buy me pretty things and just wiggle his way in. Maybe that works for Preston girls, but not me.

"That kid just doesn't know how to stay in his lane."

Georgia snorts. "No, he doesn't. But for what it's worth, I really do think he's trying."

"To test my patience? Yeah, I got that."

She shakes her head. "No. I don't know. I just don't think this is an attack, you know?"

But it is. I already told him I didn't want his money. This is just one more way for him to cross a clearly defined boundary. I'm not allowing him to slash though this one. I never should have said all that stuff about my dad, anyway. He caught me in a weak moment. "I'm not going to do anything. I'm just going to give it back."

The drive isn't far, and I use it to go over what I'll say to him when I get there. I've settled on something like, "You can take your gift and shove it up your ass," as I'm clearing the distance between the Nerd and the shop.

A single garage bay is illuminated, a glowing ember against the shadow of twilight. I find Sebastian by a workbench, wiping his hands on a rag, hair flopping into his eyes. I work really hard not to notice the way the light catches on his hair, or the way it paints his cheekbones in sharp relief, but sometimes—these little moments where he isn't aware of me—it's hard.

It's really fucking hard to ignore how pretty he is.

He only sees me because he jerks his head, flinging his hair from his eyes. When he does, he pauses, rag still hanging from his hands. "Hey," he says, lips quirking into a smile. That makes it hard, too—the way he actually looks happy to see me. I have no idea how or why. We haven't had a single pleasant interaction. His eyes drop down to the box in my hand. "Oh, you got the—"

"Take it back," I say, thrusting it toward him. "I don't want it."

He looks at me, head tilting, eyes assessing. Then he gapes at me. "You've gotta be shitting me, Sugar. You're *mad*? Because I got you that emblem?"

"Yeah, you know what? I am." I square my shoulders, fists clenching. "What part of me not wanting your money didn't you understand? Was I unclear in any way? Because I'm pretty sure I told you—"

"It's not money, Sugar," he argues, jaw clenching. "It's a *thing*."

"It's a thing that costs money!"

He flings the rag aside, throwing his hands up. "There's no winning with you, is there?"

"It's not about winning and losing. It's about the fact I don't want," I wildly gesture between us, "this kind of thing. Between us."

His face screws up. "What kind of thing?"

"The kind of thing where..." I clamp my mouth around a dozen aborted replies as he watches me, waiting, but I can't find the words. I growl in frustration. "I don't want you buying me shit!"

He's unimpressed by this. "Well, I'm not taking it back. It belongs on the car."

Hot annoyance runs down my spine, but I reach for my wallet. "Fine. I'll pay you for it. How much was it?"

He shrugs. "It cost barely anything at all. I went to the scrap yard and salvaged it myself. It's the real deal. It's *vintage*. I'm not taking it back."

He walks back toward the tool bench and starts hanging a variety of wrenches and pliers on the peg board. I stare at him, fully aware that I'm gawking. Finally, I ask, "What's wrong with you?"

He laughs, not bothering to face me. "How long do you have? The list is pretty extensive." He holds up his dirty hand and starts ticking off fingers like he's going over a shopping list. "Entitled, self-ish, petty, way too good-looking. I have this stupid fucking temper, as you well know. I'm too competitive. Then there are the concussions, which to be fair, I can't exactly help. Fucks with your personality, though. Pretty sure my friends are tracking it behind my back." He hangs the last wrench, turning to lean against the bench, arms crossed. "Oh, and then there's the baggage, and *do not even bother* trying to unpack that shit. I mean, if you think I'm bad, be glad you haven't met my brother. He's the fucking worst."

"Jesus Christ," I mutter, trying desperately to figure out how I got involved with this guy. Oh right, he punched me. In the face.

I look down at the emblem, and who knows? He's probably lying. The whole thing is ridiculous. Sebastian wading through a sea of junk cars just to find me something like this—not money, just his time and effort—makes zero sense to me. For what? Some girl he barely knows? Some chick who hates his guts?

But the thing is, I can see it.

It's just stupid and pointlessly difficult enough to be something he'd do.

I take a deep breath. "Look, if I accept this and let you put it in the Mustang, will you promise not to buy anything else for me? Will you promise to just leave me alone?"

He stares back at me, those blue eyes sparking, searching. "That's what you really want?"

"Yes!"

Liar.

I know it's a lie in the same way telling him I didn't want him to kiss me was a lie. It's one of those things I refuse to look too closely at. Something that's just going to twist me up inside and make an unbearable situation even worse. Something I can't afford to acknowledge.

I need him to leave me alone, so I'll stop wanting him to *not* leave me alone.

But he wouldn't get it. He'd find the frayed thread and tug at it, pick at it, until it's all unraveled.

"Fine," he finally says, holding out his hand. "Give it to me."

I give him the box, and without another word, he strides over to the Mustang, opening the driver's side door. That gets my hackles up even more. That's *my* seat. How fucking *dare* he. Territorialism rushes through me and I go to the other side, hopping in the passenger seat, looking on resentfully. He's focused on the steering wheel, holding the Mustang emblem over the center.

Goddamn it.

It's so pretty and shiny. It looks right.

He slides me a grin—this absurd, smarmy tilt of his lips—like he knows exactly why I'm so annoyed. "Pretty sweet, huh? Blue ones like these are really rare. I think there was only a limited run. Usually, they're red, or red with blue."

"Why did you do this for me?" I ask, unable to hold it in. "Is this a pity thing because I told you about my dad? Because I don't want your fucking—"

"It's just a gear head thing." He cuts me off, adjusting the emblem just-so. "That's all. This is a sweet-ass car, she deserves to be spoiled a little." This idiot, talking about cars like they're people. Pretty sure that's grounds for a psych evaluation.

My shoulders are tense as I watch him work, painstakingly cleaning the metal, applying a liberal amount of adhesive. I feel even more annoyed that the emblem fits perfectly, like the empty void behind it is a scar being wiped away. It looks *right*, but everything in my body tells me this is wrong. I look around at all the little dings and scars on this thing. The knob of the stick shift has a star-shaped chip, right in the middle, that's probably older than I am. I know it's not much, but it's *mine*.

He's admiring his handiwork, wiping a rag over the shiny bubble, when he randomly asks, "Do you get tired of it?"

I frown. "Tired of what?"

"Fighting all the time."

Startled, I sputter, "I don't fight. What are you talking about?"

"Sugar, all you do is fight." The fine details of his face are lost to the low light, but I can make out the edge of his furrowed brow in his silhouette. "Mostly with yourself. I figure you have to get tired eventually. Hell, even I'm tired of fighting with you, and fighting is what I do." He pauses, adding, "Well, it's what I *did*. I mean, I've been fighting with my brother my whole life, and I could probably go another eighteen years with that prick. But you?" He shakes his head, rolling it sluggishly against the seat. "Damn, girl. You are some kind of exhausting."

My only saving grace is that he's not looking at me when he says it. Facing him head on *makes me* want to fight. His blue eyes cut through me, and he's the kind of attractive that hurts to see. But it's not just that. We're in this car, so close together, but it's never been more obvious to me that he's so far out of my reach. Even if I've been lying—even if I wanted a guy like Sebastian Wilcox—I couldn't have him. These fights with myself *are* exhausting. But the fight I'd face by giving in would be so much worse.

"Hey, Sugar?" He says my name slowly, apprehensively. When I look over, his lips are pressed into a tense line, making me wary.

"What?"

There's a long beat of silence before he asks, "Why can't people touch you?" It hangs there in the air, all sharp and too-exposed. The garage lights don't fully reach to the inside of the car, but a sliver of it catches on a lock of hair that's fallen over his eye. If I were doing less of that lying-to-myself thing, I'd admit that my fingers twitch to sweep away.

It takes me a long moment to give him this. "I just don't like it."

"Is it because…" Knuckles going white around the steering wheel, his low, rough voice grinds through the silence. "Did someone hurt you?"

You did once, I want to say.

But it's not the same. Taking a hit, leaning into the blow, that's something I'm good at. Hiding the bruises. Tending the wounds. Working through the aches. No, it's the hate behind it that gets me. That's the hurt that festers, the wound that scabs but never quite heals. As much as it pains me to admit it, I know the difference between that and what happened with Sebastian. I know he didn't mean it. I know he feels bad about it. I know, in a way, that he wouldn't do it again. What happened that night at the docks made this wild, scared storm inside of me so much worse, but it's not his to claim.

It never really was.

"Yeah," I say, swallowing around a tongue that feels swollen and parched.

He bobs his head in reply, the motion loose and unsurprised. "I hope one day you'll tell me who." When he finally turns to look at me, I feel my lungs constrict at the raging fire in his eyes. "So I can fucking kill him."

His voice, harsh and firm, sends a shiver down my spine, and I don't doubt for one second that he means it. It should scare me. It should grab onto this particle of anxiety sitting dormant in my chest and pull it out, bring it forward. This is worse than anger. This is purpose and promise, a threat of a vengeance that isn't even his to give. It should be terrifying.

Instead, it makes my belly spark with a different kind of nerves.

I wish I didn't have to lie. I wish I didn't have to trade one fight for another. Leaning into blows is something I'm good at, but I wish I weren't. I'd rather feel the things currently going on in my chest—these fucking fantastic, blood-blazing things—and be good at leaning into them instead. I'd rather see that hard, certain look roaring in Sebastian's eyes and just… fucking do something about it.

Because *god*, he's right.

I'm so, so fucking tired of fighting.

It takes a fraction of a second for Sebastian's face to change when I lean in. When it does, slacking into a shocked expression, I don't give him time to put voice to it. I clear the space between us and press our mouths together.

This should be stilted and halting. I haven't initiated a kiss with a guy in a long time, and Sebastian is clearly caught off guard, lips parting on a surprised inhale. But there's nothing halting about it at all. Our lips slide together like puzzle pieces. He tilts his face to surge into it so smoothly that my stomach dips.

I hear him shift, and I can feel his hand lifting to my face in that way I can always anticipate a touch. He stops before it makes contact—before I can ever flinch away. It must land on the steering wheel instead, because I can hear the creak of the leather when he grips it.

I try to focus on his mouth and not the panic that threatens to bubble over. On the warmth and how into it he is. On the way his tongue licks against the seam of my lips and slowly enters my mouth. This isn't the erratic, impulsive boy I've watched fight and race his way through life. His movements are strong and sure, full of careful intent. The fight might rage on inside my chest, but it's so easy to sink into him, lost in the rush of sensations; heat, smell, taste, the sound of the Mustang's old seats creaking beneath us.

I pull back to catch my breath and see the blue of his eyes glazed over.

"Sugar," he says, my name a low whisper, reverent. "Please don't run from me. Not this time."

I don't want to. I want to hold on to the good feelings. The warmth underneath the anxiety. The crazy zings happening between my legs. The impulse to sink deeper and deeper. I push a breath from my lungs in a long, tremulous exhale. The fear and self-doubt and worry are there, but there's something else, too.

Defeat.

"Oh, fuck it." I climb over the gear shift and clamber into his lap. I capture his lips with mine before he can do more than inhale.

My kiss is aggressive and vaguely hostile, punishment clear in the way I crush myself into him.

He instantly surges back into the kiss, all defiant tongue and soft lips, meeting my fight with one of his own. The hard length of his cock presses between my legs when I settle against him, and I grind down, thighs trembling. He groans hot and rough into my mouth, and I can feel his hands lifting to grab my hips.

I rear back, panting, "Rule number one," and wait for the inevitable. An argument. A confused expression. A look that says I'm crazy.

But he sits there beneath me, chest heaving, and just nods. "Hands to yourself, yeah, yeah, got it, just—" He lurches forward to capture my lips, and I let him, licking back into his mouth.

The rules here aren't even, though. I put my hands on his shoulders to steady myself and get lost in running them down his chest, feeling the expanse of his defined muscles. He breaks away just to drop to my neck, pressing hard, wet, open-mouthed kisses up to my ear. With my eyes closed, I grind down on him again, chest hitching when his hips buck upward in response.

"Jesus, Sugar," he rasps. "You're so fucking beautiful, you know that?"

You're a fat, ugly bitch.

Lazy, ungrateful freak.

Stupid little cunt.

The slurs I'm used to echo past Sebastian's question. My skin prickles, waiting for the blow, the kick, the stinging whip of a belt against my back.

But he kisses my mouth, and his lips are warm and soft. There's no pain following the words, and I rub against him, seeking the good feelings, the temporary rush of euphoria that I can normally only give myself. Sebastian's hand reaches out, but not for me. He grabs the back of the passenger seat, fingers curling tight around the top as he lifts his hips into my rocking grinds.

He mutters things between kisses. Idle, mindless, impossible things. "Knew you wanted this." He licks deep into my mouth.

"Been hard for you for weeks." A kiss to my throat. "Christ, I wanna fuck you." A long, sucking lip lock. "Come on, let me fuck you."

I fist my hand in his shirt, grunting, "Shut. Up."

Incredibly, he does.

He lets me ride him like this, rocking against the hard cock I can feel beneath his jeans, and it's sweltering. I can feel a bead of sweat running down the small of my back. Sebastian's skin is like fire. His mouth works greedily over my neck and lips, taking and taking, like he's afraid it might get snatched away, so he's grabbing whatever he can.

I press my palm against the foggy window when a whimper slips past my defenses, sliding into his kiss. He makes a sound back, something guttural and unrestrained, and the throb between my legs grows into an urgent pang. He feels so hard between my legs, he has to be getting chafed or crushed, but he keeps thrusting into it, breaths coming in ragged spurts.

When I take a chance to open my eyes and finally look at him—at his red cheeks and swollen lips and glazed, heavy-lidded sex-eyes—it's almost enough to send me right over the edge. But that's not what triggers the coil to spring.

It's the way he's watching me so closely. There's a sweet sort of agony in his face, like the way we're rocking against each other hurts, but there's also a flash in his eyes. A sharp delight. Like someone who's being given something they *really* wanted. Like he's enthralled by it. Like maybe all those sweet, dirty words before weren't just about getting into my pants. Like maybe he actually does think I'm beautiful. Someone worth having.

That's what takes me to the precipice, sending the wave of an orgasm shuddering between my legs. I'm quiet, gulping my pleasure down, but Sebastian is anything but.

He bites out a sharp, "Oh, fuck," and groans, slamming a fist into the ceiling. His hips thrust harshly upward, lifting me with him. His razor-sharp jaw tenses and then he exhales, head falling back on the seat.

He never looked away from me once.

It's in that post-orgasm haze that my stomach drops. The panic floods my chest like rolling waves, building and building. I fumble away from him, limbs shaking.

"Hey, hey, no," he rushes out, tensing beneath me. "Sugar, just wait."

I push against the driver's side door, releasing the latch and tumbling outside. Too stunned by his own orgasm—or possibly the simple fact that I'm just a freak—he doesn't move quickly enough to stop me. And like I should have done when I first walked into this garage, I run, and never look back.

13

SEBASTIAN

SUGAR VOSS WANTS MY DICK.

Just thinking about it kept me up all night—both my dick and my brain. Even three jerk-off sessions later, I'm still thinking about it. About Sugar. About how she totally wants my dick.

Sure, she ran away after getting a small preview of it, which is unfortunate. With girls, I'm usually the one bailing after the post-orgasm glow fades, but you know. Whatever. I didn't do anything wrong here.

She kissed *me*.

She climbed into *my* lap.

She wanted *my* dick.

And yeah, she looked fucking gorgeous when she finally let go for a second and let me help her feel good. For a moment there, she actually stopped fighting. Whatever the hell it is that always holds her back was just... gone. Fucked off to orgasm land, I guess. But then just as fast, the wall was back, and there she went. Skittering away. Again. Leaving me with spunk-soaked boxers.

The problem is that I'm just really—fucking monumentally —*confused* here.

I can't get it out of my mind when I walk into Dr. Ross's class the next morning. Naturally, my eyes go right to her seat. It's not like I wasn't always checking her out before, but now everything's jacked up to eleven. I know what she tastes like now. I know what she looks like writhing in my lap. I know that her cheeks get crazy pink when she's turned on, a lot like when she's pissed off. Most of all, I know the way her face looks when she comes, and fuck. It's breathtaking.

I'd almost written off having her altogether. She wasn't budging. I was just making shit worse and worse, and weirdly, if I couldn't fuck her, I still wanted to know her. Now that she *wants my dick*— fuck, I'm so pretty, not even the Ice Princess herself can resist this shit—all the cards are back on the table.

If I thought I wanted her bad before, then now I'm like a man possessed.

I cross the room, eyes sweeping over her, taking in the soft curve of her calves in direct contrast to the worn leather of her combat boots. Her hair is shielding her face like a curtain, so I can't make out her expression. She's been wearing this wide leather wrist cuff and it undulates as her fingers twirl a long strand of her hair. I want to ask her *what the fuck*, but there's no time.

Dr. Ross will be walking into class in about thirty seconds, and as much as I'd love to corner Sugar and demand to know why she bolted like that, I've got other shit to worry about. I take a moment to enjoy the very last of my 'Sugar Voss wants my dick' elation, because I'm pretty sure that's about to come to a swift end.

I whistle, catching most everyone's attention, but it's Elana and Afton I point to, jerking my head toward the hall.

Afton holds my gaze and pinches her cheeks, getting them all red.

Then, she starts crying.

Like full-out sobs, snot and tears and all. It's borderline scary how she can do that shit on-demand, but I give her a loose, appreciative salute as she rises from her seat. Elana swiftly moves to follow her, both of them disappearing into the hall to distract Dr. Ross.

I gently close the door behind them.

A good female-drama crying jag will probably buy us five minutes.

Reynolds is in the back, already raising his chin at me in acknowledgement. Right-o. Time to find the lucky victims. Not that it's hard. Pierce's crew all sits in the back corner, clustered together like a goddamn knitting circle.

I snap to get their attention, ignoring all the other prying eyes. "Pierce, Tharp, Brennan. Get out your phones and line up against the wall."

The three of them blink back at me like morons.

"What?" Pierce says, face blank. "Why?"

I shrug. "Because I asked so nicely. Chop-chop, fuckwits."

Brennan crosses his arms, reclining back in his seat. "I don't know what this is about, but I'm not one of your sheep."

"The thing is, I'm tired, I'm hungry, and I'm doing this in front of someone I don't particularly want to do it in front of." I gesture vaguely at Sugar, knowing she's watching me. Knowing this is probably going to erase all the work I've done in convincing her I'm not some asshole bully. It fucking sucks and I'm not in the mood for it. "So how's this? Either you get out your phones and line up against the wall, or Reyn and I will come back there and get them ourselves." I leave the threat unspoken, but it still comes through.

Reyn pipes in, "I guarantee to you that this is the only way you leave class today with phones still in your pocket."

Pierce is first because he's a pussy. Tharp follows because following is what Tharp does. Brennan puts up a token protest, but ultimately lumbers from his seat, face angry-tight.

"This is bullshit. You're not the campus police."

"Police," I say, sending Reyn a grin. God, these guys are lucky I've had so many orgasms in the past twelve hours. Otherwise, this impulse I'm feeling to feed this motherfucker his own teeth might be too much to resist. "Ah well, we could call the police instead. They'd probably be really interested to see what you've got on your phones. Pretty sure that kind of video gets you put on a list, best case." I know instantly that *they* know what this is about. They all go shifty and start lining up against that wall real damn quick. "Go on, unlock them. Faster would be nice."

Dr. Ross isn't going to suffer Afton's histrionics for too much longer.

Reyn and I double-team it, going through Tharp and Pierce's phone first. The video of Georgia—recorded during her Freshman year—is there. This thing has been following her around for years now. You can't see her face. No one except the Devils actually realizes who it is. But Georgia knows. She knows whenever she hears guys talking about it just whose tits, moans, and ass they're whispering about. She *always* knows and it fucking destroys her, every single time. Apparently, these three had been 'discussing' it a couple days ago, sending her into a tailspin.

No one fucks with a Devil or a Plaything.

No one.

So I delete it. But I also go into his media history and cloud storage to make sure there aren't any copies there, either.

Brennan's phone is a goddamn landmine. "Jesus," I groan, seeing way too much of this guy's dick. "That's just nasty."

"You know who the girl is, don't you?" he asks, laughing. "It's one of your friends, isn't it? Probably not Afton. She's too leggy. Caroline's too mousy, and there aren't enough scars for it to be Van—"

His head slams back against the wall, but it's not my hand around his throat.

It's Reyn's.

"I'm sorry," he says, teeth gnashed, nostrils flared, "kind of seemed like you were going to say something about my girl. Go on. Continue."

The class behind us is charged and all gaspy, shifting forward in their seats, eager for a fight.

I let out a low whistle, head shaking. "Done fucked up, Brenny boy."

Eyes bulging, he wheezes out, "I wasn't going to say anything!"

"And you're going to stop guessing at who it is," I advise, slamming his phone into his chest. "Because the day you figure it out, is the day I beat your ass so badly, you won't even be able to remember there was a video at all. We clear on this?" I look at Pierce and Tharp, waiting for their nervous nods. "Good shit." I give Reyn a pat on the shoulder, but he doesn't let up on Brennan's throat. "Dude, strangle him to death or let him go, I don't give a fuck either way, but let's move this along."

He releases him roughly, giving him one last shove into the wall. "You're all fucking disgusting for watching that shit." He thrusts a finger at Tharp. "One of these days, she's going to come forward and report it. You remember that the next time you're passing around porn of a freshman like the sick fucks you are."

"Oh shit," someone in the class whispers. "That girl's a freshman?" Georgia's video is a thing of Preston legend. Every straight dude has probably seen it by now. Fuck, *I've* seen it—long before I knew who Georgia even was.

The whole thing is broken up when steps sound out in the hallway. The three sickos all dart to their seats, but Reyn and I take a more casual approach, striding leisurely down our respective rows.

I can't help a testing glance at Sugar as I pass.

She's staring right back at me, face paled and slack. I give her a tight, thin smile in response, but she sits there frozen, eyes tracking me as I move past.

I slide smoothly into my seat just as Dr. Ross enters the room.

The lecture might as well be given in the form of radio static for all I absorb of it. I'm too busy freaking out about Sugar on multiple fronts. She didn't look mad. She didn't really look like anything at all. Surprised, maybe. A little wary. She sure didn't look like she wanted my dick. And now I have to untangle all her reactions to me. Like when she glances at Dr. Ross and I catch the profile of her face, teeth pressing down into that plump, eager bottom lip...

Is that about what happened last night, or what she just witnessed?

Fuck, this girl doesn't need a knife. She's going to kill me by means of just existing there, inches away, still as a statue, not giving me a goddamn thing to go off of. All I can see is her shiny, dark hair tumbling down her back. Her posture is ramrod straight but slanted toward her desk, *away* from me. I get the occasional whiff of her honey-scented shampoo, but that's it.

The bell rings, snapping me back to reality. My classmates move quickly, packing up their things, still whispering about the little show at the beginning of class, but I sit back and watch Sugar, trying to figure out what's going on. I let her leave first, watching as she slings her messenger bag across her chest. Her skirt bounces with every step that carries her away from me. I inhale, finally able to breathe something that isn't laced with honey, resigned to getting on with the rest of my day, not knowing a damn thing.

And then she looks back over her shoulder.

At me.

Fuck.

Fuck.

Fuck.

Me.

I jolt from my seat and pause to give Dr. Ross a grin, "Have a good day."

"I will," she replies, adding, "you stay out of trouble, Mr. Wilcox."

"Always, Dr. Ross, always."

Except here I am, following Sugar Voss down the hallway, looking for trouble. I see her at her locker and walk up.

"Look," I start, eyes roaming the hall unseeingly. "I know that probably looked bad, but you have to believe me. Those guys deserved it. And I didn't lay a hand on any of them, which to be honest, was pretty generous considering how much I wanted to."

She doesn't say anything for a long moment, and I get more and more tense as the seconds tick by. If that put her off—for the sporadic, blink-and-you-miss-it seconds she's ever *on*—then it'll suck.

But I wouldn't have done a single fucking thing differently.

Finally, she puts a book into her locker and turns to me. "That whole thing was about..." She looks around shiftily and there's something in her eyes. Something perceptive. "...about someone we both know. Wasn't it?"

I prop a shoulder against a locker, shrugging. "Can't say."

The corners of her eyes tighten as she assesses me, and she looks suspicious. Wary. Tense. But she doesn't look pissed off. She doesn't look like she hates me. "Because if it were, then I'd probably understand."

"Yeah?" I ask, trying to keep the relief from my expression.

She nods. "Probably." She does this thing where she wets her lips and I can't help but watch, eyes glued to her mouth. Sugar never wears lipstick, but sometimes her lips are a little shiny, like she's wearing something convenient and utilitarian. Chapstick.

I wonder what it tastes like.

She turns back to her locker, like that's it. Like that's all there is to say.

"Are you really going to pretend like nothing happened yesterday?" I ask, voice low enough not to attract attention.

She freezes, turning slowly, barely glancing at me through her hair. "Yesterday was a mistake," she says, voice quiet and thin. "A regret."

"You didn't look very regretful when you were grinding down on my dick."

She struggles with her massive biology book, trying to leverage the weight of the other things in her locker. I reach in and pull it out, handing it to her. She takes it and slams her locker door, then starts off down the hall.

This time, I run after her.

"No way," I yell, catching up to her. "You don't get to run off again."

This time, the majority of the hallway glances our way. I even see Sydney zero in on us, so I'm sure it'll be all over ChattySnap in ten minutes flat. I know I should let this drop. Pushing the matter isn't going to lead to good, grindy, orgasm-inducing places, but I just can't leave it like that.

"Come on," I say, jerking my head toward the door that leads outside. She finally turns to glare at me—the ice princess returned. I tilt my head at her, shoulders dropping. "Please."

Sugar probably relents more out of annoyance than anything else, but I hold open the door as we step out to the underused, covered walkway.

The instant we're alone, she asks, "Why are you so fixated on me?"

I look her up and down, deciding that nothing but complete earnestness is the best tack here. "Because you're sexy. Strong as hell. Really bitchy. What can I say? You tick my boxes."

She gathers her hair back, away from her face, looking flustered. "If all that shit in the Cliffs never happened, would you even pay me any attention?"

It's a valid question. "I saw you before I got in the fight with that asshole, you know. I noticed you; the blue hair and the big eyes." I look down at her mouth, then back up. "I wanted you then, too. I picked a fight with that guy half because he was being a dick to you, and half because I wanted to impress you. I saw you. Just like I see you now."

That answer doesn't soothe her like I'd hoped. If anything, she looks unnerved. "This isn't something I can do, Sebastian."

"Yeah, you can. You did it last night. Did it pretty well, too. Just do it again." I shove my hands deep into my pockets. "I'll follow the rules, whatever they are."

She laughs darkly. "Something tells me you're not that hard up, Wilcox."

"Christ, Voss. You really don't know anything about me." I can get pussy anywhere, anytime. All these hot sparks just looking at this girl sends up my spine? Only one person can give me that. "Not yet, but you can."

Sugar eyes for me for a minute, her hand squeezing the strap of her messenger bag. She doesn't look particularly accepting of any of this, so I brace myself for a blow—physical or otherwise. Mostly I expect her to walk away. Maybe run. She'll probably tell me to fuck off and stop harassing her, once again.

It's okay.

I've got stamina for days.

But for the second time, I'm not prepared when she pushes up on her toes and brushes her hot lips across mine. It doesn't take me long to seize it, to lean hard into her kiss, sending her stumbling back. She lands against the metal door but doesn't flinch away. If anything, she just bounces off it, right back into me.

I place my hands beside her head, palms flat against the door, knowing that if I want this to continue, I've got to keep them to myself. I tower over her, kissing her back with greedy, wet, sucking kisses. Fuck, she tastes just as good as I remember, tongue licking forcefully against mine. My heart beats wildly, banging hard against my chest. All I want in this moment is to feel the rest of her, but I know better. Jesus Christ, I know better.

Across campus, the bell in the tower chimes, a warning that our next class starts in five minutes. As hard as it is, this time I'm the one to pull away first, stepping back and giving her space. Her mouth is shiny and red, her chest heaving.

Being around this girl is a fight against my instincts—against all my impulses—and the best thing for me to do is walk away before I give into every one of them.

~

"How's the jaw?" Ben asks when I take a seat between him and Caroline in the Devil's Lair.

"Shut up," I reply, slinking down in my seat. "Don't pretend a chick or a dick hasn't wanted to slap that smug expression off your face before."

"Maybe, but not after I kissed them."

I scowl and ignore him, waiting for the meeting to start. The Devils mingle around like we're waiting for a pep-club meeting to begin or something. Emory glances at the time impatiently, ready to start. He shoots Carlton a dark look when he strolls in late. Like everyone else, I'd gotten the black envelope in my locker this morning with a time written on a small card. After the rites last fall, we don't meet as often. We still hang, of course. Hell, we're probably closer to each other than most of us are to our own families. But it's been a while since we'd received an official notice.

Tyson bursts though the door next. His hair is still damp, and he carries the strong scent of chlorine. "Sorry," he says, grabbing the seat next to Elana. "Practice ran late."

He'd been recruited last year from Northridge for the diving team. It's probably the first time a non-legacy has ever been initiated into The Devils, but we're living in a new world order. I mean, hell, the Playthings are all equal members as well.

"No worries," Emory says, eyes sweeping over to Carlton. "At least you have an excuse."

"Dude." Carlton shakes his head. "I told you I had some business to attend to."

"Yeah well, I'm not into your business. Especially when it holds the rest of us up." Everyone here is perfectly aware that Carlton is Preston's resident drug dealer. Everyone also knows that Vandy spent two weeks in rehab dealing with her painkiller addiction. "You wanted to be a Devil. That obligation comes first."

"Jesus Christ, Em—"

"Stop!" Vandy says, shooting them both glares. "If you guys want to fight about this, do it on *your* time. Stop wasting ours."

Reyn's hand hangs easily over Vandy's shoulders, his fingers grazing the cuff of her sleeve, and I roll my eyes. I guess at some point they were hiding their relationship, but I can't imagine them being anything other than joined at the hip. It's not that I don't approve. Reyn takes good care of her and she's totally obsessed with him. They make a solid couple. It's just that after what happened with Sugar today, seeing all the handsy bullshit is grating on my nerves a bit.

"Can we get started?" I bite, my arms crossed over my chest. "I've got shit to do."

Emory narrows his eyes at me, but I just stare back, ready to be done with this. He sighs. I mean, what did he expect? He wanted to be the leader of a bunch of entitled assholes.

"The homecoming prank was awesome. We carried it off without a hitch. But now it looks like one-off. There are so many rumors and speculations about who did it, and as I'm sure many of you know, there are people trying to take credit."

Afton snorts. "I heard some bitch in fifth period claim it was this group of guys on the wrestling team."

"Same." Ben adds, "There are a few kids trying to act like they know who did it or were directly involved. Obviously, we can't say anything, right?"

"Right," Reyn says in a hard tone. He's on probation, and if word gets back that he had anything to do with the prank—which involved breaking and entering, tampering with security and video equipment and vandalism—he'd be massively fucked. He looks up at his best friend, Emory. "What do you want to do?"

Emory gives his best evil grin. "I think another prank is in order. Basketball season is in full-swing. The men's varsity team is doing well, right? They'll probably go to the playoffs. I'm thinking one of those games is where we should focus our attack."

"Elana, Aubrey, and I will be there," Afton says. "Cheer and dance squads. So we already have an in."

"That's what I'm thinking." He nods at Ben. "You're in the band. They go to all the games, right?"

"Yep."

"Okay, good, that's a solid lead. We'll spend the next few weeks working up a plan." Emory looks out over the group. "Everyone down with that?"

The general consensus is yes, and when it's clear that's the focus of the meeting, I stand quickly, ready to get the hell out of there. My brain's already at the shop, elbow-deep in a half-rebuilt transmission. I've slipped one arm into my jacket when Georgia approaches me. The expression on her face doesn't bode well. We'd decided not to tell her about what went down this morning, but maybe she found out anyway. People at Preston do love to yap their goddamned mouths. It's not that Georgia's a weak person—not by any means. But sometimes the smallest reminder of that video is enough to ruin her entire week.

"Georgia," I say, piling on the charm. "How are you this evening?"

At least she looks better today. She didn't go all out with the makeup and hair, but she's put together, bouncing back. "Stuff it, Wilcox," she says, arms crossing. "What happened with Sugar?"

I blink in surprise, realizing that glare isn't even about the guys with the video. "Wanna be specific?" I ease my other arm into my jacket and zip up the front.

Georgia rolls her eyes. "I know she came to see you last night. She was really pissed about that little gift you sent."

"Yeah, she came to the garage. We discussed it and agreed to put the emblem on the 'Stang. So what?"

Her eyes narrow at the word 'agreed.' "Then why did she come back more upset than she left?"

Oh.

That.

Question of the century, obviously. I'd been right about Sugar all along. Something about her is broken. More specifically, someone did the breaking. It was so fucking hard to keep my temper in check when she admitted that someone hurt her. I'm not an idiot. Whatever happened, it was bad. Bad enough that now she can't even stand being touched, and how fucked up is that? I wasn't lying when I said I wanted to kill them. If she ever tells me who did it, I'll stop at fucking nothing to make them pay. People think I'm all about the violence because I'm a restless, aggressive, fucked-up rich boy. They aren't wrong, they just aren't completely right, either.

The thought of someone hurting a person who doesn't deserve it always gets my hackles up. It makes this tense, red-hot thing in my chest roar to life like a screaming engine. There's a reason I was so hard on myself after hitting Sugar.

But there's only one answer to Georgia's question. I rake my hair back in frustration, pitching my voice so the others don't hear. "I don't know what's up with that girl, G. She's so damn hot and cold. She hates me, but she's always around. She's always telling me to be better, but gets mad when I do something nice for her. She's fucking exhausting."

Even Georgia can't argue with that, shoulders drooping. "Look,

I don't know her that well yet, but one thing is obvious. Sugar acts strong and mean, but she's hiding some serious baggage."

I look around at my fellow Devils and Playthings, gesturing. "Who isn't, right?"

"I think hers might be a little more sensitive than what you're used to, is all." She touches my arm, pleading, "Just be careful, okay?"

I cut through the remaining Devils, passing Reyn and Vandy, and head upstairs. At the top I pause, bending down on one knee, fussing with my shoelace. This uncomfortable, shitty idea is brewing in my head. I hear heavy footsteps on the stairs and look down to see Reyn. I stand and push the door open. "You headed out or waiting for Vandy?"

"I'm leaving," he says, striding forward. "She's going to ride with Em."

"Cool." I look both ways and make sure no one is around to see us leave. Worst case, Dewey sees us and starts snooping around, but anyone spotting Reyn and I exiting the Devil's tower together will start the rumor mill. Luckily, the coast is clear.

Halfway across the quad, he says, "So what's got you in such a pissy mood tonight?"

"Nothing." I clench my fists inside my jacket pockets. I know Reyn and Vandy had to work through a lot of shit to really get together. Baggage, jealousy, a psychotically overprotective brother and parents. This dude had to work for his girl. I respect the hell out of that, and right now I need his advice. "Can I ask you something?"

He cuts his eyes my way. "You can try."

Squinting into the distance, I try, "There's this girl…"

"Sugar, right." He gives a sharp nod. "I think all of us know by now that there's 'this girl', Bass."

"Well, you know we have that history. Beyond Preston shit," I elaborate, raising my eyebrows meaningfully. "It's not a great situation, what happened with her over the summer. I've tried to apologize but it doesn't seem like it helped much."

He glances at me, chuckling. "Is that what an apology looks like these days? Shoving your tongue down a girl's throat?"

"Seeing as how she wants my dick, I figured it couldn't hurt. Minor miscalculation on my part."

"She wants your dick?" He looks at me like I'm crazy. "She acts like she wants to decapitate you and put your severed head on a spike in front of Hayden as a warning to the others."

"I know, right?" I can't help the dopey grin I give him. "Be still my beating heart."

"You're a freak," he says, head shaking. "I've seen my share of trainwreck relationships, but whatever you two have going on is toxic. My advice? Run."

Yeah, I'm not the runner in this relationship. "Come on, Reyn. I'm pretty sure no one thought you and Vandy could get past your history, but you did it anyway."

"Fair enough." He pauses. "I'm just giving you a hard time, anyway. I guess I get it. Sugar seems tough. Those are the best ones. Makes everything sweeter when it works out."

We're nearing the fork in the path. He's going to his car, but I've got to go back to the dorms before I can escape to the shop for a few hours. "Yeah, Sugar is definitely tough. No doubt about that." I rub the back of my head. "I figure you, uh, have some experience with winning over a girl who had every right to tell you to fuck off for good. Any *real* advice you want to offer a fellow Devil?"

Reyn exhales, a puff of fog streaming from his lips. "Fuck, I don't know, man. Me and V are different. But I think..." He looks down at his keys pensively. "The main thing is that you've got to show her that she can trust you. It took V a long time to get there. We took things slow." He grimaces. "And when I say slow, I mean two-snails-fucking slow. I let all the physical stuff be on her terms. It was up to her when we kissed or fooled around, when we fucked. I just gave her the reins."

"So you let her grab you by the balls, huh?"

"Sure did." He shoves his hands in his pockets and doesn't look embarrassed to admit it.

"You're telling me I have to back off, basically," I grumpily conclude, "and wait for-fucking-ever."

Reynolds leans back against his Jeep, tilting his head toward where Em and Vandy are hopping into Em's truck. "You know, when me and V were first messing around, we couldn't be together yet—not really. We had to keep it a secret and a bunch of other bullshit. I think we were both worried we wouldn't wait on each other. So we made these promises."

"That you'd wait," I guess.

He shakes his head. "I think we both realized this thing we were doing would just be too hard, you know? Sydney was just starting to sniff around, and I guess V was kind of torn up about it. Because Syd would have been easy for me."

I counter, "Syd's easy for anyone," and Reyn just laughs.

"Yeah. So Vandy made me promise." He holds out a palm, sweeping it across the campus in the distance. "Anyone but Sydney."

I wince. "Yikes."

He nods. "Yeah, I was kind of fucked up about it. But I had her make a promise, too." He gives me a long, meaningful look. "Anyone but *you*."

"Hey!" I playfully shove his shoulder. "Fuck you, I would have treated that girl like a queen."

He snorts, but there's a smile flirting at his lips. "I know. That's exactly why I made her promise. But the more I think about it, the more I know you and Vandy wouldn't have lasted a week."

I argue, "I don't want Vandy, dude. She's like my sister."

But Reyn ignores it. "Because you wouldn't have had the patience. Not for her. So I need you to really ask yourself if this girl is different. Is this just about trying to get under her skirt, or is this something you're actually willing to commit to? Is she worth it to you?"

I don't even have to pause to think about it. "She is."

Reyn shrugs. "Then if she's worth it, you've got to be patient—especially if you've fucked up already. Let her set the rules here. Let her drive this thing. Stop making it all about your dick, Wilcox. I know you. You never back down from a fight. But you can't fight something like this into submission." He ticks off, "Don't jerk her around. Don't play games. Don't bail when shit gets rough. Don't keep shit from her. Christ, they do *not* like it when you keep shit from them."

I nod, thinking. "I can probably do that." He arches his eyebrow and gives me a look that says he definitely does *not* think I can do that, but whatever. "Thanks, man," I say, holding out my fist.

"No problem." He bumps his knuckles against mine. "Good luck with not thinking about your dick for five minutes."

I walk backwards, holding out my arms. "Bet I could manage ten."

"Oh yeah," he replies. "Get used to cold showers."

I flip him off, but he just laughs and walks off.

❦

I'm almost back at my dorm when I text Georgia.

S: Is Sugar in your room?

G: Why?

S: I need to talk to her.

G: She's not here. I don't know where she is.

If she's really not in her room, then I suspect I know where to find her. I detour from my dorm and head across campus. My phone buzzes again as I walk toward the dining hall.

G: Stop poking, Bass.

Yeah, that's like asking a dog to leave a bone.

G: She doesn't need your shit.

Sugar may not need my shit, but she wants it, just as much as I want hers.

Or fuck it—I need her. Whatever this thing is always pulling me toward her, I'm not going to cast it aside. It's not in my nature. I tuck the phone away and walk around the side of the brick building. Sure enough, in the faint light of the sunset, Sugar sits on the stump, quietly trying to coax the cats to come to her.

I hang back for a minute, watching her interact with the cats.

161

There's a bag of treats hanging in the hammock of her plaid skirt. Lucy, the most at ease, eats a treat right out of her fingers, while Abby circles closer and closer. Even Hades has made his way near, sniffing around the treats she's tossed in the grass. The longer I watch, the more it starts to click. Patience. Building trust. Letting them take the lead.

Abby's getting a little closer now. I'm watching the way the light is playing against the soft curves of Sugar's lips when they slowly quirk, a small half-smile slanting her mouth. I thought she wore sharp fury well, but this—a small, secret thread of happiness brightening her face—is what she should always look like.

Fuck, she's gorgeous.

I take a deep breath, trying to settle this itch to go and do and *have*, and stride across the grass. The cats see me first, Hades jumping back a few feet and running to the closest bush. Abby starts in my direction, undoubtedly hoping for a can of food. Sugar looks up, startled, the smile instantly twisting into the hard, flat line of a grimace.

By the time I'm a few feet away, the cats have scattered, and Sugar is standing, looping her backpack over her shoulders.

We stare at each other for a bit. Too long. Desperate for something to do, I take my pack of cigarettes from my pocket and light one, tossing the pack over the distance between us.

Just like last time, she catches it easily, regarding it with a blank stare. Reluctantly, she lights her own.

"So," I start, but she just shakes her head.

"Yesterday was my fault. I don't even know how to explain my behavior, or what the hell even..." she searches for the words and lands on, "I don't know what came over me, but it was my fault. It never should have happened."

"I disagree," I tell her, blowing a stream of smoke from the side of my mouth. "I think it was awesome, and I want it to happen again. Preferably pantsless, but, you know. However I can get it, count me in."

Her cheeks turn pink and she ducks her head, eyes fixed to the toes of her boots. "It can't."

I force my feet to stay where they are, shoving a fist deep into my pocket. "But what if it can?"

Emotion flickers across her face and it's too much—too fast—to catalogue it all, but there's definitely conflict. Irritation. And if I'm not mistaken, sadness. "Trust me, Bass." So softly that it's almost a whisper, she says, "If I could, I would."

My insides clench and I replay her words in my head to make sure I heard them right. "You would?" I clarify.

"Yeah." She says this like it's something grim and sad, but when her eyes flick up to mine, all I see is loss. "I think so."

It takes everything, every ounce of strength and impulse control I have, not to lunge at her and *take*. If any other girl gave me a green light like that, no matter how muted, I'd be all over them. All. Fucking. Over. But I count in my head, mentally chanting 'patience, trust, control' over and over. When I feel like I've got it together, I ask, "What would it take to get you to trust me? To let me prove myself to you? To get another kiss like that?"

Her laugh is bitter, laced with the smoke that swirls around her head. "A fucking miracle, Wilcox."

In an effort to lighten the mood, I try, "Well, I *have* been known to make a few girls feel like they're walking on water." She rolls her eyes, but I see it. It's happening. Her lips curve just slightly, a small, exasperated smile that makes my chest feel utterly weightless. "You know, for someone who doesn't like to be touched, you're pretty good at it yourself."

The smile disappears. "That's different."

"How?"

She shrugs, flicking her cigarette and watching the ashes tumble to the ground. "Because it just is."

I want to know why, although I think I already do. It's got to be a control thing. She wants it—maybe even needs it—and this is something neither she nor Reyn really get about me. They think I can't handle not being in control—that I can't hold back—but they're wrong. I've held back for way lesser people than the girl currently standing across from of me.

"Sugar," I say, willing her to meet my eyes. When she does, I hold her gaze, because I need her to know that this isn't a fight. "Please, give me a chance. One chance."

She looks up at the sky, groaning, "Sebastian, you don't—"

"We can do it on your terms. We can play by your rules. If I fail, then I'll leave you alone forever. Promise."

She shifts on her feet, swaying back and forth, and my heart leaps into my throat at the awareness she's considering it. I don't push. I don't beg. I suck a drag from my cigarette and play it cool— at least on the outside. On the inside, I feel like I'm either going to vomit or run like hell and pretend this never happened.

She finally sighs, tucking a strand of hair behind her ear. "I'll think about it."

"Fuck, really?" I blurt, before instantly tamping it down.

"But if I let this happen," she adds, pointing her cigarette at me, "and you screw up, then I'm holding you to that promise. And it has to be real. No more of this pushing and prodding bullshit. You'll have to really fuck off."

I nod, sure that she means it. One fuck up and I'm done—*we're* done—and I'll have to accept it. I watch as she walks away, turning the corner around the building. I'm aware that there's only one option here; not screwing up.

14

Sugar

"What do you think of this?" Georgia asks, holding the poster up to the wall.

I'm on her bed, munching on a slice from the pizza we'd ordered. I tilt my head, scrutinizing. "Maybe a little to the left."

She slides it over a little before securing it, nodding. "Yeah, that's better."

We're staying in tonight, which isn't a surprise. Georgia's been a lot better since that night Emory and Aubrey came to cheer her up, but she's still laying low. After the shitshow I witnessed in Dr. Ross's class yesterday, I think I might understand why.

I'd never ask. If it's true—if some absolute asshole recorded them having sex and then leaked it for the whole world to see— then chances are, she's a stickler for privacy.

It makes sense, though.

A couple weeks back, I'd been trying out a new lens Mr. Lee had loaned me. I was in here snapping some random test shots and decided to get one of her. She was at her desk, mirror propped up on a stack of books, sweeping a shimmery green eyeshadow over an eyelid. When she heard the click of the shutter, she completely freaked out.

It's not like she was naked. In her tank top and skimpy little sleep shorts, she was still wearing more than she had been the day she took me swimming. But she still wrapped her blanket around herself, pale-faced and wide-eyed, and told me in no uncertain terms that I'm to never, *ever*, take pictures of her.

She wasn't mean about it. She just looked scared shitless. So I pulled out the film, effectively ruining every shot in it, and threw it in the trash, right in front of her, no questions asked.

Now, I get it.

"Okay, now you need something soft," she says, stepping back to admire my side of the room. Apparently, I hadn't been putting in enough effort to make my mark on it. I could frankly give a shit, either way. This dorm room is nice. It has nice people and it's safe. But it's not really home. I'm not sure I have one of those at all.

I suspect, however, that this is just a project she's taking on to stay distracted, so I've been playing along. "What do you mean?"

"You know, textures," she says, flopping down belly-first onto my bed. "Maybe some plushy pillows, or you could drape a sheer curtain over your headboard. Lots of options."

I look to my left, and then my right. Georgia's bed has eight pillows. Some are pink. Others are fluffy. One has sparkly sequins. "Don't take this the wrong way, but do I look like the kind of girl who has decorative pillows and sheer curtains?"

She pauses with her slice of pizza halfway to her mouth. "Hm. Good point. Maybe some razor blades, then." When I take one of *her* decorative pillows and throw it at her, she ducks, laughing. "I don't know, punk isn't really my aesthetic. I like soft pillows. They're good for a lot of things." She wiggles her eyebrows and I snort in response.

I hear what the other girls say about my roommate in the halls. Slut. Whore. Easy. Yeah, Georgia does have a lot of sex. But she's really respectful about it. I know she has guys in here every time I have a meeting with the photography club. I've started to schedule my time outside with the cats, just to give her some more windows, although I'm not sure she's noticed. This is not to say that she needs our dorm room to have sex. On many occasions, I've seen her come back to the room, rumpled and blissed out. I don't know exactly where she goes, or who she does it with, but you know what?

More power to her.

Get that dick, girl.

One of us should be able to.

I scowl down at my pizza, trying to work up the nerve to ask the question that's been niggling at me for days now. "Hey," I start, tossing my crust aside. "Can I ask you a personal question?"

Georgia, who I know is private, who I know never gives certain parts of herself, answers with a breezy, "Sure."

I pick at my chipping nail polish—a dark, shimmery silver Georgia had insisted on last week. "So you've hooked up with Sebastian, right?"

I can see her jaw falter, mid-chew. "Uh, yeah?"

I nod, having already known as much. "I was just curious—I mean, I was wondering..."

"There's nothing there," she interjects, misunderstanding me. "Sebastian and I are just friends. Neither of us wants to go there, trust me."

"No," I say, head shaking, "I get that. I do. I was just wondering, like. Uh. You know. What he's *like*."

Her eyebrows climb her forehead. "*Oh.*"

My face screws up. "Yeah."

She sits up now, folding her legs beneath her. "You want to know what Sebastian's like."

"Yes."

"Sexually."

I drag a hand down my face, groaning. "Just fucking kill me."

"You have nothing to worry about," she says, slicing her hand through the air. "Sebastian is a great hookup. A little spoiled—okay a *lot* spoiled. But the guy knows what he's doing and he's um, generous."

I wholeheartedly regret initiating this conversation. "That's not really what I meant." One good makeout session with him told me everything I needed to know on that front. Sebastian has experience. He probably makes the heavens sing when he's with a girl. I bet there are fucking cherubs fluttering around, and fireworks, and sudden cures for terminal ailments. "I was more wondering, in the sense of, you know, whether or not he's, like…" I rub my hands on my thighs, feeling my cheeks heat. "*Rough*."

Georgia coughs, but quickly recovers. "Oh, geez. Bass? No way."

My responding, "No?" is mostly dubious, but there's a thread of hope in there, too.

"I mean, if you're into that, he'd probably be good at it. I mean, he does have that underlying energy, but my baseline read of Bass is that he's just really…" Her face screws up in thought. She ultimately lands on, "Fun. He likes to have fun."

Fun.

Sex to Sebastian is *fun*. Of course it is. I bet he likes that—playful girls who giggle and like to be touched and have a grand old time. I haven't giggled a day in my fucking life. What the hell does he want with me?

Georgia suddenly looks sick, hand pressing into her stomach. "I shouldn't be talking about this. I wouldn't want him telling people about what I'm like when I hook up." Oh, fuck. She's going to freak out.

I hastily counter, "You singing his praises about how good he is? Please. He'd lap that shit right up. Probably buy you some earrings to go with that bracelet."

She only looks mildly mollified, even though it's true. The man's ego is already big enough, but I doubt he'd take any issue with seeing it inflated a little further.

It kind of kills the mood of the night, though. Georgia turns in early and I feel a little shitty about it. But I had to know.

I had to know, because a couple hours later, I'm still *thinking*. Georgia sleeps across from me, mouth parted with her arm hanging off the bed. I've learned quickly that she's a deep sleeper, unlike myself. I've tossed and turned since I was a little kid—usually consumed by anxiety about my dad on deployment. Even when he was home, I couldn't stop thinking about him not coming back home. Then one day he didn't. And after that, I had a new reason to toss and turn and always sleep with one eye open. I doubt I've gotten a full, unimpeded night's rest in my entire life.

None of that is the focus of my restlessness tonight, though. I'm still obsessing over Sebastian's offer. And that's exactly what it is; obsession. He wants one chance to prove himself—an opportunity to show that I can trust him. What does that even mean? I don't trust anyone. Especially volatile, smug, eighteen-year-old boys who like to have fun in bed.

Although most eighteen-year-old boys do not look like Sebastian Wilcox. They don't have that wild, caged-animal glint in their eyes. He's got a need for trouble, and it looks like he's decided I'm the kind of trouble he wants to get into. I've spent a long while avoiding guys, with all their touches and sleazy offers of companionship, but with Bass, it's different. It's not just that he's so attractive. It's not even his weird, uncomfortable intensity. Just, at some point this sharp, heightened awareness of him became less about being afraid of him and more about....

Something *else.*

Something that's almost as scary, almost as painful, but far more appealing.

Reaching under my pillow, I pull out my phone and open ChattySnap, searching for his profile. I open up his page, confirm that Georgia's still sleeping, and quietly, *secretly* browse his account.

Naturally, it's mostly selfies. The most recent is a picture of himself in front of a mirror, showing off his cut and defined body. He's looking down at the phone, tongue trapped between his teeth, lips pulled up into a cocky grin. There's a video of him working out at the gym, lifting weights, that's a little older. The rest are either photos of his car or candid, random shots from the shows. The farther I go back, I catch some lacrosse stuff. Photos of him sweaty, dirty, tired-looking, but satisfied after a win. He may be erratic and impulsive, but he knows how to commit to his body, his hobbies, his passions.

I scroll back up to the recent picture—the one with him shirtless in the mirror—and stare at it for too long, eyes raking over his muscles, following his abs down to the waistband of his low-slung sweats. My hand creeps beneath the covers, so yeah.

I guess this is happening.

Before I can slip my hand into my pants, a direct message pops up.

Bass: Saw your profile was live. Can't sleep. You?

I stare at the message for a long moment, frozen. Do I want to open this door? Isn't it already open?

Sugar: No. I can't sleep either.

Bass: I should come over, help you relax.

Sugar: Doubt my roomie would be into that.

Bass: Georgia? She wouldn't care, but if that's a problem...you know I don't have a roommate.

My stomach reacts in a series of somersaults. I keep replaying Georgia's words in my head, over and over.

"Oh, geez. Bass? No way."

I don't trust him. Not yet. Maybe not ever. But Georgia?

I type the next sentence out in a rush, pressing send before I can reconsider.

Sugar: Too bad I don't know where your room is.

His response is instant.

Bass: Cresswell. 408. Code #2289

I stare at the text on the screen. What a presumptuous idiot. Does he really think I'll just march over to the boys' dorm in the middle of the night for what amounts to a booty call?

He's right.

I keep telling Bass that he's fixated on me, but the truth is that I'm equally fixated on him. This fucker is like the guy-equivalent of an earworm—a song that gets stuck in your head, all day, all night, and you end up looking it up and listening to it just to find out *why*.

That's the real reason I slide out of my bed, making sure not to wake up Georgia, grab my jacket, and quietly exit my room.

The distance is short, since our dorms are side by side. The risk of getting caught seems high but I *feel* high. Maybe I want to get caught—probably the only thing that could jerk me back to my senses. But even after I push in the code and climb the stairs to the fourth floor, no one stops me. I walk down the quiet, dim hallways unnoticed, passing the silent rooms of sleeping boys, down to the one on the end; 408.

My heart pounds in my chest when I get there. I look at that door and think of who's behind it, and what waits for me on the other side. I stand there for a long, torturous moment, willing my feet to retreat. "Fucking insane," I mutter to myself, taking a step back. I'm about to turn away when the door opens, revealing Sebastian in the gap.

"I was hoping you'd come," he says. Or I *think* that's what he says. All my senses are focused on his bare chest and the fact that, under the ladder of abs and the cut muscle shaped like a 'V,' all he's wearing is loose cotton boxer shorts.

He's practically naked.

I'm still looking right at his bare chest when I admit, "I have no idea why I'm here."

"No?" he asks, with the tilt of his head. "Because I think you do."

He steps aside and I slowly, reluctantly, enter his room. I realize it's more like a suite once I'm inside. He has a small living room with a gray couch and armchair. A flatscreen is mounted to the wall, a bunch of gaming instruments piled haphazardly underneath. Through the hammering in my chest and the blood throbbing in my ears, I hear the click of the door closing behind him.

I swallow loudly, realizing that I didn't even bring my knife. It's a ridiculous thought. If I really thought I'd need it, I wouldn't have come in the first place.

No.

There's only one way to approach this.

When I turn to face him, I shrug out of my jacket, throw it aside, and then push him down onto the couch.

He looks more satisfied than surprised as I straddle his lap. "See?" he says, leaning in to plant a slow, wet kiss to my neck. "You know exactly why you're here."

The feel of his lips beneath my ear makes me shudder and I

exhale, pushing down on him. His cock is already growing hard beneath me, stirring a sharp heat between my legs. When he turns his face to me, I take his lips in a kiss, and it's not like before. It's not *rough*. It's calculated and full of intent. His warm breath fills my mouth, and then his tongue, sliding smoothly between my lips.

I lean into it, my hardened nipples pressing against the thin fabric of my tank, drilling against his hard chest. I groan into his kiss, feeling the rush of desire, the heat of his body. Sebastian's skin is fire—so much warmer than my own—leeching through every scrap of fabric separating us.

I don't follow when he falls back, staring up at me with heavy-lidded eyes. His hand reaches out to clutch the dogtags swinging between us, giving the chain a light tug. "Can I touch you now?" I jerk back, the chain digging into my neck as I do. There's a roll of anxiety threatening to drag me under and Sebastian flinches against me, but doesn't chase. "You can say no. I might ask, but that doesn't mean I'll—you can say no."

"No."

His face falls—for just a moment—but it's quickly replaced with a restless sort of want. He slings each arm against the back of the couch, the muscles across his chest, taunt and teasing, hands out of reach. "So tell me what you want, what I can do. I'll follow it to a T."

I stare at his mouth, those soft lips that feel so good against my overheated skin. I run a thumb over his bottom lip. "Just kiss me."

He doesn't argue, surging up to recapture my lips. Fuck, he's a good kisser. I bet he's good with his hands too, when he can actually use them. I try not to think too hard about it—about things I can't have—and focus on this. The little rumble in his chest when my teeth rake over his lip. The way his head tilts, shoulders shifting to guide the kiss, like he doesn't even need hands, because this— mouths and bodies—are enough.

He's solid and firm beneath me when I writhe against him, and I'm feeling the same restless want I'd seen on his face moments earlier.

It's not enough.

He looks startled when I spring to my feet, but it doesn't last long. His tight, puzzled expression falls slack when I whip my tank top off over my head, throwing it aside. His eyes dart to my chest and linger there, hands fisting against the back of the couch. The feel of his gaze is as intrusive as if he was touching me, but it doesn't hurt. There's no malice, only want.

He mutters a slow, appreciative, "Goddamn."

"Kiss me," I say again, feeling the prick of my flushed skin.

He nods, caught in a haze, but then snaps out of it, standing up and giving me a blistering, hungry kiss on the mouth. I step closer, and *oh god*.

There it is.

Flesh to flesh. Touch. Sensation.

I gasp, "Wait," and hold him there, nice and still. The feel of his hot skin against so much of mine makes something collapse inside of me, tumbling into a sweet kind of chaos. He looks confused when my forehead drops to his chest, maybe even worried, because suddenly I'm trembling. He stands there frozen, arms out, like he's about to be assassinated or something. "Just... wait."

He obeys, still as a statue as I soak in the feeling of a body against mine. The way his chest expands and contracts, the feel of his skin, the warmth, the *life*.

Texture, my brain supplies in the form of Georgia's voice. *Now you need something soft.*

"Did I do something?" he asks, voice stilted.

I shake my head, not knowing how to explain that I haven't touched anyone—*really* touched anyone—in so long, that I'd almost forgotten what being up against another life felt like. I swallow thickly. "No, I just needed... I needed..."

Instead of answering, I stretch up on my toes—the hard, sensitive nipples sliding against the hard planes of his chest—to capture his lips in an urgent kiss. He falls back into the moment like he never left it, and maybe he hadn't. His cock is hard, arrow-sharp in his thin shorts. He doesn't linger on my mouth long, having been given permission to explore.

He guides me with his body to swap our positions, nudging me back to the couch. I sit and he drops to his knees, palms flat on the cushions. I can tell he's getting a little keyed up now, knuckles white with how hard he's fisting them as he sucks a kiss into my neck, and then my shoulder, something greedy and possessive in the way he boxes me in. He burns a hot trail down between my breasts and I don't stop him. Even when he pauses there, his warm breath feathering over a peaked nipple, his blue eyes raise to mine—a question.

I don't say no.

His tongue flicks out, sending a spark of fire across my skin.

"Oh, god," I gasp, arching into him.

"Your tits are fucking amazing," he says, clamping his mouth around the peak. I lean my head back and run my hands over his shoulders. They're smooth and strong. Powerful. From this vantage, I can see the corded muscles flexing in his back as he dips his head to take me in his mouth, assaulting my nipple with quick back-and-forth flicks of his tongue.

I learn quickly that Sebastian doesn't need his hands to work magic. Just feeling this—watching him—is enough to make me squirm, hips bucking unthinkingly. The movement makes him pause, and he rocks back, reaching down to squeeze the tenting in his shorts.

Roughly, he says, "We could fuck, you know." His dark eyes hold mine, even as I watch him stroke himself through my periphery. "I can do this. I can fuck you without touching you."

I feel myself lock up. I'd come here expecting to make out, and even that had held an air of impossibility. My voice comes out too sharp, panic bleeding through. "I'm not fucking you, Sebastian."

He hurries to say, "No? That's cool, that's fine." He taps the cushion, and then, "Can I pull down your pants?"

I'm still for a moment, thinking. It's so intimate, so exposed. Full on vulnerability. Aside from my back, all my worst scars are there. Is he going to ask questions?

Sebastian must sense my hesitation because he exhales raggedly and runs his hand over his face. "I don't know how to do this, Sugar. If you can't tell, I want you really fucking bad." He grimaces. "But I made a promise. Tell me how to keep it."

His admission of how much he wants me sends another wave of desire through me. Instinctively, I lift my hips again, this time pressing my fingers between my legs. He watches my every move, lips parted, tongue darting out. Feeling stupid, I yank my hand back.

He says, "Yeah, yeah, do that again."

I try to play dumb. "Do what?"

"Touch yourself. Do it again."

He watches me like a hawk, eyes zeroed in on my hand. My heart pounds hard in my chest. What I am I doing? Why does he get under my skin like this? I don't know why, but just the heat of his eyes on me is enough to send a flood of red-hot want, right to my core. I want to see that flicker of hunger in the deep blue of his eyes. I want to control him with my movements.

I place my hand flat on my belly, fingers tucked under the waistband of my pajama bottoms. "Like this?" I ask, knowing good and well there's no right or wrong in this moment. There's just lust.

"Yeah, just like that." He falls back on his ass, knees bent and parted. His dick is ramrod straight, pressing against his shorts. "Touch yourself the way you'd want me to."

I inch my fingers down, still covered by my pants, and graze my fingertips over the hot bundle of nerves at the crux of my body. I inhale sharply, my stomach rising and falling. I keep my eyes on Sebastian while he leans back on one hand and reaches inside his shorts. A moment later he's exposed himself, the throbbing, long length of his cock. He slides his hand down the shaft, but his eyes remain on the spot between my legs, my hand shifting beneath the fabric.

His actions cause a cascade in my own body. I get slippery and wet, hips rising into my own movements, setting a rhythm. Watching him watch me, watching him handle himself with such defined expertise, just makes me wish I could have said yes. His desire is exposed in every part of him, the darkening of his eyes, the tensing of his jaw, the sharp line in the muscle of his forearm. Heat blooms across my skin and I finally lift my hips, lowering my pants over my knees. When I part my legs and touch myself again—over my panties—Sebastian groans in approval.

"Christ, I want to—" He seems to bite back the rest, jaw clenching. I watch as he rolls his thumb over the tip of his dick, alternating strokes of hard and soft. I can see the sticky fluid at the top. I lick my lips and mimic his motions, rolling my clit with my thumb, applying pressure, then letting up. A rhythm forms between us, bolstered by the sound of our heavy breathing, the noises building in our chests.

"Touch your tits," he demands. I have no idea where he gets off telling me what to do, but I do it anyway, spurred on by the tightening in my belly. I massage one breast, then the other, causing a sensation that jolts straight between my legs. He falls back on his elbow and flicks his nipple between his fingers, shuddering in response. "Jesus."

I've been thinking maybe it couldn't happen—me getting off in front of someone like this. But the orgasm builds in my belly, a coil tightened with every flick, rub, and stroke. Sebastian's jaw tightens and his abdomen tenses as his motions grow more erratic. I can't take my eyes off of him; his face, his body, the way his muscles flex the closer he gets.

Fuck, he's got a nice body.

"I want to see it," he says through gritted teeth. "I want to see you come, Sugar, let go. Let me see you just fucking let go."

My body has never cooperated with my desires. If anything, we're in a constant battle. But there's something about Sebastian's tone—his demand—that I physically react to. The orgasm spreads through me in waves of warm pleasure that drag me under, hazy, sweaty, overcome. I sink my teeth into my lip to bite down my whimpers as it shakes through me.

True to his word, that is all Bass wanted to see. He comes quickly, violently, seizing on his cock in a final gripping tug. "Fuck, fuck, fuck," he mutters, ropes of white, sticky fluid, dripping down his fist and pooling on his taut stomach. I lean back against the couch, the feeling slowly returning to my limbs, and then we both sit there, panting.

He mutters a low, "Good shit," head still thrown back, eyes closed, body limp.

I take the opportunity to pull up my pants and root around for my shirt, having to stand and walk a few steps to bend down and collect it. It's cold in here now, or maybe it's just me. Maybe it's just this frenetic, chilling feeling returning to the pit of my chest, making me shiver and shake.

When I turn around, Sebastian's watching me, a strange look on his face. He immediately looks away, removing his shorts and using them to wipe away the spunk.

"Is this the part where you bolt?" he asks, and there's a *fuckton* of things happening in my head right now, but mostly I'm just staring at him as he stands, stark-ass naked, completely unashamed.

I sputter out an unnecessarily hostile, "What?" and he sighs, tossing his boxers aside.

"Nothing. Just wait here a second." He disappears through a door and I shift from foot to foot, thinking about how much I don't want to bolt.

I mostly just want to feel his bare chest against mine again.

When he returns, he's dressed in a pair of sweats and a thick, comfortable-looking pullover. He shows me a pack of cigarettes and jerks his chin toward another door. "There's a window in the bathroom."

That's how we end up sitting on the counter on either side of his sink, a squeaky exhaust fan to our front and the sound of chilly January wind to our backs.

He lights a cigarette and passes it to me, watching as I reluctantly take it, careful not to touch his fingers. "Looked like you needed it," he explains.

I don't know what the hell that means, but I suck in a drag anyway, letting it burn my chest. His eyes look about as tired as I feel, but he seems more relaxed than I've ever seen him. Loose. Unguarded. Apparently, the post-orgasm version of Sebastian is something to behold.

"Can I ask you something?" he says, watching the stream of smoke as I aim it out the window.

I tuck my knees closer to my chest. "Depends."

"On?"

"Can I ask *you* something?"

He looks surprised that I'd want to. "I'm an open book. Shoot."

So I do. "Why aren't you with Georgia?"

He lets out this soft, quiet laugh. "Not my type."

"You're friends, so you like each other," I argue. "You've already hooked up with her, so you're obviously attracted. You're protective of her. You buy her gifts."

He raises an eyebrow. "Jealous?"

For some reason it makes me angry, and I'm starting to suspect a part of that is that it *does*. "Maybe I don't want to get into something that's going to end in some CW love triangle bullshit. I like Georgia. She's the closest thing I've had to a friend since middle school. So if there's anything there, then I want out now."

He plucks the cigarette from my fingers before I can bring it to my mouth, lifting it to his own. "Georgia is nice, and pretty, and yeah, she's my friend. I've got her back. Not because we fooled around or because I'm into her, but just because that's what I do for friends. I do the same for V or Caroline. Part of having Georgia's back is knowing that we aren't long-term material and not ruining a good friendship over something that's just," he makes a dismissive gesture, "never going to click. It started as a dare, for real, and after that we shut that shit down."

I don't even want to know what that says about whatever he's trying to drum up with me. Casual, experimental sex isn't something I do.

Well.

Until now.

"Good."

He adds, "We never fucked," and I stop him.

"Not my business. Ask your question, it's getting late."

Despite being the one to ask permission, a frission of dread seems to pass over his eyes. "You don't have to answer," he says, passing the cigarette back to me. "I was just wondering what happened to your back."

I freeze, cigarette still outstretched between us. Fuck. How did I let him see that? How did I possibly forget about the ugly, criss-crossed mess of marks from Doug's favorite belt? Fucking careless, stupid, sex-fueled bullshit. "Nothing. Long story."

"Okay," he replies, instantly backing off. "Why don't I ever see you around with your camera."

Blindsided by the sudden change of topic, I ask, "What?"

"You're in the photography club. You took that picture of Abby." He shrugs, loose and unbothered. "Just seems like you'd be taking more pictures."

At least this is easier to answer. "I don't really know anyone here —except Georgia. Vandy, I guess. Can't leave campus much, so not much opportunity for landscapes. Everyone in the club takes the same four pictures of the campus."

"Hey," he says, smirking, "if you need a subject, all you need to do is ask."

I roll my eyes. "Yeah, cause that's what the world needs; more pictures of you shirtless, admiring yourself in a mirror."

His eyebrows shoot up his forehead, smile widening. "Have you been stalking my profile, Sugar Voss?"

Jesus. Shouldn't have clued him into that. "I should go," I say, standing. Orgasms clearly turn into me a mindless fount of drivel.

He doesn't argue, but he still looks smug, even when we're slipping into our coats and he's leading me down the quiet, dark hall. It's cold outside, the harsh opposite of what I felt back in his room. The urge to press into his side, to feel his arm wrapped around me, is so foreign that it takes me the walk to Hayden to even realize what it is.

When I do, I wrap my arms around myself instead.

He walks me to the door, and I can't help but wonder if it's still a walk of shame if he's escorting me. I'm not sure, but I'm thinking not. I don't feel shame, anyway, I just feel weird and hyper-aware, like anything could suddenly happen in this strange, dream-like moment I'm finding myself in.

Mostly, I feel a sense of relief. No one—not even Sebastian—could possibly understand how big a deal that was for me. To be with someone like that. To touch someone like that. To expose myself to him like that.

I climb the steps and he asks, "So... did I do it?"

I frown, both at the reluctance in his voice and the words. "Do what?" A lot had just transpired between us.

He gazes up at me, the edges of his face softly illuminated in the fluorescent light of a distant lamp. "Did I prove myself to you? Did I fuck it up?"

I step back down to his level, thinking it over. He followed my rules. He was patient and calm. He pushed but wasn't intimidating. He asked for things I couldn't give him, and he wasn't a dick about being denied.

He was... *nice*.

In lieu of an answer, I pitch forward, brushing my lips against his in a slow kiss. He leans into it, and there's a strange intensity to the way he lingers, our noses pressed close, and I think *here*.

This is where he'd touch me, if he could. Maybe he'd cup my cheek, or tuck my hair back, or just wrap his arms around me.

He pulls away, burying his hands into his pockets instead. "Good night, Sugar."

"Good night, Sebastian." I turn away, disappearing inside the warm, dark building.

15

Although it never really goes away, my tense, agitated restlessness has substantially faded by the time I walk into school the next day. There's nothing like a good orgasm to take the edge off, and my most recent was pretty damn explosive. I keep thinking about how that's just from jerking off and watching Sugar. I can only imagine what having sex with her will be like.

Yeah, *will*.

That's something I'm determined will happen, even if it's going to take more time and chasing than I'd usually expend on a girl. I can wait. What I've come to realize is that Sugar isn't just *any* girl. She's special. A marathon, not a sprint. Sort of like my sweet Jasmine; I'm going to have to put in the time to get her engine humming.

I go to my locker, half-zoned out, still thinking about the way Sugar looked on my couch last night. Shit, even the type of girl I'm used to popping would have run like hell if I'd asked them to touch themselves like that. So many girls are shy and insecure. But not Sugar. I can't quite figure her out. She's scared of being touched, but she's also not inhibited. Somehow all her wires seem crossed, and I plan on figuring out how to fix her the way I'm fixing the Mustang.

"Hey, Bass."

I turn and see Sydney, suppressing a groan.

"Syd. What's up?"

She leans against the locker next to mine. "I heard there's a car meet up tonight. You going to be there?"

I'd gotten the text from Carlton late last night. "Yeah, I think so."

"You think maybe I could get a ride?"

I grimace. "Yeah, I'm not sure about that. I've got a shit-ton of work to do this afternoon over at the garage and I'm not really sure when I'll be able to get downtown."

She scoots closer, tits pushed out. "I could come keep you company at the garage. Watch you work."

I step back and close the door. "Sorry. Merle doesn't like visitors at the garage. He barely tolerates me being there and I'm paying for it."

"Oh, boo." Her bottom lip sticks out and she rests her hand on my chest. "I thought you and I had a good time when we hung out before."

No, I had a spell of total lack of judgment. I can't even blame the concussion—it was long before that. The problem with Sydney is that she's vindictive and a total shit-stirrer, but most of all, she doesn't take rejection well. Reyn is a perfect example. She tried to blow up his relationship with Vandy when he wasn't into her. My problem is that I didn't say no the first time, so now I have to finagle every fucking interaction with her into a carefully diplomatic refusal.

"Things are kind of crazy right now, Syd. I'm still healing from that concussion, and I've got a lot of work to do down at the garage, along with school and everything."

"I'm starting to think you're avoiding me, Bass."

Like the fucking plague. I swallow back my irritation. "Maybe I'll see you there tonight."

Her eyes light up like I've just agreed to a date. *Fuck.* "Definitely." She leans forward and whispers in my ear. "Keep an eye out for me, I'll wear something special."

Jesus.

I glance over her head and see Sugar walking toward the arts building. The reaction is instantaneous, a heavy warmth rolling like waves down my limbs, my cock tingling in anticipation. That's the problem when you've been naked and sweaty with someone you're into. Your body just wants it again and again. I definitely want it again with Sugar, which pretty much hammers the nail in the coffin with Syd. I've had a little fun with her too, and I have zero interest in going back down that road.

I slam the locker door, mutter, "Whatever," and walk off. I make a beeline toward Sugar. As I get closer, I realize she's fussing with one of those ancient cameras.

"You know there's one of those on your phone," I say, once I'm a few feet away. "Digital, fits in your pocket, easy to edit."

She looks up from the lens, and I see a pink blush spread across her cheeks as the memory of what we'd done last night flickers in her mind. I'd give anything to kiss her right now, claim her in front of the school, give her a Devil's mark, but the way she clutches the camera to her chest like a shield tells me to hold back on my impulses.

"Digital is fine for amateurs, selfie-takers, and moms at the park." She expertly attaches the lens, pressing some levers and locking everything into place. "Real art needs a real camera."

"Yeah, but that's a lot of work." I pull out my phone and take a quick snap of her.

"Hey!"

I glance down at the photo. Her eyes are shrewd, mouth slanted wryly, and she's holding the camera sort of aggressively, like it's a gun or something. Her cheeks are also still flushed pink. She's beautiful. I shove the phone back in my pocket, out of her reach. "See? So much easier."

She shakes her head and starts toward Dr. Ross's class. "Funny. I'd think if anyone would get it, it'd be you."

"Me? Why?"

She slides me a sidelong glance. "I've seen your ride, Bass. You could have bought some flashy, quiet, easy car, but you went vintage and put in the work. That must have taken a lot of time and patience, attention to detail. I know you're like this whirling dervish of chaos, but I bet when you're really into something, you don't just want the easy way. You want to do it right."

In one sentence, Sugar managed to completely verbalize how I feel about her, and she doesn't even realize it.

She steps ahead of me and I grab the strap on her bag, gently tugging her back. I jerk my head to the side, encouraging her to follow me to an empty computer classroom. For once, she doesn't fight back, not even looking super cagey when I ease the door halfway closed.

Even still, I make sure to walk around her, not blocking her exit. "I wanted to, you know, make sure things are still good with us after last night."

She gives me a cutting look, even though her blush intensifies. "Do I not seem okay?"

"Seems like every other exchange we've had was pretty heated, and you haven't threatened me in a while. Figured I'd check in." I glance over her shoulder to make sure no one is coming in here. "Although, I guess last night was pretty heated, too."

"I'm fine," she says, hands still clenched around her camera. "Remember how I'm the one who came to your room?"

"Yeah," I say, staring at her mouth, "you definitely came, alright."

Her eyes narrow. "Are you *looking* to get threatened again?"

"Whirling dervish, remember?" Unable to stifle the impulse any longer, I dart forward and steal a kiss. It's brief, but the heat of her mouth against mine is worth the fleetingness. Her eyes are still blinking closed when I pull back. "Listen, there's a car show tonight. Do you want to go with me?"

Her forehead creases, probably processing the fact I've jumped subjects again. When she doesn't reply right away, I wish I hadn't asked. Too much? Too fast? Too eager? I'm in a world I'm not sure how to navigate, with a girl who's impossible to read.

"A car show?"

Feeling defensive, I reason, "You said you couldn't get off campus much to take pictures. I just thought there might be some good opportunities." It's only partially a lie. Mostly, I was thinking about how much I want her beside me again, looking all pretty and bitchy in my passenger seat.

She doesn't seem unopposed, though. "Is it the same place as last time? I did see some cool graffiti I couldn't get to."

"Nah," I answer. "But this place has way better graffiti anyway. You'll love it."

She gives me a cynical look. "Will I, now."

"Definitely," I answer, feeling frenetic all of a sudden. "So you'll come? With me?"

Jesus. How desperate did that sound?

Apparently not too much, because she gives me a small smile. It's a little pursed, like she's trying to hold it back but can't. "Yeah, I'll come."

Ah, fuck. That smile gets me. "Can I touch you?"

The smile falls. "No."

But I just nod, having figured as much. Her dog tags are lost somewhere beneath her uniform, so I can't even fidget with them like I usually would when I get the urge to touch her. My eyes roam over her. "What about your hair? Can I touch your hair?"

Now *that* definitely sounded desperate.

She chews on her lip, eyes sliding shiftily to the side. "I don't know." Her eyes flit back to me for a moment and there's something wary in them, like maybe she's bracing for me to ridicule her for not knowing.

I don't. "Can I try?"

"Uh..." She ducks her head to look at it—her hair—resting over her shoulders in a waterfall of shiny-black. "Okay."

"Yeah?" I reach out slowly, watching her eyes track my hand, and touch it. It's cool and soft, silky. When I run my fingers through it, sweeping it off her shoulder, she makes this sound—this little hitch of breath—and her eyes flutter closed.

I take the opportunity to duck in, pressing a gentle kiss to her jaw, right in the place I'd decked her that night at the docks. I linger there for a moment, inhaling the soft, honey-laced scent of her, before carefully pulling back.

When her eyes open, she looks all at once anxious and dazed.

"I'll meet you in the parking lot at nine," I say, giving her hair one last stroke.

She gives a slow nod. "Yeah, nine."

I leave the room first, trying to figure out exactly when I decided to ask Sugar on a date and how in the world I got her to say yes.

THE DRIVE DOESN'T TAKE LONG.

I spend it with one eye on the road and the other on Sugar in the passenger seat. She looks fucking amazing in her denim jacket and holey jeans, that strip of skin on her thigh still taunting me. But every time I look at it, I also see a little dot. Birth marks? Scars? I'd sort of seen them last night in my dorm room, when she'd taken off her pants, but my brain wasn't exactly firing on all pistons.

Not until I'd seen her back.

Nothing. Long story.

I glance at her and she's looking down at the gear shift, blankly staring at the way my hand rests on the knob. There's no point asking about it. Best case scenario, she'll just duck the question. Worst case, she starts backing off. That's okay, though. It's not like I'm in any hurry to unload all of my shit on her, either.

"Are you hungry?" I ask, shifting down to idle at a stoplight in front of the bridge we raced under last time. "We can grab something on the way, or—"

"I'm not hungry." It's not said unkindly, but still feels like a rejection. And, then, quietly—almost begrudgingly, "But maybe something to drink."

I instantly pull into the nearest fast food place, ordering us both a soft drink in the drive-through. "There," I say, watching fixedly as she wraps her lips around the straw. "Now it's a date."

She sputters. "This isn't a date, Bass."

Fuck, I love it when she calls me Bass.

I reason, "A predetermined meeting between two sexually attracted people, which includes the consumption of something edible and-or potable? That's a date." I give my drink a long slurp, concluding, "And if you put out later, it could even be a good one."

She rolls her eyes, but I can see the faint bloom of pink on her cheeks. "You're hands down the most insufferable motherfucker I've ever met."

I flash her a winning grin. "Thanks."

"Does that actually work for you?' she asks, reclining back in the seat, looking perfectly at ease. "Badgering girls into getting on your dick?"

"You tell me."

"I'm never going to fuck you," she says, but even though it's firm and brooks no argument, it's lacking that tight, angry tone she usually says it in.

I wonder if she really believes that. I sure as shit don't.

"Sugar, I need you to know..." I start, watching her lips around that straw, my dick stirring. "I'm really into you. Like, *really* into you. Into you enough to badger you for a piece of that fine ass, and trust me, that's not something I've lowered myself to for anyone else." She's frozen, her eyes falling to my lips when I lean closer, voice a low, soft purr. "But if you spill that drink in my car, you'll be walking that fine ass back to campus."

Her slack, hypnotized expression instantly vanishes, replaced with something disbelieving and annoyed. "Shut up and drive, Wilcox."

Laughing, I obey.

Turning past the cracked and weathered 'For Sale' sign, I enter the wide expanse of the parking lot. The huge, vacant building sits in the middle, windows boarded up and overgrown weeds climbing the brick walls. A few cars are idling down by the shuttered department store, along with a growing group of spectators.

"This is where everyone is meeting tonight?" Sugar asks, peering out the front window. "The mall?"

"The *abandoned* mall," I clarify. "It's been boarded up for years.

It's a good spot. The view's obstructed from the streets, not many houses around, lots of space."

She stares at the mall, eyebrow quirked. "It's a little creepy."

I grin at her. "Well, then I'll just have to keep you safe."

That comment makes her give me this bitchy look, but I don't miss the way her cheek quirks, another one of those secret smiles pursing her lips. Fuck, it drives me crazy knowing that Sugar Voss, maybe even a better fighter than me, can't even fight this.

She totally digs me.

I grip the steering wheel and lean over the center console. She watches me carefully, eyes darting to my hands then back to my mouth. Her tongue darts out to lick her bottom lip and she meets me in the middle, kissing me with her soft, sweet mouth.

I pride myself on being a good kisser, but Sugar is a challenge. She makes me feel sloppy—rushed—wondering if I'm going too hard or too fast or not hard enough. But she keeps letting me do it, so I think it's probably not the worst she's had.

Wait, has Sugar been kissed before? God, I know nothing about this girl.

A stream of lights parades down the lot, interrupting my thoughts and the kiss itself. "Unless you just want to park over here all night—which, for the record, I'm totally fine with—I should probably go get a spot."

She brandishes her camera, only meeting my eyes in fits and starts. "Go get your spot. I came here to sweeten up my portfolio, not neck with you like a nineteen-fifties schoolgirl."

I internally curse, but I'm also into her being here with me— beside me, all sweet and sour in my passenger seat, like a shiny prize—even without any necking. I shift the car into gear and the muffler rumbles as I make the slow drive across the parking lot. I find a good spot between a tricked-out Honda and an old El Camino. I hop out of the car while Sugar fusses with her camera, taking the opportunity to open the door for her. She looks up at me in surprise, blinking.

I offer her my hand.

She looks at it for a long, hard minute, and then back at me. I don't know how this whole thing works. I can't touch her—not with my hands—but she can obviously touch me. She could touch my hand, couldn't she? But she doesn't, so I pull it away, stuffing it into my pocket and moving aside for her to climb out.

"So," she says, her voice a little more quiet than usual, "tell me what's going on here?"

I pointedly don't mention the hand thing. "Everyone circles up where we can check out each other's cars, see the new detailing or mods. If we want to race, we'll throw our names in the pot." I point to a guy over by a souped-up Toyota. "That's Darren. He figures out who's racing who. If there are bets on it, he'll take the money."

She looks around, following where I point. "People bet on the races?"

"People bet on everything," I say, taking a chance to reach out and stroke my fingers though the hair covering her shoulder. She just watches, unflinching. "Smart people bet on me."

She studies me suspiciously for a minute, and I feel the heat creeping up my neck. Is this going to be one of her deal breakers? It's not fighting, but it's still illegal. "I thought you were into cars because you like restoring them."

"I do," I say, shrugging, "but I think you know me well enough by now to see that I've got a competitive streak. I can't fight. I can't play lacrosse. What else am I going to do? Racing fills a need." It feeds the wild craving I have inside for a rush, a chase for the win. It strikes like a match, burning bright, and it's not as good as fighting—it's not explosively physical—but the high of having conquered something through fuel and fire is close enough to do it for me. "I'm good at this, Sugar. I'm also smart. I know how to handle my car, who to compete against, and what kind of bets to place. When I race, I'm here to win. I'm not here to do something stupid."

She gives me a wary look. "Some people would consider anything dangerous and illegal like this stupid."

"Then they've never experienced the thrill of going a hundred and forty miles an hour and the sweet, sweet feeling of victory."

She rolls her eyes. "Are you planning on racing tonight?"

"No."

She levels me with a look. "You sure about that?"

"Yes. I promise." She looks instantly relieved and I'm thankful that I'm telling the truth. "I came to show off the new glass-packs on Jasmine, that's all, plus—"

But my words die in my throat, because in the distance, I spot a familiar head of blond hair. My reaction is instantaneous—a sharp, twisting recoil deep in my gut.

No.

Fuck no. No fucking way Heston is here right now. Only he clearly is. There's no mistaking my brother, over there checking out a neon green Mazda like he has any goddamn right to *be here*. This is mine. And here he is with his slimy fucking hands all over it, the one thing of mine he hasn't touched and tainted.

Jaw clenching, I suddenly remember Sugar. My stomach sinks in realization that I'm wrong.

There's something else he hasn't touched yet.

I try to keep my voice casual. "So, things are about to get technical and boring for a few. Unless you want to hear about how much Rich paid for the wheels on that El Camino, you may want to take the opportunity to go take some photos."

She wrinkles her nose at the idea of listening to car talk. "Good idea. I think I see a good spot to hang." She holds up her camera to look through the viewfinder and I do everything I can to keep my expression neutral, but it's getting hard. Heston spots me just as she smashes her finger on the button. *Hurry hurry hurry.* Moving with the speed of molasses, she slings the strap of her bag over her shoulder and says, "I guess I'll see you in a little bit?"

I give a jerky nod. "Yep, go document the seedy underbelly of my life. We'll catch up later."

My smile drops the instant she turns, and I bend, pretending to inspect something on Jasmine's wheel well. I furtively track her progress across the lot, holding my breath as she crosses paths with Heston. His head swings when she passes, eyes glued to her ass, and the acrid taste of fear mingled with rage climbs up the back of my throat. I know better than to let him see that, though—to see that I care.

When he approaches, I stand and brush off my hands to face him.

"Hey little bro," he says, offering me his fist.

I stare at it for a brief moment, then bump back. "What are you doing here?"

He shrugs. "Smoking a little weed, placing some bets. I heard you were coming tonight, so I knew I'd have a sure winner."

I'd seen it coming, but it still tosses me about inside, a sudden, chaotic storm of fury. Can't let him see, though. I can *never* let him see. "Sorry, man. You wasted your time. I'm not racing tonight."

He laughs, lips quirking into a smug grin. "Tell that to Darren. Your name is on the docket."

I turn slowly, feeling dangerous. "My what? I didn't sign up to race tonight. My car isn't ready, and I haven't done any intel on the competition."

He waves dismissively. "I'm sure you'll be fine. Use your instincts."

My instincts are telling me to punch Heston in his stupid fucking face, but I suck it back. Darkly, I guess, "You signed me up."

His eyes give me a scathing onceover. "Fucking right, I did. Your little break from fighting has put a serious damper on my expendable income. You need to get your ass out there and hustle a little."

"And whose fault is that, dumbass?" Anger licks under the surface, turning my constant undercurrent of irritation into a full-out rage. "I'm not racing for you tonight, Heston. Not now, not ever."

He snorts and shakes his head. "You're seriously trying to blame that bump on your head on me? You agreed to that fight, got that guy all riled up. I just helped the odds along."

"You tossed him a fucking *bat*."

"I made ten large," he argues. "You were getting too good. Had to shake things up a little."

"Shake things up." I laugh without humor, glance across the

parking lot and see Sugar crouched atop a pillar, taking a wide shot of the show.

Heston's eyes follow mine, carefully assessing the crowd, before flicking back to mine. "Get your ass on the course, and you better fucking win."

"And if I refuse to?"

He shrugs easily. "Then I guess I'll have no money to support my lifestyle and I'll have to move back home with Mommy."

That's the thing about Heston. He can't take me. More than once, Emory has asked, "Why don't you just kick the shit out of him and get it over with?" I could. Heston doesn't fight with fists. Too unseemly for him. He fights like this—through others. He takes apart everything you care about and destroys it, bit by bit.

Yeah, I could kick his ass.

And then what?

He knows just how to get me to cooperate. For years, our mother has been my Achilles heel and he fucking knows it. But this time there's something else at stake—someone else—and I just promised her I wasn't racing tonight. I've only just barely been given a glimpse at earning Sugar's trust and now Heston wants me to blow it? I run my hand through my hair and curse my life and the fucking rock and hard place I've been thrust into.

"Bass! I've been looking all over for you."

I look up at the sky and wonder if I really am cursed.

"Hey, uh, Sydney," I reply, "this really isn't a great time—"

"Oh, you're Heston, right?" she says innocently, like she doesn't know him. Everyone knows Heston. He used to run the school with the previous set of Devils. He looks down at Syd, eyes zeroed right in on her cleavage. It's January and cold as balls out here, but Sydney still has managed to show as much skin as possible. My brother looks like he wants to bury his face in her tits to warm up. Jesus Christ.

"Have we met?" he asks, offering his hand while still obviously ogling her. I swear to god, she pushes them out further.

"I doubt it," I interject. "Sydney is a *junior*. You know, not even eighteen yet."

"But not illegal," he replies with a wolfish grin. "You go to Preston?" She nods. "How have we never met before?"

"Because sophomores weren't on your radar when you went to school with us."

He looks at me, eyes narrowed, trying to figure out what Sydney means to me. The answer is 'jack shit', but just because I'm not into her doesn't mean I think she should be thrown to Lucifer himself. But, unfortunately for Sydney, I've expressed the slightest defense. Heston won't be satisfied until he defiles something he thinks I want.

"Sydney," he says in a slow drawl, eyes raking down her body, "my brother and I need to work out a few things before he races tonight, but if you'll go wait over there, we can watch together."

Her eyes brighten and she nods. "Yeah! I'll be waiting." She gives me a glance. "Good luck, Bass."

"You too, Syd," I mutter, knowing this won't end well.

She walks off, ass swishing back and forth. I look back at my brother and he's still watching her go. "Damn," he says, licking his bottom lip, "where have you been hiding that one?"

"I'm not hiding anything. Sydney is... well, a friend at best, but not even that. And you should stay away from her. She's a shit-stirrer. Nothing but trouble."

His eyes hold mine, like he's trying to discern if I'm holding back on him—downplaying my relationship with her. "You know I have a thing for trouble."

"Well that's it, Bro. Capital T. Your funeral." I glance over at the car. "Seriously, I don't think Jasmine is in the right condition to race tonight."

"Well, you better get her in the right condition, because the bets are locked in and I'm not losing all my money because you pussied out." He leans forward, face set into a hard scowl. "I told you the conditions. I need the money. If I don't get it, I move back home. Your choice."

There's always a third choice, scratching like a tiger in the back of my head, willing me to bury my fist in this fucker's face. But even setting our mom aside, this fucking concussion has me vulnerable now. It wouldn't take much from him. One calculated hit could cause more damage to my already-pressing head injury and end my lacrosse season, or worse. Also, I think, eyes darting over to where Sugar is photographing some graffiti on the side of the building, I'll lose her for sure and I can't do that. Not now. Not when it's barely started.

"You know what?" I hiss, shoving a finger into his chest. "Fine. But you can't ask me to do something like this last minute again. I fucking mean it."

He doesn't respond, just grins widely, smugly, knowing he's won —again. He strolls off, making a beeline for Sydney. It takes every-thing in me not to chase him down and pummel the life out of him. Instead, I get in the car and crank the engine, backing it out of the circle and driving it around the corner of the building. I get back out, slamming the door and popping the trunk for my tool kit. I've got about twenty minutes to do some last-minute tweaks on the engine.

"Fuck!" I shout, scraping my knuckle on the hood latch. I wish he couldn't get to me like this, but he does. Every fucking time. My chest gets tight, blood pumping through my veins like lava, nerves firing so rapidly that it makes it hard to even uncurl my fists. My teeth ache with how hard I'm gnashing them and my head throbs with the pressure of it all, vision tunneling.

Unthinkingly, I pick up the tool bag and hurl it across the parking lot, scattering tools with an echoing clang. "Fuck! Fuck! Motherfucking fuck!"

But I don't stop there. When it comes to Heston, this burning, furious thing inside me won't be satisfied until I've hurt—someone else or myself, it doesn't give a shit. I strike out without really thinking about it, being driven by the knowledge that this car is just one more thing—one more tool—for my brother to use.

His.

The first blow is a hard punch to the hood. I kick out mind-lessly, smashing the front side panel. Over and over, the dull thuds of my fists and boots sound in my ears, and it's not enough. I grab a tire iron and slam it into a door. My muscles scream as I beat it into the car's body, not out of exertion, but out of this rabid need to thrash and destroy. It's like being hooked up to an exposed light socket, a constant feedback loop of shock and strike.

Everything.

He ruins fucking *everything*.

The more damage I see, the more I want to cause. I lop off a sideview mirror and keep slamming forward, raising the tire iron over my head to take out that fucking window next.

"Sebastian?"

I feel a hand on my back and I spin around, iron still held high.

Sugar's standing there, face morphing into wide-eyed terror as she shrinks back, throwing her hands up. "Sebastian, stop! What are you doing?! Stop!"

It's like the switch on that socket gets flipped. One second I'm boiling over with rage, and the next, I'm cringing away from it. She's so small next to my car, up against my anger, that I suck in a shocked breath. The wave of emotion ebbs, pooling in my gut like a bitter, toxic waste.

"Jesus fucking Christ, Sugar! I could have—" If I'd hit her again? My life would be fucking over.

She's still staring at me with those eyes. Those huge, alarmed, *frightened* eyes. "What the fuck is going on?"

"I—" There are no words for this. No excuse can transform this into anything resembling sense. There's just me, with all my flaws, laid bare for her to see. I'm coated in sweat, still panting, the result of my outburst imprinted like scars upon the car, and I think *yeah*.

That's it.

She's going to run now. That stunt in Dr. Ross's class was bad enough, but she could forgive it, because it was for Georgia. This? This is the exact kind of crazy, nonsensical, indiscriminate violence she'd accused me of. The perfect display of 'I told you so'.

I wait for her to bolt.

Amazingly, she doesn't. "What happened?" My knuckles burn and I flex them, wincing in pain. "Goddamn it, Bass, talk to me!"

Turning to brace my hands against the top of the car, I struggle for air. "I can't fight him. God, I want to, so fucking bad, you have no idea. But I can't. I can't risk it, but I just..." I'm shaking and it's not even just the anger. It's that I could have hurt her. It's that I'm wedged in this place I can't get out of. It's that I'm such a fucking slave to it all, unable to control this storm that's always raging inside of me. "I hate him so fucking much."

I choke on the words, hands balling into tight fists. It's like I can't fill my lungs anymore, breaths coming in shallow, barely-swallowed pants. I flinch at the sudden weight of her hand on my back, and I feel her flinch back in response

The weight returns almost instantly. "Take a deep breath."

I inhale sharply, but it's like razor blades in my lungs. Her arms begin winding around me, slow and careful, testing. I don't know what to do with the warmth of her chest against my back, the press of her cheek against my shoulder.

"Breathe with me," she says, chest expanding and contracting against me.

My body falls into the same rhythm as she guides me through a full breath. When I truly feel like I can breathe again, I shudder an exhale, hanging my head to gaze down at her arms around me.

Softly, I ask, "Can I touch you?" and I feel her stiffen.

"Sebastian," she says, voice low and strained. "Please don't make me say no to you right now."

I nod, head feeling heavy on my shoulders, and push back from the car. The loss of her warmth against my back is like a physical pang. "Thank you."

She's shifting from foot to foot, looking cagey. "Who is this 'he' you keep talking about, and what does he have to do with beating the shit out of Jasmine?"

My jaw clenches. I don't want to tell Sugar about Heston. I don't want her to even know he exists, like just having him in her head would be enough of a violation. I sure as hell don't want him to know *she* exists, but there's a shit-ton of damage I have to clear up if I want her to keep touching me like this.

"My brother, Heston," I explain, kicking a screwdriver toward the back of the car. "He's forcing me to race tonight."

She shakes her head, looking away. "I have a hard time

believing you, of all people, could be forced into doing anything. So how does that work, exactly?”

I make a long, winding gesture. “It’s this whole long, complicated family history that I don’t have time to go into now. Let’s just say I have absolutely no choice but to race. And *win*. If I don’t…” I look at her, willing her to understand. “If I don’t, then I’d be putting someone in danger.”

Concern furrows across her forehead. “Danger? Who?”

I take another deep breath. “Just... someone important to me. Family.”

A flicker of emotion sparks in her eyes, but she just nods. “Then I guess you have to do what you have to do.”

My head jerks back in surprise. “You won’t be mad that I’m racing when I promised not to? Or that I just fucking flipped out and almost hurt you again? Or that I’m clearly everything you said?”

“I’m not mad about anything right now.” She holds my gaze unflinchingly. “If you think that racing tonight is that important, then whatever. That’s your business. But ...” Her eyes move to the car, forehead creasing. “That was some seriously out of control, batshit tantrum. It just... it just freaks me the fuck out. What the hell? Jasmine means everything to you.”

I look over at the damage, and shrug, voice flat. “It’s just a car.”

She gapes at me, wide-eyed. “*Just a car*? Bullshit. You put your own labor into it, Bass. Don’t act like this car means nothing to you. You were going to make me walk back to campus just for spilling a drink in it.” She shakes her head. “I don’t believe that. Not for one second.”

In the distance, engines rev, creating an echo against the cement building and flat parking lot. A voice carries, announcing the start of the races.

“I have to go,” I tell her, bending to gather the tools off the ground. “Do you want me to find you someone to catch a ride back with?”

Her head tilts, confusion evident in her frown. “What do you mean?”

I toss the tools in the trunk, feeling raw and tired. "Well, I figure the chances of you wanting to ride back with me are pretty slim, considering that I fucked up and—"

She steps forward and kisses me on the mouth. The feeling is instantaneous, a burst of warmth through my body. Sugar ends the kiss almost as soon as it starts, pulling back and swallowing anxiously.

I touch my lips. "What was that for?"

"Luck," she says, burying her hands in her pockets. "I guess whatever's going on with your brother can't be solved tonight. But if you need to keep someone safe, then do it." Her eyes are full of steel and the shadow of a secret, like we're conspiring against something bigger than ourselves. "*Always*. You get me?"

I stare at her, stunned, feeling both steadied and unmoored by this one tiny girl. She has every right to bail on me—to be afraid. But the racing, what happened in class for Georgia, *Always*. When it comes to protecting someone, maybe Sugar gets it.

It's a more solid form of forgiveness than our truce ever was.

16

I watch Bass's car idle at the starting line over by the boarded-up Food Court. The crowd has grown since we first arrived, people of all ages hustling for a good place to spectate. It's a strange, awkward mishmash. There are a few teenagers that look way too young to be out here, and then older gear-heads who should probably be at home with their wives and kids, and plenty of others who fall somewhere in between. It's the same kind of vibe as last time; loud engines, air thick with exhaust, the occasional fireworks. The sulfur mixes with the clinging scent of weed, and heavy bass from portable speakers bounces off the buildings.

It's a straight up party.

I take a deep breath and work my way toward where I spotted Georgia earlier, sitting in the back of Emory's truck. Like always, crowds like this stress me out, but tonight it's hard to really dwell on it. Instead, I dwell on Bass and what I just witnessed.

Because he beat the shit out of his car. His *car*. The car that he named and talks about as if it were an actual person. The car that, according to him, he'd built himself, through blood and sweat, without any help from his parents, something that's completely his.

It's not that it didn't scare the shit out of me, because it did. Seeing him like that, all raged out, fists flying, made the hairs on the back of my neck stand on end. Every nerve in my body was screaming at me to run. Each time he made contact with the metal of the car, I could almost feel it, remembering what it's like being on the other side of that raw, angry power.

I should have run.

Instead, I squared my shoulders, marched up to him, and stopped it.

Stupid.

Completely, inexcusably, ridiculously stupid.

It just wasn't *like* him. And knowing that, deep in my bones—knowing him well enough to understand this—was enough to drive me forward. People don't just go around hurting the things they love for no reason. Not unless they're complete psychopaths. Sebastian is a lot of things, but I've seen a real psychopath. I've lived under the heel of one for long enough to know the signs.

Sebastian Wilcox, for all his impulsive, hot-headed nature, isn't *that.* This guy's got some serious shit going on.

I didn't want to run from him, I wanted to sink inside him. I wanted to cool his fire and be warmed by it, at the same time. I wanted to cut away all his frayed edges and see him still again. I wanted to pull him back from the chaos, because I've been wrong. *So fucking wrong.* That look in his eyes—angry and feral, yes—but also so full of anguish, is one I know well enough, and why shouldn't I?

Until a few weeks ago, I'd seen it in the mirror, every goddamn day. I just *needed to know.* I needed to know that someone like Sebastian, so strong and sure, could grasp that anguish and conquer it. Because if Sebastian Wilcox can't, then what hope do I have?

I've spent the last twenty-four hours practically gagging for a chance to feel him against me again, solid and alive. That part was easy, winding my arms around him, coaching him to breathe with me, our bodies flush. He was so warm, so strong, even on the verge of falling apart. Hearing the pain in his words, the admission that he was caught up in something bad with his brother. The guilt for going back on his promise to me. His need to protect *someone.*

It's that warmth that I carry with me as I cut through the crowd to reach my new friends. I tuck into it like I'm hiding behind a shield, the tingling sensation of Bass's body against mine. For so long, touch has been something so bad, so painful, that I truly forgot that it could also feel like this: good and pure and so warm that I just want to fall into it and stay there.

I already can't wait to feel it again.

"Hey, you're here!" Georgia says, when I finally reach her. She shifts over, giving me room to climb into the truck bed.

Aubrey and Emory sit on the top of the cab, his arms wrapped around her shoulders from behind. Along the sides of the bed, a few other kids from school are hanging out. I give them a small nod, watching Carlton sneak a sip from a longneck.

"Where have you been?" Georgia asks.

"Talking to Sebastian," I explain, looking toward his car. I brought Mr. Lee's zoom lens, and it's not great for such low light, but I can just get Sebastian in frame, close enough to see the way he's looking out the windshield, intense and eerily still. I press the shutter without thinking.

"Holy shit." I can hear Emory shifting behind me, a slow inhale sucked through his teeth. "Is that Jasmine? What the fuck happened to his car?"

Carlton adds, "Oh, shit! She's all busted up."

Lowering the camera, I mutter, "He's racing and isn't very happy about it."

"He is?" Emory says, glancing back at Ben. "Did you bet on him?"

Ben grins back, patting his front pocket. "Got it in at the last second. Sounds like he was a late addition."

I slide him a cutting look. "He said his brother is making him race."

They all look at me and Emory frowns. "Wait, you're saying Heston is here?"

"I guess."

"Where?" Georgia asks, looking around. I'm not imagining the way her expression shifts to something tight, hunted.

"I saw him a few minutes ago," Aubrey says. "With Sydney Rakestraw."

Emory's eyebrows shoot up to his hairline. "Seriously?"

"Yep."

"Jesus, not that I'd put anything past Heston, but since when does he sniff around high school girls anymore?"

I look to Georgia to get her reaction to all of this, but she's uncharacteristically quiet. I ask, "This Heston guy... is he really all that bad?"

She ducks her head, hiding her face. "You know I love Bass. I mean, I've told you repeatedly to give him a chance, so obviously I'd vouch for him. But Heston?" She shakes her head. "That guy is a fucking psychopath."

Carlton overhears and pipes in, "Hey, go easy on the psychopath community. Pretty sure even they don't want to claim him."

All of this is putting some of Bass's meltdown into perspective.

"It's about to start," Ben says, nodding toward the parking lot.

"Do you mind if I stand up so I can get some pictures?" I ask, looking at Emory.

He looks surprised I'd bother asking. "Go for it."

The set up tonight, while still make-shift and temporary, is less primitive than a straight drag race down the street like the first time I came. There's an elaborate course, set up with cones and a few metal barricades. It's hard to tell where the lines are, but it seems to arc all the way across the big parking lot, and loop back around.

"It's one lap," Ben says, noticing me surveying the course. "Whoever finishes first or without crashing, wins."

I spot the Shelby—Jasmine—nose up to the line. Nerves spin in my stomach and I focus on my camera, the crowd, anything to keep my mind off what's about to happen. I've seen Bass drive. I've seen him fight. I've seen him handle *himself*. I know his reflexes are good, but he didn't exactly seem at his most level-headed. All that pent-up anger behind the wheel of a two-ton moving ball of steel doesn't feel safe.

The flicker and glint of sparkles catches my attention and I press my eye to the viewfinder, watching through my camera. Someone is walking out in front of the two cars, but the most prominent thing I can make out about them is the fact they're dressed in sequins.

And then, they turn.

I don't bother trying to hide my smile. "Fuck me, is that...?"

"*That* is Micha Adams," Aubrey says, her tone tinged with a similar awe. "He'd posted on his ChattySnap account that he was going to be here tonight and had a surprise for everyone."

The kid saunters up to the beam of headlights, a red cloth hanging from his hand. His outfit is a sparkly red and gold, and his eye makeup matches flawlessly. The headlights hit him like the catch of sparks, practically making him glow. He looks like a smirking phoenix.

"He's the flag girl—er, boy?" Emory declares or asks. I'm not sure he knows. But this kid, Micha? He knows. Goddamn, he's glorious out there. My lens zooms in on him like a magnet, and through it, I can even see Sebastian grinning at the sight.

Micha raises the flag in the air, and everything goes suddenly still and silent. The two engines rev, and Micha has to know that everyone is watching him, waiting. Just like that, this little freshman holds a whole parking lot of party-goers right in the palm of his hand.

His arm drops, flag slicing through the air.

It's a blur of smoke and the sharp smell of rubber at first, the two cars squealing off. Georgia and her friends spring up to watch, and I inch out a bit to avoid the press of their bodies. Sebastian's car is a blur of blue as it approaches the south side of the building where I'd been photographing graffiti earlier, and then they both disappear around it.

I can still hear them though, the roar of their engines bellowing to us against the concrete. Everyone turns to the north side of the building, waiting in anticipation. My camera's sensor isn't good with high action shots, so I don't bother. I loop it around my neck and wait with everyone else, and I don't even know what the fuck.

Suddenly, I'm wanting Sebastian to win this thing so badly, I can taste it.

Ironic that it's the first time I truly feel a sense of belonging in this place, all of us poised as one with bated breath, a strange patchwork of unified eagerness. The first car to come around the building drifts in a long, skilled slide of rubber and exhaust, and at first, it's hard to tell which car it is. It doesn't matter, though.

I know it's him.

Jasmine careens around the track and the other car follows closely, gaining speed. My insides feel stiff and electrified as I watch the cars push and pull. Emory's shouting, "Come on, Bass!" and Ben is emitting some truly embarrassing, screeching sort of sounds, but I can barely hear them over the sound of my heartbeat.

In the end, Sebastian passes the line of worn, jagged spray paint on the pavement in a whir of wind and the crowd's celebratory shouts.

I deflate in relief at the victory,

"Not too shabby," Carlton declares, "for a last-minute entry."

Post-race is almost as much pandemonium as the first time, just with less cops. I pull back, not wanting to get into the push-pull of the people as they scatter about, even though I feel a weird spike of annoyance at the way everyone swarms his car. These people don't actually understand. None of them saw him right before, that crackle in the air around him, like the electricity of a thunderstorm.

But as much as Bass claimed he didn't want to race, he's all bright eyes and winner smiles now, revving his engine *obnoxiously*. I take the chance to snap a few shots of him like this—he *had* offered himself up as a subject after all—hair pushed back to reveal his manic eyes and smooth brow.

He's bombarded with admiration the second he exits the car, palms meeting in high-fives, fists bumping fists, a couple girls straining up to plant kisses on his cheeks, people hungry to gain a scrap of favor from the victor, as if such clout might be catching.

I mutter a deep, "Ugh," under my breath and look away. That's how I get a better view of Sebastian's brother as he strolls across the parking lot, all long legs and arms, squared off at the top with broad shoulders. He's strikingly handsome, and now that I know they're related, I can see it in their similar features; sharp cheekbones, defined jaw, blue, aristocratic eyes. Heston is more refined than Sebastian—less rough around the edges. I can't see him in a street fight, or racing a car, or even punching a girl, but there's a dark glint in his eye, a twist to his lips, that feels cruel even at a distance. His arm hangs over the small shoulder of a girl. I'm assuming it's Sydney, the one they were talking about earlier. I've seen her around school before, talking shit—talking about Sebastian—just plain *talking*. She doesn't make it a secret that she's into him.

Feeling restless, I gather up the courage to cut through the crowd toward the guy in question. He's leaning into the driver's side window, grabbing something from the console. As soon as he pulls back, I start, "Aren't winners supposed to do some kind of lap around—" He turns and walks away, like I'm not even there. "...the track," I finish lamely.

I stand there, blinking in his wake, heat licking up the back of my neck. Heston and Sebastian approach the betting table at the same time. When the two brothers meet, a flicker of something rolls between them. There's a high five, but while Heston's is firm and sharp, Sebastian's is loose and unenthusiastic. Whatever that look means, it's lost when Heston grabs a stack of cash from the bookie and holds it over his head as though he's the one coming out of this victorious. The stack is easily three inches thick and would probably be enough to pay for the Mustang repairs and a month of Preston Prep combined.

I turn and walk away. There's something uncomfortable and heavy settling into the pit of my stomach and it's frustratingly *not* simple. I'm remembering how I don't actually belong here. I'm thinking of the way Sebastian's eyes lit up when everyone was fawning over him before, but just passed right over me, like I was invisible. I'm feeling pissed the fuck off—mostly at myself—for actually feeling this way about it.

Because fucking *ouch*.

That really did sting.

I keep walking, thinking that maybe I'll find Georgia or Emory for a ride back to campus. I don't know Ben or Carlton that well, but maybe well enough that I'd chance riding back with them. I'm still mulling this over when I hear the familiar rumble of the Shelby approaching from behind. It rolls up next to me, Sebastian leaning across the passenger seat toward the open window, one hand on the steering wheel.

"You looking for a ride?" he calls, eyes tired.

I look forward, not stopping. "I don't know. Am I?" Inside, I cringe at the way it comes out, all bristled and aggressive. Too transparent. I'm letting this guy have way too much power over me.

I can see his face harden in my periphery. "You're pissed."

"Oh?" I ask. "What gave it away?"

He mutters a low, "Goddamn it," under his breath. "Come on, don't make me do this."

I stop, biting out a sharp, "Do *what*?"

The car pauses next to me. "The thing where I chase you around and beg and scrape. I'm not actually all that good at it, in case you haven't noticed."

I level him with a look. "Trust me. I have."

He taps the steering wheel. "So?"

I take a deep breath, open the door, and get in. That stack of cash he won is sitting on the center console like a spent bag of fries from McDonald's. Stiffly, I ask, "So? How much did you win?"

His eyes dart down to the stack of cash. "That? I don't know. Just chuck it out the fucking window."

My face screws up. "What?"

He waves dismissively. "I don't want it, it's dirty money. Throw it out."

A bitter laugh bubbles in my chest, spilling into the enclosed car. "God, you're such an entitled prick. Why did you even bother racing if you didn't want the money? Maybe one of the other guys could have actually used it instead of treating it like used tissues."

He tilts his head and narrows his eyes at me. "You know, an hour ago, you were kissing me senseless and wishing me luck. Now you're pissed because I won? I told you I didn't really have a choice."

He thinks I'm pissed about the race. I don't necessarily correct him. "I don't know," I tell him, and I'm not lying. "Watching you out there, I admit it. You have a gift. And your brother? From what Georgia and the others say, he's a piece of work—"

He snorts. "That's the polite way of saying it. He's a fucking sociopath."

"But this whole world—the money and the gambling and the illegal shit—I didn't sign up for that. I don't belong there. I'm going to Preston to get away from a shady life, not to make a new one. If I wanted to spend Friday nights with a bunch of delinquents, I could have stayed in the Briar Cliffs."

He pulls the car to a lurching stop at a light, fingers tightening around the wheel. "I don't know what you were expecting. The people here aren't magically functional just because we have more money. We're a fucking mess, Sugar. We're barely eighteen and you wouldn't believe the kinds of skeletons we already have in our closets. All this shit—the money, the nice cars, the fancy-ass school—it doesn't erase our problems. It just makes the problems more expensive and easier to hide." He looks at me, something hard and intense in his eyes. "People can't *touch you*. I don't know what that was like for you back in the Cliffs, but here? Fuck, Sugar, we've barely asked any questions. Why do you think that is?" Before I can answer, he tells me, "Because not facing our problems is something we're really fucking good at. You really think you don't belong here? You think being from the Cliffs make you better or worse than us? You're wrong."

He speeds away from the light and I don't answer. It's true that I'd had expectations of Preston and the sort of people who went there. But knowing people like Georgia, like Vandy, like *Sebastian*, has dispelled a lot of them. Maybe he's right. Maybe everyone is fucked up in their own way and the only things that really divide us are the arbitrary notions that our problems are somehow more insurmountable.

"So is that what I am?" I ask, knowing that this heavy, churning feeling in my stomach has nothing to do with the race. "One of those problems you don't want to face? At least, not in public."

He glances at me, quick and confused. "What are you talking about? I faced up to what happened that night, it's not like—" He goes suddenly silent, eyes flashing in realization. "Oh. You think I blew you off back there."

"I don't need to think," I argue, feeling tired. "You did blow me off."

He scoffs. "It's not like that. I just had to deal with my brother."

I give him a blank look, trying to figure out how the two are even connected. "Whatever."

He pauses, turning to give me a slower, calculating look. "Huh. I didn't realize that about you."

"Didn't realize what?"

He shrugs, shifting gears to pass a car. "That you could be insecure."

My jaw drops before clenching angrily. "Fuck you."

"Not in a bad way," he says. "You're always so hard and tough, you just don't put out that vibe. Plus, most of the time I sort of figure you don't even like me that much. But if I didn't know better, I'd say I hurt your feelings."

"Please," I mutter, scowling out the window at the passing trees. "Don't flatter yourself, Wilcox."

He stops at another light, grimacing. "Wow, it's so bad that I'm 'Wilcox' again?" When I don't answer, he curves tiredly over the wheel, car idling. His voice comes out quiet and ragged. "I don't like my brother knowing my business. The way I wanted to kiss you back there would have aired it all out for him. It wasn't personal."

Exasperated, I meet his gaze, but all I find are weary eyes and a set jaw. "You're a dick, Sebastian."

His eyebrow raises. "Sebastian now. Getting warmer, eh?"

I roll my eyes. "Hardly."

"Look," he says, dragging a rough hand down his face. "I've been chasing your tail for weeks, and most of that was done under the risk of serious personal harm. I'm not a subtle guy, Sugar. If I want something, I don't beat around the bush about it. I've told you that I'm into you—that I want you. Don't let one little bullshit moment put doubts in your head about it."

I argue, "Actions speak louder than words."

He bursts, "Yeah, you're right," and then he kisses me. It's a hard kiss, full of defiance and promise. He's wrong about me being hard and tough—so fucking wrong—because the way he licks into my mouth just then makes me feel anything but.

The way I feel instantly mollified and set at ease is even scarier. "The light's green," I mutter.

He sighs against my lips. "If only." He drives for a while and I watch the passing scenery, feeling oddly—embarrassingly— relieved. I have no idea when I went from wanting this guy to leave me alone to feeling relief when he assures me he won't. After a bit, he breaks the silence with, "You realize you're going to have to come to all my races now, right?"

I pull a face. "What? Why?"

He shoots me a toothy grin. "I won, baby, and that makes you my good luck charm." He picks up the cash and hands it to me. "In fact, you should be the one to take it. You earned it."

I toss it back. "No way. I'm not taking your dirty money."

"Then pick a charity." He shrugs, leaving the stack of money discarded in the console.

"Plenty of good causes out there. Maybe there's a girl who needs her car fixed up, or I don't know, the cat shelter even."

I look at his earnest expression and then down at the money. "You'd really donate it to charity—and by charity I don't mean me."

"I know it sounds privileged as hell, Sugar, but I couldn't care less what happens to that money. I like racing, but I don't like being forced to do things because my brother is a fucking dickhead."

I purse my lips at the money, secretly mulling it over. "For someone who doesn't like being forced to race, you sure looked down with winning one."

"Winning is the best high I know. Even my brother can't ruin that." He smirks. "You know the best thing to do after a win like that?" He waits, obviously wanting me to guess.

I wryly take a shot. "Give your winnings to disadvantaged kittens?"

But he shakes his head. "Get massively fucking laid."

I roll my eyes. "Is that all you think about?"

"Mostly," he admits. "I am having a bit of a dry spell, I admit."

"Well, it looked like there were plenty of willing options congratulating you back there. Maybe you should get a number."

His eyebrows shoot up his forehead. "Insecure *and* jealous. I'm learning a lot about you tonight, Sugar Voss."

"I'm not jealous," I blandly insist.

He doesn't look convinced. "Truth be told, I'm all about quality over quantity. But sure, I'd settle for a blow job." I give his hopeful smirk a blank stare and he sighs. "Fine, hand job it is."

"Have fun with that."

"Ouch." He clutches his chest. "Is my game so rusty that I can't even land a sad backseat handy? And after buying you a drink and everything."

We arrive in the campus lot then, Sebastian turning his headlights off before pulling in. The car is quiet and dark when he cuts the ignition, and I'm not sure how Sebastian hounding me to get on his dick has become a surefire tension breaker, but it's a comfortable sort of silence. His hand is loose on the gear shift and after a ridiculous amount of internal strife, I lay mine on top of his, reluctantly threading our fingers together. He shifts against his leather seat, eyes pointedly fixed on our hands, but for once in his life keeps his mouth shut.

"Look, I know this is moving slow as hell for you," I say, staring at our hands, idly noting that they look good together like that. Like they fit. "I know you probably want the kind of girl who can jump in the back of your car and just...do shit with you. But...I can't. Not right now. If that's a problem, or if you'd rather—"

My words cut sharply off when he lifts our entwined hands to his lips. The kiss he plants on my knuckles is soft and so sweet that it fucking *hurts*. "Most girls look at me and see a pretty face and ripped body, and hey. They're not wrong." His lips tip into a brief, sly grin, but it melts away almost instantly. "But you saw some real shit back there, Sugar, and it's ugly—I *know* it's ugly. There's a reason I don't date. That kind of thing would have scared most girls off." He leans over the seat. "But you're not like most girls, in more ways than one, and I like that about you. Enough to take it slow."

I swallow at the feel of my hand in his. "Are you sure?"

He answers, "I'm sure I won't stop bugging you about it. And I'm sure that at least twice a day, I'll ask you to touch my dick, but I promise to not get pissy when you inevitably tell me to fuck off and die."

A chuckle bursts from my throat. "Then I promise not to get insecure or jealous anymore. Not that I am. Or ever was. Or ever would be."

"Deal," he says, kissing me in a way that already has me reconsidering getting in the back seat. But I have a feeling that slowing down isn't going to hurt Bass. It may even help him. Because tonight showed me that although going fast is something he's good at, it's not necessarily good for him. Maybe it'll be the best thing for both of us.

AT THE END of the club meeting the next day, Mr. Lee holds me back. "Miss Voss, I wanted to talk to you about your photography," he says, gesturing to my board. Every student gets a board in the studio for their works. They get wiped clean every month, with only the best of the best remaining. Because of that, mine is a lot sparser than others, not having been here long enough to really curate a collection. Most of them are my current monthly stash, plus the photo of Abbadon. Nevertheless, Mr. Less says, "I'm impressed with your submissions so far."

I stutter out a surprised, "Thank you," but pride swells in my chest. Actually getting to Preston and having them realize that I wasn't worth the scholarship has been a nagging, dogged worry of mine. It's nice to get validation. I confess, "The facilities definitely make it easier to produce better work."

He shakes his head. "Although I agree that Preston has excellent equipment and resources, that's not what I'm impressed with." He points to a photo I'd turned in the week before. It's from the first car show. The central focus is a burst of fireworks close to the gathered crowd. The overpass looms in the background, pillars of graffitied concrete stretching to the sky. "The juxtaposition of the almost brutalist nature of the bridge set up against the energy of the crowd makes for a compelling topic. Not to mention the legal implications."

I pause, wondering if my photograph is going to get someone, including myself, in trouble. "I wasn't participating. It just seemed like an interesting place to take a photograph."

"I agree," he says with a small smile. "Part of creating art is taking risks, you know. Within reason." He produces a folder from his desk. "Every year we have an exhibit for the art department, showcasing students' work."

"Like the creative corner?"

"Oh, no, not at all," he declares, handing me the binder. "This is far more prestigious. A legitimate exhibition. Usually, we manage to browbeat a whole plethora of recruiters into attending, not to mention esteemed alumni. It's the kind of visibility that the art department only sees here once a year." He watches me flip through the materials, papers full of specifications and themes. "I'd like for you to participate this year."

I look up at him, taken aback. "Really?"

"Absolutely. I think you've got exactly the kind of fresh voice that we need to see represented in the showcase this year. That is, if you think you're up to the task."

I wonder, "What exactly would that entail?"

"It'll be a lot of work," he admits. "You'll have to fill a whole wall. And it'll be a time crunch, since you're still a new student here. But feel free to incorporate some of your older pieces."

I glance down at the dates, stomach dropping. "This is in just a few weeks."

He nods back. "It is, but one of the perks is that you can use the photo lab or any other equipment you need after school or on the weekends. It's a great opportunity, Sugar. Something tells me you can handle a challenge like this. What do you think?"

A challenge? Filling a whole damn wall when I have, at most, five showcase-worthy pieces? Sure. Piece of fucking cake.

But I can't lie to myself. When he said recruiters would be attending, my initial thought was that I'd do whatever it takes to be a part of this showcase. I'm not like the other kids around here. I don't have money or connections or pedigree. All I have is my work. This is a way to get eyes on it, without the help of that other stuff.

I know instantly that I'm all in.

17

SEBASTIAN

"Now, we just need someone to steal the key," Emory says, tapping his notebook.

Caroline raises her hand. "Uh, need I state the obvious?" Everyone looks toward an increasingly stormy-eyed Reyn.

"Yeah, why can't Reynolds break in?" Ben agrees. "It's what he does."

Vandy cuts in with a sharp, "No."

Emory explains, "Reyn's taking a break from stealing for a while, so we need someone else."

"For *a while*?" Afton asks.

"My probation ends in three months, okay?" Reynolds, who has a pathological compulsion for stealing things that just might rival my own for fighting, has his arms crossed, knee jerking up and down. He looks exactly like a junkie wishing for a fix. "I made an... agreement." He says this much like someone might admit to having genital herpes.

"If he goes three months without stealing," Vandy clarifies, "his dad's going to buy him a car." But from the way she looks at her boyfriend—and the way his knee stills—I'm betting she's sweet-ened the pot. Probably with sex. Probably with some *freaky* sex. Lucky bastard.

Fuck, I wish I were getting laid.

I played it so fucking cool last night with Sugar, telling her that I was fine with taking it slow, and I am. I totally am. Might be better if it seemed like I was making a little more headway than a brief bout of handholding, though. Secretly, I'd been dead serious about that handy.

I look down at my knuckles, picking at a nasty scab—a result from last night's fight. With my goddamn car. *Jesus.* "I'll steal it."

Reyn looks at me and snorts. "No way."

I flip him off. "I can steal."

"Beg and borrow, sure," Reyn says, "But steal? You're too flashy, Wilcox. Stealing requires subtlety and patience. You're not the guy who steals. You're the guy who causes a huge distraction so that *someone else* can steal."

Emory nods. "Yeah, you're good at being a distraction."

"Excuse the fuck out of you." I point to my own face. "I'm a sweet-talker. People *like* me."

Tyson laughs. "Your own girlfriend doesn't even like you."

I raise an eyebrow. "Since when do I have a girlfriend?"

"Since you keep chasing that Sugar chick around like she's got you by the balls."

Before I can wholeheartedly debate this, Georgia pipes in, "Or since the other night when she snuck out of the room to meet you? Because I woke up and she was gone, and when I tracked her on my phone, there she was. Smack dab in Cresswell."

Everyone lets out a slow, unnecessarily dramatic 'ooooo'.

"Seriously?" I give them each an unimpressed look. "What is this, middle school?"

Elana twirls a lock of hair around her finger. "Now that you mention it, she hasn't been quite as scary lately. I haven't even seen her threaten you all week. Must be love."

I flip her off, too.

Ben laughs. "Better lock that shit down, Bass. Have you taken her to the tower yet? Put your mark on her?"

"Fuck no," I scoff. "Sugar's not *that* kind of girl." I immediately regret my choice of emphasis as I watch every girl's eyebrows climb their foreheads.

"Oh, and just *what kind* of girl gets taken to the tower?" Vandy bites out, pointing to the other girls. "Because all of us have been in there, after all."

I make a time-out signal with my hands. "Come on, you all know I'm like the most sex-positive motherfucker on the planet. I just meant that she's not the kind of girl I can afford to rush shit with."

Aubrey takes a break from staring at her phone to look me in the eye. "I like her for you. She won't take your shit."

Afton adds, "And if she did, she'd probably take it at knife point." She doesn't know just how true that is.

"Thank you for your completely unsolicited approval. If we could get back to the topic at hand? I know how to sweet-talk."

Carlton looks at me thoughtfully. "Yeah, I bet Bass could swindle."

I hold up a hand. "*Sweet-talk.*"

We'd all arrived at school an hour early to hold the meeting, so most of us are still rubbing sleep from our eyes. We've been down here in the Devil dungeon working out how this prank's going to go down. It's a fine line to walk, doing something big enough to capture everyone's awe, but not so big that it gets us busted. Hijacking halftime during one of the biggest basketball games of the season seems like the best option.

And hey, speaking of flashy...

"Well, I can't be the shirtless Devil because I have tattoos, so this is my best offer for contribution."

"Fine," Emory agrees, shutting his notebook. "At least you can afford to get in trouble if you get busted. If nothing else, it'll be amusing."

I mutter, "Ye of little faith," and with that, we all begin filtering out of the tower, careful to stagger our exits.

"Stop picking at that thing," Elana chides, batting at my hand. Without realizing it, I've picked the scab clean off my knuckle, reopening the wound. "Ew! Gross, you're bleeding." I tease her with it, shoving my hand close to her face, making her squeal and bolt to the side.

Georgia sighs. "Boys are so disgusting."

Disgusting or not, we walk together toward the school. We're early enough that there's plenty of time to do something productive before the warning bell, like organizing a locker, or finishing my Lit essay, or grabbing a bite to eat.

Like hunting down Sugar and pulling her into an empty classroom.

Unfortunately, when I find her, that's not in the cards at all.

Georgia, Elana, and I cut through the crowd. Sugar's standing in the middle of the hallway with a rapidly growing audience as some jerkoff junior towers over her, face set into a scowl.

"What's going on?" Elana asks before I can.

Sugar's eyes flick over in a rapid glance. I don't imagine the way her aggressive, tight stance loosens upon seeing me. She still looks like she's about three seconds from kicking this guy in the dick. "This asshole thinks—"

"I know you took it," he snaps. "I left it on my desk and you sit there next period."

She snaps back, "I didn't take your fucking watch."

"Then let me look in your bag," he demands, stepping close enough that my whole body ignites in anger. "I know you're hiding something."

He's right. She's got her hand stuffed into her bag like she's shielding something, but I know from experience exactly what it is. Getting caught with that knife is going to land her in deep shit.

"If she says she didn't take it, then she didn't fucking take it," I say, voice full of barely-veiled warning. Used to be people were more intimidated by me than charmed. A couple months off fighting must have put a serious damper on my ability to make shit-stains like this back the hell off.

Big mistake.

The guy doesn't even bat an eyelash, sneering down his nose at her. "God this place used to have standards. Giving scholarships to Northridge kids was one thing, but now they're letting in Cliff trash? Enough of this."

I could have let that go—maybe, maybe—but then he reaches out and clamps a hand around her wrist to wrench it from her bag, and *oh, fuck no*.

The back of his head meets the lockers with a loud clang, but I can barely hear it over the storm in my head. "You don't fucking touch her," I roar, seeing red. I've got two tight handfuls of his blazer, fists digging hard into his chest, and it's not that he just called her trash, or even that his *fucking hand* was on her when even I can't do that.

It was the sudden look of pure, spine-steeling terror in her eyes that propelled me forward.

No one makes Sugar look like that. Not me, and certainly not this piece of shit.

"*No one* fucking touches her," I seethe, knowing the crowd behind me is watching, listening. "Anyone lays a single finger on her, and I'm going to light your ass the fuck up. Georgia!"

"I'm on it," she says, knowing exactly what I'm asking her to do; lead Sugar away. Last thing I need is for her to feel more sketchy about me.

The guy looks pissed, reaching up to roughly flick a bit of spittle from his cheek. But he also doesn't push back. "She took my—"

"I didn't take it!" Sugar spits, obviously not down with being led away. "I never saw a watch. There was nothing on my desk when I got in there! If you don't believe me, then take it up with Dewey. I'm done with you. Let's go, Sebastian."

But it's not that easy. The red-hot, raging feeling that's curled around my lungs isn't satisfied, wants to bury my fist into this guy's face. My hands are screaming, balled so tightly into his jacket that the wound on my knuckles is openly trickling blood. My jaw feels locked, nostrils flared as I decide; let it go or let loose? And fuck, just the thought of letting loose tickles at the back of my brain, and I feel just like Reyn had looked earlier. A junkie jonesing for a fix.

"Come on, Bass. He's not worth it." It's her touch that does it, the warm weight of her hand falling onto my arm, not pushing or pulling, just resting there. Steadying. Understanding.

I still give him one last shove before letting go, and the way my fists send him back into the lockers couldn't be called anything less than head-rattling. It'll have to suffice. "Watch your back, motherfucker."

It's still a little bit like peeling a scab from skin, but I do it. I walk away. It's not so bad, even if I'm following Sugar down the hall unseeingly, unthinkingly, breathing through the vestiges of rage, batting them down like a slowly dying fire.

I don't even notice where she leads me until we reach the little spot by the dumpsters, but when I do, it makes it even easier to shake off this restless, frantic thing. The cats will probably come. I didn't bring any food.

"Sit down," she says, jerking a nod toward the tree stump and then folding herself down on the ground beside it.

I lower myself to the ground instead, working my jaw around something to say. She doesn't seem mad or freaked out—not like she had that day in Dr. Ross's class, or last night when I beat the shit out of my car.

She just digs into her bag and pulls out a smaller pouch, unzipping it. "Let me see your hand."

I blink down at them—my hands—and flex them into fists. "What?"

Instead of answering, she reaches out, only hesitating for the span of a breath before taking my hand in hers. "It might sting."

It takes a moment for my brain to catch up, and it's not really because of the anger. Amazingly, that's mostly gone now. But she's holding my hand in hers, resting it carefully on her bare knee, palm-down, fingertips gently grazing my knuckles. It's hard to spare a brain cell for anything that isn't the feel of her skin against mine.

I do eventually realize that the pouch has tissues, wipes, and bandages. "What are you, like a girl scout or something?"

Although I try to pretend like I'm not, I watch Sugar closely. I'm not stupid. The way Sugar acts, all of her scars, the fact that she carries bandages on her alongside the knife—these all point to something a lot worse than getting decked by some rando at a shitty river party. Whatever happened to her wasn't some one-off. It wasn't temporary.

The corner of her mouth quirks. "Something like that."

The feel of the alcohol wipe passing over the wound *does* sting. I couldn't fucking care less, though. "You should do that more."

Her gaze jumps up to mine, then back down to my hand. "Get accosted in the hallway by douchebags? I'd rather not."

I shake my head. "Smile, I mean."

Her brows pull together in a scowl, but I know it's halfhearted. Her cheeks start to pinken. "Say something worth smiling about and maybe I will."

I smirk at her. "I'll take that as a challenge."

"You would." She cleans the blood from my hand and then purses her lips as she inspects the raw, angry-red wound. "You pick scabs, don't you? That's how shit gets infected."

I shrug. "Bad habit."

Her fingers are careful but firm as she handles my hand, applying some kind of greasy ointment before peeling the crinkly backing from a flesh-colored band aid.

The cats must hear the crinkle because Hades come trotting out of tree line, nose twitching, and Lucy isn't far behind.

Sugar notices as she's pressing the bandage to my skin. "I have some treats in my bag if you want to fish them out."

I watch her skeptically. If there's one thing my mother's taught me over the course of life, it's to never go into a woman's bag. But I guess this—like the way she's touching me—is something special. Something only I'm privy to.

I use my free hand to gingerly pluck the sides of the bag open, peering at the contents. The treats aren't hard to find. "So... you're okay, right?"

She gives me a confused look. "Uh, yeah? You're the one bleeding all over the place here."

Hades circles around us and I throw him a treat. "But that guy grabbed you."

Her face shutters a bit, but she just shrugs. "Yeah."

"It scared you."

"Not really," she says, finishing up with my knuckle. She doesn't push my hand from her leg, and I don't pull it away. "Not in the way you're thinking, at least."

I watch her carefully, wondering, "What do you mean?"

"It's hard to explain." She takes the bag of treats from me, tossing some toward Lucy. Her eyes are tight around the edges. "I don't think people are out to get me or anything. It's not about that. I'd feel the same if it'd been Georgia grabbing me, and I know she wouldn't hurt me. It's not because I'm afraid of her. I'm not... I'm not a coward."

I let my thumb sweep gently over her bare knee. "I know."

She rises to her feet suddenly, eyes shifting to the side. "We'll be late if we don't hurry. That Dr. Ross really is no joke about tardies."

I rise slower, bending to grab our bags from the ground. "I mean what I said. I won't let anyone touch you. Not unless you want it."

She ducks her head but nods, voice sounding rusty when she replies, "Yeah. Thanks."

"Can I?" I ask, stepping closer. "Can I touch you?"

I can see her throat shift with a swallow. "You can touch my hair," she says, and it comes out quiet, tinted with something like embarrassment. I do it, though. I reach out and card my fingers through her hair, sweeping it away from her face, tucking it behind her ear. When her eyes meet mine, they're heavy. "You can kiss me."

I thread my fingers into her hair while I do, and it's kind of ridiculous how it makes my nerves spark in excitement. It isn't a big deal, the way I lick into her mouth while holding the back of her head. It's not the same kind of touch. It's not erotic or novel. I've kissed dozens of girls just like this, fingers tangled in their hair, guiding the kiss with the press of my palm against their scalp. But with her, it's new.

Everything with her is new.

∼

"You need to use a hammer and screwdriver to get those plugs off."
Merle walks behind me as I struggle to remove the coolant hoses
from the engine. "And don't forget to check the pan underneath,
the last thing we need around here is a spill."

"I'm not going to spill the coolant, Jesus," I mutter. I do go get
the tools he suggested off the rack and carry them back over, using
them to knock the plugs loose. Works like a charm. Merle is a pain
in my ass, but he knows his cars. A few minutes later, I have the old
radiator out and lying next to the new on the worktable.

"Now take the old parts and attach them to the new radiator,
then you'll reattach everything." He looks toward the front of the
garage at the sound of a car pulling up. "Hopefully that's Mrs.
Buchanan here to get her Lincoln. You know she needs it to get to
choir."

I should be working on fixing the dents and damage on
Jasmine, but I've kept my focus on the Mustang. Part of it is that
every glance at the Shelby is a reminder of all the shit I have to lose
if I can't keep my temper in check. That, and I'm just fucking dying
to get this car running for Sugar. She's an independent girl who
isn't used to relying on others so much. Also, I just want to do something nice for her. I want to see her smile. I want to know she's
happy about something.

Yeah, I've gone full sap.

"Things are coming along on your car," I hear Merle say. "But it
still may be a few weeks."

"A few weeks?"

My hands still at the sound of Sugar's voice.

"Give or take," Merle replies. "It's looking good, though. Do you
want to see?"

"Yeah, that would be great."

I put down the pieces of the radiator and move away from the
car. I still haven't told Sugar I'm working on the Mustang. After her
reaction to the steering wheel emblem and the money I won on the
race, there's no way she'd be down with me giving this to her. I'm
going to have to ease her into this with something smaller.

I move to hang the screwdriver and hammer back up on the

tool board and glance over as she walks around the Lincoln. She's still in her school uniform, the plaid skirt drawing my eyes down her legs. Her battered messenger bag hangs across her chest. Her eyes are coated in that smeared, sexy eyeliner, and it's only been eight hours since I kissed her but that's about seven and a half hours too long. I'd spent most of our first period sitting behind her, playing with her hair when Dr. Ross wasn't looking. At one point, I managed to elicit a visible, shoulder-trembling shiver, and I've spent all day thinking about it—about how much I want to cause another one of those shivers.

I clear my throat, getting her attention. "Hey. What are you doing here?"

She doesn't look surprised to see me, even though she says, "Oh, I thought I saw Jasmine parked around back." She shifts her feet for a moment, looking between me and the tool board. "I came to check on the car and see if I can get Merle to let me pay him something for all the hard work he's doing."

Behind her, Merle grins like the Cheshire Cat, loving the fact he's getting the praise for all my free labor.

"Don't even think of paying him yet," I reply, shooting him a look. "Never pay a mechanic in advance. Wait until you're satisfied with the job."

The bell on the office door chimes and Merle says, "That has to be Mrs. Buchanan. How about you show Sugar all the work *I've* put in on the Mustang."

I ignore him and gesture with my arm toward the car. "It would be my pleasure." We pass the table with the radiator and I point it out, then take her to the open hood. Her jaw drops when she sees the clean, non-rusty interior.

"How the hell..." she breathes, gaping down at the engine. "It's like completely new!"

"Well..." I touch a few things, feeling excited. "Not completely, but new to *this* car. A lot of these parts are salvaged and just cleaned up. It's amazing how this old stuff lasts. Way better than the disposable, plastic shit they use nowadays." I jerk my thumb over my shoulder. "Once that shiny radiator is back in, it'll look even better."

"I can't believe it." She runs her hands over the clean additions. "Merle has done such a good job, I don't know how I could ever repay him."

Jealousy wars with pride in my chest, but I manage to keep a cool exterior. "He's a pro, alright."

She leans against the front of the car and asks, "So, hey, those kids in my photography club, the Adams twins? Do you know much about their family?"

I grab a rag and wipe off my hands. "Micha and Micheala? Yeah, big family. I know they're all adopted. Their oldest daughter, Gwendolyn, graduated last year. They have another daughter and son, but I don't really know them much."

"The parents... they're the ones who gave me my scholarship so I could attend Preston." She reaches into her bag and pulls out an envelope, the top torn and wrinkled. "They invited me to this dinner so they could meet me." She looks weirdly anxious when I take it, eyes fixed to the paper.

I skim the details. Dinner at a nice restaurant in town. Seems pretty informal. "Are you going?"

She twists the strap of her bag in her hand. "I don't know that I have a choice."

"Well, for what it's worth," I say, tapping the paper against my palm, "they all seem like nice people. Not really your average Preston type of family, if that helps. Gwendolyn's dating my brother's former best friend, Hamilton."

"Former?"

"Oh, yeah. Definitely former. Hamilton and Heston were kind of the kings around here last year. Well... kings of the Devils. But then Hamilton fell for Gwendolyn, and my brother didn't like her, so he stirred up a bunch of shit." I shake my head at the memory of it all. "Anyway, when is this dinner?"

She chews on her lip. "Next week." I'm not sure what she's so nervous about, but it's plain as day in her eyes that she is.

I hand the invitation back to her, boldly offering, "Do you want me to go with you?"

She stills, eyebrows rising. "What? You mean like... as my date?"

"I might not look like much, but I clean up well." I spread my arms. "I'm absolutely escort material. Use me."

"You'd do that?"

"Sure."

"I don't know..." She pushes off the car and paces anxiously. "You really want to go to a stuffy dinner with me and a group of people neither of us really know? Especially if there's bad blood between their daughter's boyfriend and your brother?"

"First of all, I'm not Heston." I reach out and grab her dog tags when she paces by, stopping her in her tracks. I've noticed that, more and more, she's started wearing them outside of her shirt, almost like she's indulging my impulse to touch some part of her. I use it to gently tug her between my legs as I lean against the car. "Second of all, like I *keep saying*, people find me endearing. *Including* parents. I'm likable as hell. Everyone really needs to stop underestimating my talent for sweet-talk."

She rolls her eyes, but I see the small tug of a smile on her lips. Damn, I just want to kiss her. I don't, instead tucking her hair behind her ear. "We can figure that out later. Is Georgia waiting for you?"

"She dropped me off," Sugar says, holding my stare. "I was actually hoping you'd give me a ride back to school when you're done here."

"I can do that," I answer, still thinking of that shiver from class, "but how about we go for a drive first?"

Her eyes dart to my mouth then back up. Yeah, she wants to kiss me, too. "A drive, huh?"

"Yeah, I know this place that might be good for taking pictures. A nice view. Thought I'd show it to you."

She purses her lips like she's thinking about it, but I already know she's down long before she responds, "Okay."

"Let me go clean up and we'll go."

I do my best to scrub off the grease and oil, then change clothes in the back room. When I walk out, Sugar's leaning against the Shelby, her dark hair showing tints of red in afternoon sunlight. Fuck, the sight of her against my car, staring into the distance as the wind blows her hair around, is a better view than anything else in this town.

I open the door for her, taking the opportunity to catch a whiff of her hair, and then slide into the driver's seat. I crank the engine and look over at her, grinning to myself.

"What?" she asks, shifting in her seat.

I shrug. "I just like seeing you over there."

I cut off the main road and head over the bridge that leads across the lake. There's a quiet spot that overlooks the dam and I slow the car, parking under a large oak tree.

We get out and walk around to the front. I watch her take it in, feeling electrified when her mouth curls into a surprised grin. There's a wide view of the lake out here. In the golden glow of the sunset, it looks like a nice summer day, but it's January and the trees are bare. There's a chill in the air and I see her shiver, but it's not exactly the kind I'd been hoping for.

I take off my jacket and offer it to her. "What do you think?"

"It's fucking killer," she says, blinking down at my jacket. After a moment of hesitation, she reluctantly accepts it, draping it around her shoulders. "I wish I had my camera."

"We can come out again sometime," I assure.

"None of the other people in the club have this view of the campus. Is that the bell tower?"

"Yep." The top of the tower peeks out of the trees. "The Devil's Tower. Or the Stairway to Hell. It has a few names."

"Georgia said not to go up there with anyone unless I wanted to. Something about a secret society. Any idea what that's about?"

I send her a smirk. "I could tell you, but you know how secret societies work. I'd have to sacrifice you after, probably in some dumb and unnecessarily sexual ritual with really bad Latin, swearing fealty to Satan, yadda yadda."

Sugar would make a kick-ass Devil. She already fits in with all the playthings. She's got balls of steel and is sharp as a tack. She has secrets. She has courage. But there's no way that's going to happen with only a semester left. The idea of taking her up in that tower and branding her with the mark is definitely appealing.

She leans back against the hood of the Shelby, something I would have thrown a goddamn fit about two days ago. Now, Jasmine is so battered and bruised that it seems stupid to care. "I watch Dateline, you know. That's not really the kind of joke you want to make when you've got me alone in a deserted place."

"It's not as sinister as they like to make it seem." Resting against the car beside her, I explain, "The way it works is that the Devils take girls up the stairway and mark them in the tower."

"Mark them?" she asks, head tilting curiously. "How?"

"Well, if they're really dating or serious it'd be something visible, like a hickey." I push back her hair and press a slow kiss to the skin under her ear. I don't mark her, but I'd be lying if I said I didn't want to. "Or it may go further with a hook-up. Blow jobs, hand-jobs, even full-on fucking."

Her face screws up. "While people are right outside?"

I laugh. "The thrill of possibly getting caught is part of the fun. Or so I'm told," I add quickly. "The Devils were officially disbanded last year—mostly because of my brother—but traditions die hard at Preston. Someone may be up there getting marked right now."

She turns to hold my gaze. "Have you ever been up there?"

That is not a conversation I want to have right now—if ever—but getting Sugar's trust is important and I don't want to lie. "On a dare. Last year."

I wait for her to ask who I was with, but she doesn't. She just nods, seeming unsurprised. "We have a place like that back home, too. Well, kind of."

"Yeah?"

"It's called Cliff Cave. Really original, right?" Rolling her eyes, she explains, "It's *the* place to hook up. It's kind of a rite of passage to lose your virginity up there, but god knows why. It's cold and dark and wet, and smells like a mossy armpit. I could have come up with a million better places to lose my virginity."

I look at her, head jerking back in surprise. Surely, she can't be saying... "What, you've been up there?"

But she nods, looking nonplussed. "Toby Catchall. Halloween, junior year." Her nose wrinkles. "He kept calling it 'Clit Cave', which is hilarious considering he couldn't find one with a map and a compass. He was nice, though."

"He was nice," I echo tonelessly, eyes fixed to hers. "Are you fucking kidding me?"

She frowns. "What?"

"You let some guy fuck you?" I push off the car and walk three paces, only to double back. "Some guy named *Toby*? I mean, what the fuck?"

She glares daggers at me, jaw clenched. "First of all, I didn't *let* some guy fuck me. You say that like I just laid back and *let* someone go to town. Pussies aren't shiny toys that girls just lend out. And secondly, one of your past hook-ups literally lives with me, and you're going to be salty that *I'm* not a virgin? You have no fucking right!"

"Georgia and I did not sleep together," I clarify. "And I don't care that you're not a virgin. You said no one could touch you, I just figured—"

"Oh, you *figured*," she snorts. "Well excuse the fuck out of me for managing to grasp a shred of something resembling a normal life before I became a total freak."

I step between her legs and gently wonder, "So what was so special about Toby?" She doesn't lean away from me, but she doesn't lean into me either, even when I reach down to clutch her dog tags. "Look, it's not that I'm salty or mad. I get people having a past, it's not about that. I just really fucking need to know why you tried for him, but not for me."

Her face puckers up angrily. "Fuck you, Sebastian. I *am* trying. No one here has touched me as much as you."

"Every time I ask, you shut me down," I point out, fighting the urge to just *take*. "And that was fine—I was okay with waiting. Only now I know there's a fucking Toby, and you apparently told him yes, so I'm just wondering." I don't know what she sees in my eyes —frustration, need, more patience than I probably possess—but it deflates that tight, bristling anger in her posture.

"It wasn't always like this, okay?" She looks away, eyes troubled. "It's always been bad, but lately, it's just... worse. There was a time I could handle being touched. I didn't like it, but I could push through it. And then..." But she trails off, leaving it hanging.

I already know it's useless to ask, but I try anyway. "What happened?"

To my surprise, she meets my gaze, and there's steel there. There's bitterness, too. "I met some *asshole*."

Fuck, I don't want to voice it. I don't want to even think about it. Part of me is scared of my own goddamn head, like what if knowing sends me off the edge of something that's too hard to pull back from? I don't back down from facing it, though. That's not how I'm wired. "Did he do... *things* to you."

She looks so taken aback that her face twists in a way that might be comical if I weren't basically asking if she's been *raped*. Then, she barks a quick, incredulous laugh. "Jesus, *no*. He just punched me in the fucking face."

Now it's my turn to be taken aback. "Wait—what?"

"I don't know why," she says, eyes dropping to my hands. "Just after that night, it's been un-fucking-bearable. It's not like you mauled me. And it hurt—of course it hurt—but it wasn't so bad. It just made it all worse."

I let go of the chain, stepping back. "This is my fault?"

"No," she says. "Not really? It's like I said, it was already bad. You just—"

"Made it worse," I finish dully, turning to stare out over the lake. Like it wasn't already bad enough that I hit her, now I bear the blame for this, too. Pretty fitting, I guess. I've always been good at fucking things up—making things worse—before even realizing that I want them.

Her voice is gentle when she says, "I know you didn't mean to."

"That doesn't exactly help you, does it?" I give her a tight smile, but inside my head, there's all this shit brewing. Because I couldn't leave it alone before, but now that I know that I'm at least partly to blame? *Fuck.* "Let me try."

"I can't."

"I'll be so fucking careful, Sugar. If it's bad, I'll back off. I'll—" When she shakes her head, I plead, "At least *think* about it?"

"Think about it?" She lurches up from the car, eyes wild. "You would not fucking believe how much I think about it! It's all I've thought about for weeks! I've tried before, Sebastian. It never ends well."

Determined, I argue, "You've never tried with me. Maybe I'm different. Maybe that's why I can kiss you and touch your hair. If I made it worse, then it's fluid. Maybe I can make it better, too."

Softly, she says, "You can't fix me."

"Not if you don't let me *try*."

"Jesus Christ," she mutters, burying her face in her palms. "You're like a fucking dog with a bone." Her hands fall, slapping loudly against her thighs, and she's got this look on her face. Like she just tasted something bad but she's about to go in for another bite. "You know what? Fine."

18

"FINE."

His jaw, which has been tight with frustration, eases as he asks, "What? Really?"

"Yes, really," I agree, holding my arms out wide, smile tight. "Let's do this. Where do you want it? Up my shirt?"

He looks taken aback. "I was just thinking like... little touches, on the reg. It doesn't have to be one big *thing*."

Jesus, the thought is horrifying. Not that Sebastian wants to touch me regularly, but that I'd have to feel the repercussions of it so often. "You want a shot to prove yourself, then let's go for it."

He shuffles around for a second, and if it weren't because he's about to put his hands on me, it'd almost be cute—Sebastian looking all bashful and shifty, like a kid about to shoplift for the first time. "Uh. Okay."

I hadn't been joking about him going up my shirt. I figure that's what this is all about, anyway. A guy like Sebastian is used to being with girls he can fool around with. Touch, to him, is probably just about sex. Makes no difference to me. A touch is a touch. The result is always the same.

He finally steps up to me, and it's cold out here—colder by the second as the sun sets—but he doesn't even have a single goosebump. His eyes stay fixed to mine as he lifts a hand, reluctantly nudging a curled finger beneath my chin. That's not so bad, just the soft pressure of a knuckle. I swallow in response, but it doesn't make my chest feel like it's imploding in fear. Bolstered by this, he ducks his head to press our mouths together, thumb sweeping out to graze the edge of my jaw. I push back against a flinch, surging into the kiss instead. Distantly, I'm going to miss this being enough for him. Just the warm press of our mouths, the way our tongues slide wetly, how we breathe one another, taste one another.

It was nice while it lasted.

His other hand dips into his jacket, still hanging absurdly from my small frame, and gently—so carefully that I'm already regretting what's going to happen—slides around my waist.

He never stops kissing me, which is good, because if he weren't, I wouldn't be able to pretend. I can almost hide the way my body stiffens, have gotten used to clamping down on the tremors, biting back the gasp. He falters, but doesn't stop, pressing my body to his as he palms my lower back in an embrace.

I can't remember the last time someone tried to hold me like this, but my body's reaction is an old, familiar thing. I barely get to enjoy the warmth of his chest, the way his arms feel, swallowing me up, shoulders curved into me like a shield, before it happens.

I try so hard to hide it, to kiss back and force this to be tolerable. My lungs are on fire, head screaming. It's all I can do to take myself out of the moment, to crawl back to the safe, isolated place in my mind that watches but isn't a part of it. I don't touch him back, because I know he'd feel the way my hands shake, aching to both push him away and drag him closer.

He doesn't notice.

If anything, the kiss and the way I'm taking it, just works him up more. The hand on my jaw goes from gently caressing the skin there to cupping the side of my neck, fingertips pressing firmly into the hard tendon and fluttering skin. He makes this rough, excited groan, hands pushing me closer, capturing me, trapping me, clutching me.

But it's impossible to remain in that place—the safe, back-of-my-mind place—when I want this so badly. I want to feel the way he touches me. Even if it's bad, I still want to feel the weight of his arm around me, the warmth of his skin. I slam back into the moment in a rush of panic, a hard, terrified lump wedged into the back of my throat.

He doesn't fight when, with a sharp turn of my head, I lurch away, stumbling from his hold.

"Stop," I gasp, unnecessarily. He's already frozen there, palms in the air, but I still walk away from him, just in case.

Just in case that feral, eager thing in his eyes is too much to fight.

I crouch on the ground there, knees tucked up beneath my chin, and try to breathe. They're awful, shuddery things. My heart is going off like a goddamn jackhammer, and it's stupid—oh my god, it's so fucking stupid—but I have this crystal-clear image in my head of Doug's hands, just like that. Rough, big, stained with grease, grabbing my neck, choking me. The look in his eyes when he did it, so fucking full of hatred, like he wanted to kill me, but something flimsy and indistinct was holding him back.

It's not fair, but it's like my blood cells are turning themselves inside-out to get away from the ghost fingertips—Doug's, Sebastian's, my brain doesn't care.

I barely register Sebastian coming to crouch beside me. He doesn't touch me or watch me. Through my periphery, I can tell that he's just lingering there, waiting, silent as I try to wrestle this fear back into the dark pit of myself.

When I can speak again, I say, "This is a waste of fucking time. It's just going to make us both more frustrated."

"Do you know what happened when I tried to change the battery on the Shelby?" he asks. I stare down at my hands, trying to hold back a hot tear, not interested in one of his car discussions. "It was supposed to be an easy fix, something I could do quickly, but the old one was corroded and completely welded to the inside. My instinct was to rip it out, but Merle told me that if I did that, I'd fuck up the connectors, make a bigger mess, and possibly burn myself on the acid. So, I had to slow down and use the right safety gear, gloves, goggles and all that shit, then use the correct solutions to clean off the corrosion. Something that should have been easy, a fast repair, took time and deliberation to do it right."

I chuckle darkly. "Are you saying I'm corroded and broken inside?"

"I'm saying that I have way more patience than you give me credit for." He shifts a little, ducking his head to catch my gaze. His face falls at the sight of my tears. "We can do this, Sugar. You and me? We're not like other people. We don't give up and we don't break. All you need to give me are the right tools and the opportunity. Can you tell me what happens when people touch you?"

I shake my head, but Sebastian is right. People like us don't get to run from our problems. It's not the way we're made. I think about it, closing my eyes and searching. "It freaks me out, like something bad is going to happen, or—it's just the idea that you could—not that you would—but when... with your hands, and it feels like my body isn't... mine? Just for a while, like you could do something, or take something, and it's not really *you*, it's just this idea of it all, when it's... it's scaring me, and I can't talk myself out of—and you might... I don't know, go too far or be too much, and it just makes me sick." My face feels hot, cheeks flaming with embarrassment. "That made zero fucking sense. I'm sorry." The last part comes out too soft, spoken more to the wind blowing in from over the lake than the man I'm apologizing to.

But Sebastian just looks curious. "That's... I think I get it."

I give him a skeptical look. "How could you?"

"Okay, I obviously don't *get it*, but I think I get what it's about. You like to be in control, right? That's fine, that's so fucking..." I watch the wheels turn in his head, like this is a very exciting break-through. "Will you let me try again? I have an idea."

My shrug is passionless. "Whatever."

"Perfect." He plants a hand on each of his knees, levering

himself up. "Come on, I have a blanket in the back seat." Not knowing what the hell a blanket has to do with anything, I follow him mindlessly to the car. He opens the door for me, and I climb inside. A moment later he's inside, slamming the door behind him, shutting out the cold. On the floor is a canvas bag. He unzips it and pulls out a soft thermal blanket.

Raising an eyebrow, I can't help but ask, "Do you use this often?"

"My mom made me put it in the car when I bought it. She got stranded in a snowstorm in high school and almost froze to death." He takes the bag and folds it over, creating a pillow, and props himself back against the door. "Of course, it doesn't snow much down here anymore, but she worries a lot, and it's just easier to give in if it'll give her peace of mind."

That admission is why, under all that pretty, entitled, tough-guy exterior, Sebastian is hard to read. One minute he's a pushy, demanding brat, and the next he's doing something sweet like feeding stray kittens or humoring his mom.

Once he's situated, he says, "Come lean against me."

I drag my eyes down his body, dubious. "Like, my back against your chest?"

He reasons, "It'll help warm you up, and there's like, two solid layers of clothes between us. Three with the jacket."

I take a deep breath, and scoot my butt back, nestling myself between his legs. He then reaches over us, covering both of our bodies with the blanket. To be honest, I'm not even sure I need a blanket at this point, my skin is so overheated from the anxiety and embarrassment of it all. I still haven't fully leaned back, my back and arms stiff and rigid, but I also feel the radiating warmth of him behind me. Sebastian's skin is always so warm, like a human heater. And there's also his scent; the combination of clean, soapy boy, and the oil and grease from the garage. My body, like always, is at war. I'm caught in an internal battle of want versus fear, when his deep voice fills the car.

"All I'm going to ask you to do is trust me."

I do as he asks, feeling a little better after talking it out. I believe that Sebastian wants to treat me right. I'm just not sure he can. I look down and see that his hand is passively by his side. He hasn't made a move yet, which is reassuring. Running my hands down my thighs, I take a deep, steadying breath, and fully lean back.

"You okay?" he asks. I nod, taking another breath and settling against the lean length of his body. We sit there for a moment and I feel his breath on my neck and hear my heart pounding in my ears.

It feels nice to be against his body again and I exhale shakily. "So, what's your big idea?"

"You take the lead." He holds up his hands, fingers wiggling. "Hold my hands and just put these babies wherever you want. I've seen you touch yourself, Sugar. You know what feels good and what doesn't."

All I've really wanted for weeks now is to feel Sebastian's hands on me, so it's not like I don't want to try. Resigned to this all going horribly once again, I reach up and place my palms on the back of his large hands, linking my fingers through his, bringing them closer for inspection. They're warmer than my own, rougher, and even though he washed them, I can still see the faint lines of grease under his nails. His knuckles are still busted up from that night of the race, and he's got a thin scar beneath one of his nails, jagged and pale. His fingertips are wide and blunt, raspy near the thumb, like there's an old callus.

For once in his life, Sebastian is completely passive as I observe his hands. The only movement I feel is the rise and fall of his chest behind me. Slowly, I move his hands down to the top of my thighs, over the blanket still separating us, and rest them there.

My breath stalls in anticipation of the dread that always hits, but this isn't so bad. It's not even against my skin, and Sebastian is still—so still that it feels like he's stopped breathing, too. Reluctantly, I grip his hands and run them down to my kneecaps.

Nothing.

I do this a few times, getting used to the weight and feel, warmth spreading through my body. I use his hands to push at the blanket, exposing my skirt and my legs down to my knees, because I have to know. There, I pause, taking a few deep breaths.

The feeling of his rough palms against the skin of my thighs is like a trembling fire. I brace myself against the coming tide of panic, but it never comes. Instead, it's just skin and touch and the heat of him, so alive against me that it makes my shoulders sink into the cradle of his own. I repeat the motion, half intoxicated by the sensations and half terrified—not of the touch, but of losing it again.

"You okay?" he asks, his mouth next to my ear. A shiver rolls up my spine at the raggedness there.

"Yeah," I breathe.

"We can stop here if you want to."

"No, no, I'm good," I insist, moving his hands back up my thighs, my skirt catching from the drag. He tenses, but for once, I don't. This—me moving him how I want—is *working* for me. There's no clutch of panic, no fear, just the glide of his palms over my skin.

I fall into a pattern of breathing, my rhythm matching Sebastian's, and continue to stroke his hands up and down my legs. Fuck, it feels amazing, but also strangely fragile, like maybe the smallest error could shatter it all. Thankfully, there are none. Even when I spread my legs and sweep his hands inward, all of his calloused roughness against the soft skin there, I mostly just feel ridiculously, incredibly, *painfully* turned-on.

He shifts beneath me, the hard press of his cock obvious and obscene against my ass, and I freeze.

"Sorry," he says, a hoarse chuckle bouncing his chest, "but there's no turning off how my body reacts to you."

"It's okay," I reply, secretly enjoying that there's something else I have control over in this situation. Sebastian wants me and that's a double-edged sword, one that grows both blunter and sharper as the minutes pass. "My body reacts to you, too." And Jesus Christ, is it fucking ever. My hips keep twitching with the instinct to writhe against him, desperate for some friction.

He tenses again, his breath catching in his throat, and I use the surge of power to continue on more boldly. In for a penny, I figure.

I peel off the jacket, revealing the fitted red uniform shirt, and sink back into him, resting my head on his shoulder. I leave one of his hands on my upper thigh while moving the other to the crux of my neck, carefully trailing his fingers over the sensitive skin. Feeling victorious at the lack of panic, I tilt my chin up, pressing a kiss to the underside of his jaw. Warmth rushes down my body, sensations coming from all sides, something that would normally overwhelm me, but instead, I just want to roll around in it.

"You can unbutton my shirt," I tell him, kissing the column of his neck.

The muscle at the back of his jaw is taut beneath my lips. "You sure?"

I nod. "Yeah, I think—*yeah*."

His restraint is visible in his fingertips as he gingerly tugs my shirt from my skirt and slowly slides each of the tiny red buttons, one by one, though the holes. I have no doubt if he were being left to his own urges, he'd just tear it off, but true to his promise he takes his time, pausing after each button, giving me the chance to back out.

I don't.

When he peels the sides away, my open shirt reveals the satin and lace of my black bra and the taut, pebbled nipples beneath. Sebastian's hands hover in the air, arms tensing, and I slide mine over his again. Like we agree, I direct him, moving his hands to my breasts. His chest has stopped moving, his breath caught somewhere deep inside, hands frozen, like he's afraid to move.

I squeeze his hands and he breathes out a low, "*Fuck yeah. Is this…?*" When I nod, he lets out a stream of whispered, knee-buckling things, right into my ear. "God, your tits are fucking amazing, Sugar. Been thinking about them—about the night I had my mouth on them. You liked that, didn't you? I know you did. I could see how wet you were."

I gasp at the feel of his hands on my tits, back arching into his warm palms. He's been so diligent about letting my hands move his own that I feel the rebellious sweep of his thumb against my nipple too late to feel anything but just… really fucking good about it.

I've experienced a lot of sharp, painful touches in my life. But touches like these? Spine-melting, leg-trembling touches that are all about sex and pleasure? Never. Hardly even with Toby, who was nice but impatient. Not even with myself.

No, these touches are *new*.

My brain almost doesn't know what to think of Sebastian having dominion over my tits. Good or bad? Fuck if I know. But there's no pain association, no instinct to flinch back, even when I hesitantly slide my own hands away.

I reach over my head, sliding my fingers behind his ear and into his hair. He pauses, but only for a moment, sensing the significance of the gesture. He starts soft and slow, testing, feeling the weight of me in his palms, and all I can do is let my head loll back on his shoulder, covering myself in the feel of it.

His lips press into my temple and slowly his hands start to massage my breasts. "Good?" he asks, as I fight the urge to buck my hips.

"Yes."

"Do you want more?"

I nod, pressing my nose into his shoulder.

"You have to use your words, Sugar, or I can't do it."

I look up into his brilliant blue eyes, searching for the smug asshole I've been dealing with for weeks. That person isn't there. This is just the guy who wants to make me feel good.

"I want more, Bass," I tell him, arching my back. "Please."

He reacts instantly, his big thumbs circle my nipples over the bra, then dip beneath to roll over the hard peaks. The rough pads of his thumbs grazing over my bare nipples sends a shockwave between my legs, warm and wet. I rotate my hips, desperate to relieve some of the pressure, which forces my ass to grind against his erection. He shudders behind me and lifts his hips into the motion.

Everything about this moment feels good—right. The pacing, the amount of pressure. When he'd told me that he could take his time and do it slow, I didn't really believe him. I wanted to, but I've watched Bass lose control more than once. What would make this different? But here we are, my body on fire as he continues to taunt and tease my nipples.

He stills when I reach for one of his hands, letting me drag it away, down my belly. "What...?" he dumbly asks when it lands on the inside of my thigh.

Instead of answering, I guide it right to my hot, aching center.

He drags in a deep, shuddering breath. "Oh, fuck *me*."

I grind his hand against me, bucking up against it, and the sound I make might be embarrassing, but I can hardly care. The friction and warmth are perfect, and if his fingers twitch, then I don't hold it against him.

I drop my knees open and rest there for a moment, and there's no way he can't feel me throbbing against his palm, aching and desperate. Slowly, I pull my hand away, leaving him there, letting him take control of it, of making me feel good.

These hands can do a lot more than hurt, Sugar.

His words float back to me from that night, and I can still hear them perfectly—have been secretly obsessed with them ever since they were spoken. My hips rock up against his still palm, giving me a flash of his big hand against my black panties.

"Come on," I say, straining up to press my mouth to his slack jaw. "I can take it."

His blue eyes are hooded, fixed to the space between my legs, watching his own hand against me. When he finally moves it, fingertips brushing over the bundle of nerves hot under my damp panties, I moan.

His eyes flick to mine. I'm not sure what he sees there, but suddenly he's all business, fingers massaging expertly against my clit, watching me squirm against him. "Christ, you're so fucking hot, Sugar. I can feel it—how hot and wet you are. You like it, right? You want me to keep going? I can stop if you—"

"If you stop," I grind out, "I will cut your fucking balls off, Bass."

"Well, yeah," he says, like this is entirely reasonable, and then takes my mouth in a hot, slippery kiss.

I already feel too hot for the blanket, for my clothes, but the way he presses against me sends my temperature higher and higher, belly coiling tight as my hips move with his hand. His other hand palms at my tit again, and it's amazing, the way he's able to have his arms around me like this, and all I feel is the white-hot spike of want that's driving me crazy.

Every time his fingers dip low, I can feel how soaked my panties are. I know he can feel it, too. I know that every time he drags his fingers back up, it's because he wants me to chase them, to take what I want.

I know when his fingers dip beneath the fabric of my panties that I'm excruciatingly impatient. "Yes," I say before he can ask. "Please, just—"

He watches me, eyebrows knitted tight as his fingers slip between my folds. "Goddamn."

I don't know what makes me shudder more—the ragged, strained note in his voice, or the feeling of his rough fingers sliding up and down my pussy. He moves them slow, testing, almost like he's getting to know it, acquainting himself with the feel of me. On one of those long passes, I buck my hips up, encouraging, and he hisses out a breath when the tip of his finger sinks inside me.

He goes still and I kick a foot out for leverage to push him deeper. "More," I gasp, hands fisting in the blanket. "What the fuck do you need, an engraved invitation? Just take it slow, okay?"

There's a rumble from deep in his chest, and like I ask, he goes slowly, sliding his finger inside. "Is this okay?" he asks, pausing. I nod. "Words, Sugar."

"Yes, it's okay." More than I thought, I like the way the pressure feels as he fills me up, pushing against the walls. He takes my approval to heart and slides in further, not stopping until it hits the knuckle. He shifts around a bit, curling his other hand around my ribs, holding me close as his finger retreats and dips back in. It doesn't make sense. The way he's holding me... if this were another person or another time, it'd be sending me running away. But right now, all my body seems to care about is the hot throb between my legs.

Sebastian fucks me with his finger, deep and slow, the heel of his palm pressing against my clit on each thrust. I'm such a fucking mess of 'almost there' and 'don't stop' that when he slides a second finger in, all I can think is how much I want more. But as much as I'm making sounds—god, the most embarrassing fucking little cries—I know he's a mess, too. I can feel him hard beneath me, moving his hips in tandem with mine.

"I told you I could make you feel good." He groans, breaths coming as choppy as my own when his lips rest against the shell of my ear, voice like gravel. "Bet you could take it. We can—just like this. I have a condom." I don't even have time to really think about it before he hastily adds, "Fuck, forget I said that. I just wanna make you come. Can you come for me, Sugar?"

With a sharp gasp, I slam my hand over his, pressing him hard against my clit, deep inside me. If I thought my cries were embarrassing, then the way I shake apart as I fall off the precipice is truly next level. He clutches me against his chest, the muscles in his forearm rippling as his hand works between my legs, yanking my orgasm from me like a willingly stolen thing.

"Perfect," he rasps into my ear. "So fucking perfect. You take it so good. That feel good, baby?"

I never would have thought listening to a guy talk during this would make it all better, but it does. Listening to Sebastian's want, his desire, is ridiculously hot and I whine as the vestiges of my orgasm ripple through me, surging and waning at the motion of his hand. I bat at it when it becomes too much, too sensitive, but alternately feel the loss acutely when he takes it away.

Sebastian didn't come, I know he didn't, but he deflates just like if he had, the two of us sprawled out in the back of his car, trying to catch our breath. The windows have all fogged over and the car smells thick with sex.

It takes approximately three minutes for that hand he has wrapped around my ribs to start feeling less like one of those good sex things, and more like something that's trapping me.

He doesn't fight when I spring upright, almost braining myself on the roof. "You okay?" he asks, reaching out to touch me, but thinking better of it at the last second. "Did I—was it too much?"

But I shake my head, turning to give him a tired smile. "No, it was... *God*. It was perfect."

I can practically see his ego inflating right in front of me. He wedges an arm behind his head, eyes dragging down my open shirt. "Told you so."

〜

"So, things with you and Bass are working out?"

I glance at Georgia as we walk from our third period class. She'd been asleep when I got home the night before, and I left early to go check on the kittens and give them a little food before class started. It's the first time we've seen one another since Sebastian finger-blasted me at the lake.

"Um, sort of." By 'sort of' I mean 'yes'. Like 'shout it from the top of the mountain' yes. What transpired between the two of us in the backseat of his car was nothing short of a miracle, but Georgia's question does make me wonder... "Why? Did he say something?"

Do I look different? Can she tell? What made her ask?

"Well, when I dropped you off at the garage yesterday, I didn't expect you to come home right away, but I didn't realize you'd be gone that long." She gives me a coy smile. "People can do a lot of things with that much time."

"We just hung out," I say, fully aware that my cheeks are blistering. "And you know, got to know one another better."

"Mmmhmm," she says, pulling open the front door of the building. "That's definitely my favorite part of getting with a guy. The 'getting to know one another' phase can be very sexy."

Georgia has no idea that sex wasn't even the biggest part of what happened between me and Sebastian. The simple fact he and I had been able to work through my fears and aversions was bigger than she could possibly grasp. Sure, he fingerbanged me within an inch of my life, and the resulting orgasm was a thing of poetry, but that was just the cherry on top. A delicious, sweet, knee-quaking cherry.

I wonder, "Do you ever get past the 'getting to know one another' phase? I ask that out of curiosity, no judgment intended."

"Honestly, not if I can help it." She grins. "Like I said, it's the best part. Why would I want to mess that up by getting into all the icky stuff?"

She splits off toward her locker, adding that she'll see me in the dining hall. I approach my locker on the opposite side of the hall, unlocking it and opening the door. I do a double take when I see the contents, thinking I've opened the wrong locker. I close and re-check the number, but this is definitely my locker. Someone must have put their shit inside by mistake, because on top of my math book is a shiny, brand-spanking-new laptop. It's rose gold-colored with the charging cable tucked carefully next to it. I look around to see if anyone is watching, but they aren't. I open the laptop, just hoping to find out who it belongs to, and it springs to life, an image appearing on the screen. It's a photo of a kitten. Abbadon, to be exact. It's *my* photo.

No fucking *way*.

I grab the laptop, shove my science book inside, then slam the door. I head straight out of the building and across the campus to the dining hall. The table where I normally sit is half full, Reyn and Vandy already there, along with Caroline and Ben. I march up.

"Has anyone seen Sebastian?" I ask.

"I saw him and Dean Dewey walking down the hall before second period," Caroline says, looking up from her study guide. "Something about him lurking around the lockers on the junior hall between classes."

"Motherfucker," I mutter. "Well if you see him—"

"Hey, you got my gift," he cuts in, reaching out to gently slide his hand down my arm, just like he had yesterday when we parted. I guess he'd been serious about getting me used to his touches in small, measured doses. This one doesn't make me want to hurl, but I still flinch. He uses my distraction to swipe the laptop from beneath my arm. He holds it up, face lit up with a beaming grin. "I thought about going for black, because you know, you really work that whole edge-lady vibe, but rose gold is just so much shinier."

He looks around the table, seeking approval. "Right? Don't you think?"

Reyn's eyes dart between me and Sebastian, an amused grin twisting at his lips. Vandy kind of looks like a deer in headlights. Meanwhile, I'm about two seconds from completely losing my shit. I swallow back the rage.

"Can I talk to you for a minute," I ask in a calm, collected tone. "Alone?"

He tilts his head, delayed awareness spreading across his face. "Now?"

"Yes, now."

I spin on my heel, hightailing it through the students that are still coming in the door, not waiting for him to catch up. It doesn't take him long though, and I hear several people telling him to watch out and to slow down as he chases after me. Once I'm in the hallway, I stop and hold out the laptop.

"I can't take this."

"What? Why not?" A deep line creases his forehead. "I mean, no offense, but your laptop is a piece of junk—you were saying last night that it can't handle all the photos you need to store on it and that the battery dies in like twenty minutes flat. This one won't have those issues."

My whole body clenches up in frustration, remembering our discussion in the Preston parking lot. I'd just had a fucking epic orgasm ten minutes prior, which apparently turns me into a pile of goo, and there'd been a moment there where I'm pretty sure neither of us wanted the night to end. But mostly, I didn't know what to *do*, how to act, or what to say.

Hence, some truly stupid word vomit about how I needed to write up an essay on my dinosaur of a laptop.

"It's like a two-thousand-dollar laptop, Bass. That's ridiculous."

"What's the big deal? I have the money to spare, and I want you to have it." He watches me thoughtfully before adding, "I didn't buy it with betting money or anything. Swear."

I pinch the bridge of my nose. "That's not the point. It's too much, and you and I... I mean, come on. We hardly know one another."

His expression turns incredulous. "Hardly know one another? How can you even say that after what we did yesterday?"

"Shhh!" His voice is loud, boisterous—too casual about it all. I hiss, "Don't just go shouting about that in the fucking hallway!"

He looks around, eyebrow rising at the complete lack of students milling around. "You think any of these people don't think we're already boning? Because trust me, that ship sailed the first time people saw us talking in the hallway. Or is this about yesterday? Are you having regrets or something? Because last night was fucking aces, and I know you know it."

My face already feels like the surface of the sun, and I don't care that there are only two people in the hallway, far out of earshot. I still lean in close to say, "This isn't about that. I told you not to give me money or gifts!"

"That was before." He points it out like this has all been some huge misunderstanding. Like, obviously when you fingerbang the hell out of a girl, you're suddenly allowed to start buying her expensive consumer electronics. "I wasn't your friend then."

"You're not my friend *now*."

He gives me one of those slow, smarmy smiles. "Nah, I guess I'm not. But I'm definitely *something*, and it's a little friends-adjacent, don't you think?" He reaches out to tug at my dog tags. "Why are you freaking out?"

"I'm not freaking out," I argue, even as his eyebrow raises skeptically. "I'm not. I just..." I shove the laptop at him again. "I can't take this. It's too expensive and just... way too much. It's *too much*, Bass."

He looks down at the laptop but doesn't take it. Instead, he rocks back on his heels and says, "You know, I've worked really hard to understand you, Sugar, because there's something about you that has me so fucking infatuated, it's borderline embarrassing. You're fun and sexy and snarky as fuck. I don't care that you drive a shitty car, or that your boots are scuffed, or that your laptop is old. I actually *like* all those things about you, and you want to know why? Because they make you who you are. It's the true *you*. You don't apologize for it and you aren't someone who tries to hide it. I accept it all, even when some of those things have historically been a massive pain in my dick."

He touches my arm gently, making a point. "But you have to be willing to accept the true me too, and I'm sorry, but a part of that is being stupidly rich. I'm talking trust fund, stocks and bonds, off-shore accounts, type of rich. At least my father is, and his father was, and there's just no end to the fucking money, and that's something you have to accept if we're going to be together." I open my mouth to argue but he holds a finger to my lips. "Seriously. Money means fuck-all to me. It isn't going to go away, and as long as I have it, I'm going to shower you with gifts, because that's what my mother taught me, not to be greedy, to share what I have and give freely. No-strings-attached gifts to the people I care about is just how I roll."

He bends down and kisses my forehead before turning and walking back toward the cafeteria, with that same cocky swagger that's impossible to hate. The embroidered devil on the back of his jacket is the last thing I see before he vanishes around the corner. I hold the laptop against my body, realizing that part of what bothers me the most is that Sebastian is always giving me something; the decal for the Mustang, rides when I need them, help with the kittens, and yeah, okay? I admit it.

The epic fucking orgasm, too.

It was this huge, monumental thing that I thought I might never get to experience with another person. I'd written off ever being able to feel like that. I'd already accepted that no one would ever touch me like Sebastian does, and not even just what happened in his car, but also what happened after, and again today. Someone willing to be patient, to not give up, to keep touching me like this, even when it's hard—even when I can't accept or return it in the way I'd like—is the biggest gift of all.

It's just that I have nothing to offer in return.

Maybe, I think as I head toward the art hall, I need to stop refusing his gifts and figure out the best way to even out the scales.

19

SEBASTIAN

Sitting at the end of the long table, I try once again focus on my turkey sandwich instead of thinking about sex. It's like a fucking sickness, all of a sudden. People always talk about that statistic where guys think about sex every three-point-something seconds, and fucking hell. A three second reprieve is actually sounding really good.

The glaring eyes of the other Devils are a helpful distraction. I haven't said a word to them since I'd spoken to Sugar in the hall, but they're all a bunch of nosey bitches, so in between absurdly detailed daydreams of sinking my hard dick into a wet pussy, I brace myself for their commentary. For once, they may have gotten the hint, because no one says anything until Aubrey asks, "My dad said he'd see if he can get use of the box seats at the stadium for the Twenty-One Pilots show. Anyone want to come?"

"What night?" Carlton asks, as if he has anything else going on.

"Wednesday. We'd have to drive into town, but there's free food and stuff."

"Sounds fun," Vandy says. "Reyn, you want to go?"

"Eh, they're a little too emo for me, but free food sounds good."

"They're not emo," Georgia argues, narrowing her eyes at him. "I'm definitely in. Do you mind if I ask Sugar? I know she's into them because she has a sticker on her lap—" My gaze flicks up to hers and she rolls her eyes. "Come on, Bass. Did you really think she wouldn't get mad about you buying her a laptop? She got pissed about the little thingy you got for the car. Not everyone can be wooed with money."

"I'm not trying to woo her. That laptop she lugs around is a piece of fucking trash. I was trying to—" I throw my sandwich on my tray and stand. "Forget it. You wouldn't get what I was trying to do."

I kick the chair back under the table and grab my tray.

"Where are you going?" Georgia asks, taken aback. "Wait, are you seriously mad?"

I give her a look and keep going. I'm not mad. I'm just... I don't even know. Too full of energy. Irritable. Wound up. I need to work out, fight, race, do *something* with my hands. I thought waking up at the ass crack of dawn and driving twenty miles to the closest Apple store to buy something shiny for Sugar would settle this buzzing beneath my skin. Maybe help me think of something other than finding a nice, warm hole to get my dick into, too.

No fucking dice, on either count.

I storm out the door, feeling the tension coil in my chest. Being with Sugar is pretty much the only thing that's helped me feel better these past few days. But then last night, feeling her tight little body writhe against mine as she let me touch her—let me *inside* her —was such a fucking thrill. I've been thinking all morning about one phrase to sum it up: Sexual adrenaline. That's all I've got. It fits. I almost came in my pants just from watching her, head thrown back, mouth opened in a soft, tortured cry as she came apart on my fingers.

I've never wanted to fuck anyone as badly as I wanted to fuck her right then. I couldn't stop thinking about how easy it'd be to work my pants down, roll a condom on, and just sink into that tight, wet heat of hers. God, and I would have made her feel so good, too. She has no idea.

But that was the point. Reyn had been right about that. I need to stop making everything about my dick. That whole thing was about showing Sugar just how good I could make her feel. Bad enough that I'd already caused her pain—had already been the catalyst to her being unable to handle touch at all—I had to count my dick out of the game.

Yeah, it was hard.

Literally.

Limping back to my dorm with balls bluer than a smurf was a new low for me. I jerked off though, and it was... fine. Even if the back of my teeth are set on edge, even if I'm still hard *all the damn time*, even if I can't stop thinking about it—pussy, pussy, dick, dick, fucking, fucking...

It's *fine*.

I took second period to deliver the laptop, skipping class to get it up and running for her, setting that cute as fuck picture of Abby as the screen-saver, and leaving it in her locker, just so. But because my luck is just swinging that way recently, Dean Dewey caught me 'skulking around the lockers suspiciously'. It took me an hour to talk my way out of that one.

 I don't know what I expected. Maybe a thank you? A smile? A kiss? A hug, if I was really fucking lucky?

I wasn't expecting her to get all pissed about it, that's for sure. Okay, that's not true. Sugar getting pissed is like her default factory setting. Maybe she's right. It's too fast. We barely know one another. I'm, predictably, misreading the situation. So what if we hooked up? No one knows how non-committal those things can be better than I do.

Since I've already skipped one class today, I see no real reason to go to any more. I decide to head to the garage instead. Jasmine needs a little TLC and I've been neglecting her for another woman. Typical.

I'm almost at my car when my phone buzzes with a text. My heart skips when I see it's from Sugar. A photo. I recognize it instantly as one she took right before Heston came over at the car show. I'm staring straight at the camera, my eyes as bright as

Jasmine's paint. There's no mistaking the slight tension pulling at the corner of my eyes or the tight set of my jaw. There's the hint of fear in my eyes that she can't know was worry that Heston might see her. I wouldn't say I look weak, but in that brief moment, there's a chink in my armor. If I can see it, then so can she.

I stare at the photo for a long moment and then reply back.

Bass: This guy is hot. Kind of a broody bastard but still sexy.

Sugar: He is pretty good-looking. I probably should get all over him. Too bad he's not here and I'm down in the photo lab all alone.

I freeze, keys in hand, eyebrows climbing my forehead. I take a furtive look around the lot before responding.

Bass: A pretty girl like you, all alone? That doesn't sound safe.

Sugar: Maybe there's a broody bastard out there that wants to come keep me company.

Yeah, that's an invitation, and one I don't plan on squandering. I jog across campus, darting behind the tower to stay out of Dewey's line of vision, and then over to the arts building. I open the door and head down to basement level where the studios are located. The photography lab is marked and I try the door, but it's locked. I take a photo of the door and send it along with a text:

Knock Knock

My heart's hammering from both the running and the anticipation. Fighting with Sugar isn't something I wanted to do today, but I brace myself in case I've misread the flirtatious nature of the texts. I'm not crazy, right? That was flirting. No way that wasn't flirting!

The door swings open and Sugar stands there with her dark eyeliner and sexy mouth.

The instant I say, "I heard someone down here needed a broody bastard to protect them," I regret them, because *Jesus Christ,* Bass, where did all your fucking game go? But she lunges forward and grabs me by the jacket, pulling me down for a searing kiss.

It takes me by surprise, but not for long. I kick the door closed with my foot and thread my fingers in her hair, cupping the sides of her head. I do my best to be gentle, but it's hard with her body pressed all up against mine. I've been hard for a good sixteen hours. There's no telling my dick to calm down.

"I may have overreacted this morning," she says between kisses, "about the laptop."

"And you're apologizing by bringing me to your lair to seduce me?" I duck down to suck a wet, open-mouthed kiss to her warm throat. "This is definitely *not* going to teach me a lesson about not buying you gifts."

My dick strains painfully and I take a deep breath. Sugar's initiated things before and I've tried my best to encourage her to take the lead, but it's getting so fucking hard to rein things in. I've never spent this much time trying to get into a girl's pants. It usually comes easy, freely. This whole plan to sit back and wait for her to want it is fucking killing me.

To my relief, she takes a step back, her hazel eyes raking up and down my body. She places her hands on my chest, then slides them up to my shoulders and pushes my jacket off.

I lean my back against the door and take a chance.

I cup her neck, stroking my thumb against her jaw. She blinks up at me, mouth red, but doesn't flinch away like she had the other times. Maybe it's working, this whole idea of random, small, regular touches. Before it has the chance to evolve into something bad, I trail my hand down her chain, reaching for the dog tags and rubbing the raised letters. "Not that I'm complaining, but want to tell me what's going on?"

She looks up with wide, clear eyes. "Yesterday was a really big deal for me, Bass. I'm not sure you get it, because you probably do shit like that all the time, but—"

"I've never done anything like *that*," I cut in, needing her to know.

She rolls her eyes. "You've fingered a girl before. That wasn't the work of a novice."

I sweep her hair back, arguing, "I've never done it just for her, just because I wanted to make her feel good. I've never taken my time like that. Pretty sure I've never done anything with a girl and not busted a nut." I give her a significant look. "And definitely never in the backseat of my car."

Her mouth curls into a grin that's probably a shade shier than she'd admit to. "Yeah?"

"Yeah. Think of the upholstery." I laugh when she playfully pushes my shoulder. "Is this your way of trying to thank me for completely rocking your world?"

She scoffs. "You're so pathologically full of yourself, it's impossible to thank you for anything without feeling annoyed about it, but basically? Yes." She does look annoyed, but beneath that low brow and slanted mouth, there's also something else. "The point is, the laptop. You've already given me a lot, Bass. Too much."

I drop my head down and graze my nose over the shell of her ear. "I told you, giving is in my nature. It's not a big deal for me."

"Well, it is a big deal for me." Her hands are now flat on my stomach. "And I'd just feel better if things weren't so one-sided."

I feel my eyebrow inch up my forehead. I wonder if she can tell how much she helps me. Sure, I'm a little—okay, a *lot*—sexually frustrated, but for the first time in my life I'm being forced to slow down a little bit, and it's not the worst thing in the world. Actually, the rewards are pretty fucking sweet.

"Sugar," I start, trying to come up with the words to explain all that to her without looking like a pussy, "if this is about you feeling like you owe me something, then you're dead fucking wrong."

"Not owe," she clarifies. "Just... even. Meeting you in the middle. You made an effort—you made me feel good—and I want you to give me the chance to do the same. I don't know how it'll shake out, but you can be chill. I know that now. You can be—"

I must suck in every atom of air to say, "Fuck yes, so chill," and I'd probably be halfway out of my pants by now, but I'm kissing her instead. She makes a small, surprised sound into my mouth, but it doesn't sound disagreeable. Going by the way she kisses me back, deep and breathless, she's all for it.

I reach out to curl a hand around her hip, braced for her to twist away, leaving my grip loose. But she doesn't. I wonder if she's realized yet that it's easier when we're like this, licking into each other's mouths, bodies pressed close and hot, buzzing with the promise of pleasure and the frustration of not getting it fast enough. She doesn't flinch away like she does in the halls.

But I wouldn't be me if I didn't push it.

I drag a hand up the arm she has wound around my neck, gently tugging her wrist away. She pauses when I press her hand to the front of my pants, but doesn't pull away.

She squeezes.

"Oh, fuck," I sigh, letting my head fall back against the wall. "Fuck, I've been hard *forever*."

Her mouth is hot against my throat, voice low as she rubs my dick. "What do you want? The door locks from inside. No one's going to come in."

The way she's palming my cock has my brain too focused on the thought of a tight, wet hole to think twice about saying, "I want to fuck you."

Luckily, she takes this in stride. "We're not fucking in the photo lab, Bass." Right. Not realistic. I look down, but she's watching her hand curl around the tent in my pants, mouth parted as it strokes up and down. "I could do this."

"Yeah." *Fuck yeah*, she could. Even a hasty hand job through my pants would probably make me bust the best nut I've ever had. But, "Can you suck me off?" I'll probably cringe about it later, but right now, I don't even give a damn.

She gives me a wry look, and I'm wondering if a blow job is unrealistic like fucking. My brain isn't exactly operating at peak capacity. But she just says, "Hey, tone down the romance, Nicholas Sparks. I'm a sure thing."

"Uh," I say stupidly, "sorry, I just meant, if you wanted to."

She doesn't look upset, though. If anything, she looks almost as horny as I feel, teeth sinking into that plump bottom lip as her fingers move up my shirt. She toys with the hair below my navel, dropping her eyes to watch.

"Take off your shirt and maybe I'll think about it."

I've never gotten out of a shirt so fast in my fucking life.

"Jesus," she says, reaching up to press her palms against my bare chest. "You've got such a nice body." I'm not sure why she says it like that—like me being ripped is the source of her greatest annoyance—but the way she sweeps her hand down my abs tells me it's anything but.

"Did this hurt?" she asks, running her tongue over my collarbone tattoo in a way that makes my dick twitch angrily.

"Nah," I answer, winding my hand into her thick, dark hair.

She hums against my skin, fingers dipping teasingly beneath my waistband. "Really?"

"No," I snort. "Of course it hurt. Like hell."

Tension coils in my lower belly and it only tightens further when she bends, placing hot kisses on my stomach. I hiss, feeling my abdomen cave. The sound forces her to look up with those big hazel eyes, and I touch her cheek. I realize that coming in my pants wouldn't be the worst thing to happen to me that day, but god, having my cock in her mouth? Having those pink, puffy lips around me as I come? I'm *this* close to begging for it.

Instead, I just make a little suggestion.

A suggestion in the form of two heavy hands on her shoulders, pushing her to her knees in front of me.

She gives me a long-suffering look. "With smooth moves like that, it's a wonder you get any action at all."

"Hey, that's some of my best work."

The impulsivity flares and I take her hands with mine, shifting them to the button on my pants. She holds my gaze as we thumb it open together, waiting until we've worked my pants down my thighs to shift her attention to my dick, hard and straining toward her.

I suck in a loud gasp when she touches me for the first time. Her palm is soft, her fingertips warm. Like she'd done with me, I take the lead, stroking her hand up and down the shaft, rolling her thumb over the tip, showing her what I like. Her fingers dip down to my balls and I shudder out a groan.

"Fuck." I look down at her kneeling on my bunched-up letterman jacket. She's staring at my throbbing cock like she's sizing it up, wondering if she should take a go at it. I lift her chin so I can see her face—her mouth—those lips. The plea is out of my mouth before I can reconsider, "Please?"

She continues to run her hand up and down my length, toying with the skin, applying pressure. Her cheeks bloom a delicate, vivid pink. "I will, I just haven't ever—"

"There's no wrong way, Sugar," I grind out, shoulders pressed against the door for support. I lay my hand on the back of her head, encouraging her in the form of a polite nudge. "Use your tongue, not your teeth." My dick jerks with an eager twitch, hips jutting forward, and she bats my cock away, pulling a face. "What?"

"You." She grabs me by the base, and I exhale. "Even your cock is pushy and entitled."

"You have no fucking idea," I mutter, pulling back and plunging forward. The tip grazes her lips, leaving a trail of sticky pre-cum. Her tongue darts out and licks it, making my balls seize. I reach down and thumb at her bottom lip. "Come on, I'll go easy."

Those lips create a circle and slowly I push inside, watching closely as she takes me in. Our gaze meets and I see the spark of something flicker inside her eyes. When she bobs her head up and down once, running her tongue up and down my length, I know sure as hell it isn't fear. It's the glimmer of desire.

It's hard not to just fuck her mouth, especially as I watch my dick disappear and reappear with her slow, teasing rhythm. Even though she's never done it before, she isn't shy about meeting my eyes when she pulls back, and she isn't reluctant when she takes me back in, letting me hit the back of her tongue.

There's already a fine tremor going through my thighs as she works me, a hand curled firmly around my base. Fuck, her mouth is hot, even hotter when she just... *twists* a little, creating the sweetest drag up my cock. I stroke a hand over her hair, careful, easy. No girl I've ever met has liked being force-fed my dick, and Sugar will probably hang me by the balls if I tried. Instead, I just thread my fingers into her hair and let it rest there against her head, feeling the way she surges and retreats.

She gets a little bolder as she sucks me, learning what makes me groan, what makes my chest expand with a shaky inhale, what makes my legs tremble. She moans around a mouthful of my dick and I spit a sharp, "Fuck," as I watch, reaching down to graze a thumb over the corner of her full mouth.

She blinks her dark eyes up at me, pupils blown wide, and a sudden stream of words spills from my mouth.

"So goddamn gorgeous, Sugar. I think about this all the time—being with you, making you look at me like that. You're wet for this, aren't you?" Another moan around my dick makes me shudder. "You'll let me finger you again, right? You were so hot last night, letting me inside you like that. One of these days, I'm going to fuck you so good."

She does this thing where she pulls back, tonguing at the head of my dick while her hand pumps me, and my toes start curling with the way my balls draw up.

"You need me to pull out?" I ask, trying to keep my voice even and completely failing. Her eyes flick up to mine, blinking once before she sinks back down on my dick. No, of course not. Sugar might have reservations about sex, but it's about touch, not this—not about getting dirty and *taking*.

Still, when my belly begins tensing with the impending wave of sweet, sharp relief, I bite out a low, "It's coming."

She makes a low, rough sound in response, and it sends me careening right over the edge. I have to yank my hands away from her and shove them safely behind my head, fisting into my own hair to make sure I don't do it to her. It hits me like a sledgehammer, an animalistic sound being ripped from my chest as my dick starts pulsing hot waves of cum between her slick lips.

My vision goes white, just for a moment, and I think I must rip out some of my own hair when she *sucks* it right from my dick, mid-nut. I watch, slack-jawed and breathless as she lets my spent dick slide from her mouth.

I pant out a weak, "Damn, girl," and she looks up at me, blank-faced. Then, she swallows. "Holy shit, you just—" She just fucking kills me.

When she finally speaks, her voice is rough. "Your jizz tastes vile."

"Please, my jizz tastes like fucking sunshine." I flap a hand at the sink in the corner. "You could have spit it out."

"I needed a time-efficient solution," she says dryly, but I'm not dumb here. I can see the way her hips kind of... squirm.

"Let me finger you again." My dick is completely spent, but it still twitches at the thought of it.

She doesn't miss it, curving an eyebrow at my cock. "And get that thing all revved up again? Let's give him a break."

I protest, "But—" and she levels me with a look.

"This was for you. Later, okay?"

Later. Something to look forward to. I can live with that.

Probably.

Coming down off that high takes longer than I'd expect and I'm still sweaty and breathing hard when I pull her off her knees. I tuck myself back in my shorts and straighten my pants. She doesn't flinch when I run my fingers through her hair, setting back to rights all the places I'd ruffled up.

"I have an idea."

"I'm sure you do," she replies. "What kind of idea?"

"I'll keep buying you expensive things and you keep giving me blow jobs like that. It's a completely acceptable trade."

Her lip curls in half-hearted disdain. "You just described a hooker, Bass."

"Hooker," I shrug, "or girlfriend. Whichever one, I want it on the regular. For real."

She looks up at me, forehead creased. "Girlfriend? I thought Sebastian Wilcox didn't do girlfriends."

I clutch her dog tags, pulling her into the space between my legs. "Well maybe Sebastian Wilcox just found someone worth calling his girlfriend."

Her eyes search mine, like she's doing the long-division of it, wondering how those pieces fit together. *Just fucking fine*, I want to say. "In no universe would my boyfriend be someone who refers to himself in third person."

I roll my eyes. "Don't reject me. My fragile ego couldn't handle it."

"Your ego is about as fragile as a lead anvil."

"True," I concede. "Is this about the thing you said earlier, about needing romance? Because I could romance the absolute *shit* out of you, girl. Flowers, candy, switchblades, I can really do it up right."

She groans, tipping forward to rest her forehead on my bare shoulder. "Oh god, that was basically like a challenge to you, wasn't it?"

"Yep." Cautiously, I wind my arms around her, leaving them loose around her hips. The way she stiffens tells me that this isn't like before—it's not one of those horny moments where it doesn't bother her as much. This is a bigger touch, stronger than I've ever tried before. I give her room to pull away or shake me off.

Instead, she lets out this full-body shudder and presses closer. Even though her breath hitches, chest trembling against mine, she lets us freeze like that, and it's not like she's okay with it. I can tell she's scared, that it's doing something bad to her, to be held like this.

I try to pull away, but her hands fist into tight balls against my ribs. "Just wait," she says, voice thin, but full of determination.

I don't know how she works through it. In a perfect world, it'd be instant, because I'm me and she's her, and we fit together easily, effortlessly.

Neither of us live in a world like that.

We live in a world where we have to fight, so that's what we do. I fight against the impulse to tighten my arms—to take what I want, just because it should be mine—and she fights against whatever makes this so unbearable.

It must be ten minutes of us standing like that before her breath starts evening out. Even then, I still don't move, shattering the silence every now and then with a heavy gulp, trying so hard not to fuck it all up. My muscles are screaming with the urge to fidget, to move, but I close my eyes and will them all to relax, to wait for her to finish the battle.

She turns her head to rest her warm cheek against my chest, and when I chance a look at her face, she looks tired.

"I think... yeah. I think I'm good." Tired and *relieved*. "Thank you. For waiting. For letting me see."

Still frozen in place, I ask, "See what?"

"If I could do this," she says, sinking into my chest, "without feeling afraid."

I take a chance, finally moving my arms around her more firmly. She doesn't react beyond pressing closer. "It's not the chore you seem to think it is."

She lets out a long, shaky exhale, but I can tell this one isn't about fear or exhaustion. Her eyes flutter closed when she says, "I could be your girlfriend."

My lips spread into a grin as I look down at her. "Yeah?"

She opens one eye to glare at me. "Buy me flowers and I'll shove them up your ass."

"Noted."

When she kisses me again, the anxiety and anger and ever-present irritability slip away, and I know that no decision that makes my chest feel this light could have been a mistake. Sugar Voss is mine and I'm completely willing to be hers.

20

Other than Netflix romcoms and the occasional trashy romance novel, I have no idea what to expect in a boyfriend—especially from a guy like Sebastian Wilcox. He's unpredictable in a regular situation, but being the public object of his affection? Let's just say I better adjust quickly, as well as everyone else in our orbit.

"This is fucking weird," I tell him, trying not to be overwhelmed by the stares, the whispers, and the way my heart flutters anxiously as we walk down the hall, his fingers threaded through mine. That alone had taken me a minor five-minute freak-out in our little space behind the dining hall to adjust to. "Even on my first day here, people didn't notice me this much."

He grins, giving our hands an obnoxious swing. "What can I say. I've always been a fascinating point of interest at school. Now you're fascinating, too."

I roll my eyes, because it's become apparent someone has to try to keep his ego in check, but he's not wrong. Sebastian is incredibly popular. "Maybe we should play with the idea of non-public displays of affection."

"People are jealous," he scoffs as we slow by his locker. He doesn't untangle our fingers as he spins the lock, and I'm secretly grateful. As much as I'm whining about the reactions, if I'm going to be someone's girlfriend, I want to be able to do disgusting shit like hold hands in the hallways. Weathering small meltdowns to achieve it could get exhausting. "Certain people at this school, who shall remain nameless, have wanted to lock me down for years, and then all of a sudden this new chick shows up. A sexy, badass, hot-as-*fuck* new chick. They're wondering what makes you different from all the others."

So am I, I think.

He opens the door to his locker and I barely get a glance at a black envelope taped to the inside when he tilts his head toward me. "There's no way in hell I'm not claiming you in public, Sugar. There's something you have to understand about Preston. These people are vipers. Left unchecked, they tend to get a little ruthless. Everyone here needs to understand that you're mine."

His words are archaic and borderline offensive. But I'm not going to deny that he's already made an impact. Ever since the day he slammed that jackass against the wall and made it perfectly clear that no one was to ever touch me again, I've been given a courteously wide berth. And while the thought of someone thinking I 'belong' to them halfway makes me want to slap them in the face, knowing that everyone considers me his does have this way of making my stomach flip enticingly.

"Maybe everyone here needs to understand you're mine," I counter, fully expecting some crass reply.

Instead, I get a slow, heated look, those blue eyes boring into mine. "Maybe they do," he says, dipping down to give me a kiss that's absolutely scorching. The background hum of the other students grows, like they're watching and shocked at what they see, but if Sebastian notices, he doesn't show it. Even when he licks into the seam of my lips, hips nudging mine back into the lockers, he only seems eager and horny.

Just his usual self, then.

He pulls away with a groan, reaching up to graze a thumb against my wet bottom lip. "If I didn't have this useless fucking meeting with my college counselor, I'd drag you somewhere a little less public to show you just how much I am—*yours*, I mean."

When he turns back to the contents of his locker, yanking out a binder and swinging the door shut, I notice that the black envelope from before is gone. Maybe I'd imagined it. I certainly haven't really been thinking straight lately.

"I guess you'll have to go all caveman on me later," I say, reluctantly tugging my hand away. "I have an after-school photography club meeting, anyway."

"What time do you want me to pick you up for dinner?" He says it so casually, so unbothered at the fact he's spending an hour with near-strangers just to be my date.

"Six-thirty," I answer, reaching up to fidget with my dog tags. It's a weird new habit I've fallen into ever since he began doing it. "But can you get me at Vandy's house? She's taking me home after the meeting so I can borrow something a little less 'holey and angry'. Georgia's words, by the way."

"Sure," he says. "Six-thirty. It'll give me some time to get a little work done down at the garage."

We continue to stand across from one another, and I get this ridiculous vision of us both sitting on either side of a phone, saying, "No, *you* hang up." *Vomit.* Maybe I do know how to live a rom-com.

Bass looks around the hall, then meets my gaze, and I know instantly what he's going to do. He snakes a hand around my waist and pulls me to him. It's getting easier every time he tries, but it still makes me freeze up, lungs constricting. He doesn't give up, though. "See you at six-thirty," he says, kissing me on the lips and releasing me quickly enough that the thread of anxiety in my chest never gets the chance to graduate into anything bigger.

I watch as he walks off, transfixed by the sight of his back disappearing into the throng of students.

"You've got a little drool on your chin," a voice says from behind me. I spin and see Micha and Michaela. Their expressions are caught somewhere between smug amusement and abject jealousy.

"Ha ha," I say, but discreetly wipe my lips anyway. "Funny."

"I knew all that was bluster a few weeks ago. You thought he was hot all along, didn't you?"

"I never said he wasn't good-looking," I mutter, adjusting my bag as we walk toward the arts building together. "Just that he has stupid hair."

"And that he's vain," Michaela adds.

I snort out a laugh. "Like him being my boyfriend has changed that at all? Please. Narcissus himself would look at that guy and think, 'a bit much, yeah?'" Nevertheless, I do relent, "But yes, I may have reconsidered some of my opinions on Sebastian."

"Mmhmm," Micha says, studying his nails. Each is painted a different color. "Please tell me you're bringing that eye feast of man meat with you to dinner tonight."

My jaw drops.

"Micha!" his sister cries before I can say anything. "You're fourteen. He's eighteen. You realize that you're jailbait."

"Just because he can't look at me doesn't mean I can't look at him. *Closely.* Don't pretend like you didn't want to know if he was coming."

"Enough," I cut in, eyeing the two of them. Michaela's eyes cast down guiltily. "I'd been planning on bringing him, but not if you're going to make him feel weird all night. I'll tell him to skip it." Micah's mouth forms an 'O' and snaps shut.

His sister says, "We'll behave. Promise."

I raise an eyebrow at Micha and he sighs. "Fine. I'll control myself."

"Good."

"But," he says, smiling coyly, "can I just ask one thing?"

"You can ask," I reply warily, "but I may not answer."

"Okay," he says, glancing at his sister, who gives him a nod of encouragement. "Exactly how soft is his hair?"

I laugh, and because they are fourteen and absolutely adorable, I tell them the truth. "Soft as a baby kitten."

~

Vandy had an assignment for the newspaper, so I told her I'd meet her near the Devil's Tower when I was finished with photography club. While I wait, I walk around it, noticing a small plaque that claims it's the oldest structure on campus—once part of a church that burned down in the 1800s. I'm sure the people who built this thing as a religious icon would be delighted to know its legacy for becoming a teenaged debauchery sex den. I pull out my camera and take a few photos of the historic details—the arched windows and stonework. It's a popular subject in the club among the kids who can't get off campus, like me. I suspect Mr. Lee knows exactly why.

"Hey," Vandy says, walking up with her slow gait. "Thanks for waiting. The basketball team is the focus of our next issue and I needed to do a few interviews." She looks at the camera in my hands, shoulders falling. "Aw, man, I should have had you take the pictures. Mine are never very good."

"I'm not sure how great I'd be at athletic photos," I admit, snapping the cap over the lens. "I'm sure yours are fine."

Two girls pass on the other side of the tower just as I start in the direction of the parking lot. "Seriously," one girl says to the other, "let me see it."

"No," her friend replies. "It's not a big deal."

They stop abruptly and Vandy's hand clamps around my wrist and yanks me back. Startled, I whip around and jerk it away from her grip. She drops her hand with an apologetic look and gestures for me to come back around the side of the tower. She whispers, "Sorry. I just...can we wait until they're gone?"

I glance back at the two girls who have stopped in the pathway a few feet away, then back at Vandy. Her back is pressed against the tower, but she looks more annoyed than scared. I recognize the girls instantly; Sydney and her friend Fiona.

"Syd and I used to be best friends," Vandy explains quietly, "but there's a lot of bad blood between us since a bunch of dumb drama went down the fall. Seeing her just makes me so mad. It's easier to avoid her."

"Sure," I say, in response. If anyone understands the desire to stay out of someone's way, it's me. I lean next to her, but still have a pretty good view of them, and it's hard not to overhear their conversation.

"If it's not a big deal," Fiona says, face stony, "then it shouldn't be a problem for you to show me."

Sydney shifts her backpack from one side to the other. "It looks worse than it is."

Fiona crosses her arms over her chest and stares at her friend. "Syd, show me."

Sydney's exhalation is annoyed but she lifts up the hem of her shirt with one hand while pulling down the top of her skirt with the other. A large, purpling bruise splays over her hip and waist in the shape of fingers. My heart lurches into my throat, making it momentarily hard to breathe. I know that kind of bruise. Not an accident. The pit of my stomach aches as I look at it.

"Jesus Christ, Sydney," Fiona gasps, peering to look at the bruise. Sydney drops her shirt and moves her hands protectively over her waist. "He did that to you?"

"You say that like he meant to hurt me or something. He got excited," she replies flippantly. "I can't help it if I have that kind of effect on a guy."

"That's not excitement, Syd, that's...." Fiona swallows, "that's not cool."

I have to agree with Fiona on this one.

"Look, he's older. More experienced. Passionate." She gives Fiona a pitying look. "One day when you're actually, like, *having sex*, you can have an opinion, but until then? Stay out of my business."

Fiona's jaw drops but Sydney has already started walking down the path. A moment later her friend follows, I guess willing to let the condescending tone slide. I glance over at Vandy and see that she's also heard the entire conversation. The look of annoyance is gone, replaced by something I can't discern. "Do you know anything about that?"

"No," she replies, "but with Sydney you never know what's really going on. She's not known for her honesty. Telling lies, twisting truths, and spinning drama is pretty much her brand." She pushes off the tower and starts toward the path, her foot dragging on the cobblestone. I definitely don't have a handle on the inner workings of all the interpersonal dynamics around here—who's a liar, who's a sneak, who's a narc—but I do know one thing.

That bruise is real and whoever put it there is dangerous.

~

"Thanks for doing this," I say, once we're up in Vandy's bedroom. It's so clean and bright that I'm almost afraid to move in case I accidentally stain something. "I've never had to go to this kind of dinner before. I'm guessing, aside from my Preston uniform, my usual ensembles aren't going to cut it."

Georgia had made this perfectly clear, but doesn't have much to offer me in the way of options until she goes home for the weekend. Luckily, Vandy and I are about the same size, even if our styles are miles apart.

"Farmhouse is a pretty low-key restaurant; it's got this whole 'farm to table' vibe. Everything is organic and locally sourced," she says, walking over to her closet. "So it doesn't need to be too dressy, but it never hurts to make a good impression."

That means it's going to be dressy.

'Dressy' to rich kids like Vandy and Georgia probably includes a ball gown, but to me, it's anything that rules out jeans or leggings.

She flings open the closet door and *Jesus Christ*. It's easily the size of my bedroom at home. It's jam-packed with clothes of every color and function. She has more shoes on one shelf than I've owned my entire life. I'm doing everything I can not to judge the Hall's expensive, massive home. Vandy has visible challenges and if the rumors are true, has had some major struggles. Just because you're rich doesn't mean things are perfect, but damn. What I wouldn't give to have grown up with this much space.

I peek my head in but feel too anxious about ruining something expensive to actually enter. "Do you know the Adamses?"

She flips through the hangers, stopping occasionally to consider a piece of clothing. "Actually, I do. Mrs. Adams is a kick-ass lawyer who really helped Reyn out of a jam last year. I know there's like, this preconceived notion that people like them are just do-gooders and over-compensating for something, but they're a really great family. They actually believe in helping people."

I snort. "Then what are they doing sending their kids to a school like Preston?"

"Hey!" She gives me an affronted look, but then laughs. "We're not all bad, but I get it. Trust me, the Adams kids have suffered more than their share of abuse from the dickheads at Preston. All I know is their parents are both alumni and the kids actually choose to go." She pulls out three different dresses, sizing them up. "Thank god, can you imagine how dull things would be without Micha?"

I smile, remembering our conversation from earlier in the day. "He definitely marches to the beat of his own tuba."

She flutters past me in a whirl of fabric, tossing things onto her wide bed. "The only thing you need to really know about their parents is that they appreciate genuine things. So you should choose whatever here is most 'you'." She plants a hand on each hip, nodding her head in approval at the selection she's curated.

I gnaw on a nail as I look over the choices, instantly nixing something unapologetically pink. There's a dark purple dress that could work, edged in a fine-looking lace around the neck and sleeves, but it's too nice. I'd spend all night worrying about staining it.

There's a black, knee-length dress that flares out prettily, but also looks perfectly plain. The neck scoops a little lower than I'm used to, but the fabric looks nice and hardy—no delicate lace or fussy material. It wouldn't be completely weird to wear my boots with, either.

"I think that's my guy," I say pointing to the dress.

She doesn't look surprised. "Good choice! And don't worry, I have a good bra to go with it."

I change in her closet, feeling awkward as I stuff my tits into the bra. The awkwardness only amplifies when I get the dress over my head, feeling it swish around my knees, and then look down. *Holy shit*. My tits are unreal in this thing. I spend a moment adjusting the waist before submitting myself to Vandy's inspection.

She gives a gleeful clap. "You need a necklace—oh, a choker! And some earrings!"

Resigned to being a sentient mannequin, I let Vandy deck me out in some of her jewelry, making sure she isn't giving me anything even remotely valuable.

"I got this as a free gift with another purchase, it's literally nothing,"

I stay painfully still as I hold my hair up, letting her secure the necklace. The thing about Sebastian being a stubborn bastard is that I'm beginning to realize he may be right. Every time he touches me, it's a little less awful. It's not always a big thing. Usually, they're little grazes, light touches. In Dr. Ross's class, he almost always spends her lectures playing with my hair, running his fingers through it, winding it around a wrist, sweeping it back off my neck. Sometimes, it's enough to make me shiver at the feel of it, sparks flying across my nerves like pyrotechnics.

"Thanks," I say, fiddling with the cord. I take a moment to come to terms with the fact that a pair of dog tags doesn't exactly go with the ensemble. With a tight inhale, I lift them over my head, feeling uncomfortable as I tuck them into my bag.

Vandy waves off my gratitude. "I should be thanking you. We all should. Bass has really been different since you came along. Less frantic and reckless all the time."

I feel doubtful about that, but maybe his friends don't realize just how much Sebastian trying to get with me was *also* reckless, in its own way. "He still races and stuff," I argue.

She gives me a look. "Well, yeah. Bass is gonna Bass. But he's also not coming back to school every weekend with a split lip and two black eyes. Or impulse buying a bunch of useless crap. Or getting trashed every Monday night with Carlton and his buddies. Or going out of his way to get shoved in the hall. I mean," her expression turns thoughtful as she peeks out her curtains at the driveway below. "Some of that is the concussion. He really is trying to be better, so he can get back to playing. But there's a difference between the way he was white-knuckling it before and how he's acting now. He actually seems... settled. Happy."

"That might not have anything to do with me," I insist, even though a part of me hopes I'm wrong. I want to be the one to make him better, the way he makes me better. The way he can touch me and wait for it to be bearable so I can actually enjoy it. The way I was able to let Vandy's fingertips brush my neck before and not have a complete meltdown about it.

She just shakes her head. "Trust me, it does. You're dating now, right? Like for real together?"

I feel myself flush at my stuttered confession, "Uh, yeah, we're... together. Whatever that means around here."

Vandy laughs. "Why? What does it mean where you come from?"

"A lot of sex, fighting, and statistically, an unplanned pregnancy?"

She pulls a face. "Well, for the record, anyone can get condoms at the health counselor's office. Preston's never been conservative where sex-ed is concerned. But usually, dating at Preston involves a lot of secrecy, because our parents are the biggest drama llamas of all. At least you and Bass don't have to worry about that."

Great, something else to worry about. "Yeah, I'm sure his rich parents will be thrilled to learn he's dating Cliff trash."

"Hey," she says, frowning. "Don't talk about yourself like that. And I've never known the Wilcoxes to interfere in their kids' lives like that. They're pretty hands-off."

"That's good to know." The last thing I need is some ornery rich parent all up on my shit about their precious son. "So, any other tips for this dinner tonight?" I ask, nerves flaring up again.

She flaps a hand. "No, you'll be fine. But word to the wise? Take your change of clothes with you, just in case." She gives me a wink.

"Okay," I say slowly, gathering my things. *Just in case*. Whatever that means. "I should probably go wait for him outside. The muffler on that Shelby is so loud we'll be able to hear it two blocks away."

When we get on the porch, the sound of a ball bouncing on the driveway greets us. Emory and Reyn are running around the driveway's basketball court playing one-on-one. Emory glances over his shoulder at us, pausing for a double take when he sees me dressed up. It gives Reyn the opportunity to knock the orange ball out of his hands, but then he stops in his tracks, eyes fixed on the driveway. I turn to see what he's looking at and notice a sleek silver car idling behind Emory's big truck.

"The fuck is that?" Reyn says, no longer interested in the game. His eyes are glued to the car. "Is that a 911? If that bullshit HOA is on my nuts again, so fucking help me..."

But when the driver's side door opens, the first thing I see is that trademark blond hair. Bass steps into the light, and he's almost unrecognizable. He's wearing a dark gray V-neck sweater with a white collared shirt underneath. My eyes travel down to the well-fitted dark jeans and brown lace-up shoes. It's all topped off with a black wool coat.

"*Damn*," Vandy mutters, voicing exactly what's lodged in the back of my throat. Prep school Sebastian is pretty. Greasy, unkempt, race car-driving Sebastian is undeniably hot. But this? Date Sebastian? He's so handsome it fucking hurts.

Micha is going to *die*.

"Man, where did you get that car?" Emory asks, as both boys approach him—well, approach his car. Sebastian lets them pass, eyes zeroed in on me. Despite the cold, I feel hot, prickly, overwhelmed. He strolls up, gaze raking over me. "Hey V," he says without looking at her.

"Bass," she says, sounding a little flustered herself. "I've never seen you looking so..."

"Appropriate?"

She gives a wry chuckle. "Sure, we can go with that."

"You ready?" he asks, bending to pick up my bag for me. "I'm afraid if we wait any longer, McAllister's drool is going to fuck with the paint on the car."

He holds out his hand and I take it, glancing over at Vandy once more. "Thanks, again."

She nods and mouths, "Call me later."

Bass walks me to the car and opens the door for me. Once I'm inside, he crosses the front of the car, says something to the guys, and bumps their fists. I don't miss something passing from Sebastian's hand to Emory's. Whatever it is, Emory gives a salute and they wander back down the driveway.

When we're both inside, I ask, "What's with the car? Where's the Shelby?"

Sebastian's jaw moves as he smacks on a piece of gum. "I ran home to get a change of clothes for tonight and figured my other car would be more suitable for the occasion. You know, less noise, a little more comfortable."

I run my hand down the soft leather. "It's gorgeous."

"Nah," he replies, reaching out to run a warm hand down my thigh, "*you're* gorgeous. Fuck, Sugar, how the hell am I going to make it through dinner when you're going to be sitting next to me like that?"

I breathe through the spike of anxiety that ebbs at his touch, but it's a brief, mild thing. I don't tell him, because his ego is already the size of the moon, but the feeling is entirely mutual. "Guess this night is going to be a challenge for both of us."

"You have no idea," he replies, pressing a button to start the ignition.

I look over at him in his nice, crisp clothes, hair flawless, jaw clean-shaven, and can't help but ask, "Hey, could you do me a favor?"

He cocks an eyebrow. "In case I haven't made it clear, I am completely down with favors." His smirk is pure obnoxiousness. "Sexual or otherwise."

Ah, there he is.

I roll my eyes, even though I'm fighting my own grin. "Just stay still for a second." I twist in the seat to root around in my bag in the back, pulling my chain from the pocket. The thought if it sitting in this car—so far away from me all night—makes my stomach churn in the worst way. Sebastian does as he's asked, remaining perfectly still as I lower it over his head, even if his eyes drop to watch it fall against his sweater. There's a question in his eyes that he doesn't voice. I answer anyway. "I can't wear it with this fancy get-up. Just... keep it safe?"

He blinks in surprise. "Yeah, I can do that." Giving me a pointed look, he even lifts it, tucking it securely into his sweater. It's not the same as it being against my own chest—it's not the same as always knowing it's there—but it's almost as good.

Sebastian protects what's important.

21

Sebastian

I chose to drive the Porsche on a whim, snagging the keys out of the drawer by the garage on the way out. I'd really only gone home to get a clean sweater and a pair of shoes that weren't covered in grease, but I'd doubled back at the last second. It's not like I stole it or anything. It's technically *my* car—the one my father bought me last year—the nice, flashy, approved vehicle that represents our family's status. It's not that I don't like the car. It's a fucking Porsche. It's a *nice* fucking Porsche. What's not to like? But it's just so easy. Driving it always makes me feel like a pampered, spoiled little brat. That's more Heston's gig.

But I chose to drive it anyway, because if there's one thing I can do, it's level the playing field for Sugar. Driving this car and wearing these clothes is one way to do that. She doesn't come from money like me, which is something I like about her. But in this town, that has a way of setting you apart.

But now that we're pulling into the restaurant parking lot, I begin wishing I'd driven the Shelby, self-inflicted dents and all. The Adamses aren't like other Preston families. For one, they actually want their kids. Secondly, they believe in good causes and genuine people. The fancy clothes and car, all my money, it's a part of me, but it's not who I am. I'd rather be getting down and dirty below the hood of a car than sitting on Italian leather. They'd probably appreciate that, not shun it. Chances are, flashing my status around the Adamses will probably make them like me less.

"You okay?" Sugar asks, squeezing my hand. "You look worried."

"Yeah, I just...I hope coming with you wasn't a bad idea." Somehow, I've become more nervous about this dinner than she is. I just want them to like her, like I do. God knows why.

"Why would it be a bad idea?"

"I told you there was some bad blood between Heston and their kids. He pulled a pretty mean prank on Micha last year. I just hope they don't think I'm like him. I don't want them to judge you for being with me."

She just snorts a laugh. "Bass, Micha is your number one fan, and Michaela is a creepily close second. I don't think either of them are holding a grudge against you for whatever dumb shit your brother pulled."

Which of course is half the problem. The Adamses don't hold grudges. They're too good for that. And even if the twins are Team Bass, my charms do have limits. *Fuck.* I scrub my face and nod, "Well, it's too late to turn back now anyway. I'm starving and you look hot as fuck. No way I'm letting you go in that restaurant without me."

She gives me a sour look. "What exactly do you think is going to happen? Like men are just going to start jumping me or something?"

"Maybe," I say, shooting her a grin. "Or maybe I just need everyone to know that I'm scoring with the hottest girl in the room."

Her sour expression flattens into something vaguely amused. "That, I can actually buy."

I exit the car and walk around to open the door for her. She looks so pretty, so perfect, the last thing I want to do is fuck this night up for her. I help her out of the car and give her a kiss, but don't let my touch linger. I'm starting to learn that there are times and places to make my testing touches. She's probably got enough nerves as it is.

"Sebastian?"

My fingers tighten around Sugar's and I turn toward the familiar voice.

"Hamilton." I'm genuinely surprised to see him, but there he is, in all his bitchy glory. I offer my hand, fighting the urge to wipe my palm on my pants before I do. Instead, I flash a grin at his date. "Gwendolyn, nice to see you."

Gwen looks pretty—not as pretty as Sugar, but just... better. Better than she had last year, back when she was always stone-faced and dead-eyed and avoiding everyone. Not that she was at fault for that. When the head of the Devils tells everyone to pretend you don't exist, that's exactly what happens. And then, apparently, you end up dating him.

Weird fucking place, Preston.

Gwen narrows her eyes like she's trying to place who I am. In that moment, if I could wipe my genes away, I would.

"Babe," Hamilton says, arm slung casually around Gwen's shoulder, "you probably never met Sebastian. He's Heston's younger brother."

"Oh," she says, recognition clicking in. "Right. Wilcox."

"Same last name," I assure her, "but the similarities stop there." His eyes dart over to Sugar and I turn to her, smiling. "So, believe it or not, we're here to meet your family. This is Sugar Voss, recipient of your parents' scholarship."

"Oh, you're Sugar!" Gwen's expression softens. "I really love your work. The black and white one of the cemetery with the flags was really provoking."

"Thank you," Sugar replies, tucking her hair behind an ear in an uncharacteristically shy gesture. Despite that, I can still see the spark of overwhelmed pride in her eyes.

Gwen's phone chimes and she looks down. "I think the rest of the family is already inside. I hear you've already made an impression on the twins. You can meet everyone else, too."

I peek into the large front window, internally cringing at what awaits us inside. The whole fucking family came. Even the older brother. Even *Skylar*. At least that's one sin that's not hanging around my neck.

"Sugar, walk with me. We can talk art while the guys catch up."

I release Sugar's hand and watch her walk off. I drag my eyes away from her and look at Hamilton, who's watching me closely.

"How's lacrosse?" he asks in a clear display of shooting the shit.

"Starts in a few weeks. I'm waiting to get cleared from a concussion."

"Ah, right. I won two hundred bucks at one of your fights." He looks me over, assessing me. On anyone else, it'd look like an attempt at intimidation, but I know Hamilton better than that. "Guess that's how you got the concussion."

"Yeah, something like that." I take a stab at the elephant lurking in the parking lot. "Look, I know we never really hung out or anything. Heston pretty much preferred me to be as far from his orbit as possible. But just so you know, I'm not anything like him. You seem to have a pretty good grasp on Gwen's family, so if you think that me being here will damage Sugar's reputation with them, I should bail now." I rake my hair back, blowing out a hard breath. "I really like this girl, so the last thing I want is her being judged on an association with my asshole brother that doesn't even exist."

"They're not like that," he says, twisting at the waist to peer in the window. "I mean, fuck, I'm petty as hell, but Gwen's family? They even forgave me, and you know how much of a shit I was to Gwen. They'll probably just see any association with Heston as another reason to take her under their wing. They love adding a new wayward soul to their flock." He laughs, dark eyes flashing. "Hell, why do you think they like me so much?"

"Okay." I nod, feeling a little bit of the tension easing. "Okay, good. That's a relief."

"How is your brother, anyway?"

"The same," I reply, giving a bitter, tight-lipped smile. "I avoid him as much as possible, truthfully."

He looks toward the door where the girls just walked in, face set into a pensive frown. "Have you told him about her?"

"Fuck no," I reply quickly. Maybe too quickly. "You know how he is. First sign of a weakness and he grabs hold."

"Yeah, I know." He shakes his head. "Your girl looks tough on the outside—I guess she'd have to be to deal with the assholes at Preston—but bro. *Bro*." He gives me a significant look. "Underneath that, she's really got that fragile, lost thing going on, you know?"

Irritation at him sussing out Sugar so quickly puts me on edge. "The fuck does that mean?"

"Gwen's family is the least of your worries. Your brother will sniff that shit out in a heartbeat." He holds my eye. "If you know what's good, you'll keep him away from her."

I already know this. It's why I kept him away from her at the car show. But hearing Hamilton say it—Hamilton Bates, who was such a terrible bastard that he was the only one at Preston who could keep my brother in line—just cements my determination.

I exhale and nod. "Yeah, of course. Thanks for the advice. And look, not that it's worth much, but I'm sorry about what he did to Gwen and Micha."

Hamilton holds up a hand. "Don't apologize for that sack of shit. That's his baggage, not yours."

By the time we walk into the restaurant, I'm seeing Hamilton Bates in a whole new light. He still seems like the same prissy little shit he always was, but he's grown up a lot since high school. He doesn't even mock me when I hold the door for an elderly couple exiting.

Meeting the rest of the family is a bit of a whirlwind. Sugar, seated to my right, looks like she's already been caught in the storm of it. There's a tightness around her eyes that tells me someone touched her—probably a handshake, maybe even several. And I was outside dicking around with Hamilton Bates. *Fuck*.

She just gives me a thin smile when I take my seat though, having given my own handshakes. Being so focused on her discomfort does have the advantage of taking my mind off everyone realizing I'm a Wilcox.

Micha reaches across the table to tap the table in front of me. "I told them not to touch her."

His mom's eyes widen. "Oh goodness gracious. You know that I completely forgot?"

"We weren't supposed to touch her?" the oldest son—Brayden—asks.

Michaela offers, "Everyone at school knows it."

Sugar looks like she wants to crawl into a hole and die. "No, it's fine. I'm okay."

I jump in, "So Micha, Michaela, you're in the photography club too, right? I haven't really given Sugar the chance to talk about it much. What all do you do?"

Michaela tilts her head, voice a perfect deadpan. "We take pictures."

Her twin scoffs. "No, we do more than that. Critical theory, color theory, you name it. Mr. Lee has been on this wild composite photography kick lately. Sugar's stuff has been really good this week. Not as good as mine," he clarifies, making sure everyone at the table has ample opportunity to roll their eyes. "But still really good. I'm guessing because she has that fancy new laptop."

I raise an eyebrow at her, not even trying to hide my smugness. "Yeah, she's really good, right? There's this one picture she took of our cat—I mean, not *our* cat, but one of the cats we feed. I wanted to buy the print for my mom because she's always hassling me to send her pictures of the strays at Preston. But Sugar totally shot me down. Probably smart. I'm sure it'll be worth like tens of thousands of dollars one day."

Sugar blinks back at me, face slack with surprise. "You never told me you wanted that for your mom."

I just shrug, shaking it off. "I have a camera on my phone. It'll do, even if it's not 'true art'."

Gwen and her mom go off on some tangent about a wildlife photographer they met in Africa. Sugar seems appropriately engaged in that—he's apparently a big name in the industry—so I dig into my salad, trying my best to follow along.

It isn't until Skylar asks, "So do you know where you want to study next year?" that I start to worry for her again.

Apparently, I don't need to. "Well my absolute dream would be

Yale. Their fine arts program is second to none. But my more realistic dream is probably SCAD. The counselor at Preston helped me apply to a lot, though, just in case."

Mrs. Adams's face lights up. "Oh, SCAD is lovely. Such a beautiful city. But I wouldn't sell yourself short on Yale. They'd be lucky to have you."

Sugar shrugs. "It's a really competitive school, so I doubt it. Can't hurt to try, though. SCAD is still—"

I lean in to interrupt, "What's SCAD?"

"Savannah College of Art and Design," Sugar explains to me. "The campus is fu—reaking amazing."

"Better than Preston's," Mrs. Adams says, "and that's saying a lot."

"What about you, son?" Mr. Adams asks. "Got your eyes set on a particular school?"

I answer easily. "Ah, the appeal of academia is lost on me. I'm going to spend a few years travelling the world instead."

The Adamses don't look the least bit put off by this, even if Sugar shoots me a curious glance. Mrs. Adams even raises her glass to me. "That's an equally valid experience. Learning from the world, giving back what you take, living on your feet. I had a couple years abroad in South Asia before law school, myself."

Maybe they could have a talk with my dad to that effect. He's not as sold on that whole validity thing. He hasn't forbidden me or anything, but he's still set Preston's counselor on me like an attack dog.

Sugar and I share an awkward smile, glossing right over the obvious implications of what those kinds of plans might mean for a relationship. It's early—too early to start thinking a future together —but whatever is happening between us is also too intense to completely ignore it.

Nevertheless, we try.

The dinner goes well enough. Hamilton gives me his number before we depart, even though I'm not sure what I'd ever have to talk to him about. How much of a dick my brother is? I guess contacts have been built on less.

Sugar visibly deflates once she's in the car. "That didn't go so bad. Right? It didn't seem like they hated me."

"They didn't seem to hate you," I agree. "In fact, they seemed to really like you, and buckle up, because I'm pretty sure you might have more of these in your future."

She groans, but then looks abashed about it. "It's not that I don't like them too, it was just a lot of work."

We're halfway across town before I finally begin, "So, hey. There's this thing tonight."

She looks instantly wary. "What kind of thing?" The way she says it makes it clear she's expecting a race or something equally as sketchy.

I shake my head. "Nothing like that. Every now and then, we all like to get together at the lake. There's usually a bonfire. Beer. Weed. Music. The usual. It's really low-key, not crazy like the car shows."

She chews on her lip for a moment. "And by 'we', you mean...?"

"The group," I say, trying to find a way to sum up the Devils without outing us as *being* Devils. I'd already taken a chance of passing Emory what I'd stolen from Miss Weathers—Preston's college counselor and holder of the keys to the drama department—right in front of Sugar earlier. I need to be careful. "Georgia, V, Em, Reyn, etcetera and so forth."

"Oh." She looks relieved, and then thoughtful. "Is that why Vandy told me to bring a change of clothes?"

"Probably." I haven't clued them in on her coming yet, but it's probably obvious. These things are for Devils and their partners only. Sometimes Tyson brings his girlfriend, and Elana had a guy she was into for about five minutes. Ben's too on the down-low about liking dick to ask whoever he's been hooking up with, but everyone would be chill about it. Bringing Sugar tonight is an obvious move. "What do you think?"

I can sense her eyes on me, like she's searching, wondering what the deal is. The truth is, I've never brought anyone to one of these things. Before Sugar, the closest I'd ever gotten to legit dating was probably attending a middle school dance with the daughter of someone my dad was chummy with. Asking Sugar to come with me to this is a bigger declaration than taking her to dinner tonight, or kissing her in the hall.

Which is why when she says, "Okay," it's a big freaking deal, even if she doesn't know it.

~

SUGAR CHANGES on the ride up, right beside me in the passenger seat. It's a bit of a struggle to watch the road instead of the increasing amount of bare skin that flashes in my periphery, but I do my best.

Still get a nice little glance at those tits. She rolls her eyes when I whistle, but goddamn. Her cleavage has been killing me all damn night.

Emory cheers when we arrive. "'Bout time, you fucker!" From the sound of it, plus the way Carlton has lost his shirt—*plus* the way Afton looks annoyed—it's clear these guys are already in the thick of it.

Reyn tosses me a beer, giving me a nod. "All good?"

I nod, knowing he's asking about the dinner. "Ran into Bates, actually."

Emory nods. "Where Gwen goes, he goes. Guy's got it bad."

They all laugh about it, but I know better. To people like me and Hamilton—guys who come from fucked-up, dysfunctional families—the Adamses are a real nice picture. I can see why they took him in, and I can see why he let them.

We settle into a spot in front of the fire, and Sugar warms her hands. "They were nice. Really normal." She stares into the flames, and there's a sadness there. I'm pretty sure it's reflected back at her when I nudge her shoulder, finding her gaze.

"Want a beer?"

Her nose wrinkles. "Not a fan." To the group, she asks, "Hey, is it cool for me to snap some candids? I promise to avoid any legal proof of contributions made to the delinquency of minors."

Carlton instantly starts flexing. "Yeah, gotta document this!"

Sugar gives him an exasperated look that almost makes me jealous. I'm used to seeing that directed at me. "It's not candid if you're *posing*, jackass."

Despite getting everyone's permission, she mostly spends the next ten minutes pointing her camera at the fire itself, even walking around it to get different angles. I watch her like that, transfixed at the way she seems to disappear in it, hair hanging around the camera like a veil as she presses the shutter in random intervals that make me wonder what she's seeing. Jealousy flares again as she points it at the others. Ben, in the middle of a story that involves way too many lewd gestures. Emory as he and Vandy share a whispered discussion across the fire. Reynolds, as he watches them. Afton and Elana as they play a game of rock, paper, scissors for designated driver.

When her lens finally gravitates to me, she's on the opposite side of the fire. Her figure is distorted with the heat of the flames, but I can see her freeze, surprised that I'm looking back at her.

The way she presses the shutter just then is slow, full of intent.

She returns to my side and puts the camera away. "Do you do that?" she asks, nodding to the blunt being passed from Caroline to Tyson.

I shrug. "Yeah. Why?"

"Just curious." Her dark eyes spark with the reflection of the fire when she turns them on me. "I'm kind of different when I'm high."

I reach over to sweep her hair away from her neck, delighting in her responding shiver when I scoot closer. "Different how?"

"Looser, I guess. Less anxious." She gives me a meaningful look. "Touchable."

I search her eyes, finally catching on. "Really?" At her nod, I raise a hand, snapping my fingers. "Ty, puff puff pass!" Everyone bitches about me fucking with rotation, but he hands it over, because he knows what's good for him. I take a long drag from the blunt before nudging Sugar's chin with a gentle knuckle.

She rolls her eyes when she realizes why I'm holding it in. "I know how to hit a blunt, you giant dork." Despite that, she purses her lips, sucking in the smoke as I exhale it. She's such a trooper too, doesn't even cough. I guess girls in the Briar Cliffs aren't exactly sheltered little princesses.

On the third shotgun, Carlton must give up on the blunt, because he starts rolling another one. Sugar and I are happy to share what's left of this one, and I can tell when it hits her, because she starts to get really floppy, head lolled back on her shoulders.

"That's some good shit," she says. Luckily Carlton doesn't overhear, otherwise we'd be subjected to his Ted Talk on why loud is overrated. "Back home, we don't usually get the good stuff until all you rich fuckers show up for the summer."

I take one last drag of the blunt, throwing the roach into the fire. "At least we share."

"Mmm," she moans. "You know what would be sweet as fuck? A back rub." When she finally opens her eyes, bloodshot and glazed, she bats her lashes at me, mouth curling into a wicked grin.

I gesture at the space between my legs. "Your wish is my inevitable blue balls."

She snorts a laugh, but clumsily scoots herself in front of me, settling between my bent knees. Even though I'd caught her drift about weed making her all touchable, I still wait a moment after resting my hands on her shoulders, anticipating her going stiff.

I knead my thumbs into the muscles, thankful for Carlton's personal stash more than ever when she melts back into me instead. The curve of her jaw is loose and I can just barely make out the silhouette of her lips parting as I work the muscle. She's got a lot of knots back here, carrying way more tension than she should. I take to the task just like I might to working on the Mustang. Methodical. Careful. Uncaring of time or space, just setting out to make something better.

She sinks back, her head finally falling on my shoulder, eyes dropping closed. "Oh my god, that feels good." She makes this little moan that, as predicted, makes me hard as a rock. The others aren't really paying attention beyond the occasional glance when something funny happens, gauging our reaction, so I start moving lower, digging my fingertips into her middle back. She writhes with the motion, feeling soft and serpentine against the cradle of my body.

It's reminding me of that night in the backseat of my car, and without really thinking about it, I move to her lower back, dipping beneath her jacket and shirt.

The fire is nice and toasty—Caroline always builds the best fires, and shit around here got a lot better when all the guys finally accepted it—but I can still feel Sugar's shiver at the lick of cold wind across her back. I peel off my wool coat and drape it over her front, and for once, she doesn't fight. She just curls her fingers in it and lets me make her feel good.

She doesn't even resist when I wind my arms around her middle, arms warm against her narrow, bare waist. It's nice, not having to worry about touching her as little as possible. She's pliant like this, a soft, malleable thing in my arms. I watch her face, the way the fire cuts against her cheekbones, eyelashes fluttering above them, when I reach for her tits. I know she'd taken that bra off in the car. I caught more than a flash of glowing skin and dark nipple as she shed it.

They're soft and heavy in my hands, warmer than the rest of her, and when her eyes blink open, catching mine, I'm expecting her to give me a little smile before saying something vaguely violent.

Instead, she just says, "Your hands are nice."

I give her tits a little squeeze. "Yeah?"

"I always thought so." She hums in response to my hands' massaging. "When they're not hurting, that is."

I frown, ducking my head to press my lips to her temple. "I wouldn't hurt you again."

"I know." She arches her back into my palms, seeming uncaring that I'm just sitting here playing with her tits in front of everyone, squeezing them together. "Vandy told me. She said you've been different."

"Different?"

Her nipples are hard, but she doesn't have that heavy-eyed, horny look. When her eyes meet mine, they're just curious. "Because you aren't always angling for a fight with other guys anymore."

"Oh." I stare thoughtfully into the fire as my hands work her over. "Yeah, I guess I haven't been feeling that itch as much."

"She thinks it's because of me."

I give her tits a little squeeze. "It is because of you." At her confused look, I quietly elaborate, "It feels like... having a stuck throttle. I'm always trying to find a place to point the car, trying like hell to decelerate for a bit. I usually end up crashing, which technically works. The car stops, but it's this split moment of chaos and twisted metal and destruction. But being with you is like having a wide open, uphill road." I sweep my thumbs over her pebbled nipples, watching her closely. "Deceleration without the crash."

That shit sounded like the deepest, most profound thing I've ever said.

For about five seconds.

Then I bury a laugh into her hair. "That sounded stupid as fuck. Ignore it."

"No," she just says, brows knitting together. "Is it weird that it actually made perfect sense?"

"Not if you're as stoned as we are."

She sends me the loosest, most beautiful smile. "I'm glad to be your uphill road, Sebastian Wilcox."

I press a soft kiss into the skin beneath her ear. "Thank you."

I can tell when I walk into her rooms, package shoved beneath my arm. I'd come to drop off the Porsche and pick up the Shelby before heading over to the garage for the day. I've just about finished with the mechanical repairs on the Mustang and need to get started with the interior. I've already set up a date with the best upholsterer I know, fully prepared to pay out of pocket. There's no avoiding it.

"Sebastian!" Mom says, rising to greet me. Her eyes are wide and clear, smile coming easy today. "I was hoping you'd drop by soon. Everything's so quiet around here without you kids kicking around."

"Feeling good today?" I ask, pleasantly surprised.

"Fantastic," she replies, patting my cheeks. "Here on business?"

"Just swapping cars. And I wanted to give you something." It'd been propped against my door this morning, no note.

Mom looks appropriately surprised when I hand it to her, turning it over in her hands. "Oh, I hope you didn't buy me anything. You know I have enough—"

"It didn't cost a single dime," I assure, dropping onto the sofa. "It was actually a gift from someone else."

She opens the paper with a curious expression that instantly softens when she sees the contents. "Sebastian, it's lovely! Is this...?"

"Abbadon," I explain. "Might finally get to catch her soon."

"My word, look at this!" She holds up the framed photograph. "It's such a good picture. So professional-looking!"

I was worried at first it might make her sad. Abby is a hungry, pregnant, scared stray. But the photo really is that good. It perfectly captures her warrior spirit, the strength and survival. "It was taken by an actual photographer," I explain.

"You know where this would go perfectly? The bedroom." Mom has a whole wall full of black and white photographs in there, which is exactly what I was thinking of when I saw it. "How are the other ferals doing? Has this one had her litter yet?"

"Not yet," I say. "But I suspect it'll be pretty soon. Sugar and I are checking on them every day."

"Sugar?"

I point to the frame. "The girl who took the photo. She feeds them too."

"And her name is Sugar?" Her smile is bright and delighted. "What a beautifully unique name."

"It fits the owner," I offer.

Mom tilts her head, studying me for a moment. I do my best to keep my expression noncommittal. I hate it, but no one in this house needs to know about Sugar. My conversation with Hamilton confirmed that last night.

"And how are you doing?" she asks as she sits on the loveseat in the sun. A stack of paperbacks and an ashtray sit on the end table. She reaches for her pack of cigarettes. "How are your classes? Your last report card looked good."

"I'm holding on. Dr. Ross is a hardass, but I should get an A." As much as I hate academics, I'm still good at it.

She frowns at the language but says nothing, tapping out a cigarette. "And lacrosse?"

"Still waiting for the all-clear." I lever myself to my feet, rocking back on my heels. "Tell Dad if he wants to donate to the athletic association, now would be a good time."

She shakes her head. "You don't need your father's money to get back on the team. Just take care of yourself."

"I will," I say, giving her a kiss on the cheek. "I need to run, though."

Her smile wavers, but doesn't disappear. "Okay, sweetheart, but you bring that girl around when you're ready."

"What girl?" I ask, blankly.

She shakes her head, more observant than I give her credit for, and opens her novel.

I head down the hall and duck into my room to grab a pair of boots out of my closet. As I step back out and shut the door I hear, "Hey there, little brother."

The hair on my neck stands on end at just the voice alone. The sight of him standing in my doorway makes my stomach want to turn inside out. "Heston. What are you doing here?"

"My mini-mester isn't over for a few more weeks. Just chilling here until the frat house opens back up." He gives me a weird grin and the resulting paranoia makes me wonder if he heard me talking about Sugar to mom. Luckily, he just says, "Anyway, I found something to entertain me while I'm in town."

"Oh yeah?" I mutter, grabbing my keys off the dresser. "What's that?"

"That sweet little thing you were flirting with at the car show." My stomach drops, mouth turning bone dry. He reaches into his pocket and pulls out his phone. "Sydney Rakestraw."

I frown, even though it feels like my heart just restarted. "Sydney? Dude, I told you. Jailbait. She's a junior."

He shrugs, uncaring. "Seventeen's legal. And hey, she doesn't fuck like she's a junior."

"Jesus," I mutter, tossing the clothes from last night in the laundry. "Sydney is a mess. I don't know if that's really who you want to get involved with. She's always causing a shit-ton of drama. She tried to stir shit up with Vandy and Reyn last fall."

He narrows his eyes. "What, you jealous I got to her first?"

I snort, biting back the response that I actually had been there first. I'm not proud of that drunken hookup, though. "Fuck who you want. I'm not jealous."

Because he's obsessed with the sense of competition that only exists in his twisted head, the expression on his face says he doesn't believe that at all.

"You should be," he says. "Check this out." He holds up his phone, and although it's pretty clear from the jump that I'm watching porn, it takes me a second to get past the slapping flesh to figure out what's going on. It's a girl on her stomach, face covered by her hair, neck turned sideways. A hand cinches around her neck as he stands over her, pounding into her aggressively. A queasy feeling builds in my stomach. I can't see his face any more than I can see hers, but there is one identifiable mark. A devil tattoo, on his bicep. My brother's tattoo. He grins down at me. "Damn, this girl lets me do whatever I want to her. You missed out on this one."

"Are you sure she's into that?" I ask, unable to look away for a reason I can't quite put my finger on. "It looks like she can't breathe."

"She's into whatever I'm into. That's what makes it so good." He turns off the video and slides his phone back in his pocket. His eyes narrow. "Are you judging me or something?"

Yes. Of course, I'm judging you, you complete fucking psycho.

But I don't say anything. What can I? If I defend Syd, he'll think I'm jealous and make it twice as bad for her. Acting aloof is probably the best thing I can do. He'll get bored soon enough and head back to school, where he can terrorize college girls. Shit. *That* doesn't make me feel any better.

I suck in a breath. "I think you probably should stop showing people a video of you choke-fucking a high school girl if you don't want to get slapped with a charge. Does she know you have that?"

He laughs. "I told you, she's a freak. She *asked* me to record it."

Honestly, it fits. Sydney films, and streams, ninety percent of her day. From brushing her teeth to her late-night ramblings and dance marathons, Sydney loves to document every little fucking thing. If anyone would want visual proof she'd had sex with my brother, it would be her.

"Whatever. As long as you're covering yourself," I say, heading to the door.

"One more thing."

I pause, feeling the annoyance and irritation build in my spine. "What?"

"There's a fight coming up, a big one up in Peachford. People are coming from all over to be in it."

I sigh and press a hand against the door jamb. "I can't. You know that."

"Can't or won't, doesn't cut it, baby bro. The winner's pot is going to be epic. You've been out of the game long enough that people are talking." From the pinched look on his face, it's obvious what he thinks of this. There's a reason he never wanted me crossing paths with the Devils back in his day. The thought of me being more popular—more wanted—always made him the mean-est. "They asked for you specifically."

"I don't need any money." I swallow, adding, "You're not my manager, Heston. Stop acting like it. I'm not fighting for you or anyone else. I'm done with that shit."

I step into the hallway, adrenaline and fear pumping in my veins. 'No' isn't something my brother is used to hearing, but it's time. If Sugar can let me touch her, every single day—if my mom can wake up some mornings with that sunny smile of hers—then I can shut Heston down.

I get to the stairs and as I take the first step, his voice rings out.

"I see you've got some new friends over there at Preston."

I turn slowly, keeping my face blank. "I don't know what you're talking about." Only now, I'm starting to realize that he's been fucking Sydney, the biggest loudmouth I know. She absolutely would feed him intel from inside the school.

Intel like his brother having a new girlfriend.

I'm expecting it so much that when he says, "I hear you're getting pretty tight with Vandy," it takes a suspended moment for it to really sink in.

I laugh.

And then I keep laughing.

"Fucking hell, Heston. If you want to go after Vandy, then it's your funeral. Emory and Reyn would absolutely smoke your ass." Of all the people I worry about, Vandy is near the end of that list. Sure, she's a sweet little thing with her own vulnerabilities. But she's also completely locked down.

Heston's face goes dark at this, eyes flashing angrily. "You don't want to fuck with me, Sebastian. You're going to be in that fight."

I volley back, "No, I'm not," and I know from the storm in his eyes that it's a mistake—something that's going to bite me in the ass. There's no escaping Heston's abuse. Not for me. Not for Sydney. But there's one person I'm determined to protect and I'll do everything I can to make sure that he never finds out Sugar exists.

22

"Shhh."

"*You* shhh."

"I'm trying to be quiet."

"What do you think *I'm* doing?" he asks, making as much noise as a bull in a china shop. After weeks of patience and ten bags of treats, Lucy and Abby have finally grown comfortable with us. At least, until Sebastian drops the metal can of food on the sidewalk, sending them all scurrying off. "It's fucking cold as balls out here. My fingers are frozen."

"Give it to me." I hold out my hand, and he drops the can in my palm. I push my nail underneath the tab and pull it open. The cats perk up and slowly stalk back over. I bend over and scoop out half the food into one of the containers on the ground, then place the rest in another.

Straightening, I don't even flinch when Sebastian wraps his arms around me from behind. It's not as easy as it was a couple days ago, when I was baked off the blunt at the bonfire, but it's also not as bad as it used to be, either. There's a moment of panic at being held, but as I'm coming to learn is best, I face it head-on instead of locking it away.

This time, it only takes a couple minutes for it to pass.

Sebastian pushes his fingers under my shirt, and I flinch for an entirely different reason. "Jesus Christ. Your hands *are* cold!"

"I need you to warm me up," he says, lips against my neck.

"At least your uniform has pants," I grumble. "If anyone needs warmed up, it's my skirt-wearing ass."

"At your service," he says, voice full of innuendo.

His fingers dip below the waistband of my skirt, stroking against the skin. I'm not sure how I can go from panic, to relief, to squirming with desire so quickly, but Sebastian seems to bring it out in me. Every time he's near me, touching me, the fire in my belly gets a little hotter, a little wilder. The idea of someone touching me like this used to repulse me, but now I find myself wishing for it—dreaming about it—all the damn time. It's becoming a huge distraction, though not an entirely unwelcome one. It's nice to look across the quad and see him standing with his friends, knowing the fingers he's gesturing with are mine, in a secret sort of way.

"Lunch will be over soon," I say, turning to graze my lips against his cheekbone. "But maybe after classes are over, we could... you know."

He turns his head to catch my gaze, blue eyes sparkling in the afternoon sun. "We could what?"

My face heats, but I hold his gaze. "Go back to your room. Hang out for a bit."

He holds my stare and I see the gears turning. It's been hard to find the time and privacy for what I want, between school and clubs and Sebastian spending so much time at that garage.

To my surprise, he lets out a long, annoyed groan. "You've gotta be fucking with me, girl. You finally want to fool around, and I have to go to that goddamn game?"

I grimace, looking away. "Oh, I forgot about that."

"Trust me, if it wasn't completely mandatory, I'd be all over that." He gives my hips a squeeze. "You should come to the game, too."

The whole school is pretty caught up in the basketball team making it to the playoffs. I've been bombarded with banners and school spirit all week. "Didn't you say you had to hang out with your lacrosse 'bros' or something?"

"Just for the first half. Coach is very into team camaraderie."

"Basketball is boring," I sigh, resigned to another night without Sebastian's hands on me. "I may just use the time to work in the lab. I need to get the last few pieces ready for the exhibit anyway."

"What exhibit?"

I shudder when his fingers move, wiggling enticingly lower on my stomach. "It's this thing Preston does every year. For the Arts Department?"

"You're in that?" His fingers still. "What am I talking about, of course you're in that. Your stuff is fucking awesome."

I roll my eyes, even though my face gets hot again. "It's just a lot of pressure because most of the kids here have like years' worth of critically approved pieces, so I've been playing catch-up."

What's most embarrassing to admit is that, more and more, it's starting to look like some of my best stuff revolves around Sebastian himself. Abby, the first car show, the shots taken of him at the mall. I'd even gotten Georgia to drive me out to that spot that overlooks the lake for a nice landscape shot, and I'm itching like fucking crazy to develop the photos I'd taken the night of the bonfire. Part of it is that Bass actually gets me off this damn campus, but I know that's not all of it. Every picture of him—every picture taken of something in connection to him—comes out heavy and dark and full of something that almost hurts to inspect too closely.

"Well, who said you needed to come watch the game?" He licks under my ear. "I'm thinking we can make out under the bleachers."

I watch the cats sniffing at the food, squirming as his fingers hit a ticklish spot. "Getting fingerbanged in a sweaty gym beneath five hundred peoples' asses is not the prize you think it is, Wilcox."

He laughs. "You tell me when you're ready to get banged a different way and I'm all in."

Bass and I haven't had sex yet, but with things building the way they are right now, it feels inevitable. He makes no effort to hide how much he wants it. He doesn't ask quite as much as he used to, but he doesn't need to. I can see it in his eyes when we kiss, in the impatient buck of his hips when we're pressed close together, his cock always hard and insistent.

I've grown accustomed to some part of his body always being on me; his mouth, his hands, the press of his hard erection into my thigh. He's like a vampire, but instead of blood, he feeds on touch. Also like a mythical creature, he's got me under his thrall, and it takes every ounce of energy to not just spread my legs and tell him to *come on, already*. The truth is that if he got me under the bleachers, I probably would let him do whatever he wanted to.

"You go to the game," I decide, because when I finally get to have Sebastian, it'll be somewhere quiet and private where I can really enjoy him. "I'll see you later."

He sighs long-sufferingly. "If you change your mind, you know where I'll be. Honestly, it's probably for the best. I *am* supposed to hang out with the lacrosse team. No chicks allowed." He releases me and I clean up the trash from feeding the kittens, while he dumps the water container then refills it from a bottle in his bag. He taps at the bowl. "I'm a little worried it may freeze overnight."

"We can check on it, if it does." This cold snap is supposed to last through the next week—with even the possibility of some snow. The memorial for my father is next week, so freezing temperatures and snow sound about right. The day he was buried, it rained so hard that the dirt from the grave turned into a river of red mud. Unfortunately, that set a precedent. There's no way my mother will let us out of it for a little snow. "We need to keep an eye on Abby, too. She needs to be warm when it's time to deliver."

We've talked this over a few times, trying to figure out a way to sneak the cats into the dorms. Georgia is allergic, so my room's out. Bass has his suite, but he's worried about getting them up four flights of stairs without one of them freaking out and getting loose. Thankfully, there's still some time to come up with a plan.

Speaking of plans...

"Oh," I say, as we walk back toward the main part of campus. "And can you ask Merle if he thinks my car will be ready by this weekend?"

Sebastian shoots me a wary glance. "Why? You need a ride somewhere? I can drive you."

"I do have an appointment," I admit, shaking my head at his offer, "but it's just been a while since I left it with him. Even if he actually wants to work on the car, it has to be a nuisance at this point."

Sebastian waves this off. "Are you serious? He's into it, not to mention totally anal about getting everything just right."

"I don't want to take advantage of his generosity."

A flicker of tightness crosses Bass's face but quickly vanishes. "You're not taking advantage. Trust me, Merle doesn't do anything he doesn't one-hundred-percent want to do. I've seen this guy turn down harder cases than you. I'm sure it'll be finished soon."

I purse my lips, unconvinced. "If you really think so."

"I don't think, Sugar. I know." He walks me right up to the front steps of Hayden, bouncing on his toes against the cold of the wind. "So, if you're not coming to the game, maybe we can hang out after?"

I hum in thought. "If I get everything finished in the lab, *maybe* we can hang out." It'll be too late to risk much, but at this point, I'm willing to take anything.

He dips down to kiss me, tongue sweeping between my lips, thumbs pressing into my hips. I link my arms around his neck and slowly lose myself in him until someone loudly clears their throat.

"Gross, get a room." We pull apart and see Georgia down at the bottom of the steps, smirking at us. "Not *our* room, mind you. I need to get ready for the game."

Bass and I say goodbye for real and I head up to the dorm room with Georgia. I sit on the edge of my bed while she sorts through her black and red spirit wear for the game. The sight of it makes my head ache—or maybe it's just all the tension I'm carrying.

She glances over at my long sigh. "Are you okay?"

"Yeah. Just overwhelmed, I guess."

"With Bass?"

"No." I pick at a sticker on my phone case. "I've got that show-case in a couple weeks, plus I need to go home for this family thing next week and I'm totally fucking dreading it."

"Oh, I can relate to that. My cousin is getting married this summer and we have this huge shower coming up. It's a couple's shower, which means I should bring a date. My mom is already obsessing over the fact that I don't have a boyfriend, always going on about how I need to try harder. My cousin is super perfect and she's marrying a doctor, so I figure it's going to be one huge 'dump on Georgia' party. It's the last fucking thing I want to do."

Although that does sound terrible, it doesn't quite compare to having to see my abusive stepfather to celebrate my father's death.

"Are you taking Bass home with you?" she asks, while pulling a white tank top over her black bra.

I wince. "Yeah, that's part of the problem. I haven't told him about it. I'm not sure how he and my family would get along."

"Because he's super rich and they're," she gives me an apologetic look, "not?"

"That's a part of it. It's just..." I wedge my nail under the sticker edge. "See, my mom's husband and I don't really get along." Understatement of the fucking century. "And you know how Bass can be, so..."

But her expression turns comprehending. "Overprotective? Mouthy and hot-tempered? Voted most likely to cause a massive scene by JD Power and whoever?"

"Yes, those things." I nod, falling back on my bed. "And truthfully? My stepfather isn't much better. I can see it going badly. I just don't want him to think I'm ashamed of him or something. This is definitely a case of *them* being the problem, not Bass."

Georgia pulls on a pair of skin-tight, black leggings. "Bass has changed since you got here. Believe it or not, he seems to have calmed down, at least a little. The irritation and anger flare-ups seem to happen less, and I haven't heard anything about him fighting lately—officially or unofficially. Mostly he just seems really into you. Who knew this whole time he just needed a fine piece of ass to focus all his energy on?" Sending me a grin, she pushes her feet into her shoes. "Just talk to him. Bass knows more about fucked-up families than he may have told you. Now that I think about it, if you want to loan him to me for the shower, I'll take him."

I don't expect the flicker of jealousy to rise in my chest, but it does—hot and furious. "Georgia, I like you a lot, but so help me—"

"Kidding, I was kidding!" she adds quickly, heading toward the door. "Sure you can't come to the game tonight? I hear it's going to be pretty epic."

"I'll try to swing by after I get some work done."

"Don't wait too long," she says, then steps into the hallway and closes the door. "I'm telling you, there are some things you don't want to miss at Preston. This game is one of them."

~

I try my hardest to focus on my work, sorting through the photos I plan on using in the exhibit. My mind is on other things— home, my mom, my dad, Doug. Carrying Sebastian over to that world, *my* world, hadn't really crossed my mind, but with our relationship intensifying, I don't know how I can keep it from happening forever. My gaze keeps going back to the photo Gwen mentioned at dinner; the one of the cemetery and my father's grave. I hate the idea of going to celebrate my father while Doug is there. He pretends to be respectful—my dad was a hero, after all—but I know he's jealous that my mom still honors him every year. He dotes on her all day and I get the brunt of his attitude. That's what finally makes me realize that I not only want Sebastian to go with me, I think I need him to.

Thinking about all this dries up my creative mood, and I put away the equipment. If Georgia is right, I shouldn't be down in the lab during a major social event. I lucked out with this scholarship and I should take advantage of every opportunity. I'm part of Preston Prep now, stupid basketball games included.

I lock up the lab and head across campus to the gym. I show my ID to the woman at the entrance and she waves me in. Inside is a clash of color; red and black against the cool silver of the opposing team. From the chatter around school, the Devils are poised to win the entire championship with this game against Sparrowood Academy. Even up in the Briar Cliffs, the rivalry between these two elite schools is well known. I doubt the Academy will go down without a fight.

When I enter the rowdy gym, the clock is counting down to halftime. I search the stands for a familiar face, but it's all a blur of red and black painted faces and chests, devil iconography, and electrified energy. The players run down the court, shoes squeaking on the sparkling hardwood. A ball flies past my face and I yelp before darting up the nearest bleacher. I take the first empty seat that I find, heart pounding from the close call, and take a deep breath.

From up in the bleachers I have a better view of the gym. The cheerleaders are along the end, cheering and shaking their shiny pom poms. Afton is in the middle, more super model than cheerleader. Down the row I see Aubrey, and then Sydney and Fiona. I recognize Elana with the dance team, their lithe bodies in motion with the music being played by the marching band. There's a Devil mascot, some poor shirtless student, painted red with a head covering mask, roaming up and down the sidelines, working the crowd into a frenzy. He waves a flag adorned with a grinning Devils face. In the chaos, I keep an eye out for familiar blond hair, but even though I see a few of the other lacrosse boys, I can't find Bass in the crowd. I pull out my phone and text him, hoping that he'll see my message and come find me. If not, I make a plan to hide out here until things clear out at halftime and make my escape.

Preston Prep is up by four when the buzzer blares through the gym and the players jog off the court. I'm about to make a break for it when the game announcer's deep voice comes over the speakers: *Don't leave your seats now! One lucky winner will get a chance to play for a big cash prize! But, first, let's give it up for the Dancing Divas!*

A deep tempo fills the gym, techno music bouncing off the walls, and the cheer and dance squads rush to center court, falling into line. I drop back down, feeling like I should watch Afton and the other girls I've become friendly with. Some guy near the court shouts, "Afton! I love you!" as they stand in position. She doesn't flinch at the attention, but I notice her eyes dart down the court. I follow her gaze, and see the Devil mascot's return, flag raised in the air. The girls on the floor begin their routine, while the Devil strides across the court. That's when I notice he's not alone. Seven other masked devils swarm the gym floor. None of them are shirtless, some are clearly girls. When the crowd sees them, the energy in the room amplifies. The guy next to me says, "Fuck, you see that?" to the person next to him.

"What?" his friend asks, searching the court.

"The main Devil's flag. It's not the Preston Prep logo. It's the Devil logo, like from homecoming."

I look at the flag and realize it doesn't have the smirking devil on the front anymore. It's a circle with a pitchfork in the middle. I've seen that symbol before. Once on Georgia's back, and of course, on Sebastian's chest.

Leaning over, I say, "What does that mean? It's a Devils logo?"

He gives me a weird look but nods at the court. "Secret Society bullshit. I don't know if it's real or just a bunch of kids trying to claim it, but I think it's hilarious."

Just then, the lights go down. *Way* down. In their place is a hot, red glow, the noises of the crowd swelling in excitement. For a moment, I wonder if I've fallen asleep in the photo lab and this is all just a very weird dream.

The seven Devils position themselves on the floor beneath the student section. Each has a bundle in their hands. Someone screams, "T-shirts! Up here! I want one!" Because no one can resist a shitty, free T-shirt, not even rich kids with unlimited access, the crowd gets even more worked up. All of this goes on while the squads finish their routine. The main, shirtless Devil hands the flag to one of the other masked Devils and picks up a cordless microphone. He jogs to the center of the court, passing cheerleaders and dance members with confused, wary expressions on their faces. He comes to a stop near Afton. I don't know the girl well but the expression on her face isn't one of confusion. If anything, she looks amused, and definitely not surprised. There's something in the Devil's swagger, the confident walk that sends a tingle up my spine. It only intensifies when he lifts the microphone to his mouth and shouts, "Hail to the Devils!"

"Hail to the Devils," the cheerleaders, dance team, and half the crowd repeats on cue. I look around, glaring at the look my neighbor gives me. Sorry that I'm new here and didn't get the memo on crazy chants, asshole.

"Hail to the Devils!" he shouts again. The microphone has a modulator, making the voice unidentifiable. Once again, the crowd cries back. "We've come to give one lucky student a gift from the underworld. Who wants a shot?" Once again, the crowd roars in approval. The Devil paces back and forth, peering up the bleachers to say, "If you get a shirt, hold onto it until it's time to reveal them all at once!" The crowd rumbles with excitement and the masked devils start running up and down the bleachers, tossing shirts to people. The main devil strides off the court, a bundle tucked under his own arm. My eyes are glued to him, and even though he's wearing a mask, I get the strong feeling he's aware of me. The guy next to me stands, waving his arms to get picked. "Over here! Hail to the Devils! Over here!"

I sink down into my seat, hoping no one thinks we're together, and keep an eye on the main mascot as he climbs the bleachers, two steps at a time. A moment later, he stops directly at my row. I stare at his red, painted abs.

"Yesssss!" my neighbor shouts, pumping his fist in the air, then leans across me to grab the shirt. "Hand it over."

"Not you, dumbass," the Devil says, blocking him with a solid thrust of his hand. "Her."

"Me?" I say, completely confused.

"Her?" the guy says incredulously, then tosses his hands in the air. "Damn it, I never win anything." He slumps in his seat, defeated.

Behind the mask, dark blue eyes bore into mine. I swallow. "Um, can I pass?"

"No." He shoves the shirt in my hand and vanishes back into the crowd and down the steps.

A moment later, the Devil joins the others back on the court and Afton hands him the microphone. He puts it to his mouth and shouts, "Can we get a drumroll?" The drum section, led by Ben, obliges the Devil's demand and a loud drumroll reverberates through the high-ceilinged room. The cheerleaders shake their pom poms and the dance team wiggles their spirit fingers. The whole room is abuzz, transfixed on the Devil below. "Everyone stand up and unroll your shirts!"

The guy next to me nudges me with his elbow. "Well?" he demands, looking way too excited. "Open it, open it!"

I narrow my eyes at him but stand, pulling at the ribbon holding the shirt in a tight roll. The T-shirt unfurls and reveals a smirking devil on the front. I hold it up, like everyone else forced to participate in this charade, showing it to the gym. I feel a hand on my elbow and glance down, yanking my arm away.

"Look at the back," the guy says, nodding at the shirt in my hands.

I hold it up and see that, on the back, it says in bold font, *"You've been marked by the Devils."*

"She's got it!" the guy screams, jumping up next to me. "Sugar Voss has been marked by the Devils!" He sounds as excited as if *he* were the one to get it.

I stare at the guy, wondering how he knows my name, but then realize I'm the new girl. Everyone probably knows my name. It doesn't matter. The whole place goes a little crazy, and the next thing I know, I'm walking down to the center court, feeling annoyed and weirdly suspicious about the whole thing.

Afton meets me in the middle and hands me an envelope. "Congratulations, Sugar," she says, giving me a wink. Before I can say anything, the buzzer blares, announcing the start of the second half, and I'm shuffled off the court with everyone else. I try to locate the main Devil, but the crowd is too thick and the band's too loud, and then Georgia's smiling face appears.

"Oh my god! You won!" she cheers, holding her hand up for a

high-five. I listlessly slap it. She drags me out to the lobby, and I hear the referee whistle and the game starting back up.

"I guess?" I say, feeling overwhelmed. "Do you know who that was in the mascot suit?"

Georgia's smile stiffens, but she just says, "I think Johnny Weider is the mascot, right?" I don't know who Johnny Weider is, but the guy in the mask definitely had familiar blue eyes and abs. "Did you open your prize?"

I look down at the envelope in my hand. I hadn't. I figure it's probably a gift certificate to The Nerd or school bookstore. At least that'd be the kind of thing they'd give away at Briar Cliffs, or—who am I kidding. Nothing is given away for free in the Briar Cliffs. I open the flap and peer inside. It's a check. For a thousand dollars.

I look back up at Georgia, who still has that wide grin on her face. "Holy shit, girl! That's amazing. You *are* a lucky devil!"

I stare at the check. Sugar Voss is a lot of things, but lucky isn't one of them. That game was rigged and I'm pretty sure I know exactly who decided to give me the mark; the Devil himself, Sebastian Wilcox.

23

"Tell anyone and I'll hunt you down," I say to Johnny Weider, as I shove the mask in his lap. I take a moment to really assess the situation, and yeah. It looks pretty bad. He has a black hood over his head and his wrists are zip-tied. But it's not like we roughed him up or anything.

"Tell them what?" he asks, voice wobbly under the single equipment room's lamp. "I have no fucking idea what's going on, you psychos!"

Carlton and I grin at one another. We'd basically kidnapped Johnny and held him hostage during the prank so I could commandeer his mascot outfit. Everyone else was able to do a quick change, but I have to hit the locker room shower and clean off the layers of thick red paint. And I'd thought my tattoos would get me out of anonymous showboating. I'd overlooked the possibility of body paint. Emory, who had been the second choice, conveniently remembered.

If everything is going according to plan, Afton, Elana, and Aubrey are keeping up the façade of having no idea what just happened, Caroline is wiping all evidence from the video surveillance, the other guys are back in the lair, hiding the evidence, and Georgia is handling Sugar, who is probably already trying to return the prize.

I clean up quickly, watching the paint run down the drain like a bloody massacre. There's no time to fuck around, I have to get out of here before the final buzzer. Once I'm clean, I hop out, get hastily dressed, and push out the side door to head across campus to the tower.

"Leaving early?"

I jerk to a stop at the sound of a voice and turn. Sydney Rakestraw leans against the stadium wall, the same one Hamilton and Gwen spent a month of detention painting last year before my brother and the old Devils got themselves disbanded for vandalism. Her knee is bent with her foot propped up behind her, vape pen in her mouth. Classic Sydney, always trying so hard. A cloud of smoke cloaks her face followed by the cloying scent of cotton candy. The last thing I want to do is stop and talk to her, but I can't help thinking about her in the video Heston showed me.

"Hey, Syd," I say, coming to a slow stop. "Why aren't you inside?"

A flicker of annoyance crosses her face, but she lifts her chin defiantly. "I'm waiting for someone."

"Heston?" I guess. When she doesn't deny it, I add, "I heard you were seeing him."

"From who? Him?" she asks, a little too eagerly. She pushes off the wall. "Did he mention me?"

If she only knew. It's awkward coming face to face with her after seeing the video, having seen that pinched, panicked look on her face as my brother brutally fucked her. She's an annoying shit-stirrer, but I mostly just feel bad for her. "Syd," I start, running a hand down my face. This is not a conversation I want to have. "You know my brother is bad news, right?"

She laughs and takes a drag from her vape pen. "I know he's sexy and popular."

"He's also an abusive asshole."

Her jaw clenches, but she blinks and recovers. "You had your chance to have an opinion on who I date. I don't really give a shit about what you think now." She barks out a mean laugh. "And you're one to talk. You and Little Miss Hot Mess are quite the couple. You're both freaks. You think you're so much better than your brother? Don't think I don't know what you did to her, and here the two of you are, boning anyway."

Hot, instant anger rolls up my spine. "I'm nothing like Heston," I grind out, fists clenching around the strap of my bag. "What happened with Sugar was an accident. When I'm with a girl, I treat her right. Heston doesn't know the first fucking thing about it."

She blows a long plume of smoke from her lips, pursed, smile full of bitterness. "Oh, I know exactly how you treat a girl."

I look at the girl in front of me, trying so hard to be unaffected by everything mean and harsh and cold that she's turning into it herself. "Sydney," I say, willing her to believe the sincerity of my words, "I never wanted to hurt you. I just wasn't feeling it. I'm sorry if I didn't handle it right." For a moment, that aloof exterior of hers cracks, eyes going round and sad. I almost feel bad about taking advantage of it. "Heston wants to hurt. It's what he likes. You understand that, don't you? Maybe you're into that, maybe you aren't. You're right, it isn't really any of my business." I give her a long, meaningful look. "Just like what happens here at school—whoever I might be seeing at the moment—isn't any of his. Know what I mean?"

Instantly, any trace of vulnerability in her expression slams shut. "So that's what this is really about."

Fuck. Subtle has never been my strong suit. "You told him about me being friends with Vandy."

Her eyes spark in anger. "Vandy is shit, and you know what? I'm sick of all you fawning all over her like she's the second coming. She's not so special. You'll figure that out when she stabs you in the back, just like she did to me."

Her words are cutting and make me want to fight back, because Sydney Rakestraw is the last person to bring someone's sense of loyalty into question. But I don't bother, because I'm realizing now that she didn't tell Heston about our friendship because she was pissed at me. It was because she's pissed at Vandy.

She scoffs. "I don't give a shit who you're boning, Bass. Fuck a light socket for all I care. I'm on to bigger and better things. Emphasis on *bigger*."

Telling her about the video is on the tip of my tongue, but I swallow it back. What if it was consensual and she's into that kind of thing? It's not impossible. Syd's always been a little wild, but that video…there's something about it that just bothers the shit out of me, even if it was consensual. I waver, but know that she's right. Who am I to judge?

"Good luck," I tell her. "Go inside and get warm. If he shows up, he can find you in there."

She rolls her eyes. "Whatever, Sebastian."

Her nose is red from the cold and there's no doubt she's freezing her ass off, but I walk off anyway. I cut across campus and back over to the tower. Emory is just inside the entrance.

"Shit, did anyone see you come down here?" he asks, looking over my shoulder. It's cold as a snowman's dick, so I push past him and jog down the staircase to the Devils lair.

"Nah, I doubled back. But I think the Admin is still in the gym trying to figure out what the fuck just happened." I don't mention Sydney, because what is there to say? I enter the room and see that other guys are already down here in the process of changing. None of them went all out with the body paint like I did.

Jesus. Altercations with Sydney aside, what a fucking rush.

Part of it was that I'd finally—*fucking finally*—gotten the all-clear from my doctor earlier that day. No more worries about being careful all the time. No having to coddle myself. No sitting on the sidelines anymore, restless and agitated.

But a bigger part was just pulling something off with my boys. With my girls. It's been too long.

"Good job, man," Carlton says, changing shirts. He'd been one of the other masked devils and the hair around his temples is still damp with sweat. "I hope someone gets a video of the Headmaster's expression when he realizes his halftime show was hijacked."

Emory walks into the lair and shuts the door behind him. He approaches me, fist out. I bump mine against his and he grins. "Dude, you should've been the mascot all year. You killed it!"

I scoff. "That's a pussy position. I'd rather be on the field than on the sidelines."

"How do you think Sugar took being the winner?" Tyson asks. "She looked a little stunned."

"Oh, she's going to be pissed. She's probably already trying to return it," I reply. "Too bad that money came out of our funds and not the school's. There's no one to return it to."

"Have you said anything to her about it?" Reyn asks, buttoning his shirt. "You know, the Devils."

I give him a stony look. "I'm not a squealer. You know that."

"What if she recognized you?" Emory asks, eyebrow arched. "You were right in front of her—half naked. You think she didn't recognize your body? She would, right?"

It's a loaded question, and I don't know why Em doesn't just come out and ask if Sugar and I have had sex yet. He probably doesn't want to be on the other side of my temper if it doesn't land right.

"If she recognized me, I'll deal with it."

The others leave first and I change quickly, wanting to go up and find her. To be honest, I wasn't even expecting her to come to the game. If that happened, we wouldn't have given away the big prize at all. Everyone agreed to give it to Sugar. None of the other assholes around here deserve or need it. I know the way she'd see it, though—as charity.

My phone buzzes and I pick it up.

Sugar: Leaving the gym. Where are you?

I type out my response: *Wait there. I'll be there in a minute.*

Pulling on my jacket, I head up the stairs, locking the door behind me. I shove the key in my pocket and step outside the tower. Walking fast, I turn around the curve of the building toward the gym, but stop when I see a shadowy figure a few feet away, with their arms crossed over their chest.

"Jesus Christ," I mutter, clutching my hand over my heart.

Sugar steps into the light, revealing her narrowed eyes and taut jaw. "I know you're the one who gave me that money."

I observe her for a moment, the camera hanging around her neck. She doesn't seem to go anywhere without it nowadays. She's also looking at me like she's figured everything out. "I don't know what you're talking about."

"Cut the shit, Wilcox." Ouch. *Wilcox.* "That was you, in the Devil mask. You're the one who gave me that shirt."

"Babe," I say, following a deep exhale, "Johnny Weider is the mascot. He's out there right now."

She doesn't look even remotely convinced. "One? Don't ever call me 'babe'. Two, I've seen your abs, and now I've seen Johnny Weider's. Not even in the same fucking ballpark. That was secret society stuff. You're one of them, aren't you?"

A few students walk toward us and I wait for them to pass. I want to tell her. For the first time in my life, I want to tell someone everything. I can't, though. I took an oath.

But earning Sugar's trust is important.

With my hands in my pockets, I rock back on my heels. "What if I was? Would it matter?"

Her face smooths out from the scowl, even if she still looks frustrated. "I'd be mad that you rigged that contest to give it to me."

"But not about me being in the group?"

"I don't care about some dumb rich kid club," she insists, waving the envelope around. "That's not the point. We've been over this, Bass. The point is that you shouldn't use your money—or power—to give me things."

I take a step closer. "I hate to tell you, Sugar, but that's the point of power. You wield it however you want. But let me make one thing clear. *If* I was a Devil, I wouldn't mark you with a t-shirt. I'd want to mark you for real, somewhere that everyone could see." I reach out and run my thumb along her jaw, eying the perfect spot. "I'd want everyone to know you were mine."

Her eyes dart to my mouth, then back up. Her throat bobs with a swallow. "People know we're dating. It's not a secret."

"Being Devil-marked is different."

"How?"

Fuck, but it's so hard to explain. To someone on the outside, the tradition must seem dumb as hell, but to us, it's a big deal. Tyson can never mark his girl. Not until he comes clean about everything, and he probably never will. It's not just about giving someone a hickey. It's about the way Reyn and Vandy, or Emory and Aubrey, are completely connected. It's about letting someone in—all the way in—because the risk is too big to waste on some minor fling. The Devils are more than some silly high school secret society. For most of us, we're more family than our own flesh and blood.

"Do you really want to know?" I ask, weirdly nervous about her answer.

"Will it hurt?"

"Not if I'm doing it right."

I expect her to tell me to fuck off, presumably after she rips up the check, but she doesn't. She just looks up at me with those big hazel eyes and says, "If you were a Devil, and if I'm really your girl, it only seems right for you to treat me like it."

Just hearing her say it sends a rush of heat through my body. I slide my fingers between hers and look both ways to make sure we're alone. Part of being a Devil is being sneaky. Sure, the whole world can see the mark, but they don't need to know where and when I'm giving it to her.

I open the tower door and pull her inside, shutting it quickly behind me. It's cold and I keep her close as we walk up the stairs, as much for warmth as just to be near her. I turn on the flashlight on my phone, showing the way up the old stone stairs.

"This is where the magic happens?" she asks, eyes dubiously taking in the space. I know what she's thinking. It's not so special. For all its reputation, it's still just an old, musty, cold tower.

"This is it." I wrap my arms around her and nod up to the beam. "If we go through with this, I'm supposed to add another mark under my name."

"Another?" her eyebrow raises. "How many marks are there?"

"None that matter," I tell her, nosing into the warmth of her neck. "There are different ways to mark someone. It can be the kind you can't see, like sex, or it can be the kind you can see."

"Like what?"

I lick and kiss down her neck. "Hamilton Bates always marked Gwen with a hickey under the ear. Sparked a shit-ton of rumors."

Her voice is reedy, shaking. "That seems antiquated."

"You're at Preston. It's never been a bastion of progressiveness." I lift up her hair and kiss the top of her shoulder. "I heard that Reyn wanted Vandy to get that tattoo on her inner thigh. Just for him."

"What about you?" she asks, pressing her chest against mine. "How would you show the rest of the school that I'm yours?"

"Well," I drop my mouth to the smooth skin in the dip in her collarbone, lathing the spot with my tongue. "I'd probably buy her shit, like a new laptop, or stuff for her car, or... you know, something super sexy like cat treats."

She gives a silent laugh. "That does sound like you."

I open my mouth against her, sucking gently at first, getting her used to the coming pressure. She gasps when I really clamp down, pulling the skin in my mouth. Her hands fist in my shirt and I can't even handle the sound she makes as I suck in slow, hard bursts—something airy and hungry. I pull back, blowing over the wet skin, and she shivers. Her hips push against mine and my dick twitches in response.

"There," I say, running my finger over the hollow. "All done."

She looks overhead at the beam, eyelids heavy. "That'll get you another slash?"

"Yeah," I grin, unable to tear my eyes away from the bruise. "I'd go for another one if it wasn't so damn cold out here." I kiss the mark, then her jaw, all the way up to her mouth. Unable to help myself, I guide my hand up her side, running my thumb over the swell of her breast. Her nipple is peaked, hard from either my touch or the cold. I've been thinking about them ever since the bonfire, the way she let me hold them in my hands, play with them, get to really know the weight and softness.

I groan into the kiss, cock aching, and I know I'm kissing her too hard—too much, too fast—but I can't help it, tangling a hand in her hair, breathing sharp, quick clouds into the air around us with every pant. "You taste so fucking good."

"Yeah," she replies, sucking on my tongue with just as much fervor, "you taste good, too."

It may be cold, but I'm burning with the way I feel right now, buzzed and barely restrained, electric with the way her body feels against me. I could do what I want to Sugar up on this staircase and earn another mark, but that's not what it's about or what I want. I want her splayed underneath me. I want to take my time. I want to taste every part of her body. I want to be inside her, around her, against her.

I pull back, cupping her warm cheeks in my hand. "You really want to know what it's like to be with a Devil?" I ask, rules and oaths and obligation lost in a haze of lust.

Her eyes ping back and forth between mine, lips red when a soft, "Yes," passes between them.

"Do you trust me?"

She blinks and my heart pounds, more scared of her answer than anything else.

"I do."

24

"Turn around," he says, the cold making his breath fog.

I shiver but turn, facing down the curved staircase. He asked me if I trust him, and I do.

I'd tucked the T-shirt I won at the game into my jacket pocket and he pulls it out. A moment later, he's lowering it over the top of my head, covering my eyes. I reach up and stop his hand. "What are you doing?"

"Blindfolding you."

I pause at this, but ultimately take a deep breath and nod. *Trust.*

I wasn't even entirely serious about him being a Devil. Mostly, I figured he'd sweet-talked the pep club into letting him hand out the prize. It's a big stage, lots of attention and opportunity for bragging rights. But when he brought me up to the staircase, and I saw the initials and the gouged markings on the beam, I'm realizing just how right I'd been. I have questions, too many to put into words at the exact moment, but then he started kissing me, sucking on my neck, and whatever I wanted to know slipped away in a haze of want.

It's this new thing, this *hunger*. I've been impatient with it all night, even when I was pissed at him for trying to, once again, give me money. Even when he brought me up to this nasty tower to mark me, like I'm something to be owned, I still burned with it, because it's true.

Sebastian does own a part of me.

He folds the cloth over itself three times, making visibility impossible. It's all hilariously dramatic, but when his warm hand closes over mine and he slowly leads me down the staircase, I realize that whatever is going on right now is more than just theatrics. I could see it in his eyes earlier, when he asked me up here. This means something to him—something significant. Sebastian has been working hard to prove to me that I can trust him. Perhaps this is just another step, a bigger one than all the ones before it.

We reach the landing at the bottom of the stairs and I hear the creak of the tower door just before feeling the cold bite of wind on my cheeks.

Grand gestures aside, I still roll my eyes behind the blindfold. "Is this really necessary?"

His thumb brushes over my hand. "It's a *secret* society, Sugar. I took an oath. There were candles and chanting and scary mother-fuckers in masks, the whole nine yards."

I stop abruptly, voice a rushed whisper. "Wait! I don't want you to do something that might get you in trouble. Whatever this is that you're involved in, it's important. I don't want to screw that up."

His breath warms my ear. "Do you know how they pick the Devils?"

My forehead scrunches in confusion. "No?"

"There's something special about us," he admits. "I'd like to say it's because we're the smartest, strongest, and brightest at Preston Prep, but that'd be bullshit, honestly." He continues walking, leading me carefully over the soft ground. I wonder if anyone is out here to see us. If they are, he doesn't seem concerned. "It's because we're brave. Ruthless. Devious. We have our own secrets and sins. All of us have baggage and a hunger for something bigger and better. Joining the Devils was the best thing that happened to me, because I found my people." He spins me around. I now feel the heat of his breath on my lips. "That is, until I met you."

He guides me across the grass until he stops, and I hear a door creak again, similar to the last one. The temperature doesn't change once we're inside, but I hear the scrape of metal against metal, then the spring of a lock. Once again, we head down a narrow staircase.

I wrinkle my nose. "It smells like my grandmother's basement. Are you taking me to an underground murder room or something?"

He laughs, voice smooth and dark in my ear. "Or something."

Trust, I keep chanting. *Trust, trust, trust.*

I hear the sound of a heavy door opening and he guides me over a threshold. This room is warmer, less musty. "Keep that blindfold on for one more second, okay?"

"Okay."

Butterflies fill my stomach as I hear him moving around the room. My senses are heightened, and I detect the sound of a match being struck, the scent of sulfur following close behind. I wrap my arms around my body, feeling self-conscious, like maybe his eyes are on me right now, watching. Anything could be going on here. Maybe we aren't even alone. Maybe this is part of an elaborate prank. To be fair, Bass had caught me up in a prank once already tonight.

"All done," he says, suddenly in front of me. I feel his fingers brush my cheeks, and he pushes up the shirt. The first thing I see is his handsome face and brilliant blue eyes, but I look past him, into the room. It's small and cramped. Candles flicker around the space, giving it a shadowy glow. The ceilings are low, and the back wall is covered with various Preston memorabilia. Some of it looks pretty old. I can't decide if the ambiance is romantic or eerie, until he takes my face in his hands and kisses me.

Okay, then.

Definitely romantic.

"Are you going to get in trouble for bringing me down here? I mean, we could have gone back to your room."

He shrugs, pressing a slow, sucking peck to the corner of my lips. "What kind of Devil would I be if I didn't break a few rules?" His fingers move to unzip my jacket, the sound loud in the quiet room. I don't hesitate to push his off his shoulders, watching as his arms shake it off. "My room's too far away, anyway." A kiss to my jaw. "Too many people." A kiss to my lips. "Want to concentrate."

His hands return to me instantly, growing more insistent and greedier than usual, and I'm grateful for it. I always feel him holding back, being careful, even though I can sense the whirlwind happening beneath the surface. It's the same focused chaos I feel for him, like I need to grab hold of whatever I can, keep him close.

Now, he deepens the kiss, a hand coming down to palm my backside as the other threads into my hair, pulling me closer. He swallows my surprised moan, taking a hard handful of my ass and grinding into my hip.

"Too rough?" he gruffly asks, and I remember that conversation I had with Georgia, nervous over him being rough, too selfish and physical and mean. I shake my head, wondering how I could have ever been afraid of this. Of his hands being too needy, too determined. Of being something he wants badly enough that he *is* being a bit rough.

There's nothing scary about it.

His arm slides behind my back and he lifts me, carrying me across the room to a worn leather couch in the corner. Anticipation blooms in my stomach, a mixture of worry over how far he wants to go, and the deep, building understanding of how far I'm willing to let him take it.

Sebastian wants sex and has never been shy about it. I can't even count how many times he's asked, alluded, insinuated. There's a part of me that knows I'd say yes if he asked right now, but that same part also knows how terrified I'd feel. He wants sex. He wants to *fuck* me. He wants it so bad that he even has the good grace to not seem annoyingly impatient about me shutting him down all the time.

But maybe that's the end of the line.

Maybe, once he finally gets it, the shine will wear off. Maybe then he'll see me for what I am. Mediocre, at best. A lost, angry girl with more issues than National Geographic. A burden, a hassle. Nothing really special. Something already conquered. Unexciting, unimpressive.

Like this, when he hasn't had it yet, he just looks captivated. He pushes me down on the couch, laying me back on the cool, slick surface. Somehow, he manages to get my shirt off and kick his shoes to the floor before climbing between my legs. Despite the hungry kisses and greedy touches, this isn't the wild, impulsive Sebastian I've come to know. This one is calm and collected—determined—eyes drinking me in like a prize, something to be slowly savored.

He grazes his fingertips over my lace-covered breast. "Did you know your tits are absolutely perfect?" he asks, palming them. "Like, they fit absolutely perfectly in my hands. Not too big, not too little." I don't reply beyond a hitch of breath as I arch into his hands. I can't, because it feels so good.

I lean my head back against the padded arm of the couch, over-whelmed by his touch. He presses his face in my cleavage, burying himself in my flesh, then yanks at the cup of my bra, tugging it down so my breast spills out. He squeezes them together, and I feel the heat of his mouth—his tongue—as it licks between them and then latches around a nipple, sucking and tonguing the peak.

Needing to feel him, I push resolutely against the hem of his shirt, seeking the heat of his skin. He rears back and reaches behind his neck, yanking his shirt over his head.

Fucking hell.

Talk about perfection.

Bass's upper body looks carved from stone, a conglomeration of fine genetics and hard work. I run my hand up his abdomen, over his chest, and then lurch up to kiss the Devil symbol inked there. A big piece of Sebastian, one I didn't fully understand until the game and the stairway and right now, clicks into place. This is why he walks around like he owns the place. This is why his classmates love him. This is why he gets away with murder.

He's Preston royalty.

I look up into his face and see that he's watching me closely.

"Thank you for bringing me down here," I say quietly. "I know it's a big risk."

His lips are a bright, vivid pink, eyes darkening as he holds my stare. "The first initiation into the Devils," he begins, propping himself up with a hand beside my head, on the arm of the couch. The other hand glides over my chest, across one breast, down to my ribs. "We had to tell our worst sin." His fingertips climb back up, eyes flicking down to watch its ascent. "It was recorded, so that if any of us spilled the secret, the people in charge would leak it."

My stomach sinks, even as I surge into his touch. "Mutually assured destruction."

He nods, blond hair falling into his face. "Do you know what mine was?" I shake my head, sucking in a slow breath when he bends, pressing a lingering kiss to my jaw. "You." His fingers replace his lips, blue eyes boring into mine. "This. What I did that night."

My stomach sinks even further, but this time it's a bittersweet sort of ache. "Sebastian," I say, reaching up to cup his cheek.

But his jaw just tightens as he says, "I don't want to have any secrets between us, Sugar. I want you to trust me."

I run a thumb over his cheek, nodding in understanding. "I do."

"Good." His tongue darts between his lips and he places a hand on my lower stomach, pushing me back against the cushions. "Do you trust me enough to make you feel good?" His fingers curl around the waistband of my leggings and his eyebrow raises. "I know you hate it when I do shit for you, but I really, *really* want to do this. Just let me..." He seems at a loss for words for a moment, lips forming around an aborted reply. "Just let me show you. Please?"

I nod, pushing past the twist of anxiety in my chest. "Show me."

He peels off my leggings, struggling to get the tight fabric over my feet. "Fucking spandex," he mutters, before going back for my panties. His frustration makes me laugh, easing a bit of the intensity. I do trust Bass, more than anyone else, but letting him take control of my body like this is hard for me. It's the loss of control and security, sure. But it's also something new to begin craving. Something new to miss when it goes away.

Despite my agreement, my body fights against me like usual, knees clamping shut once I'm bare. Bass sits before me and kisses each knee before stroking up and down my legs, coaxing them to part. "Can you relax for me?"

I take a deep breath and let my legs fall apart, one against the couch, the other on the seat. This time, he runs his hands up my thighs, eliciting a spark that travels to my core. He switches to gentle kisses, while kneading his fingers into my thighs. I focus on his shoulders, the way the muscles tense and retract, the tattoo inked around his collar. I feel his eyes on me like a branding iron when they rise to my center, a soft groan pouring from his chest.

"So fucking hot, Sugar." His eyes flick up to mine as he moves closer, and when his tongue flicks out and swipes against my clit, I seize and grab for his thick blond hair.

"Oh!" I gasp, pulling harder. He hums in response and flattens his tongue, coating my pussy with wet warmth.

It's hard to reconcile, the squirming feeling of wanting to both let him in and shut him out. My knees keep wanting to close, even though my hips happily writhe into him, giving him more of me. He takes it in stride, curling a hand around my thigh and easing it away, spreading me, tongue working me over in expert ways.

He whispers things as I watch him, breathless and captivated. "So fucking gorgeous. Do you like that?" Some of it is completely nonsensical. "I want to, but I won't. I'm not gonna ask." Sometimes he'll mutter a low curse and reach down to squeeze the tent in his pants. Mostly, they're sweet things, though. Sweet and dirty things. "Been thinking about this for days. Always so fucking hard for you."

When his fingers join the party, two sinking right into me as his tongue works my clit, my knees don't even think of closing. They just spread wider and wider, until I'm nothing but an open mess of whimpers for him, hand fisting into his hair.

Fear fades into a tingling, good sensation and I lift my hips into his face. Sebastian reacts by sucking my clit with his open mouth, and it's all so good, so right, that whatever I'd been worried about, whatever part of my body had been *not cooperating*, completely vanishes. I barely have time to enjoy the weightlessness of it—the '*oh god, I'm coming*' part of it—as the orgasm rolls over me quickly, furiously, and I buck into him with a loud cry.

Sebastian breathes hot and heavy against my body until the spasms stop. Then he jolts to his knees and unbuttons his jeans, reaching inside. Through the foggy, post-orgasmic haze, I watch as he runs his hand over his erection in jerky, fast strokes. When he slides a finger back inside me, hooded eyes fixed to where it disappears, still gripping his cock, I don't even have the presence of mind to feel weird or self-conscious about it.

His eyebrows sort of collapse as he fucks his finger into me, like he's imagining it's not his finger doing it. Like he wants to fuck me so bad that it doesn't even take much to pretend this is his cock.

He doesn't ask, though.

Maybe all that talk before wasn't so nonsensical, after all.

It's not the first time I've seen him do this, but we're long past the slow foreplay we'd experienced that night in his room. He's so close I could touch him if I wanted to, almost hovering over me, and if I could, I'd catch up to his quick movements. But by the time I shake out of the haze, he's pulling his finger out of me, jaw tensing, eyes slamming closed as he heaves forward. His hand jerks to a stop. "Fuck," he grunts, spilling over his fist, dripping hot and sticky on my stomach. His eyes open and he looks down with a grimace. "*Fuck*. Fuck, Sugar, I didn't mean to…"

"It's fine," I tell him, pushing up to watch the hot cum dribble down my belly. I reach for his neck and pull him down. "It's fine." I kiss him, because it *is* fine. The fact that he did that for me, and that I got to see him go there… it isn't even gross. If anything, it just makes me like it even more, wearing him like this. Marked, again.

Bass grabs the discarded blindfold-shirt and uses it to clean himself, then me. When he returns to me, settling back between my legs, head resting on my chest, a stillness settles over us. We're still breathless, my knees bracketing his ribs, and when I run my fingers through his hair, he hums.

"This is probably super shitty timing," he says, propping his chin between my breasts to gaze up at me. "Because we're down in a dungeon, and I just jizzed all over you like a goddamn animal—" He laughs when I clamp my hands over my face, groaning. He reaches up to tug a wrist away. "But the fact that you trusted me enough to come with me, to let me do that, even though you..." The skin around his eyes goes tight, tongue darting out to wet his lips. "And because you're not scared off by literally everything about me, I just..."

"Just what?" My heart is pounding so hard in my chest, I can't help but wonder if he can feel it.

Blue eyes bore into mine when he says, "I think I'm falling in love with you, Sugar."

My mouth parts in shock, chest blooming with a sudden, fierce heat. He stares back at me, frank and sure, like he's not even waiting for me to say it back. Like I could ignore it and it wouldn't bother him one bit.

I don't.

Voice trembling, I reply, "I think I'm falling in love with you, too."

Some girls would get mad about the words '*I think*' being added into it, but I get it. Love doesn't come easy to people like us, especially when it's muddled inside all these feelings—all these fears. What do I know about love?

His eyes, reflecting the flicker of candlelight, say the same thing.

"Don't move," I whisper, keeping still as possible as my hand roots around on the floor in front of the couch. Sebastian, who probably hasn't stayed still a day in his life, does exactly that. And when my hand grabs hold of what I'm looking for, raising it between us, his only reaction is a slow, soft blink.

The camera's *click* is the only sound in the room.

It's true. I know fuck-all about love. What I do know is that Sebastian makes me feel safe. He makes me feel beautiful and sexy and strong, like I'm not just someone to be suffered. Like I'm someone to be wanted and had and cherished. I just hope that I give him back as much as he gives me.

~

"IF IT SNOWS, are you still going home?" Georgia asks as we get ready for class. It's Wednesday and the memorial is scheduled for tomorrow. Of course, the weather forecast is terrible—the first and probably only time this year we'll get something like snow. Down here though, it's more likely to be ice that results in power outages and slippery roads. You'd think my mom would change the day for the memorial, but I doubt even a nuclear winter would compel her. As if my dad will know we had to change dates.

"I don't have much choice," I tell her. "If I don't show up, my mom will lose it. It's really important to her."

Sometimes, I still wonder why I care. I'm eighteen now. I'm an adult. I don't live at home. I could never speak to her again, and it'd be perfectly legit.

"Have you asked Bass about the Mustang again?"

"Yeah." I pull my gloves on, sighing. "Honestly? He's being kind of weird about it. He says it's almost ready, but that there's no way I can take it on the road yet. Whatever the fuck that means. I just need it to be drivable."

"Hmm," Georgia says, wrapping a scarf around her neck. "Are you going to ask him to go with you? I mean, I'm still happy to loan you my car for the day if you need it."

I give her a tight smile. "Thanks. Let's see what the weather does first. I should have a better idea this afternoon."

As we step outside, the cold, blustery air slaps against my cheeks, and I feel the first droplets of precipitation. "Jesus," Georgia gasps, pulling her scarf over her mouth. "I'm going to run to the library and get the books I need for my exam next week. See you later, okay?"

I wave as she runs off, ready to get out of the cold myself. I trek across campus, head ducked low against the wind and rain. Running up the steps of the main building, I slam right into a hard body. Two hands steady me and I look up, prepared for an impromptu meltdown at some random guy clutching my arms.

The panic flares and dies so suddenly that my head spins a bit. "Oh. Hey."

Bass's blue eyes peek out from under a black stocking cap. It's my first time seeing him since we departed last night, on the steps of my dorm, Sebastian giving me a slow, lingering kiss before watching me disappear into the building. From the way he watches me, eyes softening, I suspect he's remembering the same thing.

I think I'm falling in love with you.

A bitter chill of wind cuts between us, breaking the moment. "I was just coming to find you," he says, guiding me out of the way of a few classmates walking up the steps. Forehead wrinkled with a frown, he glances toward the dining hall. "I went to check on the cats this morning. Give them fresh water and a few snacks. I'm actually sort of worried about Abby, though."

From Bass's calculations, she's already been pregnant for almost three months—the amount of time it takes for kittens to gestate. "Did you see her?"

He shakes his head. "That's what's got me worried. She hasn't been shy about coming around lately. If she goes into labor and that ice storm hits..." He rips off his cap to rake his hair back, then instantly shoves it back over his head. It's a useless, fidgety gesture. There aren't a lot of soft edges to Sebastian Wilcox, but this is one of them.

"Come on," I say, taking his hand. "Let's go look for her."

He glances at the building. "What about Dr. Ross?"

"She'll get over it." I pull him forward. "Or, fuck it, right? We'll pay for it later, but I'm willing to take that risk."

He shoots me a sharp grin, following me quickly cross the quad, looping around to the back of the dining hall. The air smells like bacon and burned toast, and as soon as we arrive, Lucy and Hades make an appearance. I get the treats out of my satchel and hand them each a few, just to keep them occupied. I make a clicking noise with my tongue, calling out for Abby, but Bass is right. She's not coming. We wait there, calling and clicking, even shaking the bag of treats as loudly as possible, but even though Lucy and Hades are practically dancing to get more, there's no sign of her.

Bass ducks behind the dumpster and emerges a moment later with a blue cat carrier.

"Where did you get that?"

"The other night on the way back from the garage, I stopped at the pet store for some extra food. I grabbed it."

"Good thinking."

We split up, each of us searching a different part of the area. I comb the tree line, holding out treats and hoping I'm not just spooking her off. Bass searches around the building, the ducts, the gutters, looking under the dumpster.

"Sugar," he calls softly, fingers snapping in my direction. He nods down at an area between the recycling bins. I quietly walk over, pulling a few treats out of the bag. When I get close enough, I finally see her, tucked between the blue containers. Sebastian shifts anxiously. "Do you think you can get to her?"

"Maybe?" I bend down and tentatively hold out the treats. She's warmed up to me a little lately but she's still timid. The fact that she doesn't even flinch or hiss makes me worry most of all. She's not in a good place. She sniffs the treat but doesn't eat it. "Hey, sweet Abby girl, we're going to get you somewhere warm and safe, okay?"

I know cats don't like it when you come at them from the front, but from this position there's no other option. I glance up at Bass. "I think if you move that container you can grab her from behind. I'll block this side so she can't run."

"Good idea." The rain starts coming down harder now, and from the sound of it hitting the concrete and grass, little *plinks* instead of drops, it's already beginning to ice over. I get the cat carrier and move it to the area we need Abby to go. He looks down at me and asks, "You ready?"

"Yep." I wipe a cold drop off my cheek. She's not going to give us more than one chance, and once she's exposed to the ice coming down, she's going to bolt and go god knows where.

Bass carefully shifts the bin, closing up one entrance and making another. He then pushes it forward, forcing Abby to move or get crushed between them. It's enough of a threat to get her moving, and she stands, backing her swollen body toward the carrier. When she gets close enough, I grab her gently and push her inside, slamming and latching the door quickly.

I exhale and look up at Bass's grinning face. "Good shit."

"So," I reply, standing, "what do we do now?"

Abby makes a low meowing sound, and I peek inside. We may have caught her just in time.

Bass grimaces and says, "I'm not sure."

"Your room?"

"Have you been around a cat giving birth?" he asks. I shake my head. "Well, it's probably loud and I'm pretty sure even with a suite, my neighbors would hear." He scratches the back of his neck. "Don't you have your family thing tomorrow?"

"I'm supposed to, but with the weather and not having my car back yet…"

He nods, brows knitting together in contemplation. "I think we can solve that. We can take Abby back to my house, which will put you closer to the Briar Cliffs. I can drive you up there tomorrow." He watches me closely. "If you're okay with that."

I'm struck with surprise that he so willingly wants to take me to his home. That he so willingly wants me to take him to mine. I'd been determined not to have Sebastian meet my family, particularly Doug, but the time for stressing over either has passed. Desperate times call for desperate measures.

As if on cue, Abby gives another long howl. Whatever I think about tomorrow, right now she needs to get somewhere safe, and Sebastian can provide it.

"Yeah, let's do it," I tell him, even though the idea terrifies me. He must sense it, because he kisses me on the forehead and tells me to meet him at the car once I've grabbed my stuff. Life put Sebastian Wilcox in my path, and there's no way to avoid introducing him to my family.

I just hope that everyone can survive.

25

Sebastian

If I had to picture a scenario of me taking Sugar—or any girl—home, it would not have been to the soundtrack of a howling cat about to give birth.

"Holy shit," Sugar says, peering into the crate, "Abby *really* does not like being in this thing. Is it much further?"

"Nah, we're almost there." The ice is coming down harder now, the tiny pellets bouncing off Jasmine's windshield. I'm as confident as anyone can get about driving, but I'm still tense and anxious. Maybe it's the fact I'm carrying precious cargo that makes my hands clench, white-knuckled around the steering wheel. After we pass two accidents, I'm ready to get off this fucking hellscape of a road.

It feels like it takes forever for the stone pillars marking the entry of my driveway to finally come into view. I turn in, following the long path toward the house, and can't help but sneak a quick peek at Sugar, trying to anticipate her reaction. Sugar knows enough about me and my family's financial status to expect a nice house. But exactly how nice is relative.

Even I'm aware that our house isn't only *big*. It could almost be qualified as a fucking compound. We could house a cult in here and no one would be the wiser. Any other girl would be impressed as hell, would probably want to jump straight on my dick when they realize just how loaded I am, but Sugar? She may decide we should go back and stay in that shitty motel off route 64 instead of accepting the reality of my family's wealth.

I'm already anticipating some pushback about the Mustang. Probably a lot of pushback. Maybe even more of like a shoveback. I'd planned for it to be done by now, and it mostly is. Mechanically, it's completely solid, all rebuilt. I even took a chance and replaced the sound system, all by myself—new wiring and all. I sent the dash façade off to a guy in Nebraska, the best of the best for restoring those things, and paid someone from out in Thistle Cove to re-do all the flooring. But this cold weather has made painting the exterior impossible. I just need a few warmer days and I'll have that Mustang looking shiny and new again. I've been excited about it for days now, having gotten the seats back from the upholsterer yesterday. My grand plan is that it'll look so perfect, so fucking amazing, that maybe my girl will only be a *little* bit pissed when she finally finds out I'm the one who restored it.

Hey, a guy can dream, can't he?

I pass the old course greens and the little entry gate, seeing her look out at the various buildings we pass. Most of them are guest quarters. My dad likes to entertain here on a regular basis. There's a cottage tucked against the tree line behind the house he just refurbished and expanded last year. For all that my dad is gone most of the time, he fucking loves this place, dolls it up whenever he gets the chance, like the biggest jewel in his crown.

I feel her go very still next to me when the main house comes into view. I risk taking her hand to squeeze it, wanting to remind her that she's here with me—and that one simple fact means she belongs.

I pull the car around the looping drive and stop right in front of the house. I peer up at it through the window. "Home sweet home."

"This is your house." Her hand clutches the handle on the top of the crate. "Not one of the ones back there?" She looks over her shoulder, back at the buildings we passed on the way up. When she meets my gaze again, seeing the look on my face, she pales. "No. You're kidding me."

I sigh. "There are eight buildings on the property—although I suspect my dad is planning to build again. Some people buy a car when they get a mid-life crisis, but my dad calls a contractor."

She gapes back at me. "I thought you lived in a gated community with a country club or something. I didn't realize the country club *is* the house."

"Used to be, anyway." I lean over and capture her lips in what I hope is a reassuring kiss. She still looks gobsmacked when I pull back. "Fair warning; it comes with *all* the trappings. Gourmet kitchens, a theater, three pools, luxurious bathrooms with double-headed showers, my troubled mother, and a cranky German head of staff who keeps the whole place afloat."

She looks at the house again, then back at me. "What about your dad?"

I wave a hand dismissively. "Nah, it's a weekday, which means he's up in New York, slaying dragons and stealing gold on Wall-street or whatever the fuck he does up there. He only really stays here on the weekend." I don't mention that Heston is back at school, and thank fucking god, because if he weren't, we *would* be staying at that shitty motel on the highway. She still looks at the house and me uneasily, like the second we step inside, everything changes. I reach out to give her dog tags a gentle tug, showing her that we're still us. "It's just a house, Sugar. It may be all pretty and intimidating on the outside, but the inside is nothing to be afraid of. Just like me." I wink and she pulls a face.

"Gross. You never stop, do you?"

"Nope. Never."

I hop out of the car, slip-sliding on the icy driveway, running around to open the door and take the crate from her. While ice spits on our face, I carry the crate in one hand and take Sugar's hand in the other, carefully guiding her up the front steps, already sprinkled with salt.

Liesel has the door open before I can reach for the knob, her thick accent calling out, "Sebastian! Oh, goodness! You're soaked."

Her eyes dart to Sugar, down to our clasped hands, over to the howling crate, and then back to Sugar again. A million questions cross her face, but she straightens her shoulders and says, "Come inside and get out of the ice."

We step inside and Liesel fusses over our wet shoes, sternly directing us to take them off. I shuck off my coat, take Sugar's from her, and see Liesel staring into the crate.

"That mama cat is close."

"I know," I say, "that's why we brought her here. Where should we put her?"

"There's space in the garage," she says.

"I'll take her to my bathroom," I declare, shutting down that train of thought now. "So she can be close to us."

She gives me a scandalized look. "Your bathroom! But the towels!" Liesel has the biggest fucking hard-on for perfectly white towels, but I'm not sitting in the garage all night, and neither is Abby. Liesel must see the determination in my expression, because she admits a swift defeat. "I've got some old linens in the laundry room that you can use."

"Thank you," I say, noticing again that her eyes dart to Sugar. She's gone silent next to me while her eyes bug out, taking in the tall, ridiculously grand foyer. "Er, Liesel, this is Sugar, a friend from school."

"Oh, a friend." Her eyebrow raises skeptically. Before she can grill me more, Abby lets out the low, deep howl of a frightened animal in pain. "Go on, then. Take her upstairs. I'll bring up the supplies."

The three of us cut through the house, Sugar quiet at my side even when Liesel breaks off from us at the corridor to the laundry rooms. My fingers are still linked with Sugar's, keeping her close. There's a small part of me that's terrified she may bolt at any moment, and a lot of it has to do with that constantly startled look in her eyes. It's not like there's anywhere to go, but rationality has never been a strong character trait for Sugar when she's panicked.

"My room is up here," I say, climbing the stairs off the kitchen. I'm propelled by her silence to continue talking, filling the gap. "My mom's suite is on the other side of the house, so Abby shouldn't bother her. Not like my mom would care. I just..." I don't finish that train of thought. I'm not sure what shape my mom is in tonight, or if we should bother her, or what kind of reaction she would have to me bringing Sugar home. Liesel barely kept her mouth shut, obviously dying to find out more. "I think the best idea is to get her settled in the bathroom. Maybe in the tub? Or is that weird? The floors are heated and it stays pretty warm in there, and look, don't worry about Liesel and the towels. I swear she sleeps with a bottle of Clorox or something. It's like her magic elixir."

I continue talking as we walk down the long hall, passing the ominous, closed door to Heston's rooms, before turning into my own. It's been a long time since I've brought anyone in here, and even then, it'd never been a girl. The first room we enter isn't technically the 'bed' part of the 'bedroom'. It's a sitting room, with a door leading to the proper bedroom just inside. When we enter, it's immaculate, thanks to Liesel's staff and the fact I live in the dorm ninety percent of the year. It's always just been my bedroom, but I'm not stupid. Most people don't have a living area in their bedroom, or a bathroom the size of a small post office, or a balcony that could comfortably entertain most of my lacrosse team.

The walls are painted slate gray, matching both the décor and bedding on the enormous king-sized bed. My mom—or really, her decorator—picked it all out. On the shelf against the far wall, there are a few items that make a halfhearted attempt at defining me. Lacrosse trophies and awards. A picture of our family from years ago, on a trip to Europe. Classic novels from all my past literature classes are stacked underneath. Over the desk is a huge Atlanta United flag. I point out the hidden flatscreen that pops out of the floor, because even I think it's cool. If Liesel didn't clean in here every week, everything would be covered in a thick coat of dust. For the first time, I realize with startling clarity that I'm not attached to much in here. Preston has become my home more than anywhere else. Aside from my mom, that's where the people I consider my real family are.

Up to and including the girl standing in the middle of the room.

Her eyes are taking everything in, and there's a little crease between her eyebrows that's really starting to freak me the fuck out. "This is your room." She doesn't phrase it as a question, but more like something she's just considering.

"This is my room," I confirm. She looks like she wants to say more, but Abby cries out again, her carrier tipping with her panicked turning. "Come on," I say, gesturing to the bathroom. "Let's get this mama cat somewhere comfortable."

"Right," Sugar says, dragging her eyes off a photo of me standing on the dock at the Briar Cliffs as a kid. In it, my hair seems even blonder, my skin dark from playing in the lake all summer. The place where the photo was taken is not far from where Sugar and I first...met.

"I have the linens," Liesel says, bursting into the bedroom with a cardboard box filled with towels and blankets. She looks frenzied and entirely out of sorts for a bad bitch like Liesel. "Don't you dare expect me to midwife these kittens, young man. That is not a part of my job description!"

Sugar steps in then, gently taking the box from her hands. "Thank you, these should be perfect."

Liesel looks ready to fuck off to parts unknown, far away from the cat about to give birth, but also hesitant to leave us alone, probably in anticipation of the mess that's going to be made. "Use the intercom if you need anything. I sent the cooking staff home on account of the weather, so all they've prepared is dinner for later. If you want lunch, you'll have to go scare something up yourself. God help us."

"Liesel," I say, halting her. "How is she today?"

She meets my gaze with a tight expression, giving me one sharp shake of her head.

I nod in understanding. "Thanks," I say, carrying the crate into the bathroom. I switch on the heater while Sugar closes the door, placing the box on the floor. She's hasty about lining the bottom with towels, but she takes a long moment to adjust them, just so. "So... any idea what we're supposed to do?"

"Not other than what I read on the internet," she says, standing up, dusting off her hands. At least she looks a little less panicked now, wearing the closet equivalent to a game face. "She should nest in the box, and when she's ready, it should all just... be pretty natural."

I set the crate down and open the door. Abby's shivering inside, another one of those low howls echoing off the bathroom tiles. I worry for a moment that she may be difficult to get out of the crate, but she's restless enough that she instantly darts out. Sugar and I look on anxiously as Abby anxiously circles the room, holding our breath when she finally approaches the box.

We both breathe a sigh of relief when, after a long interval of suspicious sniffing, she steps inside. Abby paws at the linens, turning in tight circles, and I don't know if this is what nesting is, but she finally sits down.

"She looks tired," Sugar says, frowning. "I hope she has enough energy."

Abby peers up at us with her battle-worn face, mouth opened with a sudden bout of panting. It's weird seeing her inside like this. She's an outside cat through-and-through, feral as they come. But she doesn't look scared—not of us. She must know that it's safer here.

I look at Sugar and hope she feels the same. "I guess we wait."

We don't need to wait long.

"I'm telling you," Sugar repeats, gnawing on a fingernail as she looks into the box. "We should drape something over the tub. Make it like a little cave."

"She's already had one," I point out from my spot on the counter, far across the room. "I think she's willing to grin and bear my meager accommodations."

I don't get close to the box. I'd made that mistake once, thinking stupidly—so, so naively—that I had what it takes to stomach the harsh and very gross realities of birth. Sugar still sends me a little smirk every now and then, like she's remembering the exact shade of green my face turned.

"I think… yeah, I think another one is coming." Despite all her mockery, even Sugar cringes away from it, fixing her eyes to another spot in the bathroom.

I take some mercy on us both. "Come on, let's go fuck off and let our girl do her thing."

Sugar doesn't need to be asked twice, and we leave Abby be, closing the door softly behind us. I watch her once again take in my room, walking to the shelves and eyeing it all up. It's barely two in the afternoon, so the sun is pouring in from the French doors, illuminating the silhouette of her hair in a halo. I know from dicking around on my phone earlier that classes ended up being cancelled for the day because of the ice storm, so we're not even technically skipping anymore.

"When was this taken?" she asks, eyes fixed to the photo of me at the Briar Cliffs.

I step up beside her, thinking. "The summer before sophomore year."

"This one?" She points to a photo of me on the field, taken after Preston won the championship against Sparrowood.

"Last year."

"You aren't here much," she guesses, shifting her eyes around. "Almost nothing in here is *you*." She whips her head around to look at me, eyes rueful. "Not that it isn't nice. Your house is unbelievable." When she sees the grimace on my face, she asks, "What?"

"I don't know." I rub a hand over the back of my neck. "I've never been embarrassed about being rich before," I admit.

She blinks at me, taken aback. "You shouldn't be embarrassed. I mean, I wouldn't want you to judge me by the fact I'm… not rich."

"I don't," I assure her. "You know I don't."

She nods, eyes wandering over to the balcony. "You could… I mean, if you want. You don't have to."

"I could what?"

"Show me around," she offers, bending to open her bag. "I could take my camera and—"

"Yeah," I blurt, already reaching for her hand. "There's really no one here. Just my mom and Liesel. Come on."

I show her the second floor first, avoiding my mom's wing. If she's having a bad day, then she's having a *bad day*. She wouldn't want someone meeting her—someone special to me—when she's like that. I'll have to get away at some point to go see her.

"This is our best guest room, I think," I say, leading Sugar into a suite right down the hall. "You could stay here tonight."

I've been thinking about how to broach the topic, but this seems best, showing her the enormous room, decked out with pillows and soft blankets. I can have Liesel stoke a fire in here, stock up the bathroom, make it real nice.

Real far away from me.

Sugar turns a small circle, not at all unlike Abby had a couple hours ago. "It's amazing," she says, stopping to meet my gaze. "But... do I have to? Stay in here?" She walks a couple paces toward me, head canted to the side a bit. "Can I just stay with you?"

Fuck. Thank god. "Yeah, of course. I just wasn't sure if you'd..."

"I do," she assures, sending me a soft smile.

I drag her down to the kitchens, where she stares owlishly at all the stainless steel. "Do you cook?" she asks, running a fingertip over the granite counter.

I dig my hands into my pockets, rocking back on my heels. "Point of fact, I could make you the meanest bowl of cereal you've ever fucking seen."

She barks a soft laugh. "An appetite? After what we just witnessed up there? Hard pass."

Good point.

I take her downstairs next, which is truly next level. I watch her take in the swimming pool, the sauna, the wet bar, the media room, all with a perfectly neutral face. Every now and then, I'll hear the click of her camera's shutter and look up to see it pointed at me through various baffling angles.

I raise an eyebrow. "If you wanted me to pose, you should have told me."

"I don't want you to pose," she replies, leveling me with a sure gaze. "Much like my art, I prefer you without all the bullshit artifice."

It's a shame. I could take some really hot pictures. But it seems like her lens only finds me when I'm trapped in some pointlessly complicated tangle of emotion. It doesn't bother me. I'd already given her permission to make me her subject, in any form that might entail.

"This? Here?" I point to my chest. "You're seriously underestimating my talent for bullshit artifice."

"Even so," she says, uncaring as she walks past, hand brushing mine.

I grab onto it, pulling her back. A few weeks ago, a touch like this would have probably sent her reaching for her knife. Now she just leans into it, lips curving into a smile when I press a kiss to her mouth. If I could find a way to tell her how far she's come—how brave she's been—without sounding like a patronizing asshat, I would. Instead, I say it with a kiss, tucking her against me.

We spend the entire day like that, going back up to my bathroom every now and then to check on Abby. Every time we return, it seems like she has another kitten in the box with her. Sugar lets me take her to whatever corner of the house that's still uncharted, camera going off every now and then. And if I pull her into a coat room, or a den, or a pantry for another one of those quick, stolen kisses, then she doesn't seem to mind.

She begins looking a little more at ease here, in this ridiculous fucking house, following me up and down stairs and corridors. Once, she even pulls me aside for one of those kisses, laughing when my stomach grumbles.

That's how we find ourselves eating dinner in my sitting room. It's no surprise the staff went all out; soup, bread, cheese, and dessert. We eat on the floor in front of the coffee table, legs kicked out as something loud and fast plays over my sound system.

"Wilcox," she says, chomping on a piece of bread, as she chooses another song. "Your life is bougie as fuck."

I don't argue. Much. "I spend most of my time in the dorms, so only on select weekends, really."

She gives me a wry look. "Your dorm, at your extremely presti-gious academy, with its kitchen and living room and entertainment system. Truly roughing it."

"You know," I point out, "you'd be living a bougie life too, if you let me spoil you more."

"You already gave me a new laptop and that ridiculous fucking check—which I still haven't cashed, by the way."

"I didn't give you the check," I clarify. "I chose you to get the check, but it's only like one-twelfth my own money. If you don't cash it, it's just going to rot away in the bank account. No skin off my back."

She curls her lip distastefully, but I can see the gears moving when she pops a piece of cheese into her mouth. I'm wearing her down, slowly but surely.

By the time the day starts winding down, we find a whole bundle of squirming, slick kittens nestled into Abby's belly. Sugar's hunched over the box, trying to count them.

"I think that's just her tail," Sugar points.

"No, it's got stripes. Pretty sure."

"You're not even close enough to tell." Sugar laughs at the grimace on my face as I peer over from my spot on the counter. Abby might not be birthing anything at the moment, but she's still laying in a big ole box of 'nope'. "They're so tiny," she coos. "These three look just like Hades, don't you think?"

I crane my neck to take a reluctant look. "Yep, three little voids."

"There's no way they could have survived in the ice," she says, looking vaguely upset at the notion. "Not where Abby was stuck."

I agree, "We did the right thing by bringing them here."

There's a quiet knock on the door and Liesel pops her head in. "All right?"

"Five kittens. Or possibly four and a tail. Hard to say." I watch as she smiles and leans in, ooh-ing and ahh-ing over them. For all that she was opposed, Liesel is just a big softy at the end of the day. "I think they probably need some rest."

"I brought up a bowl for some water. We didn't have any cat food, but I mashed up some tuna." She pushes in with a bowl in each hand, and I take them from her, setting them where Abby can reach them easily.

"Thank you," Sugar says quickly, earning a pleased look from Liesel. "Can I help carry these dirty towels downstairs or something?"

"Don't trouble yourself. Just hand them over and I'll take care of it." She grabs the laundry basket from the closet and drops in the used towels. She tells me, "I'm staying the night in the guest house. It's too slick to drive all the way home. If you need something —*anything*..." She gives me a soft, maternal look. "Then tough shit, pal. I'm off the clock."

"Ah, that's the warm and fuzzy Liesel we all know and tolerate." More seriously, I say, "Thanks for the help and the dinner. We've got everything from here."

Liesel takes the basket and leaves the room. It's getting late now. Late enough that we should think about settling in for the night. In my bedroom. Together. Alone.

Sugar looks down at herself, pulling a face. "I know I didn't technically *touch* anything, but do you think I could clean up a bit?" Almost instantly, she backtracks. "Fuck, never mind. All I thought to bring is the dress I'm wearing tomorrow."

"No problem, I can get you something," I offer, going into the closet that connects to the bathroom. I grab a lacrosse sweatshirt from freshman year and a pair of flannel shorts. I hand them to her and excuse myself.

When I walk into the suite off the bedroom, Liesel is still there, collecting our dirty dishes from dinner.

"Are you still working?" I chide.

"Just putting this stuff away," she insists, making to leave, but I stop her.

"So...what do you think?"

"About the dishes? You could have taken them out yourself, yes."

I roll my eyes. "I'm talking about Sugar."

Liesel gives me a soft look—without all the bullshit artifice.

"She's beautiful, Sebastian. Very polite." She glances toward the bathroom door. "She seems nervous, though."

"She's definitely skittish," I admit. "Her family doesn't have money like we do."

"Hardly any families have money like you do," Liesel reminds me, watching me closely. "I don't think you've *ever* brought a girl home before."

"I know." I scratch the back of my neck. "She's...different, I guess. I think she'll be around for a while, so I figured she should meet Mom and everything. If she has a good day tomorrow, I mean."

"I think your mom would like that." She gives me a soft pat on the shoulder. "Are you going to see her? Because I think knowing you're here would be a nice start to making that good day happen tomorrow."

Knowing she's right, I follow her out, and go to see my mom.

LIESEL WASN'T LYING. I spend ten minutes beside my mom's bed, reading her a passage from her favorite book. It's a cheap, practically obscure science fiction paperback from the eighties. I'm not really sure what she sees in it, but the part where the heroine defeats the bad guy always makes some of that dead heaviness in her eyes float away.

When I leave her, she makes a promise about getting some sleep, and she smiles. It's an ugly, rusty thing, but I'm used to it now.

I know the real smiles will return.

I'm still lost under the cloud of it when Sugar walks out of the bathroom, catching me changing out of my own clothes. I turn and see her standing there in my sweatshirt, hair wet, bare legs stretched out from the hem, looking extra small and extra sexy.

"Hi," she says, like we haven't just spent the whole day together. I don't miss how her eyes skim over my exposed upper body.

"Hey."

Her eyes dart from my chest to the bed, over to the French doors where the backyard is bathed in icy night. Her teeth bear down on her bottom lip, fingers tucking into the sleeves. The sweatshirt is from almost four years ago, when I was scrawny as hell, and it still engulfs her tiny frame, giving her this timid, vulnerable look that I know is both right and wrong. Sugar is tough as the blade she carries in her bag, and as delicate as those kittens in the other room. If I'm too pushy, too bossy, too much *myself*, she may run like hell.

The elephant in the room is that we're alone now. Really alone, for the first time. There's no Georgia in the next bed, or guys shouting down the dorm hall. We're not crammed in the backseat of the Shelby, or stealing time in a classroom or the photography lab. It's just the two of us. No restrictions. No gossipy classmates. No limitations.

From the anxious look on her face, she realizes it, too. "Should I... go?"

"Go?" I ask, eyebrows furrowing.

She gestures to my chest. "So you can change."

"Uh," I look down, realizing now that it might be too much to sleep in my boxers. "I can, if you want. I probably have some sweats I can—"

"No, it's fine," she cuts in, twisting her hair over one shoulder. "I just didn't want to—I mean, it's your space."

Not really.

Truthfully, I usually sleep buck-ass naked.

When she looks at the bed again, I offer, "We don't have to go to sleep just yet. The TV gets all the channels, or we can go to the media room. My dad has a client at Marvel, and we get all these extended cuts and everything early..." I try to read Sugar's expression, but I can't quite figure out what she's thinking or what she wants. "Or maybe you're tired? We can go to bed. Or sit with the cat some more. Or go for a swim, even." I exhale. "We don't have to do anything, it's not like—"

"Bass?" she says, cutting me off.

"Yeah?" I raise an eyebrow.

"Maybe we can just hang out for a while. You know, see how things go."

Go? There's a chance of going? Go where? Go how? Like the backseat? Like the lab? Like the Devil's Lair? Is sex on the table here? Because I won't ask. I want Sugar to fuck me because she wants to, not because I've worn her down about it. My cock twitches in disagreement and I will it to slow the fuck down. Jesus, maybe I need a cold shower. What's wrong with me?

Oh, right, I haven't had sex in for-fucking-ever and this girl turns me on like nobody else.

I push both hands through my hair, feeling more out of balance than ever. "Yeah, sure."

She climbs on the bed, giving me a peek at her ass, and wow. Okay. She *did not* put on my shorts. Fuck. This is fine. This is all good. Could be a sex thing. Could *not* be a sex thing. Either is fine. I can sleep next to that all night without my dick drilling a hole into the mattress.

Right?

She settles against the big designer pillows that always feel like they're smothering me. "Grab the remote?" she says when she notices I haven't moved an inch.

"It's in the bedside table," I say, quickly pulling down the corner of the blankets. Maybe it'll be less weirdly intense if I'm beneath them.

I look on idly as she opens the drawer for the remote, realizing too late why she's paused, staring inside at the contents. She holds up the box of condoms, raising a shrewd eyebrow at me.

"Whoa, okay, wait." I raise my hands defensively. "First of all, Liesel stocks those. My dad has a really hard-ass policy about never knocking a girl up. It's practically built into the paperwork for our trust funds. Second, if you look closely, you'll notice that it's never even been opened. I've *never* had sex with a girl in this bed. In this room, even."

'*In this house*' is on the tip of my tongue, but there had been a particularly rowdy New Year's Eve party last year that resulted in some minor hot tub shenanigans.

"Never?" Her tone is suspicious.

"Not even close. You're the only girl I've ever brought home. Why do you think Liesel was eyeing you so closely today?"

She hums, tapping the box of condoms on her chin. "I guess I figured she thought I was some girl looking to get knocked up and steal your trust fund." She gives me a sarcastic grin, but it holds more amusement than heat.

Realizing that she's enjoying seeing me all flustered like this, I snatch the box from her hands and fling it aside, ducking down to kiss her lips. She kisses me back with a laugh, leaning into me, and I fight the urge to pull her on my lap.

When we part, I say, "You can have anything that's mine, Sugar Voss. Trust fund. Kittens. I'd give you my virginity if I still had it."

"Same," she says, hand landing on my bare chest. "Well, the kittens and virginity. I don't have a trust fund."

I blink back at her, blood rushing through my body. Did she just say what I heard her say? Does that mean she wants to have sex with me? Right now? No. *No.* It's just regret over the bad time with that fucker up on the cliffs, who was nice, but apparently a really lousy lay. That's all.

I rub my face and look back at the black TV screen before I fuck everything up. "Did you find the remote?" My voice comes out a lot more even than I feel, especially given the way she's pressed all up against my side. In my bed. Alone.

Sugar doesn't move, just looks at me. "Really? You've got no follow up to that statement?"

"Um..." My neck prickles with heat. "I feel like this may be a trick question."

"I'm sitting in your bed, Bass, with no pants on." I try to look surprised, but she rolls her eyes. "Don't act like you didn't notice. I'm kind of putting out a lot of signals here."

I give her a tight smile. "I've been wrong about your signals before."

She sighs, putting a hand on my cheek to turn my face to hers. "How's this for a signal? *Fuck me.*"

I search her eyes, too scared to hope. "Don't tease me, Sugar."

"Who's teasing?" As if to punctuate this point, she pulls the sweatshirt over her head, discarding it somewhere on the floor. She's not wearing a bra. She's not wearing *anything*, except for that dark pair of panties I'd glimpsed earlier.

When she straddles me, those two perfect tits right in my line of sight, I can't help but reach up and cup them in my hands. My body, which always, *always* wants sex, triggers instantly; pulse quickening, cock tightening. It's like a crank being set into motion, but because I am trying so fucking hard here, I engage the brake and lift my eyes to hers. "You're serious?"

"Yes," she says, even though I see a seed of worry in her eyes.

I don't know where it's coming from, but I rush up to capture her lips, assuring her between deep, frantic kisses, "I'll make it good for you. I swear to fucking god, Sugar, I'll make it so good."

Her lashes flutter against her cheek. "Then what are you waiting for?"

26

His mouth is everywhere.

My lips, of course. That's where he starts. Then he descends to my jaw, my neck. There's a spot around my collarbone that gets an extended amount of attention, and then I realize it's the hickey from before.

He sucks on the skin there, renewing it.

All the while, his hands—god, his fucking hands—are all over my tits, squeezing them together so he can dip down and lick between them. It's dirty as hell, the way he looks, hungrily sucking at one nipple, and then the other, almost like he can't make his mind up which.

I'd be lying if I said I wasn't ready for him the second I stepped out of that bathroom and saw him standing there, clad in only a thin pair of boxers. It all ratchets up now, with the heaviness in the air and the way I'm rocking into his lap. I can't get enough of his eyes like this—the way they look at me, all glazed over and lazy, even when his movements have an edge of frantic mania to them, palming at my tits, and then around my waist to grab a thick, unfor-giving handful of my ass. He's soft and hard here, meeting my gaze with a slick, parted mouth that I don't hesitate to capture with my own.

The world turns upside down when he flips me, arms locked around my waist. His bare chest against mine takes my breath away, just as it had the night in his dorm. I wind my arms around his neck to hold him there, fingers curling desperately into his blond hair. I know he doesn't understand, but he doesn't make me feel weird about needing to indulge in the feeling of us, pressed together. It takes me a moment to blink out of the daze of heat and skin and touch, and by the time I do, he's already plucking at my panties.

"I want to make you come first," he says, hot and rough into my ear. "Want you nice and ready for me. Tell me," he demands, nibbling at my earlobe. "Tell me you want it."

I buck my hips into his hardness, feeling it against where I'm hot and already wet. "I want it," I breathe, voice trembling.

He props himself up on an arm to look at me, hand feathering my hair back from my forehead. "Don't let me fuck it up, okay? If I do something... I can stop." At the look on my face—Christ, if he stops, I might *actually fucking die*—he quickly amends, "I can do better, I mean. I can do it the way you want, you just have to tell me."

I give a rapid nod. "Yeah, okay."

With that, he finally drags my panties down my legs, resting back on his heels to gaze down at me. He smooths his hands up my thighs, and maybe it's because of what we did last night—because he's already seen me—but I don't feel that urge to curl up into myself anymore. If anything, I want to spread myself wider for him.

So that's what I do.

His eyes drop down to my pussy and he groans, voice low and ragged. "Damn, girl. How do you want it? You want my fingers or my mouth?"

I feel the warmth of a flush spread all the way down my chest when I respond, "*Yes.*"

He instantly moves back to get his mouth on me, hooded eyes fixed to mine as his tongue licks a wide path up my folds. I make this awful, mortifying keen that has me clamping a hand over my own mouth.

He reaches up to tug it away. "Fuck that, let me hear you."

I know it's just us here. I know from the tour earlier that his mom is so far away, a gun could probably go off in here and no one would know. Nevertheless, when he sinks a finger into me, tongue working over my clit, it's still hard to push away the instinct to muffle my whimper.

Because this is Sebastian between my legs, it's almost like he takes it as a challenge, holding my gaze as he tongues at my clit in a rapid bout of flicks, finger pumping in and out of me.

It's not long before I give in, completely unable to hold it back anymore. I dig my heels into the bed, head thrown back into the pillow as loud cries spill from my lips, arching into him. He grunts against me when my fingers fist into his hair, but I know it's not out of pain. He pulls back every few seconds to watch his finger moving inside me, muttering strained curses, before diving right back down to assault me with more of that wicked tongue torture.

Mere minutes later, I come with a sharp gasp, so surprised by the intensity of it that I have to fist my hands in the bedsheets just to feel any sense of being grounded. Sebastian is ruthless as he chases me through the shudders, watchful eyes flashing with heat, working me like an instrument until I'm a mess of squirming whines.

I collapse into the bed, breathless, like all my strings have been cut, but Sebastian is anything but. His movements are tightly controlled as he rises back up onto his knees, shoving his boxers from his hips. I watch in a daze when his hard cock springs free, bouncing with his movements as he yanks them off his legs.

His eyes travel down my naked, spent body like a trail of flames. "Fuck me, you're so hot like this." His hand runs up my thigh, over my hip. He must have found that box of condoms at some point, because he's holding one in his other hand. "You're hot all the time, but like this, all fucked out from my tongue, in my bed? Goddamn, girl."

He's still transfixed when he rips open the wrapper, resting back on his heels to roll the condom over his erection. It's a smooth, practiced motion, and when he gives his covered dick a stroke, I tug his hand away, replacing it with my own.

Fuck, he's big.

"Fuck, you're big." I instantly regret saying it. The boneless, 'fucked-out' feeling is nice, but the part where I lose my own brain-to-mouth filter leaves something to be desired.

His mouth curls into that slow, self-obsessed grin of his. "Think I'm hung, huh?"

I roll my eyes. "I don't know. I've only touched a couple dicks before."

He bends down, meeting my lips with a slick, open-mouthed kiss. I think I can taste myself on his lips, his tongue, and the spark in my belly is already trying to come back to life. "Come on," he says, nosing beneath my chin. "Can't you indulge my ego, just this once?"

I fight down a smile, feeling ticklish when his fingers graze too lightly over my ribs. "I already said you were big."

He reaches between us to run his fingers through my slickness, saying, "Doesn't matter. I can already feel how wet you are for me." He sinks a finger into me again, slow and testing, and I can feel his cock surge in my hand. Despite the playful mood, there's no missing the tightness of his jaw, or the way he impatiently knees up into the cradle of my legs, brows crushed together. "You feel ready. Are you?"

I take a deep breath, carding my fingers through the hair at the base of his neck. "I'm ready."

I feel him take himself in hand, guiding his dick to where I'm wet and open for him. Despite my assurances, he still watches me closely as he pushes forward, sinking his dick slowly into me.

It's nothing like that first time, which had felt a bit like being split open—a long, arduous sting that never quite ended. With Sebastian, it's like being filled up, holding something inside me that I hadn't even realized was missing.

My jaw falls slack on a gasp at the feel of it, and he breathes out a low, "Fuck yes," as he sinks deeper and deeper, inch by inch, until there's no space between us. He rests low on his forearms, letting me feel our chests pressed together as I get used to the stretch of him. Curling an arm over my head, he sweeps my hair back, planting a sweet, lingering kiss to the corner of my mouth.

"You good?" he asks, and even though his eyes are lazy with that lust-sex-glaze, lips loose as they pluck leisurely at my own, I can tell from the way his muscles flex and roll that he's holding himself back. "Need a minute?"

I shake my head, clutching his hips between my thighs, hands clamped tight around each of his biceps. "Just start slow."

He doesn't mention the tremble in my voice, and I'm grateful. I wouldn't know how to explain that it's not nerves. It's the complete lack of them. It's the way everything feels so confusingly *right*. It's the feel of his body against me, inside me, and how I've spent so long with that constant, gripping pressure in the pit of my chest that it's only now I realize that I don't feel it anymore. Not like this. Not with him.

His first thrusts really *are* slow—these long, dragging motions that make me feel every single inch of him. He shifts to one elbow, ducking his head to watch himself move against me and letting out a soft groan at the sight.

Palming the outside of my thigh, he asks, "Wrap your legs around me."

When I do, winding them around his waist, he sinks even deeper, his jaw going taut. "Fuck, you're tight."

I gasp out his name when his hips meet mine again, the pressure creating just the right amount of friction to make an entirely new spark of heat roll up my spine.

"Yeah," he breathes, kissing me as he repeats the motion, but faster, a little harder, like he's seeing how far he can take it. Pretty fucking far, if the way my hips buck back against him is any indication.

He gets his arms beneath me, around me, and suddenly heaves us back. I shoot out a hand to steady myself, but there's no need. He's got me in his lap now, one large palm pressed between my shoulder blades, helping me find my balance.

It takes a moment to adjust, winding my arms around his neck, but he's looking at me so desperately, a lock of hair fallen in his eyes. "Oh, god," I breathe, surprised at the way rocking against him like this is seriously doing it for me.

The hand on my back curls around my shoulder, bearing me down with each rock. "Yeah, just like that," he says, bringing his other hand to my ass, guiding my rhythm. He captures my lips in a searing kiss, never closing his eyes, even as mine flutter. "You feel so fucking good. Show me, baby. Show me how hard you want it so I can fuck you right."

I want to tell him that it's okay. That I can take it. That I'm not scared anymore—not of this. Tomorrow will be a different story. Once we've done it—once we've had each other like this—will come the worry, but for now?

For now, I want everything.

He grunts when I meet his hips hard, the sound of our skin clapping loud between us. He bites out a low, "Fuck, Sugar," fingers digging into my ass when he meets my next thrust, jerking me into his body. He sucks a kiss into my neck, breaths coming harder. "You want it like that? You want it hard?"

"Fuck yes," I grit out, wanting to feel it—all of it.

Without another word, he dumps me onto my back, hovering over me with dark eyes and tense muscles. He jerks his hips back and slams them forward.

"Oh, fuck!" I cry, scrambling at his back. "Don't stop."

Through the fog of feeling so full of him, the sounds of the headboard slamming against the wall, the way I'm crying out with each of his shallow, punching thrusts, I'm distantly aware of how beautiful he looks. The lock of hair in his eyes sways back and forth with his sure, powerful movements. He's watching me with an angry brow, but I know it's not anger he feels. I can tell in the way he keeps licking at his lips as he watches me, something sharp and satisfied flashing in his eyes every time I yelp out with abandon.

I dig my heels into the tops of his ass cheeks as he fucks me, curling a hand around his neck to bring him down for a breathless, badly-coordinated kiss. It's mostly just tongues and wild panting, and when he wedges a hand between us to press against my clit, he swallows my whimper.

"Come on," he grunts, fingers moving expertly against me. "Give me one more."

I dig my fingers into his back, trying to get him closer, too overwhelmed by the sensations happening to do much more than sob out a hard breath. His eyes keeping moving back and forth between my tits, bouncing with the motions of our bodies, and my own gaze. It's crazy, but mere minutes ago, I wouldn't have thought I could come again. Now, I can feel it building low and deep, a twisting tangle of sweet ache driving me to grind against his hand with every bed-banging thrust.

"Sebastian," I gasp, ensnared by his piercing stare, and his ragged voice husks back.

"That's right. Give it to me, one more. Come with me."

I can tell he's already close, that crease between his eyes growing tighter, but he doesn't look frustrated. His eyes shine back at me and he just looks so fucking *pleased*. Like he has this absurd amount of wealth and popularity and opportunity, but being inside me like this—his hard body with all its sharp edges plunging into me—is all he's really wanted. It's scary and breathlessly elating, like a jump from the highest cliff into the cool, chaotic waves of the river below.

When it finally happens, that explosion of white-hot everything, I claw wildly at his back, body bowed into an arch against his pounding hips. It seems like such a cliché to say I see stars, but that's exactly what happens, a burst of sparking phosphenes detonating behind my eyelids as my body clenches and seizes around him.

He buries his face into my throat as his movements grow frantic and wild, a hand curling into the crown of my hair to shove me down against his wake. From over his shoulder, I watch the muscles in his back shift and roll like a stalking feline, feel the punch of his breath against my skin when he grunts, slamming into me and trapping me there between the bed and the hot pulse of him inside of me.

I can see his orgasm ripple through his muscles, starting at the base of his back and climbing up his flexing shoulders. Still caught in the gust of my own, I idly card my fingers through his hair, soothing him through it.

His clenching muscles release all at once, but he doesn't miss a beat, wedging an arm behind me to roll us smoothly to the side. I collapse on his hard chest with a damp exhalation against his collarbone. The feeling of his dick slipping out of me makes me squirm against him, already missing it.

"Shh," he whispers, threading his fingers in my hair, tucking me up beneath his chin. "So fucking good."

We lay there for so long that our breath evens out, his palm gliding up and down my back in leisurely strokes. Sometimes he'll pause there, fingers tracing over something I can't see or feel, until he presses a kiss into my hair and repeats the circuit.

It takes too long for me to realize he's feeling the raised edges of my scars.

I'd forgotten they existed at all.

ROLLING OVER, the glare of blinding daylight creeps through my eyelids, forcing them to flicker open. I'm bundled up in Bass's comforter, engulfed in his delicious, Sebastiany smell. The day before rushes up to me like a gently crashing wave. The ice, the kittens, Sebastian's ridiculous house, and then finally having sex with him. I stretch slow and easy, waiting for an ache that doesn't come. Part of me worried I'd end up regretting not waiting longer, but in the light of day, laying here in his bed, all fucked out and reenergized, mostly I'm thinking that I want to do it again.

There'd been a couple times in the night I'd woken to the feel of him slotted up behind me, arm curled around my waist, cock hard and insistent against my ass. A couple times, we'd stirred enough to trade a few slow, wet kisses, but we never stayed awake long enough for it to escalate into anything.

350

I roll over and run my hand along his side of the bed, but it's empty and already cool to the touch.

"Bass?" I call, ignoring the flicker of anxiety that passes through my chest. I'm so used to him being there—pressed up against me and hounding me—that it's weird that he's not in the bed. A flicker of irrational panic shoots through me and I sit up and scan the room. His clothes are no longer on the floor. My eyes land on the closed bathroom door.

Duh, he's probably with the kittens.

I pull on the LAX sweatshirt and cross the room, noticing that the sun is out. The drip of melting ice taps out on the balcony, and I trip over a discarded pillow in my haste to grab my camera. There's only six days until the exhibit, and I've been like a madwoman capturing image after image. Most of them are going to be shit, but there has to be something in there worth keeping.

Outside, it's still cold as fuck, my feet stinging against the chill of the balcony floor. But in his 'yard', everything is melting. I get up against the rail to drowsily land a few shots. The branches are weighed down with ice, but beginning to lift with the thaw, like the yawn of a world waking up, stretching its arms high above its head.

It's typical southern weather, freezing enough to cause a shit-ton of problems one day, then eighty degrees the next. The good news is that the roads should be okay to drive on. The bad news is that *the road should be okay to drive on*. There's no getting out of returning to the Briar Cliffs.

Putting my camera away, I tap on the bathroom door before slowly pushing it open. The first thing I see is my reflection in the mirror. My hair is a mess, disheveled from our night in bed. I get this crystal-clear memory of Sebastian's fist wrapped up in it as he fucked me, somehow both tender and relentless. It makes me shiver, wrapping my arms around myself as I poke my head, hoping to find him.

But the bathroom is empty.

As I gather my hair up into a loose knot, I hear the tiniest little peep from the box we'd given Abby and her kittens.

"Hey, mama," I say bending down. The babies are wiggling

around, nursing on Abby's belly. At some point during the night, she had one or two more. There are clearly six kittens in the box now, all dry and fluffed up. I spend a long moment internally squealing over the cuteness as Abby lazily kneads a paw in the air, spreading her belly as if to say, '*Look what I made*'.

"You did good," I assure her, chancing a slow, cautious pet on her head. She flinches a little but ultimately pushes into it, looking too tired to keep up her street cred.

Her food bowl is empty. I grab the Preston boxers he'd given me the night before and tug them on, collecting the bowl from the floor. Her head lifts, nose twitching at the sight of it in my hand. "Let me go see if I can find you some more tuna."

Securing them in the bathroom, I enter the hallway, trying to remember how to get down to the kitchen. Left or right? This place is so big it's like a maze. Other than a door across from his, Sebastian seems to have an entire wing of the house to himself. I peer into that open door when I walk toward a staircase. The room smells like expensive, musky cologne, the kind that burns my nostrils when I inhale. The walls are painted deep blue and the furniture is a heavy, dark wood. On the floor is a pile of clothing, spilling out of a half-emptied duffle bag. Over the massive, king-sized bed, is a flag emblazoned with an image of a devil with the words, *Preston Prep Swim Devils*, underneath. Three empty beer bottles crowd the bedside table.

Heston's room, I assume.

And from the looks of the unmade bed, he'd spent some time in here.

Very recently.

The realization makes my skin prickle, knowing how much he and Sebastian don't get along. I glance back at Bass's room, wondering if I should go back inside, but Abby does need some food, and honestly, it's freaking me out that Sebastian is missing. That he left me here in this strange place all alone, after...

Maybe something is wrong.

I make the decision and continue down the hallway. I take the steps slowly, warily, the scent of pancake batter and butter wafting up the staircase. My steps falter when I hear voices below.

"So?" a guy asks, his voice deeper than Sebastian's.

"So what?" Bass replies, voice flat and low.

"Don't be dense." The other guy sounds mean, taunting. "Who's the girl you were banging headboards with all night? All the noise coming out of there, she sounded like a screamer."

I practically feel my own face pale at the realization we hadn't been as alone as we thought last night. Did he really hear us?

"Jesus, shut the fuck up." Even from a distance I can hear the fury building in his tone. "It's none of your business."

The guy hums, like maybe he's considering it. If he does, he quickly discards the idea. "I don't think I will. Bringing a chick home? Not your usual MO, baby bro." He's interrupted by the sizzle of the frying pan. "Don't tell me you even let your precious mommy meet her, because that really would be a first."

The truth is that he hadn't. He mentioned her. He talked about her a *lot*, but seemed careful—maybe too careful—to keep me away from that side of the house. I hadn't thought much of it at the time, figuring he just didn't want to disturb her, but now it feels like an intentional avoidance.

"Hes," Bass says, voice painfully tight, "I don't know why the fuck you're home right now, but trust me, had I known you'd be here, I never would have brought anyone."

"Hiding her from me? Why? Is she ugly? Stupid? Is she poor?" He drags out the last one.

"She's just a friend," Sebastian barks out.

I press a hand to my lower belly, still able to feel the lingering sensation of him inside of me from the night before. That's twice now he's introduced me as a 'friend.' Once to Liesel and now to Heston. Not at all to his mother. I know in my heart, my soul, that we're definitely more than friends. He said he loved me. My mind spirals, thinking back to how he only told me that before or after we fooled around, each time breaking my barriers a little bit more.

"You make friends breakfast after fucking them? I don't think so." Heston laughs. "Afraid she'll see me and want a real man instead of some jacked-up pretty boy, like Sydney did?"

I grip the railing, face twisting in confusion. *Sydney? Rakestraw?*

Bass's laugh is like barbed wire. "You're so fucking deluded. You and Syd deserve each other. I bet you didn't even delete that video of you fucking her like a ragdoll."

"Why would I? Our faces aren't even in it, and Sydney knows her place in our relationship."

"Relationship?" Bass asks, voice getting louder, more irate. "Everything you say is bullshit, Heston. You're not in a relationship with Sydney, you're in some kind of abusive, twisted, manipulative flirting-with-prison situation that's not going to end well for either of you. You're just too fucking sadistic to give a shit."

I blink, heart pounding in my ears, and ease down the stairs, getting to a place where I can see the two of them. Bass is standing over the industrial-sized range, pouring dollops of pancake batter on a large griddle. His movements are oddly brittle, automatic. There's a plate of burned pancakes pushed to the side, and a smudge of flour across his forehead. Despite the domestic look of it all, his shoulders are tight, face set like stone.

Heston leans against the counter with his legs crossed at the ankles, watching his brother closely. "This whole diversionary tactic is bush league. Tell me about the girl." His voice makes a shiver of fear crawl up my spine. Not a question, but a slow, threatening demand.

Sebastian cuts him a look, hand gripping the spatula. "Stay out of my fucking business." Now that I can see him, I realize that he's not just pissed off. He's nervous. When he goes to flip a pancake, his hand is clearly shaking.

"You're the one who brought her home," Heston reasons, shrugging. "It's not like I barged into your dorm and sniffed her down like a dog. You delivered her, right here to my doorstep."

"I told you, I had no idea you'd be here."

His brother just continues, "It's probably a good thing I came. You've been ignoring my texts about next weekend, but now...?"

Sebastian seems to shed some of the pretense, gripping the

edge of the counter with both hands, back swelling with his breaths. "I won't be there."

"Hm," Heston says, head tilting as he observes his brother. "Why don't I just go up and see her for myself?"

In an instant, Sebastian is in front of him, nostrils flared wide. "You go near her and I swear to fucking god, Heston…"

Heston *laughs*, seemingly happy to get such a rise out of his brother. It dies out on a long sigh. "See? You've been out of action for too long. You need it. We both know you do. You need to imagine they're all me, because that's as close as you ever get to beating me."

The air around Sebastian crackles like an impending lightning strike. Fear ricochets through me and I stumble down the step unthinkingly.

Heston's eyes whip to mine, and he's frozen for the briefest moment before his face splits into a wide, overjoyed grin. "Well, well, well, look who came to say hello."

I can see Sebastian stiffen, turning his head just enough to see me. When he does, his eyes slide closed, shoulders deflating. He mutters a low, "Fuck."

Heston's laugh rings out again as he slides away from his brother, inspecting me. "Holy shit, dude! She's in your clothes and everything! Look at her, she's so…" He raises his hands, gesturing to me, "*small*." He tells Sebastian, "Gotta level with you, baby bro, I didn't really think this whole trashy goth look was your vibe, but hey. I don't judge."

"Sugar, go back upstairs," Sebastian says from behind him, voice low and tight. I don't like the way he says it, or the way he's holding himself, or the way he'll only look at me through the corner of his eyes.

I try to catch his gaze, wondering, "What's going on?"

But Heston's eyes are widening in realization, fingers snapping. "Sugar! You're that new girl at Preston!" he bursts, looking more gleeful than ever. "The one who doesn't like to be touched."

I bristle, at both the description and the way he raises his hand, as if to brush my cheek. I rear back, but it doesn't matter.

Sebastian is already between us, shoving his brother's shoulder, lips pulled back in a sneer. "Touch her, and I'll rip your fucking arms off."

Heston stumbles, but barks a laugh at the way his brother is holding himself, tense and coiled. "And he's protective! Oh, this is good."

"Back the fuck off," Sebastian growls, and Heston raises his hands, even though his smile is all teeth. A chill runs down my spine at the sight of it. I've seen that look before. Pure evil.

"Relax, it was just a joke. I'm not going to touch your shiny new toy." His eyes cut to me, causing a ripple of something wary to course through my muscles. "Although, for the record, I have been informed by certain *qualified* parties that my dick is bigger."

I curl my lip in disdain. "Did she say your dick was bigger, or that you're the bigger dick?"

If anything, it just makes him look *more* excited. "Ooh, and she's a feisty one! Bravo." He gives his brother a slow, sarcastic applause. "Bet you a Benjamin you've got scratch marks on your back right now. I'm right, aren't I?" He laughs again.

I'm not entirely sure I get the source of what's transpiring between them, but that asshole is way too happy, and when Sebastian swipes the plate from the counter, jerking his chin at the stairs, I can't find any trace of the man I'd spent the night with. This guy standing here is completely checked out.

I follow him up, glancing back over my shoulder, where I catch Heston's eye. He stares up at me, that same dark smile curving his lips and winks knowingly. My stomach turns. Not because I'm afraid of him, but because I realize that he knows more about what's happening right now than I do.

～

We're quiet.

Sebastian rustles around the room, packing his bag, and even though he'd fucked me last night—*made love to me*, if I were capable of such corniness—you wouldn't know it by the way he's acting.

"You don't have to drive me. I can figure something out," I say, smoothing down my skirt. I'd forced down two pancakes while Sebastian pretended nothing was wrong, even though he barely tried to sell it. "I can go alone."

He adjusts the collar of his button-down, motions quick and mechanical. "I told you I would go with you. It's not a big deal."

It feels like a big deal. Every movement he's made since we came up has been perfunctory, controlled, the opposite of his nature. "If you think you should stay with the kittens…"

He pauses then, going eerily still. "The kittens." It's a long, suspended moment before he breaks out of it, raking his fingers through his hair. "I'll give Liesel a key to the room. She'll look after them."

Our eyes make contact in the mirror over his dresser and I can't hold it in anymore. "Did I… did I do something wrong?"

Did the sex not live up to his expectations? I thought he enjoyed it as much as I did. It sure fucking seemed like it. I thought I'd gotten to know Sebastian and his rolling tide of emotions pretty well, but seeing him now…

I have no fucking idea what's going on.

I just know the way it makes me feel, like I might be sick.

A line creases between his eyes and he says, "Of course not. You know my brother sets me on edge. Let's just go do this thing and get on with it."

I do know that Heston really bothers him, and it sounds like he didn't expect him to be here. I cross the room and rest a hand on his back before reluctantly sliding it around his waist—a move that even days ago would have pleased him to no end. But now, when I look into his eyes, I can't find the teasing heat that resides there. There's just a blank stare. "I know you didn't want me and Heston to meet. I get that—"

"No," he says, stepping away, "you don't." He checks the time. "We need to go if we're going to be there on time."

I exhale, not wanting to leave it like this. But he's right. "Doug will flip if I'm late."

He grabs his coat and hands me mine, arm extended. "Then let's get out of here. Get this over with."

Sebastian walks out of the room, leaving me behind. I glance over at the bed, still rumpled from the night before. A small piece of the condom wrapper sits on the floor next to the trash can. Just seeing it creates a ball of tension in my stomach.

The words, *'Let's get this over with,'* echo in my ears, as though once we're finished with this day, everything is over.

27

Sebastian

On the ride to the Briar Cliffs, I do all the shit.

I count to ten. I breathe. I count to twenty. I breathe some more. I count to fucking one hundred, and the breathing *isn't fucking helping.*

I eventually turn on the radio, trying to find something to focus on that isn't this scorching fucking rage simmering just inside my chest. He's right, is the problem. I do need it. I need someone I can build up in my head to be Heston. Someone I can beat the shit out of. It's just so goddamn hard to shake it off. This thing—this toxic fucking hatred for him—clings to me like a leech.

He threatened my girl.

Maybe she didn't hear it in all his bullshit yapping, but I did. I heard it clear as fucking day.

The fucked-up thing is that I actually woke up happy. Sugar had been beside me in bed, sheets dropped down, baring her tits as she breathed softly in slumber. She looked so fucking soft and inviting that it was almost impossible to pull away from her. But I figured after waking her up for a nice breakfast, we could get down and dirty with a second round. If the way she kept waking during the night and rubbing her bare ass against my dick was any indication, she would have been into it.

Instead, I'm sitting here in this fucking car, strangling the steering wheel as she sits beside me, still as stone.

I feel like the smallest twitch will make all of this creeping black fury inside me loose, and she'll run. She'd be smart to. It hasn't been this bad in months. Every second of the morning has been devoted to this shoddy charade that I'm not a hair's width from completely fucking losing it on something.

Because I know exactly what I need to do here.

I'll fight it. Of course, I'll fight it. Fighting is what I do. I'm doing it right now, by just sitting beside her, taking her back home. I'm clutching onto it with a death grip, even though I don't have a plan for keeping her safe.

I didn't even have a plan to keep the fucking *kittens* safe. I'm the last person who should be surrounded with all these sweet, breakable things. That's my problem. I don't plan enough. I've spent weeks twisted up with worry about what might happen if Heston found out about her, but I didn't chart a single fucking map through dealing with it. Now, here I am, staring down the cold reality of the only thing that'll make it go away.

I try the counting thing again.

I breathe.

As if the bridge is an invisible line, the instant we arrive on the other side, Sugar's urgent voice rings out, breaking my concentration. "Pull over."

"What?"

She pitches forward, hand on the dash. "Pull over. Right here, just..." She inhales, jaw clenching, and *oh shit.* "Pull over, please just pull the fuck *over.*"

I hit the brake, shooting out an arm protectively before easing the SUV onto the shoulder. She's out the door before it even completely stops, bending at the waist and losing her breakfast.

I fumble out of my seatbelt, but she holds out a hand, stopping me as she heaves again. I crane forward to watch her, frozen with indecision. It's not long though before she straightens, pushing her fingertips under her eyes, wiping at the wetness that's collected there. I clumsily open the glove compartment, pulling out tissues and wet wipes.

Stupidly, I ask, "Are you okay?"

Sure, she looks fucking peachy, vomiting her guts out on the side of the road. Real fucking bright.

When she turns back to the car, she looks paler than usual, taking four small paces back to the SUV. She closes the door with a soft click, staring straight ahead.

"So, that happened." When she takes the tissues and wipes from me, her hands are unsteady.

Distracted enough from the static of my anger to make a shitty attempt at levity, I try, "My cooking was that bad, huh?"

She fists a tissue, holding it up to her mouth. "I think it's just... nerves."

"Look," I start, feeling it beginning to build again. "I won't let Heston fuck with you. You shouldn't—"

"Heston?" She gives me a confused look, and it suddenly occurs to me that this has nothing to do with him. It's a startling revelation —like how could the earth possibly go on spinning when my brother is out there, ruining everything? For a second, it makes no sense to me. How could anything be worse than what happened back in that kitchen? The math doesn't add up. Obviously, everything is about me and my bullshit.

Fuck, maybe I actually am self-centered.

"You're nervous about being back home," I realize, feeling like a goddamn moron.

"Being home." She says this in a daze, like she's testing the words in her mouth, trying to make them fit. "Yeah, I guess I am."

Grimacing, I twist, digging around in the back seat for a bottle of water. It's cold from being out here all night, and I watch her press it to her forehead. She hasn't told me much about her life here. I know her dad was killed in action. I know he left her that Mustang. I know her mom remarried. I know Toby Fuckface exists.

And I know she's absolutely fucking covered in scars.

But she hasn't said yet how she got them.

Not like it takes a genius, anyway. The ones on her back are from being whipped. The ones on her thighs... those took me longer to suss out, but I have one exactly like it on the outside of my bicep—the result of a fight outside the Nerd two years ago.

It's a cigarette burn.

If I had to guess, whatever—*whoever*—gave her those scars is still wandering around this place.

Softly, I say, "Hey," and press a hand to her cheek, forcing her eyes to mine. "You know I won't let anyone hurt you. That's what this is about, right? I know you don't want to talk about it, but you—"

She flinches away, face blank. "Let's just go. Okay? Like you said before, let's get it over with, and then we can go home."

I watch her carefully, not missing that she considers Preston her home now. It's a precarious thing, and I should know. Preston is a fleeting shelter that has its own scars and pangs. People like me and her, we call it home, but it never can be.

Not really.

~

"Is this the place?" I ask, nodding at the wrought iron archway of the town cemetery entrance. Between the bridge and here, I've managed to talk myself into, at the very least, pretending everything is normal. At least for her. It still feels stilted and awkward, pulling this façade over all the frenetic anger that's trapped beneath.

"Yeah," she breathes, gazing out her window.

She seems content to pretend, too.

I slow the car and pull up the narrow drive. The cemetery is huge, probably the final resting place of every resident the Briar Cliffs has ever seen. Down the winding road that cuts through the gravestones, a few cars are parked off in the distance.

Sugar swallows and says, "That should be them." I ease the car up behind a white pickup truck and park. Just before I open the door, she says, "My mom makes all of us do this memorial thing.

No one likes it but her. It gets all of us tense, and my mother's husband, he..." She trails off, jaw going taut.

I let my hand drop from the handle. "He what?"

She chews out her words. "He can be a little abrasive. Just... do me a favor and ignore him, okay? That's what I do."

I nod, feeling like there's something she's not saying, but if she can let me pretend, then I can at least extend the same courtesy to her. We step out of the car, and even though it's warmer than it was yesterday, Sugar still wraps her arms around herself.

A woman bearing a striking resemblance to her starts toward us. "Baby," the woman cries, pulling Sugar into a tight hug, her weathered hand rubbing at her back. "You look so good! You've put a little meat on your bones, haven't you?"

Sugar's smile is tight and rusty. "The food at school is good."

"Should be, for how expensive it is." She brushes the hair off Sugar's cheeks, and I notice her flinch. Jesus Christ, she really hadn't been lying. She's not even comfortable with her mother's touch. "I'm so glad you made it. Any trouble with the weather?"

"No, not really," Sugar says, eyes darting back over to where the rest of the guests stand near the tombstones. She swallows, asking blandly, "How are you?"

"Good," her mom says with a rattling exhale. "You know, getting all of this together was a little hectic. Your Aunt Jane kept trying to interfere, but you know how she is. I let her handle dessert, so she backed off." She looks at me, like she's just registering that I'm here, and then back at her daughter.

"Mom, this is..." she glances at me, and even the flash of panic in her eyes is a comforting sight. She hasn't shown one ounce of emotion since crossing the fucking bridge.

I extend my hand and grin. Easier to pretend when it's just putting on some charm. Sugar will see it for the 'bullshit artifice' it is, but these people won't have a clue. "Sebastian Wilcox. I'm a friend of Sugar's from school. Pleased to meet you."

"Sebastian," she repeats, shaking my hand and arching her eyebrow at her daughter. "It's lovely to meet you, too. Honestly, I was worried about Sugar making new friends so late in the school year."

"No need to worry," I assure her, dipping my hands into my pockets. "Your daughter has won over just about everyone at Preston."

"Is that so?" a man asks, striding up behind Sugar's mother. He rests an arm over her shoulder possessively, eyes fixed on Sugar. "Thought maybe you decided not to show up."

Her mom's laugh has a nervous edge to it. "Oh Doug, you know the weather was iffy this morning. Sugar would never miss this."

I look between them, expecting an introduction. None comes. Instead, I watch Sugar's eyes lift to Doug's, see the way her shoulders stiffen, lips flattening into a grim, tense line. I watch her look at him, and there's fear there, which is bad enough. But there's also something else, and suddenly, everything begins clicking together.

I'd know that look anywhere.

It's the same sort of look she gave me, that first time we ran into each other at the garage.

Plastering a smile on my face, I offer this motherfucker my hand. "Sebastian Wilcox."

He gives me a once over before taking my hand. "Doug Dickinson." His grip is tight—it screams over-compensation, but I grew up in the world of back-room country club deals and underground fighting. I roll with it. "I see you've met my wife, Marie."

His wife. Not Sugar's mother.

"Thanks for having me," I tell her, even though I wasn't technically invited.

"The chaplain wants to get started," Doug says, glancing at his watch, mustache twitching with the glare he shoots Sugar. "We're already running late."

"Doug's right," Marie says, quickly. "Let's get started."

They walk off, but Sugar hangs back, looking up at me. I raise an eyebrow, asking, "He always like that?" even though I know now.

I *know.*

She nods stiffly. "My mom's husband. Brace for it: he's *always* right."

I realize now that she never calls him her stepfather, just her mom's husband. We walk up the small hill, and I notice Sugar's hands are tucked tight in her pockets. She'd introduced me as a friend—not her boyfriend. Maybe she'd take this easier than I thought. With each step closer to the small group of people, her shoulders tense. I watch as the wall that I'd taken weeks to tear down slowly builds back up.

"Where's the Mustang?" Doug asks abruptly, looking over our heads at my mother's SUV. "Don't tell me. That piece of junk broke down."

"It's just getting some work done," she replies, voice as abrasive as the look he gives her. "That's why Sebastian offered to drive me. The SUV seemed safer with this weather, anyway."

Doug eyes me, taking in my clothes and my car. I want to ask him how he could let his stepdaughter drive off in a hunk of junk in that condition on her own, but I swallow it back. Someone who's done what I suspect he's done to Sugar probably couldn't fucking care less.

"It's crazy, isn't it?" Marie says, oblivious to the tension, or maybe in spite of it. "Ice so late in the year. Your father would have been so amused. You know how much he loved the cold weather and snow. Especially after basic training at Fort Benning. Said he'd never experienced that kind of heat and humidity in his life and never wanted to again."

I'm introduced to Sugar's Aunt Jane and a few other people, including a few older guys in uniform. Sugar's fine with everyone, mostly, even though she's tense—except Doug. It's so goddamn obvious, how can these people not know? How can they not see?

It's not a big group and the event is entirely informal. There's an American flag folded over the headstone and people take turns saying nice memories about Sugar's dad. From all accounts, he sounds like a good guy and a bit of a bad ass, earning awards and accolades from the military for his service and bravery.

For all that I pay close attention to the little glimpse into Sugar's life, I keep one eye on Doug at all times. He's tall, probably has an inch on me, even. He's a big guy, obviously a laborer. The longer I look at him, the more I think of it—this big, grown ass man doing those *things* to someone as small as Sugar—and I practically bite a fucking hole in my tongue to stop myself from saying something.

It just gets really fucking difficult not to bash his goddamn face in.

I bide my time, though. Doug keeps his mouth conspicuously shut, his expression blank. More than once, I see him check the time on his watch. I want to ask him if he's got somewhere else to be. What's the problem, Doug? Worried about missing the game?

I keep my comments to myself.

As we approach the grave site, an eerie feeling of déjà vu rolls over me. I glance around, knowing I haven't been here before, but everything from the placement of the headstone to the American flags feels familiar. Then it hits me. She'd sent me this photo the day we hooked up in the photography lab. Go figure. I was so focused on my dick, I didn't connect the significance.

"Sugar," Marie says, "Do you have anything you want to say?"

"Um..." A pained expression pinches her face. Her fingers are pressed against her chest where I know the dog tags are laying against her skin. "Not today," she says quietly. Her mother looks disappointed but doesn't push.

Doug coughs and gives her a pointed glare. "Nothing?" he asks. "You can't think of one thing to say to your father on a day like today? Maybe a 'thank you for your service'? Thank you for providing for me and my mother? Thank you for sacrificing your-self for this country?"

"Doug," Marie says quietly, glancing around at the others. Everyone watches on awkwardly. "You know Sugar mourns in her own way. It's fine."

He shakes his head like he's been personally affronted. I glance down at Sugar and although her face is set like marble, her cheeks bloom red under the cold. I start to place my hand on her lower back but stop myself, curling my fingers into a fist.

It's hard to focus on anything else after that. Not the flowers or the nice words from the chaplain. I watch Doug, studying his move-ments, his disposition. His shoulders are broad. There's an impatience rolling off of him—not dissimilar to my own—but there's something else. An air of superiority. The kind that hasn't been earned, but still claimed. Fuck, the way it makes my blood simmer, thinking of those hands hurting my girl. I wonder if he beats his wife, too. A guy like that? Probably the only way he can feel like a real man.

I'm so tense with it that by the time the final prayer comes, my muscles are stiff and aching. Marie predictably invites everyone back to the house for lunch, an offer everyone seems willing to take.

Sugar is quiet on the way to the car, quieter still once we're inside. I pause before cranking the engine, trying to tamp down the rage that's trapped in my chest. When I notice him staring back at my car, eyes narrowed, I can't help but grind out, "What the fuck is wrong with that guy?"

She follows my gaze through the windshield, instantly swinging her eyes away. "He's just trying to get a rise out of me."

"Trying to get a rise out of you?" I take the keys out of the ignition, gripping them too tight in my hand. "He's the one, isn't he."

She doesn't even look surprised that I figured it out. She just rests her elbow on the door, fingers digging into her temple. "Sebastian, please, just—"

"He's the piece of shit who hurt you."

Finally, there's some fire in her eyes. "I can't handle you starting shit with him. Do you understand? I want to get through this, and then leave and preferably never fucking come back again."

I stare back at her in disbelief. "You can't expect me to be near this guy, knowing what he's done, and just—"

"I do," she says, voice firm. "If you can't handle it, then you can leave. I'll get another ride back to school."

"I made a promise to you back there," I insist, pointing back toward the bridge. "I'm not saying I'll start shit with him, but if he touches you? I'm going to light his ass the fuck up."

"Don't you get it!" she cries, finally turning to me. Her chin wobbles, eyes shining with unshed tears, but her face is twisted bitterly. "This is hard enough! Having to worry about him, having to walk on all those fucking eggshells just to avoid—" She clamps her mouth shut and a tear spills over, leaving a track down her pale cheek. "It's hard enough without having to manage you, too. I can't do it, Sebastian. Either I handle him, or I handle—" she gestures wildly to me, lip curling, "—all *this*. The fucked-up way you've been treating me all morning, and the fact you're obviously spoiling for a fight. I can handle one, but I can't do it all. I *can't*." She shakes her head, swatting at another wayward tear. "So if you can't keep yourself in check, then get out of here, because that's the only way you can help me."

I watch her, knowing that she's wrong, but completely unable to argue. Isn't this what I do with Heston? I manage him like a sickness, keeping people away, begging them not to make shit worse—not to let it spread.

I reach out to brush a tear from her cheek and she flinches back—hard.

"Please don't touch me," she says, face falling. "Not... not now. I'm sorry. Just not now."

My hand drops heavily, but the sound of her voice like that, the fact that just being in this place means I can't touch her... it just cements what I already know.

There's absolutely no way I can promise not to protect her.

But there's also no fucking way I'm leaving her alone at this house or with these people, especially him. I shove the keys into the ignition, cranking the engine. I make the only promise I know I can keep.

"I'll try."

~

I LEARN a lot about Sugar Voss when I step foot in her house. Probably as much as she learned about me when I brought her home. Her home is small. To say it's the size of our pool house would be generous estimate. It's clean, though—compulsively so. Marie would give Liesel a run for her money.

I feel a discomforting current of energy as we walk through the house, following Marie and her piece of shit husband through the entry. Sugar's shoulders are still raised and tight, face set into a carefully controlled expression. She looked so small in my house, dwarfed by the tall ceilings and wide corridors. Here, she should look bigger, more proportioned. Instead, she tucks her limbs in close to herself, like she's trying not to accidentally brush up against the energy of the house. Like if she makes herself small enough, she can sneak through it unnoticed.

After a long, uncomfortable moment spent shifting our feet in the living room, Marie suggests that Sugar give me a tour.

She starts at the kitchen, sticking her head into the narrow space that's already filled with people I don't know. Listlessly, she points to a small bathroom that everyone in the house shares. "My room is upstairs. Do you want to see it?" she asks, gesturing to the staircase behind a small door.

I follow her up, taking deep breaths with every step, trying to loosen the anger welling up inside of me. The walls are so narrow that my shoulders brush against them. At the top is just a squat little room. It's got a slanted ceiling, and two dormer windows tucked under the eaves.

The only place I can stand up straight without my head touching the ceiling is right in the middle of the room, but none of that matters. My eyes roam the room, greedily sucking in everything I can about Sugar. One wall is nothing but torn-out pages of magazines—stylized pictures of modeling shoots, nature, and interesting architecture. Next to the slim, twin-sized bed are shelves fitted with clothespins that have Polaroids clipped in place, close-ups of abstract textures and objects that aren't directly identifiable, but still look neat. The shelves themselves are filled with random little trinkets; a small collection of smooth rocks, a blue ribbon for a school contest, a stack of old books.

"It's like the size of your bathroom closet," she says, running her finger over a small brown dresser, "and there's no Liesel to dust every week, but—"

"But nothing," I say, slightly annoyed. "You know I don't give a shit about money."

She snorts, at least seeming a little more like herself up here. "The only people who say that are people who already have money."

"True," I concede, "but I don't judge you for it. Or your mom, or even that piece of shit she's married to." I judge him for just about everything else.

I nod to a photo tucked in the mirror of her and a few friends. In it, she's probably still in middle school and already is working the dark eyeliner. Her hair is pink, and she's wearing a jacket with fringe. Her mouth is twisted in a smirk and she looks so ridiculously badass that I have to grin. "If I'd met you back then, I would have been obsessed. Like, hounding you for a date every day."

"So pretty much like now." Insecurity flickers in her eyes. It's been there since morning and I've done nothing to fix it.

I'm not sure I can.

"Pretty much." I take a deep breath, and since I'm still fighting against what I know needs to be done, I can't leave it like that. "Look, about this morning..."

"Sugar?" Her mom calls from downstairs. "You upstairs? Aunt Jane is cutting the cake."

Her body tenses completely, shooting me an apologetic gaze. "We need to go. Aunt Jane is very serious about dessert."

I deflate, even though I know it's for the best. "So I've heard."

We walk down the stairs and she finishes up her tour, jerking her thumb at her mom and Doug's room. Across the hall, there's a second bedroom that has the words 'Man Cave' burned into a wooden plaque hanging from the door.

"Ah," Doug says, creeping up behind us, "best room in the house."

Sugar somehow manages to go more still than she has been. Her hands fidget at her sides, like maybe she's looking for something to cling to. Something like a knife.

If she's planning on responding to Doug, it's caught in her throat. It makes my own fists clench, just knowing that this girl beside me—this girl who I've never seen scared to let her own thoughts known—is too scared to even reply to him.

"Sugar," Marie calls, voice reaching down the hall. "Why don't you come help us serve this."

Sugar gives me a wary look, but Doug clasps me on the shoulder and says, "Don't worry, I can entertain your friend."

"It's cool," I tell her, flashing her a grin that's probably not reassuring in the least. "I need to hear more about what happens in the man cave, anyway. I may need one of these one day."

Sugar's glare could peel paint, but she turns and shuffles down the short hallway to the kitchen.

"Holy moley, I need a drink after all that." He lumbers past me to a small bar set up under the window. It's hard to even look at him, his big frame and imposing height. The thought of a man this size hitting on someone like Sugar...

Forget the fact that she's my girl.

Any man who wails on a woman—a fucking kid—like that deserves for hell to be a real place. I watch on, teeth gnashed as he pours scotch into a tumbler and takes a long sip.

"Would you like one?"

Doug's not so mysterious. It's a trick question. If I say yes, I'm an irresponsible, underage drinker. If I say no, I'm some little pussy who's scared of drinking like a man. I've navigated these waters before. "Thank you, but no. I'm in training—for lacrosse. The season starts next week."

"Lacrosse." He mulls that over as I picture my foot slamming into his face. "That's the one with the sticks, right? I played baseball, myself. Catcher."

Of course, he did. Lacrosse players are cocky assholes, but baseball players? They're dumb and full of themselves. As a catcher, he probably took more knocks to the head than I have. I shift my gaze to the plaque on the wall, the one that commemorates his MVP status. "Any good?"

I already know he thinks he was.

"All-State," he replies, mustache twitching with his smirk. "I figured I'd have a slew of boys one day to pass my skills onto, but life doesn't always work out the way you want it."

"My mother has two sons," I say, only just managing not to

sneer it at him. "I assure you that she'd much rather have a couple of daughters."

Doug pours himself another drink and carries it over to a well-worn chair. He sits down with a long grunt. "A little advice, son, never marry a woman who already has children. She'll put them first every time."

The pounding of my pulse echoes in my ears. "Come again?"

He swirls his drink and flicks his cold eyes at me. "How well do you know Sugar?"

"Well enough," I reply, desperately trying to hold in my temper. I hear the sound of laughter in the kitchen, hoping that Sugar is included. "Why?"

"Word to the wise on that one," he says, tipping his glass toward the door. "Get out now. Nothing but trouble with her."

My voice is deceptively even. "What do you mean?"

He tips his drink back, mustache grazing the glass. "She's an unreliable, selfish little brat. Abandoned her own mother, for one. Probably just to get out of helping around the house. And to go to that fancy school, of all places." He gives me a meaningful look. "Girl thinks she's better than she is, is what I'm saying. You seem like an alright young man. You come from money, right? Yeah, I can tell." He shakes his head. "She'll drag you down."

"Will she?" I grind out, nails digging divots into my palm.

Fucker's already too buzzed to read my tone. "Always was an ugly, mouthy little shit. I'm telling you now, keeping her in line is a full-time job, so unless you've got nothing else to do..." He waves a hand dismissively, like he's talking about the weather or something. "Not really worth the hassle, though. She's bringing nothin' to the table, unless maybe..." He gives me a slimy look, chest bouncing with a laugh. "Maybe she's good in bed. Can't imagine she would be, those twiggy little legs of hers. Got a nice set, I guess. You're lucky she got her mom's tits." He raises his glass to me like a congratulations, but I can see in his eyes that he knows just what he's doing.

This motherfucker is trying to get a rise out of me.

He has no idea just how well it's working.

I walk casually to the bookshelf, picking up a paperweight, testing it in my hand. "Look at your teenage step-daughter's tits often, Doug?"

He grins, looking pleased with himself. "Well, I do have eyes."

I tilt my head to him, wondering in a voice that I don't even recognize, "Is that before or after you put those scars on her back?"

His eyebrows rise. "You've seen my work, eh? So I was right. You *are* fucking her." He sets his empty glass aside, planting both feet on the floor. "I always did figure she'd become a slut, but a whore? Can't be putting much of a dent in your bank account, can she?"

His hand whips out to catch the paperweight when I throw it. I was aiming right for the middle of his forehead, but he snatches it out of the air, lightning quick, barking a laugh.

"Catcher," he reminds me, "but I respect the effort."

I shrug, because this isn't about landing a blow. Not yet. It's almost a relief, slipping back into this headspace. Weighing up my opponent. Calculating. Stoking the fire. There's chaos here—there always is—but there's also a sense of order to it. A routine. It takes this stuck throttle and points it somewhere safe. Somewhere it's deserved. "I'm just curious. Do you beat your wife too, or is it just defenseless girls a third your size?"

At least his movements grow a little less controlled when he bangs the paperweight onto the table beside his glass. He was clearly expecting a different reaction. "I don't break what's mine."

"You realize how little that's worth," I point out, observing him closely. His knee wobbles when he pushes himself to his feet, straightening his back slowly enough to be useful.

"You think I care what you think?" He holds out his arms wide in a mockery of welcome. "Take a shot, boy."

"Bass?" Sugar's small voice rings out in the doorway, but I don't move. I barely even blink, holding Doug's gaze as my blood pumps frantically. "What's going on?"

"We were just having a friendly chat." It's Doug who answers. "Man to man."

Sugar must sense the tension between us—it can't be even

remotely subtle—because suddenly she's in front of me, palms flat on my chest, whispering, "Please don't."

I'd move her out of the way if I could touch her. But I can't. It's because of the piece of shit standing right there, six feet away. I jerk my head to the side, cracking my stiff neck. "Sugar, go."

"No," she says, voice urgent, hands sliding up to my neck. "You said you'd try."

"I did try."

"Please," she begs, tugging. "There are people here, and—"

Doug cuts in, "Wouldn't want to embarrass us, Preppy Boy. Sugar did that enough, running away like the lazy coward she is. Not even gracious enough to speak at your own father's memorial." He's got an issue with keeping his eye on his prize, already breaking my gaze to spit at her, "You realize your mother does all this for you. She carries on with this whole dog and pony show, year after year, because she feels guilty about you losing your dad." Uncaring of the hot glare Sugar throws him, he stalks forward, pushing his sleeves up, making my hackles raise even further. "Which is bullshit. Who provided your skinny, ungrateful ass with food? A roof over your head? Clothes? And you took it for granted. What did your dad ever give you, anyway? Shitty genes and a piece of shit car. But let's honor him like a saint every year, why don't we."

Sugar lets go of me, whipping around to sneer at him. "Mom's the one who wants to honor dad. *You're* the one who's embarrassed because it may mean that you're not the center of attention for one godforsaken moment!"

His eyes flash in anger, even as he goes still. "What did you just say to me?"

"You heard me," she says, voice tough as nails, even though she's trembling—with fear or with anger. She bites out, "You're jealous. Of a fucking ghost. Of a little girl. Of anything you can't *own*. Because you're a small, petty, pathetic excuse for a man—never mind a father."

I'm so busy appreciating that fire in her eyes—her ruthless snarl—that I catch what's happening just a beat too late.

Doug's palm meets her face with a sharp crack, sending her

stumbling back, right into my chest. I catch her, but it's only a split moment before I finally—fucking *finally*—bolt forward.

The first punch is easy, even though he should see it coming. My knuckles meet his cheek, sending his head whipping to the side. He's quick to recover, but Doug's right-handed—which I know from the catch before—so I duck out of the way before his responding punch can land.

My heel meets his knee hard enough that he actually cries out, a high-pitched snarl that's sure to have gotten everyone's attention. He buckles, going down on one knee, head flying back when mine crashes into his face.

It's all a blur once I get on him, fist flying back and jerking forward. Maybe he gets one or two hits in—one to my jaw, another to my kidney—but all I see is red. Some of it's this roaring, crazy explosion inside of me, but some of it's his blood. My knuckles go numb as I hurl my fist forward, again and again. Only distantly, I can hear Sugar screaming at me to stop, but it's muddled, like it's happening underwater.

Doug gets his legs under him long enough to get me on the ground, but all I can see is that look on his face when he slapped Sugar.

Sugar, who looks so small here, in this wretched fucking house.

Sugar, who I promised to protect.

Sugar, who loves me, even though she shouldn't.

The table with the glass and paperweight tumble over when I shove him into it, glass crashing all around us. Doug's not content to stay down for long, even though I can see him tiring out, that wobble in his knee graduating to a full-fledged quiver when he tries to stand.

I'm younger and faster, and I find my footing first, using it to drive my foot into his face.

His head jerks back—there's no way that nose isn't broken—but Doug's as dumb as a box of rocks. He won't stop. It just makes me go faster and harder, knowing that he's almost even competition for someone like me, but he's content to use all that power against a little fucking girl.

At some point, he gets back up, and that's fine. I wipe a wrist under my nose, not even tired yet. I can see him huffing for breath, though. He's too worn to keep up with me—not enough stamina. I can have this motherfucker, lights out, in three more minutes.

I just need a little more time. A few more hits. A couple more kicks to the face. A little bit of time to appreciate that I've beat him. To savor the crash.

It takes me too long to realize that he's beginning to look a lot like my brother.

By the time I do, Sugar is between us. "STOP!" Her eyes are wide and panicked, but if it weren't for that, it'd just be the red welt on her cheek and the way she's crying, and I probably wouldn't be able to.

Marie is in the doorway, clutching her chest, wearing such a picture-perfect mirror of her daughter's expression that all it's missing is the welt.

That's not what stops me, though.

It's that Sugar is between us again. It's taken me twice now, but I'm finally learning that she's going to get hurt here. Holding me back. 'Handling' the two of us. Always clawing to control the situation, to remove the conflict. To get just a little fucking peace, Sugar will throw herself in front of my chaos. Every time.

I think that's the point I really stop fighting.

I stop avoiding what I know needs to be done, because people like me and Sugar can't afford that.

I lift my hands in the air, backing off. "I'm done."

Doug spits a mouthful of blood on the floor, face still twisted in fury. "You're gonna be done, boy. I'm going to fucking finish you."

Marie steps in then, and at first, I think she's going to hold him back. Instead, she rubs his back. "I'll call the cops," she says to me, face red. "So help me, I will!"

"No," Sugar bursts, eyes wide and wet. "We'll go, you don't need to—I'm sorry."

"Don't fucking apologize to them," I hiss, thrusting a finger at her mother. "You're just as bad as him."

"Don't you talk to my wife," Doug growls, irate.

I ignore him, shifting all this red-hot chaos onto her. "You knew what he was doing to her, didn't you? She's your own fucking daughter! What's he? Some piece of shit you married?"

"You don't understand anything," she cries.

"I understand enough, and if she ever comes back here again, it'll be to bury your fucking body." To Sugar, I snarl, "Get your shit, we're leaving."

Despite having gotten his ass kicked, Doug looks satisfied in a way that doesn't quite click until he says, "Don't you ever come back. You hear me, you little whore? You better pack up everything, because come tomorrow, it's all going on the lawn."

Marie flinches at the word 'whore', but she says nothing.
Nothing.

I give her a long, scathing look. "I can't fucking believe some people call my mom a bad parent when pieces of trash like you exist."

She sets her jaw and looks away, and I see it then—the spark of shame. It's not big enough for her to stop it. Maybe I was wrong. Maybe she's *worse* than him.

"We'll go," Sugar's saying. "We're going."

Upstairs, I watch, fist flexing as she dumps her things into a plastic storage bin. She's crying, but every time I try to touch her as she passes, she just flinches away, head shaking.

I never should have started this at all. Letting someone in, someone vulnerable like Sugar? That was the kind of mistake Sebastian Wilcox didn't make.

I take one last look at the bed, at the smooth quilt and the straightened pillow, and think about the knife Sugar told me she started sleeping with under her pillow. When she'd threatened me with it, I didn't really understand why she needed to carry it, but after meeting Doug? I get it. He's just another Heston. The only way out from under their thumb is to fight your way out—or fucking chop it off.

I thought Sugar came to Preston to get a jump on her education and to expand her opportunities in photography. She was actually just escaping. Unfortunately, she was doomed before she ever stepped foot on campus. We'd already crossed paths. I'd already marked her. As long as she has me in her life, there's no escaping the violence. I'm just another part of the never-ending cycle of abuse and dysfunction. She deserves better. She deserves that little bit of fucking peace she's so willing to throw herself on the line to get.

I should feel good about it—or at least as good as losing her could ever feel. There isn't a better way this could have ended. I can't be there to protect her, but I've severed a tie here. I've made it better by making it worse. Hopefully one day, she'll see that.

I'll be long gone by then.

28

THE DRIVE back to Preston is tense.

Memories of my mom keep rushing up like my mind is trying to saw the cut a little deeper. They're not good memories. There are no cute, sweet moments where she took care of me, or comforted me, or taught me something new. I know some of those memories exist, but they're long ago, from *before*, and they're buried beneath the others. Her wincing silence as the back of Doug's hand met my cheek. Her disappearing into another room when he had me by the hair, snarling obscenities at me. The way she'd turn to avoid watching him kick me in the stomach.

She didn't like that he hurt me.

She just didn't care enough to stop it.

The longer I think about it, Sebastian oppressively quiet at my side, the more I know that was the real reason the thought of coming back here made me sick. I'm scared of Doug, sure. But in a way, I'm also not. He's sadistic and cruel, but there's a simplicity to that. He can hurt my body, but it'll never go past the surface.

Not like my own mother.

I'm broken out of the thought by the sound of Sebastian's phone going off.

Again.

It's been chiming with texts during the entire car ride, but all he does is jerk an aggressive glance down to it in the console every now and then. Since I can't avoid doing the same, I know it's his brother. His name keeps popping up on the lock screen, various nonsensical messages appearing below, the meaning of them broken by the way I miss the ones in between. He's apparently one of those people who only texts in single sentences.

Winter transfer. Interesting...

Oh no, poor dad...

I'm thinking Ormewood Park...

Scholarship too! Bro, those can be fussy...

Really great tits, I'm excited...

"Look at me," Sebastian says, grabbing my attention away from the screen. I do it because it's the first thing he's said since he asked me to buckle up. "How many fingers am I holding up?"

I look away. "I don't have a concussion."

He doesn't lower his hand. "It was a hard hit, Sugar. Just tell me how many fingers."

Annoyed, I cut my eyes at his hand. "Three." And then I hold up my own. "You?"

He is the one with a history of concussions, after all.

"I'm fine," he says, even though his eye is swelling. I'd only asked once if I should drive, but he wouldn't let me. Nevertheless, he grunts out, "Two fingers."

At least there's that.

That doesn't mean I'm not pissed at him, too. "I can't believe you did that," I say, trying to fill some of the silence. His complete stillness since getting in the car has been more unnerving than the fight itself.

"No?" he asks, jaw clenching. "What did I say that day at Merle's? I said if I ever found out, I'd kill him. You knew exactly what you were getting with me. Don't act like you expected me to do nothing, because I might have been sent into that bullshit blind, but I know better now."

I stare out at the passing scenery, face growing hot. Sebastian isn't wrong. I knew coming here with him was a risk, like putting two lit bombs together in one room. Bass's fuse had already been lit that morning with the altercation between him and Heston. As upset as I am at him, I'm even more pissed off at myself. I know it's my own fault. I didn't follow my instincts. In fact, I've been outright ignoring them for weeks now.

"You're right. I shouldn't have brought you there," I concede.

"Yes, you fucking should have!" He must see me flinch from the corner of his eye, because his shoulders drop, chest expanding with a deep inhale. "But you should have told me what I was walking into. You should have told me it was him—how fucking bad it was. At least then, I could have been a little smarter about it." His bruised knuckles flex as he grips the steering wheel.

I know how he sees this. It's just like that night at the docks. Bass storms in to save the day and ends up messing shit up. He means well—I see that now—but that doesn't make it better. "I've handled it on my own for a long time, Bass."

"With what?" He asks, shooting me an incredulous look. "Your knife? The panic attacks? By not letting anyone ever touch you? That's not handling anything, it's just helping you hide the problem."

Irritation licks at the back of my neck and I flip it back on him. "Like I'm the only one not handling shit? Your whole life is one daredevil stunt after the other. Fights, street racing, pranks, police chases, concussions? You didn't even give a shit when I threatened you with a knife! You came closer, like you were daring me to hurt you!" I swallow, watching his face darken with every word. "Don't act like you'd handle it any better."

"Yeah, I'd kick his fucking teeth in," he argues, teeth gritted as the phone chimes with another ignored text. "If you'd heard some of the shit he said about you..." He's getting worked up again, and that's the issue.

"It doesn't fucking matter. That wasn't your fight, Sebastian. It doesn't give you the right—"

"The people who *had* the right weren't fucking taking it!" His hand comes down hard, loud on the steering wheel. "Your mom wasn't even—and *you*. What the fuck were you doing, Sugar? You can't let people treat you like that. You have to fucking—" He lets out this deep, frustrated sound when his phone chimes again. "You have to stand up for yourself."

"Stand up for myself?" I ask, voice dangerously low. "You think I've just been going through life, getting the shit beat out of me like some passive little chew toy? You think I just sat there and did fucking *nothing*?!"

"That's what it looked like to me."

And the thing is, I've been pissed off a lot in my life. Most of it was impotent rage, just swirling around in my chest, completely without any place to really spend it. Despite that, I'm shocked to feel that nothing—not even years spent under Doug's heel—has made me feel as irate as I do right this fucking second.

"How dare you." God, I'm fucking shaking with it, entirely unable to keep the quiver from my voice. "*How fucking dare you* imply I'm to blame for this."

He gives me a belligerent, shocked look. "I never said—"

"That's exactly what you're saying," I volley back. "Because maybe you don't know that I reported him when I was twelve. Hell, twice when I was thirteen! You obviously don't know that each time, my counselor took me home, to my fucking mother, who told her I was just acting out. Clearly, it never fucking occurred to you how shit works sometimes when you aren't the biggest name in school, so let me spell it out for you: No one fucking cares, Sebastian!" The phone chimes again and I consider chucking it out the goddamn window. "You know what each of those attempts at standing up for myself got me? I know you do. You've seen it on my back. So don't you ever fucking suggest that I did anything less than survive, because that's what I did. I survived. And that's a hell of a lot more than some people manage."

The car's quiet for a long, suspended moment. Even the person texting him seems to give us a break for this—for Sebastian to feel like shit for even considering...

"Look," he starts, but then the phone goes off again.

Fed up, I snatch it from the console to see what the *fuck*.

Saturday night

Just as I'm deciding that means absolutely nothing, another bout of texts comes in.

Or I might need a fix for my sweet tooth.

You can tell me just how good it tastes.

Or not. I'll find out myself.

I thrust him the phone, nodding to the light we're stopped at, about two blocks from Merle's. "Your brother apparently has some very urgent business regarding food." I'm thinking he'll take the stoplight to reply to the messages, but that doesn't happen.

He stares down at the phone, turns it off, sets it back in the console, and places his hands at perfect ten and two. He's looking straight ahead when he says, "Don't ever look at my phone again."

I gape at him. "It's been going off the whole drive!"

When he finally looks at me, I know that cold, empty look has nothing to do with what happened in the Briar Cliffs. This is the same expression he was wearing this morning. Shuttered and blank. "I don't have any right to your life, but you have the right to mine?"

I swallow, something heavy and bitter landing in the pit of my stomach. "What's the big deal?"

"I told you I don't like him knowing my business. I had a reason." His nostrils flare, the muscle in the back of his jaw ticking. "You should have stayed upstairs."

It finally hits me then. "This has all been about this morning, hasn't it?" I know in my bones that I'm right. That Sebastian is unpredictable and impulsive at the best of times, but his behavior today has been sharply pointed, completely lacking in warmth. "I knew something was—you've been such an asshole all day. What the fuck, Bass?"

Instead of answering me, he shifts in his seat, something chilling in his voice when he says, "You were right, you know. All that shit you said before about me chasing you, even after you pulled a knife on me like a psycho." His gaze swings to me, eyes like ice. "But did you ever wonder what it meant that you came to a new school, looking for a new life, every option open to you, and not even three months in, you're dating the guy who clocked your ass unconscious?"

I blink at him, completely taken aback. I work my mouth around about a dozen aborted replies. The only thing that emerges is, "Are you shitting me right now?"

"What does that mean?" He asks, ignoring me as we pass Merle's garage, three miles from campus. "Probably that you have shitty taste in guys. You've never been as mad at me as when I was trying to do something nice for you. So what does it mean?" He looks at me, but doesn't give me a chance to answer. "It means that dealing with abusive assholes is what you know. So I don't know, Sugar. Why have I been an asshole all day?"

The accusation lands like a blow, mostly because it's something that's been tickling at the back of my consciousness since that first kiss. I jumped right out of the fire with Doug and back into it with Sebastian—someone that, from day one, I knew had a violent temper. Until this morning, I thought everything was fine. That, despite all that ugliness and baggage, we were good for one another. What happened? What changed?

One thing.

One fucking thing.

"You want to know what I think?" I ask, already feeling sick with the reality of it. "I think you've been an asshole because maybe you finally got what you wanted."

"What are you talking about?" he asks, tilting his head toward me. His eye is starting to look bad, bruising dark around his nose.

Clarity crashes down like shattered glass. "It was all about the sex, wasn't it? I'm just another Sydney. Another Georgia. Another fucking notch on that beam in the tower."

He glares out the windshield, fists wrapped tight around the steering wheel, and doesn't even bother telling me that I'm wrong.

Instead, he shrugs.

"Let me out," I say, quiet at first. Then, louder, "Let me out," and louder, "Let me the fuck out!"

He doesn't argue, whipping the car into the Nerd's parking lot and slamming on the brakes. I feel like I fall out of the passenger side more than anything, stumbling as I reach back to slam the door. Hot tears prick at my eyes, but I won't let them fall. I've already cried over two assholes today.

Not anymore.

~

"Shit." My hands shake as I enter the code into Hayden's security keypad. The light blinks red, signaling that I've messed up again. "Shit. Shit. Shit!"

"Hey," a voice says, "did you forget the code?"

I turn around and see a girl that I recognize from around campus. "Yeah," I say, shoving my hands in my pockets and stepping aside. "Totally blanked." It doesn't help that my hands feel frozen solid. The walk to campus is bad enough even when it isn't cold as hell.

"It happens to me at least once a semester." She jabs her fingers into the keypad and the green light blinks, unlocking the door.

"Thanks," I reply, wondering how my voice can be so calm while my entire world is falling apart, piece by piece. I feel dazed as I walk upstairs to my room and, thankfully, find that the door is already unlocked.

Pushing it open, I see Georgia lying on her bed, smiling at her phone screen. I turn and determinedly face my own bed, toeing my shoes from my sore feet, hoping she hasn't noticed my splotchy face and sore eyes.

Fucking bastard.

"Oops, gotta go. Bye," she says, turning it off, sitting up to fold her legs. "Hey. How are the kittens? How was the trip home?"

I blink, suddenly remembering the kittens. I'd totally forgotten about them in the chaos. "The kittens were good when we left this morning. In good hands with their housekeeper, I think." I toss my bag on the bed. "The trip home?" My voice cracks, giving me away. "Not so great."

Georgia frowns and I hear the creak of her climbing off her bed. "Oh no. What happened?"

My whole body goes on alert, feeling her closing in, and I hold up my hand, backing away. "I wouldn't even fucking know where to start."

Respecting my personal space, she goes back to her bed, watching me sympathetically. "How about from the beginning?"

I sink heavily to my bed. The blanket is still mussed from the last time I was in it. Yesterday morning. Jesus, has it really only been one day? With a deep breath, I meet Georgia's worried gaze. "We spent the day at Sebastian's house. Abby had her kittens. We ate dinner. We—we had a good time. It was nice, you know?"

She nods in understanding. "Sounds good."

"And then, last night we…" I deflate, rubbing a hand down my face. "We had sex."

Her eyebrows crawl her forehead. "Oh."

"And it was good. Everything was good. But when I woke up this morning, he was gone."

She frowns. "What do you mean 'gone'?"

"Not gone, but like… not in the bed with me. Come to find out, he was downstairs with Heston, who said all this shit about Sydney —and was a complete dick, by the way—and also Sebastian kept introducing me as his 'friend', so what the fuck is that all about, right?"

It all comes out in a rush. The more I tell her, the more it feels like some of the weight lifts. I explain how he got so cold and distant, and how I knew he was on edge, and given how my stepfather is such a dick, there was no way Bass wouldn't get into it with him.

"To be honest," I confess, remembering Sebastian's words from earlier, "I think maybe a part of me wanted him to get into it with Doug, you know? To show him that there's someone out there who'll stick up for me. Someone that's scarier than him." I drop back on my bed, feeling embarrassed to admit it.

But it's true.

"They got into a fight?" Georgia says, jaw dropped. "And they really kicked you out? For good?"

I nod, not telling Georgia just how deep the problems with Doug go. It might not be fair to Sebastian, letting her think the fight was over something superficial, but I don't have it in me to give another part of myself away. "On the way home, we had this huge fight. It was like he just flipped." I cover my face with my hands, feeling frustrated. "God, everything is fucked."

"Where is he now?"

I sniff, dragging my palms down my face. "I think he's gone."

"What do you mean he's gone?"

I finally look at her, hoping my eyes look drier than they feel. "Like, I asked him if he was just using me for sex and he didn't deny it, *at all*, and I told him to let me out at the Nerd, and he left. He just left."

Georgia's face goes through a series of expressions—disbelief, worry, concern, anger—but when she speaks, her voice is carefully neutral. "That sounds absolutely nothing like Bass. But at the same time, it sounds exactly like Bass."

I snort, shifting my eyes to the ceiling. "Whirling dervish. I know."

"Huh?" she asks, but I just roll onto my side and grab my extra pillow, cradling it against my body.

"Did he have sex with Sydney?" I ask. "Is there something there I don't know about?"

Her mouth forms a thin line. "I don't know if he had sex with her or not, but if he did, it was a while ago. Syd's been pretty much persona non grata around here since the stuff with Vandy and Reyn went down. Sebastian wouldn't cross that line."

Yesterday, I would have believed that, but now this constant insistence that Bass is so loyal is beginning to seem like bullshit. "I know you hooked up with him," I say, pushing the words past the lump in my throat. "Did he, like, use you?"

"No," she says, head jerking back in surprise. Firmly, she repeats, "*No*. Not at all."

"He didn't just get what he wanted from you and move on?"

"It wasn't like that with us," she insists, pitching forward to catch my eyes. "It wouldn't be the same, anyway. I've seen Bass with other girls—hell, I've been one of them—and he's never gotten close to anyone like he has with you. I don't know what's going on with you two, but something about this feels majorly off." Her eyebrows scrunch together as she watches me. "You said Heston was there? What did they talk about?"

I take a deep breath. "Other than making it super clear Sebastian didn't want to acknowledge me to his brother or mother? Heston was mostly bragging about boning Sydney. Bass did say something about him flirting with jail. And something about a video."

Her expression flattens, face paling. "A video?"

"Yeah, something like 'I bet you didn't even delete the video of you fucking.'"

"That son of a bitch," she mutters, eyes flashing. Suddenly, she's shooting to her feet. "That son of a motherfucking bitch!"

I sit up. "Who? Sebastian?"

"No," she shakes her head like she's in disbelief. "Heston. I can't believe he's still doing it. I mean, he's not even at Preston anymore!"

"Doing what?" I ask, head fuzzy and slow.

She takes a deep breath, eyes slamming closed. "If I tell you something, do you promise to keep it a secret?"

"Sure."

She gives me a hard look. "I mean *for real*. No one can ever know."

I point out, "I just blubbered on the bed like a raving lunatic over Sebastian Wilcox. If you won't tell anyone about that, I won't tell anyone your secret."

She sinks back onto her bed, restless fingers twisting at her comforter. "Remember when I was having a hard week and Emory and Aubrey came around? And then Sebastian threatened those guys in your class?"

I nod, well aware of what she's talking about. I never got the full story, but it was pretty clear Georgia had been involved in some kind of sex tape or something when she was younger. The pieces add up and I bolt upright, gawking at her. "Oh my god, that video was of you and...*fuck*. Holy shit!"

She looks down at her fidgeting hands. "Yeah, it's me and Heston. Which, for the record, was technically consensual. He was older and popular, and... well, you've seen the way he looks. He was really nice at first, actually." A ghost of a smile touches her lips, but it's not a happy one. "So it's not like I wasn't into it. But when he got me back to his room, I didn't expect it to be so..." she swallows, looking a little green, "...so *aggressive*. I'd never done it that way before and it hurt. There were a few times I couldn't even breathe."

Her cheeks and nose redden, and when she looks up from her hands, a fat tear runs down her cheek. "The sex I could handle. I'd asked for it, and I liked him. You know how it is, right? I just wanted him to like me." She swats the tear away, eyes sparking in anger. "But that video. Oh my god, it fucked me up so bad. He shared it around like it was *nothing*. Like it was all just a big joke. It didn't matter that people couldn't tell it was us, because I figured it was just a matter of time before he told someone, and then everyone would know. It's almost been two years, and he still has that over me."

She sniffs and rubs her nose. "I took a semester off, you know. I told everyone I went on a study abroad, but really I was being treated for depression."

"Jesus, G," I breathe, my problems with Sebastian suddenly seeming so minor and petty. "I had no idea."

"I'm better now," she says, nodding, some of that fire returning to her eyes. "I've got a lot of really good friends who have my back —friends who know the truth and don't judge me for it." She wipes away the rest of her tears, gathering herself up. "I just didn't know he was doing it to other girls. I don't like Sydney very much, but I don't wish that on *anyone*."

"Do you think that has something to do with Bass's being such a dick today? I thought it was just about us having sex, but maybe..." It wouldn't be the first temper tantrum I've seen him have about his brother. "Maybe I'm wrong."

Georgia sighs. "I think it's worth talking to him tomorrow. Maybe he just freaked out. You know Bass is impulsive and a little rabid, but he isn't mean. It sounds like it was just a really stressful day for you both." I nod, unable to argue with that.

Georgia and I sit across from one another, quiet and solemn, because what else can a victim of a Wilcox brother do?

∼

Almost a day passes before I go looking for Bass.

It seems like he vanished after leaving me in the Nerd's parking lot that cold afternoon. I spent all of Dr. Ross's class the next morning staring at the door, waiting for him to waltz in with some weak excuse and charming apology. But it never comes. It's only later at lunch that I find out Georgia's intel—in the form of Carlton —says he never went back to his dorm room. Another source—in the form of Ben—confirms that he'd gone back home. Naturally.

He'd already skipped one day of school to go with me to the Briar Cliffs. What's the harm in taking another?

I'm impatient the whole day, annoying my neighbors with the way I keep tapping my pencil. The tension creates a bitch of a headache, stabbing like an icepick right into my temples. I wince through Econ period, but beg off my AP Lit class to go lay in the nurse's office for an hour, lights turned off, knees tucked to my chest against the ache. Probably a lingering gift from Doug's slap the day before. He got good at making shit hurt without leaving visible marks a long, long time ago.

I'm drowsy when the final bell finally rings, shuffling out of the nurse's office to meet Georgia at her locker.

As soon as I do, she gets a text. "It's Vandy," she informs me, thumb rolling over the screen. "She said she just saw Sebastian head up to his room."

My stomach drops like lead, but at the same time, I'm also weirdly excited. Despite our fight, all day I've found myself reaching for a hand that isn't there, or expecting to see him across the quad, walking toward me.

I'm pissed at him.

I miss him.

It's a lot of complex *stuff* to reconcile, and as I'm using the code to get into Cresswell, heading to the fourth floor, I'm wondering which one will win out.

Half the doors are open, revealing messy boys' dorm rooms, along with the commingled stench of sweat and bad body spray. Sebastian's door sits at the end of the Senior hall like a shiny, precious, ominous thing. I approach it with a flare of nerves, my stomach flipping, feeling queasy and unsure. I've never in my life gone after a guy like this—*wanted* a guy like this—fuck, *needed* a guy like this. I barely hear my own knuckles rap on the door, the sound drowned out by my pulse thundering in my ears.

When the door swings open, there's no one in the entry.

I shuffle my feet for a moment, waiting, but ultimately peer my head inside, searching.

Sebastian's on the couch, bent at the waist, tying a shoe. He's dressed in athletic gear, a large gym bag and equipment waiting on the coffee table. When he glances up, I wince at the color of his eye, a mottled rainbow of purple, red, and yellow.

"Uh, hey," I try. "Can I come in?"

His only response is a grunt of disinterest.

I step into the room, trying to soothe my own anxiety. "I've been looking for you."

His shoulders lift in a dispassionate shrug. "Been busy."

Okay. Guess that cooling off period didn't take.

"How are the kittens?" I ask, hoping maybe that'll ease the mood. Hasn't Abby always been that for us? A middle, neutral ground?

"Fine. Healthy. Getting spoiled by Liesel and my mom." He moves to the other shoe, yet makes no eye contact with me. "I don't really have time to talk—I've got a scrimmage."

"This should only take a minute." I take a deep breath, filling my lungs with his warm scent. "About yesterday—"

He yanks aggressively at his laces, voice low. "You really want to do this now?"

I look around the room in confusion. "*This*?"

"Talk about our feelings until we're yelling at each other again?" He flicks a hand dismissively. "No thanks."

"What..." I rear back, stunned, "I'm sorry, what's happening here?"

"What was always going to happen." He stands and smooths down his shorts, finally meeting my gaze. "Or had you really deluded yourself?"

The cold flatness of his eyes makes me take an involuntary step back. This isn't my Sebastian. This isn't the guy who kissed me, laughed with me, protected me, or... *loved* me.

This is someone else. Someone cold as stone and just as hard.

"Is this about Heston?" I ask, trying to put the pieces together—to make them fit. My brain works overtime to rationalize the man standing in front of me, blank-faced and empty.

"So, you had, then. Alright, let me clear it up for you." He bends to put something in his bag, seeming like only half his attention is on the words pouring from his mouth. "You had it right before. I chase, you run, I chase some more, you finally cave, I get what I want, and then it's over." When he looks at me again, it's with a quick, dagger-sharp glance of his blue eyes. "All clear?"

"Wait," I say, frozen in shock. Nothing has ever been less clear. "It's over? What's over?"

He shrugs, grabbing his bag and throwing the strap across his broad chest. "Move."

I blink, realizing that I'm standing in the doorway, blocking his exit. Too bad. "No. Not until you talk to me."

"I just told you how I feel." His eyebrow arches. "I know you've got some masochistic hard-on about being abused, but seriously? You want me to say that again?"

Hot anger and embarrassment rushes through me, but I try to ground myself. "No, you just basically told me that you're a dick. Bravo. Sebastian Wilcox is an asshole! But there's more to this than you're saying. I *know* there is, Bass. Is it about Heston? Talk to me."

The impassive expression on his face flickers, clouding for a moment, before returning smooth as a stone. "This has nothing to do with my brother and everything to do with the fact that if you think I'm spending the rest of my senior year coaxing you out of your pants when I could fuck any girl in this school—anyway, anytime, anyhow—you're more clueless than I thought." He watches me, face hardening at whatever he sees in my expression. "Where exactly did you think this was going? We both know I don't do girlfriends, but if I did, you know who I'd choose?" He dips in close, voice dropping to a harsh whisper. "Someone I could actually fucking touch."

I've been hit before. Punched, slapped, shoved, kicked. I've even taken a fist from Sebastian himself. But nothing, *none of those*, hurt the way this does. I look at him and I can't even see the guy I thought I was falling in love with. All I can see is the tear-blurred vision of his expressionless face and bored eyes.

It takes me three tries to inhale. It feels like the air has been knocked out of my fucking lungs. "Why are you acting like this?"

He steps closer to me, barely an inch away. "The sex was fine, just not worth all the bullshit, truthfully." He pauses and I stare at the floor, refusing to let him see me cry. "Now, I don't want to force you to move, but I will. Don't make me."

The idea of him touching me right now makes me want to wretch. I close my eyes, willing my legs to move me aside.

When I open them again, he's gone.

Gone.

29

I just want to stop seeing it.

Every time I blink, every time my attention drifts, that look on her face comes drifting back to me. The way her chin wobbled, jaw locked tight. The way she looked at me, so wide-eyed and gutted. How still she stood, how quiet.

Worst of all was that flash of understanding in her eyes, and the way she didn't even look surprised. She didn't argue. She just accepted it—just like *that*.

I kept pushing, digging that knife in deeper, hoping she'd just... fucking kick back. Pissing off Sugar is supposed to be something I'm good at. It would have been so much easier, being under the fire of her fury. It would have still hurt, but it wouldn't have been *this*.

This agonizing, hopeless throb of guilt and loss.

It's better than the alternative, though. That's what I keep telling myself. It's not a fun time, constantly assaulting myself with scenarios of the many and varied ways Heston would hurt her. He'd go for the simple stuff first. Get her kicked out of Preston. Maybe fuck up something with her mom—as if I'd care about that. But after the simple shit, he'd get his hands dirty. He'd touch her. I know he fucking would. If she's lucky, that'd be all he'd do. But it's not Heston's style. He'd probably manipulate her—it wouldn't be easy, I should know—but he's good at what he does. It might take him weeks, months, years, but eventually he'd find something to rip away from her.

That's the only thing that's keeping me breathing.

"What. Have. You. Done?"

I turn at the sound of Vandy's acerbic hiss. Except it's not just Vandy. Georgia and Aubrey each flank one side of her tiny frame, and Elana and Caroline make a solid wall behind them.

I'm fucking cornered.

Just what I need.

I try to slip into the lie—this reflection of myself who isn't a twisted, gnarled thing, as if such a thing exists. "Nothing the six of you couldn't see coming," I reply tonelessly, wiping the sweat off my forehead. The scrimmage kicked my ass. I've done my best to stay conditioned, but with the downtime from the concussion, I'm not keeping up with the other guys, and it's seriously fucking with my ability to get lost in the game. The pace on the field is brutal. It probably doesn't help that I'd spent most of last night getting absolutely tanked, alone in my bedroom at home. "If you don't mind, I smell like a jockstrap and I think we'd all be better off if I took a shower."

"No," Georgia says, her voice shaking with anger. "Not until you explain yourself. I don't know what the hell you said to Sugar earlier, but she is completely fucked up over it! She won't even talk about what happened, beyond saying you dumped her."

I run my hand through my hair, trying to maintain my aloof expression. "Look, you guys know me. I don't do relationships. Sure, maybe I had a moment of temporary insanity with Sugar. She was a challenge. She put up a fight. You know how I love a fight." I briefly consider whether or not a wink to Vandy could actually sell this, but realize she may castrate me if I did. "I couldn't resist, but you also know that, as soon as I've beaten my opponent, I'm ready to move on. Everyone knows I don't do rematches."

My eyes dart between them, wondering if any of them bought a single line of the bullshit coming out of my mouth. From the hot glare coming back at me, the answer is unilaterally no.

"Bass," Georgia seethes, "I swear to god, if you don't fix this..."

"Then what? Because there's nothing to fix. I told her it's over. I'm done with her. It was fun while it lasted, but let's face it. Sugar is way too high maintenance for me. She's..." The rest hangs on my tongue, bitter and sharp. I can't bring myself to say that she's too broken. Too damaged. I wouldn't mean it the way they'd think, anyway. There's just no way I'm making it worse than I already have. There's no way I'm letting *him* get to *her*. "She's not my type."

Georgia and the other girls gawk at me, mouths gaping like fuming fish.

Part of me is relieved they don't buy it. It's a frustrating push and pull. I need everyone to believe it—I need Heston to believe it—but the second they do, it'd probably gut me.

More than I already am, of course.

I take their silence as an opportunity to bail, turning my back on them to stalk across the campus. I think these might be the times it gets bad. Walking. Thinking. Being able to slip into my head. I thought being back on the field would make this easier, but I was wrong.

Maybe it can't *get* any easier. Maybe that's what I deserve, knowing that Sugar is walking around out there fucked up over it all. Maybe I just have to walk around like this sad, pathetic shell of a person who doesn't have a shred of control over his own fucking life because his brother is a bored, sadistic piece of shit. Maybe that's justice.

I'm just passing the Devil's Tower when I hear, "You're weak, you know."

I pause, shifting the weight of my bag on my shoulder to face Afton. She's leaning against the wall. I didn't even know she was out here. Honestly, I'm surprised she cares at all.

"You callin' me names, Cross?"

"I'm calling it like I see it. You're weak and pathetic." Her eyes rake over me, disdain dripping from her voice. "I defended you to her, did you know that? The first day of school when she left the room upset about you touching her? I *defended* you. I told her that you were a good guy. That whatever had happened between you must have been a mistake, because Sebastian Wilcox would never intentionally hurt someone."

I fist my hand around the strap of my bag, looking away. "Then you were wrong."

She shakes her head, lips pursed angrily. "You fucked up, Bass, and I don't think there's any fixing it."

I take a deep breath and meet her gaze, trying to convey a message. "You're right. There is no way to fix this—with her, *or* with you."

She arches a perfectly sculpted eyebrow. "What are you saying?"

"I'm saying that you need to do what's right here, because I sure as hell can't." Not any more than I already am. "If you want me out of the Devils, that's fine."

"I never said anything about—"

"Official or not, you're the Queen Bee of the Playthings. They'll do what you say and follow your lead." I haven't forgotten how quick Heston was to target Vandy just for being my friend. Looking at Afton now—thinking of all my brave, fucked-up, beautiful girls —I add, "It'll be best if you all stop calling me a friend. In fact, don't call me at all."

She stares at me hard and long, and when I can't take the scrutiny any longer, I turn and walk away. Walking away from Sugar was bad enough, like ripping open a part of myself and plucking out all the good bits, one by one.

Tossing away the rest is like a pitchfork to the heart.

～

It doesn't get better from there. It turns out that Sugar Voss has made an impression on my friends. Everyone is pissed at me. The Playthings. The Devils. I'm met with cold shoulders and hot glares everywhere I turn. If I thought my boys would have my back, then I'm just shy of being mistaken. Unlike the Playthings, they don't look like they want to rip my balls off.

They also don't look like they want to defend me much, either.

And they shouldn't, is the thing. It hurts, having to cast them all aside—knowing if I didn't, they'd do it for me. But knowing that Sugar's carved herself out a place here, has inspired their loyalty after only a few months...

I'm glad she has that.

She deserves it more than I do, anyway.

Even Dr. Ross, who I swear knows more about the inner workings of teenage drama than she'd ever admit, gives me a dark look when I enter the classroom the next morning.

Sugar's already in her seat, and I'd been preparing myself for this all night—if getting wasted in my room again can count as preparing—but it's still like feeling a knife buried into my chest, just seeing her sitting there. Without a word, I walk down the aisle, passing her desk, and drop heavily into my own.

She jumps at the sound of my seat squeaking on the floor, but visibly clenches tight, pitching forward.

The whole class is like that.

I still get all these wild, nagging impulses to reach for her hair. I've spent the last couple weeks playing with it in class, even having halfway learned to do a braid while Elana looked on, snickering at how lumpy and twisted it looked.

My knee bounces throughout the lecture, and I wish I could just get all these hard parts over with. Seeing each other in classes, the halls, pretending like we aren't both being singed from the inside out.

Sugar begins packing her bag long before the bell rings, and when it does, she's out of her seat like a bolt of lightning, not even waiting for the other girls at the door. I take my time, listlessly shoving my shit into my bag and sliding from my chair.

Reyn doesn't even wait around for me.

The rest of the week goes like that. I go to class, people glare at me, Sugar avoids me, I eat lunch with the lacrosse team, I go back to my dorm and get drunk until three in the morning, when I finally manage to nod off to sleep, only to wake four hours later and do it all over again.

On Friday, I'm on my way to lunch, cutting through the Arts wing, when I pass the weekly art exhibit. The twins are adjusting a piece on the display, bickering and huffing like they always do. I slow my roll, because let's face it, it's been a hard few days, and getting a little love from my biggest fans would help a lot. I stop to inspect the photo being hung—a closed eye covered in glittery eyeshadow and thick, rainbow-colored eyelashes.

"It needs to go up on the right," Micha says, hands on his hips. Michaela shifts the frame up and down. "Nope, too high. Now it's too low." He throws his hands up. "I'll just do it myself."

"I can adjust a frame," Michaela snipes, rolling her eyes at her brother.

The move forces her to look over his head, locking eyes with me. I give her a grin, expecting a smile in return, maybe a little blushing, but instead I get a hard glare.

"I think it looks great," I try, digging my hands into my pockets. "Who took this? Michaela?"

"Oh," Micha says, whipping around, eyes narrowing, "it's you."

"Yep. Just admiring your work."

The twins exchange a knowing look, then turn back to the frame.

"Do you need any help?" I reluctantly ask.

"No, we're all good," Micha says, waving his hand at me dismissively.

Awkwardly, I reply, "Okay, cool. Well, I think the photo looks great—whoever took it." Neither of them look at me, and I think maybe for the first time in my life, I've been rejected by a freshman. That didn't even happen to me when *I* was a freshman.

Ouch.

"Well, good luck with the exhibit. I know you guys worked hard on it."

"Mmhmm," Michaela says, using her thumb to adjust the picture again.

Clearly not getting anything out of those two, I start to walk off.

But then Micha calls, "Hey!"

I turn. "Yeah?"

"I thought you were different from your brother," he says, lips pressed into a tight line, "but I guess I was wrong."

Double ouch.

I continue on my way, letting the insult settle around my shoulders. I never thought I was like Heston. The idea was laughable. But the school, the Devils, even the twins all think I'm a manipulative asshole who'll do anything to get in a girl's pants and then break her heart.

Maybe I'm a better actor than I thought.

Resigned to another night of getting shitfaced alone in my room, I enter the dining hall and grab a tray. I pretend I don't feel the laser beams on my back as I carry it across the room and sit with the other guys on the lacrosse team. I keep acting like the food I'm shoveling in my mouth doesn't taste like ash, and the wise-cracking jokes I share with the guys aren't a cover-up for the fact I feel like shit.

And I know Sugar's not feeling great. Every time I manage a passing glance in the hallways, in Dr. Ross's class, I can clearly see she looks like hell. It's not just the purple smudges under her eyes or the fact I haven't seen her smile in days. It's in her hunched, defeated shoulders, and the way she sits with an empty chair between her and the others. It's how she wraps her arms around her body and keeps her hair loose, using it to shield her face.

It's in the way that, when she sits in front of me in Dr. Ross's class, she tries to make herself disappear. That wall I broke down is firmly back in place, but this time even more fragile than before. I thought when I punched her that night, when I heard her scream, it was the worst thing I'd ever seen or heard.

I was wrong.

This? The silence?

It's so much fucking worse.

I want her to fight back. Kick me in the balls. Shove that knife in my heart and end me.

"Fuck," Michael Watts says, looking at his phone. "Coach added an extra scrimmage tonight."

Peter Norton groans. "My arms are still sore from yesterday."

The guys start bitching, but the screech of a chair dragging on the cafeteria floor, and then a figure dropping into the empty seat next to Sugar, draws my attention to the Devils' lunch table. Carlton eases himself in the chair and gives Sugar a small grin.

My first response is *what the fuck*? My second is to sit back and watch Sugar pull out her blade and castrate him in front of the room. He leans into her and says something way too low to hear. I wait for her to tell him to fuck off.

She doesn't.

She ducks her head for a moment but then grins at him. She *fucking* grins. And then she nods her head in approval of whatever it is that asshat is saying. Since when does Carlton say anything worth smiling over?

For the first time in days, something penetrates this shell of gnarled numbness I've become, and I barely even think about what I'm doing. I push back my chair, plotting the ways I'm going to make him pay for even looking at my—

"Bass." A body steps in my path. I peer around them. "Bass!"

I blink and see that it's Emory standing in front of me. "What?"

"Hey," he says, giving me a weird look. "We need to talk."

Impatiently, I try once again to peer past him. "About what?"

"Tonight," is all he says. "Seven. You know where."

He gives me a meaningful look, one that suggests he's aware I was just about to beat down a fellow Devil. He's never approached me directly like that. Most Devil communication goes through the standard process. The fact that there's no envelope, and he's telling me about it plain as day in front of my teammates, means this is not a formal meeting.

Just fucking great.

"I've got practice."

"I don't care," he says, turning to walk off. "Be there."

I watch him go, and then glance back over at the table, catching Sugar looking at me. We hold one another's gaze for a long beat. My heart pounds in my ears and I wait for her to do something, to show some kind of reaction, but she doesn't.

She just turns away.

~

"Is that how you want to do this?" I ask, tearing off my gloves. "Is that really how you want this to go down?" My helmet is next. I throw it across the field. Peter Norton looks around at our teammates, hoping they'll do something. They won't, because they're all a bunch of pussies. I step toward him and shove his chest with both hands. "Are you really going to foul me like that?"

I know I'm overreacting, but it's like I can't control it. I need to get out this anger before I blow completely. This isn't even the first altercation this practice. It's the third. But lacrosse, being out here on the field, just isn't hitting the same way it used to. No matter how hard I run or how many of these motherfuckers I tackle, the wild, burning thing in my chest just isn't going away.

It doesn't make any sense. This was supposed to be *it*. I was supposed to come out here and get lost in the game and leave the field feeling... well, if not better, then at least not fucking *worse*.

"Hey!" Gus Meyers shouts, grabbing me by the shoulder. "Chill the fuck out, Wilcox."

I look down at his hand and then slowly raise my gaze to his ugly face. Fear flickers in his eyes at the grin I give him, full of teeth, and he drops his hand, taking a step back. Touching me was a stupid fucking move on his part and he knows it.

"Wilcox!" my name echoes across the field through the bullhorn. "You touch another one of my players and you're done for the season!"

Pete, Gus, and everyone else on the field waits to see if I believe Coach Pickford. Or maybe they're waiting to see if I care. I thought I would. I figured once I got this back, even if I'd carved my own heart out by fucking Sugar over so, so well, that I'd be able to immerse in the violence of it.

Now, it all seems pointless and tedious.

"Fuck it," I say. "Fuck all of this."

I walk off the field, passing the glares of the coach and the other guys on the bench. I exit the field, yanking my shirt off and wiping off my face. When I look up again, I see Ben standing nearby, hands shoved in his letterman jacket's pockets.

"The fuck do you want?"

He shrugs. "Just making sure you go meet Emory."

I scoff, stepping up to him. "Or what? You think you can make me?"

"I think Meyers is right," Ben replies, not looking intimidated in the least. "You need to chill the fuck out. You're acting crazier than usual."

I can take Ben. He knows I can take him. But where's the fun in that, anyway?

"Whatever. Let's just get this bullshit over with."

He escorts me across the field, like some kind of fucking hall monitor. When I get to the tower, he doesn't come in with me. He stands by the door, jerking his head at the knob in a stupidly persistent gesture.

I take a deep breath and head downstairs, stepping through the low entrance. The first thing I see is the couch where Sugar and I...

I grit my teeth and turn away.

I'd expected a full crew, but the reality is a lot more depressing. It's just Emory and Reyn, kicked back in a couple chairs, sharing some beers.

I go ahead and help myself to a bottle. "So where are the others? I know Ben's out there getting practicing for his career as a minimum wage bouncer. Tyson's too nice for conflict, so I get why he's out. But what about Carlton?" Bitterly, I guess, "I probably know what he's doing, considering I saw him hitting on her at lunch. Didn't take him long, did it? Bet my used condom hasn't even made it to the landfill yet and he's already taking a run at her. Motherfucker."

"Jesus, dude," Emory says, face screwed up into a glower. "What the hell is going on with you?"

"Nothing."

"Nothing?" he spits back. "You come into classes every day hungover, looking like crap. That is, when you decide to actually attend. All the girls are riled up about whatever went down between you and Sugar. Vandy and Aubrey were the ones who asked us to talk to you. Even Afton said something, and you know she doesn't get involved in trivial shit. I know break-ups suck, but this has gone somewhere toxic."

"Look," I shrug, "they're Team Sugar. No skin off my back. You know, Hoes before Bros."

"They aren't Hoes," Emory snaps. "They're Devils, and they're worried. We're all a little worried. I mean, fuck, dude, you're not exactly..." He waves a hand at me, as if encompassing my entire being.

I raise my eyebrows, waiting for him to continue.

"Stable," Reyn cuts in, clearly having no problem throwing punches. "You're not stable."

I narrow my eyes. "Is Reynolds McAllister seriously judging *my* character? Because that's like the pot calling the kettle—oh wait, someone stole the kettle. And the pot. And the whole fucking stove."

Reyn just shrugs.

"No one is judging you," Emory insists. "In fact, Georgia is convinced this is about Heston."

I clamp my jaw shut, eyes narrowing. "Georgia needs to shut her cakehole."

He ignores me. "Is it? Does this have something to do with Heston?"

I shove a hand through my hair and look away. Emory's the only one who really knows my brother. Fuck, he idolized him and Bates when they ran this joint. But I also know that Emory wanted the Devils to be better than a group of pretentious bullying assholes.

He wanted to make this into something worth being a part of. Kind of funny when I think about it—the long arm of Heston, still fucking the Devils up even after he's left.

I take a long drag from my beer before admitting, "Heston found out about me and Sugar."

There's a long moment of silence before Reyn says, "Uh, so what? What's the big deal. Did you think you could keep her a secret forever?"

"Did he say something?" Emory asks, eyebrows furrowed. "Did he threaten her?"

I think about the texts he sent me. It was an entire day of them. He found her school records. He knows she's here on scholarship. He knows she doesn't like being touched. Fuck, that one probably gets me the most. This thing I tried so hard to teach her was good and *fine*, and he's more than willing to twist it into something ugly and awful, just to get back at me for...

I turn the bottle over in my hands, pressing my thumbnail into the glass. "He wants me to fight again."

"You can't," Reyn instantly says, as if it's that easy. "Unless you want your brain to turn into swiss cheese permanently."

Rolling my shoulders, I grind out, "I know. But if I don't, he'll take it out on her. Fuck, if I *do*, he'll take it out on her."

Emory stares at me. "So what? You figured if you dumped her, he'd let it go?"

"He'll lose interest if he thinks she doesn't mean anything to me," I explain. "If he doesn't think he can use her against me, he won't bother."

"Then we go talk to him," Reyn suggests.

"Oh geez, why in my eighteen fucking years on this earth had that never occurred to me? Thank you, Reyn! In two seconds, and with almost zero insight, you completely changed my life. Jesus Christ," I say to Emory, jabbing a thumb to Reyn. "How much therapy has this guy had? Like everything can be 'talked out'."

Reyn just goes on, "Explain the situation. The concussion and everything. Work it out."

Fist clenched tight around my bottle, I explode, "It doesn't work that way with Heston!"

"You're the toughest guy I know, Wilcox," Reyn admits. "How bad can it be?"

I chuckle darkly. "You want to know how bad my brother really is? He's the asshole who kicked his best friend's girl in the face during a fire drill. He picks on little gay kids and mocks them in front of the whole school. He's the one who preys on girls, films them in vulnerable positions, and hey, if they're lucky, no one can see their face while he's abusing them!"

I stand and start pacing the room, feeling the anxiety and anger rising. "He's the kind of guy who sets up his little brother with an unfair fight that gives him a wicked concussion just to get a bigger payday. I've watched him drive our own mother to the edge of her own fucking sanity, just because she showed me a sliver of something he saw as favor."

I turn to Emory, adding, "You know that pregnant cat? The one Sugar and I have been feeding? I took her home to have her kittens, and you know the first thought that popped into my head at the thought of leaving them in the house with him?" I look at Reyn, explaining, "That he'd kill them. Just because they were something I wanted to protect, something I gave even half a shit about. That's who Heston is, and that's what Heston does. Emory doesn't even know the half of it. Being a Devil with him? That's nothing. Try living with him. Being related to him. Being someone he'll never see as anything more than competition." I shake my head, tossing back my beer. "I will do everything in my power to protect Sugar from him, even if that means breaking her fucking heart and having her and the Playthings hate me forever."

Emory and Reyn both look on, slack-jawed and still.

Reyn's the first to break out of it. "But what about your parents? You dad? He's powerful, right?"

I laugh darkly. "He is powerful, and he wields it to protect his kids, not the rest of the world."

"Aren't you one of his kids?" Emory wonders. "Doesn't he want to protect you from him?"

I shake my head, raising my arms. "Heston's his big, fat Wilcox heir. He's got the Ivy League, the looks, the prickish attitude, and the Wilcox name. My dad's been grooming him for this shit since he was born."

"So be better."

I turn a hot glare on Reynolds, feeling sort of like I want to bash his face in. "Excuse me?"

He just shrugs. "You've got all of that—or at least the opportunity to have it. Be better than Heston and your dad will choose you."

"Be better than Heston," I repeat, dumbfounded at his idiocy. "Sure, let me just go back in time and erase the fact that eighty percent of my favorite pastimes are illegal. Or that my dad has taught me fuck-all. Or that Heston was born first. That's helpful as fuck, McAllister."

"Well, you need to do something," Emory cuts in. "Are you just going to live your entire life not wanting or having anything because you're afraid Heston might fuck it up?"

"Looks like it," I say bitterly.

"That's not realistic, Bass."

"How's this for realism. You wanna know who he threatened before he found out about Sugar." I give them each a tight grin. "Vandy. Just because Syd told him we were friends. That's all it takes."

Reyn doesn't look so fucking blasé now. "Excuse me, he did fucking what?"

Emory barks a laugh. "I'd like to see him try."

I tip my bottle at him. "That's exactly why he won't. Not because he's afraid of you—he isn't—but because I'm not worried. You see, it's not fun for him unless I'm worried." I down the last of my beer, tossing my bottle on the ground.

"So that's it," Emory asks, face grim. "You're going to go back to fighting, just because that's what he wants."

I smile bitterly. "What Heston wants, Heston gets. Path of least resistance, Em. He won't stop, and if someone gets in his way, he'll bring everyone down with him." I glance between them. "Look at the Devils. Heston organized that club prank and the whole group went down. He's not afraid of cutting off his nose to spite his face. So," I continue, "unless you have something that will take my brother out for good, I can't risk it. *I can't risk her.*"

Neither of them have a response to that, which is about fucking right. He'll come after them next, and neither of them are going to risk it, either.

I don't blame them one bit.

30

Mr. Lee looks through my photos, one more time. I know from the way his lips turn down into a sharp frown what he's going to say before it's even out of his mouth. "But these two, at least?"

I don't even look at them. "No, thanks."

Mr. Lee has spent the last three days trying to convince me that the photos of Sebastian are the most compelling in my portfolio. The recruiters apparently are partial to portraits. I can't even bring myself to look at them. The most recent ones, taken during that day at his house, had been developed the night after he dumped me. Locked down in the lab, watching his face appear in a grim parade of wound-rubbing salt hadn't been my finest moment. There's just something about putting the moments on paper—capturing them, locking them away, pinning them down—that makes it easier to let go.

Or, well. That's how it used to be. Now it's just a constant reminder that at one point, however briefly, Sebastian Wilcox had managed to snare the best parts of me.

Stings like a bitch.

Mr. Lee sighs, shaking his head. "That's a real shame, Sugar.

This one, with the fire…" He doesn't make me look at it, but he does wait for me to meet his gaze. "This piece is the perfect representation of your style, the emotive nature of your work, and your skill and precision with a camera. I don't want to push you somewhere you creatively—or emotionally—aren't ready to go," his sympathetic face makes it clear that he knows enough, "but I'd be remiss in my position if I let you walk out that door without telling you that this photo should be front and center. It's your ticket, Miss Voss, plain and simple."

Internally, I wince. The photo of Sebastian, taken the night of the bonfire, has been on my mind more than Mr. Lee could possibly know. Of course, it's a great picture. It's the best fucking photo I've ever taken. I know that. Nevertheless, "I'll just stick with the graffiti."

Unable to bring myself to even look at the photos I'd taken of him, Mr. Lee and I have reached a tenuous compromise. Even though it's still like picking at a raw, gaping wound, we've decided my shots from the car shows were the best compromise.

He looks disappointed, but finally slides the photo back into the folder. "You can start setting up your exhibit on Saturday morning. I know it's not a lot of time, but you were a late addition. Can you swing that?"

I assure him I can, even though I've lost all enthusiasm for it. It's not all because of the way my chest feels like it's caving in, pretty much every second of every day. It's not all because of Sebastian. It's not even because of my mom. It's not because, in the span of a single day, I lost every bit of footing I've ever had. My past, my present, and now my future.

Mr. Lee is right. My car show pieces are good—some of them are even amazing—but most of them are just okay. Pedestrian. Formulaic. Entirely without feeling or substance. It's a mediocre display of my capabilities.

But it's all I can do.

Later that day, I'm back in my dorm, staring down at them, the spread of photos blurring into one indefinable blob of gray. It's stupid. I don't have time to keep waffling on this. The exhibit is in two days. It should be hard to dwell on the way my insides feel hollowed out when I'm so busy, but there are times when it still feels like I'm doing nothing but treading water.

Every night, before falling into a fitful rest, I think the next day will better. It can't always be like this. One day, I'll have to wake up and not feel this churning twist of grief and anger.

Hasn't happened yet.

It's pathetic. I know it's pathetic. I'm pretty sure by now everyone around me knows it, too. Hell, even Mr. Lee knows it. Every time I lay in bed at night, staring sightlessly at the ceiling, only for Georgia to suddenly lean into my line of sight with that troubled look on her face, I know she's thinking it. When Vandy links her arm with mine in the halls, determined to touch me even though it turns me into a mess of tangled things—taking it upon herself to adopt Sebastian's quest of making me better—I know she's thinking it, too. When Carlton approaches me at the lunch table, offering to slip me a little something to smooth out the rough edges, it's because he's thinking it.

I should be stronger than this. No one wants to be the girl whose whole life is consumed by some asshole guy. Especially one like Sebastian. As much as it hurts—all the fucking time, day and night—it's also so goddamn mortifying that I fell for him, hook, line, and pretty-boy sinker.

It helps that life at Preston runs full steam ahead. When I'm not in class or studying for an exam, I'm prepping for the art exhibit, or listening to speculation about who pulled the prank at the basketball game. My break-up becomes old news as other drama unfolds among the students. Things move fast here. Which may be part of the problem. Sebastian Wilcox rolled over me like a rogue wave, cloaked by the darkness of the night sky, dragging me under until I couldn't find my way to the surface again.

"Which one do you like best?" My rusty voice asks Georgia, holding out two black and white proofs. I took it the night at the mall. It's of Jasmine, mid-curve, the shape of her silhouette transforming from the sleek, organic curve to a rigid, straight line. She's going so fast that the shape is blurred at the edges. One version is a crisp black and white, while the other has kept the red saturation of the taillight's eerie glow.

"Hmm." She taps her pen against her lips. "I think I like the splash of color. It looks kind of retro, don't you think?"

I look at the one she chose, preferring it, too. Of course, I would. It'd started out as my exhibit's main aesthetic—black and white with selective pops of color—but that was back when my exhibit was still worth having.

My phone vibrates with a text and Georgia watches curiously as I read it. "It's Vandy," I explain. "She says he's at lacrosse all afternoon, so we're clear to go to the garage. She's going to pick me up in five minutes to drive me over."

Georgia frowns at the word 'he', pushing to her feet. "I'm coming, too. Let me get my shoes."

I almost ask her not to bother, but the thought of saying it feels rude. Georgia has been a good friend—a better friend than I deserve. At first, all she and Vandy wanted to do was talk about what happened. I humored them for a while, going over it again and again...

The sex was fine, just not worth all the bullshit, truthfully.

They were determined that if they analyzed every word that transpired between us—every action—they'd be able to figure out why Sebastian dumped me like that. But after a couple days, I couldn't take it anymore. Each time I went over it, repeating his cruel words, remembering his cold, flat stare, the heavy thing sitting on my chest burrowed in a little deeper. Eventually, I put my foot down and told them they had to stop obsessing over it, because *I* needed to stop obsessing over it. They aren't the ones who have to walk around with this constant, yawning fissure inside them. They don't wake up at night with wet cheeks, and in a moment of humiliating weakness, wonder why they weren't good enough. What they said wrong. What they did or didn't do. How they could have been better. If there were ever any hints that this was all just some sick game.

They don't go around wishing that he'd look at them, just once.

That's all on me.

Thankfully, they both respected my decision. But it seems like their fixation just shifted slightly to the side. Since then, they haven't stopped talking about Sydney and the video they suspect Heston has on her. This seems to have struck a nerve with both of them, and it's no surprise they're discussing it, *again*, on the way to the garage.

"It's just so crazy," Vandy says. "That day Sugar and I saw her talking to Fiona, she seemed so weirdly proud of those bruises. Right, Sugar? I mean, she acted like she was pretty into it."

"That's what he does," Georgia says from the backseat. I recognize this tone of voice from her now—low, a little too carefully controlled. She's getting pissed, just talking about it. "You're excited he's giving you attention. He's good-looking, popular, and smart. Who are you? Some nobody. You feel so lucky that he's interested, you spend most of your time with him trying not to mess it up. Doing whatever it takes to make him like you—to make him happy. You go into it willingly, and then when he has sex with you...the way he..." she swallows, "...you know it's not okay, but by then it's too late. By the time you realize what really happened, it's over and done."

"You were a Freshman, Georgia. There's no way you could have anticipated that." Georgia glances at her in the rearview mirror. "Sydney is a little older, but she's super immature. After being rejected by Reyn and Seb—*him*," she glances apologetically at me, "I'm sure she was ready to prove herself. What better person than *his* brother?"

"Do you think she knows about the video?" I ask. I haven't seen it. None of us have, but apparently, when Georgia confronted Sebastian about it, he confirmed it exists.

"I doubt it," Georgia says. "I didn't. Not until he leaked it and it went viral all over school."

Vandy straightens in her seat. "Hey, what if we could get her to go report it to Headmaster Collins? Or maybe even the police? Sharing videos like that's against the law, right? Revenge porn or something? You're both minors in those videos. That can't be legal, can it? And now it's more than just one person that we know of. You could back each other up."

Georgia's already fair skin pales even further. "I can't do that! I've managed to keep this under wraps for this long. I even went to that facility and no one knew about it. Coming out now? Everyone would know it's me. It's bad enough when they *don't*, but once they do?" She looks like she might be sick, fists pressing hard into her stomach. "I can't. I don't want to dredge it all up again."

Vandy and I share a look. Neither of us want to hurt Georgia. We don't want to hurt Sydney, either, but what Heston is doing is beyond fucked up. Maybe Vandy's right. Maybe it's even illegal.

"None of it matters anyway," Georgia says. "Emory told me they confronted, uh... *him*, about it, and he said that even if someone turns his brother in, their dad will just bail Heston out. For all we know, he's been in trouble for this before and nothing ever came of it."

A sick taste fills my mouth. I knew rich people sucked. I knew they were privileged and entitled and got away with murder. Sebastian told me that, over and over again, and I still trusted him. Sure, maybe he didn't force me the way Heston did, but he still carefully manipulated me until I broke down and he got what he wanted. Georgia isn't the only one that didn't realize she was being used by a Wilcox until it was too late.

Vandy slows the car and pulls into the garage's parking lot. My eyes are peeled for the blue of the Shelby, but thankfully, I don't see it. Most of the bays are empty, in fact.

"Holy shit, Sugar," Georgia says, pitching forward between our seats to peer out the windshield. "Is that your car?"

I follow her gaze to a car parked right out front. I'd totally overlooked it while making sure Bass wasn't here. I stare at the vehicle, knowing that's not my beater. It's a Mustang, alright. But *my* Mustang? Obviously not.

"That's not my car," I say knowingly, opening my door and climbing out. The girls follow as I explain, "They mentioned some stuff about salvaging and reproduction. Maybe they brought it as, like... an example. For reference."

While we wait by the bay for Merle to come out, they both keep shooting each other these little glances. They're a little hard to read, full of nervous energy and trepidation, but I get the sense they know something I don't.

Just as Georgia meets my gaze to say, "Okay, Sugar, look—" Merle finally walks out, giving me a tight nod.

"Miss Voss?"

I make a passing effort at a responding smile. Truth be told, being here is a little like stabbing myself in the chest, so I'd rather get it over with. "You said I could pick up my car today?"

Sticking a pencil behind his ear, he says, "Sure thing, go take a look," and gestures to the other Mustang.

I give him a long look. Maybe my car's around back or something. "Where is it?"

He looks at Georgia and Vandy, and then barks out a laugh. "It's right there! Can't miss a beauty like that, can ya?"

I look at the Mustang again. And then again. And then again. I do a quadruple take, because this can't be my car. My car is a rusted-out piece of shit being held together by little more than duct tape and a firm reluctance to actually drive it.

The car sitting in front of me is a work of art. It bears no resemblance.

"Uh," I start, reaching up to rub at my neck. "Merle? No offense or anything, but are you, like... you know. *Sure*?"

He just gives me a wide grin, raising his arm toward the car. "Go take a look for yourself. A car like that never loses itself in the pretty trim. I'm betting there's still a few tells."

I APPROACH it slowly as they all look on, eyeing the decals and shiny chrome trim. The car's painted a sleek, shimmery pewter that's both elegant and severe at the same time. I walk all the way around it, and I don't see any rust. There is a little dent—so small, most people would never notice it—right at the bottom of the driver's side door. It looks an awful lot like the one I made with my neighbor's skateboard when I was ten.

Disbelieving, I peer in the window. The seats look flawlessly upholstered with nice stitching. There's clean, black carpet on the floor boards, and the dash is smooth, unblemished, shiny and oiled. Right in the middle of the steering wheel sits a Mustang emblem.

It's a bright, blazing blue.

"No fucking way." I yank the door open, and it doesn't have that awful, screeching creak, but somehow it still sounds similar. There's a clicking to it, in the way it pulls back a bit when it's halfway open. *A tell.*

The interior is thick with the smell of the upholstery and leather. At first, I think the gear shift is new, but the closer I look, I realize it's just been refinished and buffed.

It has a star-shaped chip in the middle.

It feels like my lungs expand three sizes; a lump wedged into the back of my throat as I stare inside the car. This car that's been with me my entire life, over mountains and valleys, trunked packed with overflowing bags and bruised boxes as we moved from base to base. This place where my dad used to sit, glancing at me in the rearview with a big grin as he revved the engine, because he knew it'd make me grin back.

I look at it, so different but still the same underneath all the glamour and shine, and realize that, in many ways, I was born here. Maybe my dad is gone. Maybe my mother is gone, too. But this is my childhood—my *real* childhood—right here beneath this roof.

And it's still here.

Still standing.

Still beautiful and strong.

It takes me a long time to find my voice. It feels too big to put words to, like just trying might turn me inside out. "How...?"

"She turned out pretty nice, didn't she?" a voice says, and I turn to find Merle standing a few feet away, wiping grease off his hands with a rag. If he notices my tears, he does me the courtesy of ignoring them.

"This is too much," I say, running my hand over the roof. "I love it—every part of it is amazing—but I can't possibly repay you for this. You don't know how much I wish I could." The thought of leaving it here physically hurts. "I have eight hundred dollars, well, eighteen hundred dollars, to my name, Merle. I can't afford it."

He sighs and takes his rag, buffing out an invisible spot on the hood. "You don't owe me anything, Miss."

This isn't the work of an old dude who works on cars. This is the work of someone who truly loves their craft. This was done with careful attention to detail. "You put so much work into this," I argue, stomach sinking at the thought.

"No, I didn't," he says dismissively. "In fact, the last time I did anything even resembling work on this car was the first day it got towed in here. I haven't laid a finger on it since."

Confusion rolls through me like a tidal wave, making me momentarily speechless. "Then how...?"

"Now that you mention it," he adds, propping his fists on his hips. "Well, maybe you could do me a favor, actually."

"A favor?" My laugh is full of disbelief. It'd have to be one hell of a favor.

He nods, leveling me with a look. "Give the kid a break, Miss. I don't know what happened between you two. Probably, he did something stupid. Boys that age... we always do something stupid." He squints down at the car, completely ignoring the way my face has paled. "But someone puts as much time and care into a car like this, the way he did? That's not for nothing."

I pull in a stinging breath. "Sebastian...?"

"Like I said," Merle stuffs his rag into a pocket. "Give him a chance, would ya? He's an idiot, but he's a good kid. Worked on this girl for weeks. Seemed like every spare minute he had, he was in here under that hood. He could have fixed the mechanical parts and left it be, but..." He shakes his head, and I get the feeling this is an old disagreement between them.

"So we were right," Vandy says, coming up beside me. "Sebastian did all this."

Merle looks at her and shrugs. "From the spark plugs to the paint job. Contracted out some stuff he didn't feel as confident about, but for the most part, you're looking at his own labor here."

Vandy jabs me with her elbow, wide eyes full of awe, but I'm still too stunned to speak, staring at the car in realization. I'd spent the last week convinced that the time and patience he'd spent with me was just a con—a way to wear me down and get between my legs. But this...

This doesn't track.

Not only did he work on my car, but I know now that he prioritized it over Jasmine, who still has the self-inflicted dents and damage from the night of the race.

"Stubborn shit put a lot into this. Time, money, *three* of my tension wrenches, not to mention..." Merle gives me a meaningful look, but I don't need him to fill in the blanks.

And love.

Merle's right. Sebastian might enjoy restoring old cars, but no one does something like this—so painstakingly careful, thoughtful —for someone whose pants they're just trying to get into.

Something like this can only be done out of love.

So much comes back in a rush. All the time he spent gaining the cats' trust. The care he took for Abbadon and her kittens. The day he stopped the guys from spreading and sharing the video of Georgia. The way he used to touch me, like he was excited each time I got a little better. He bought me gifts, sure, but things he knew I needed. He was kind. Generous. I glance inside and see the new, upgraded seat belts, remembering something else he is.

Protective.

Sebastian is a lot of things, but most of all, he's a protector.

Merle hands me the keys, complete with a shiny Mustang keychain, but I barely feel the weight of them in my hands. The awareness spreads through me like a gust of warmth. Sebastian Wilcox would only hurt me for one reason.

To protect me from something else.

～

IT DOESN'T TAKE MUCH CONVINCING to get Mr. Lee's special permission to spend all night in the lab. In fact, all it takes is the sight of me, bursting into the room and collecting the folder—the one with the negatives of Sebastian—for him to pretty much give me access to whatever I need.

He looks infuriatingly satisfied about it all.

It's a long night that I spend more caffeinated than usual, but I only have one day to get everything ready. Although I'm fine with digital compositing, I've been aptly informed that a lot of the fine arts recruiters are big ole hipsters. My main piece is too important to risk it, and I do want to show my aptitude with digital skill sets, so I'm leaving that one for last.

The three really good ones from the car shows remain—Jasmine, the overpass, and a shot of twelve random-looking kids, all hanging out in front of the brick façade of the mall. In it, Vandy is talking to Reynolds. Emory and Ben are laughing about something. Afton and Elana are bickering with Carlton. Tyson and Caroline are huddled around her phone, looking pensive. Georgia and Aubrey are both looking up at a spray of distant fireworks that might not be in the shot, but I remember so vividly in my mind, I can still hear the sharp crack.

Sebastian, who holds a cigarette between finger and thumb, is staring straight ahead at the camera.

At me.

He's not the focus of the shot. He's off to the side, trapped between Elana and Carlton, the only one who looks still, as if he's waiting.

There are almost too many to choose from for my last four slots. I spend a lot of time going back and forth. There's a minor breakdown at three in the morning when my mask for a shot of Sebastian, reflection distorted by the ripples in his pool, completely falls apart.

Despite the nerves and pressure and overwhelming amount of self-doubt, I have to admit that it's good to look at these pictures again. The sight of him from that night down in the dungeon, eyes soft and sure as he gazes up from my chest, is easily one of my best.

It's going to be one of the worst to show, too.

By five, I'm finally back in my dorm, apologizing to Georgia when the glow of my laptop monitor briefly stirs her from slumber. I only have four hours before I need to start setting up my wall in the gym. Luckily, the last photo is the easiest, being digital. But it's also the hardest to look at.

I'd taken the picture through the bonfire. Sebastian's face is staring through it, back at the camera. It's as if he's been engulfed by the flames. The first time I saw it, I thought he looked like a demon, with those piercing, unnaturally bright eyes of his. Plus, the look on his face, something intensely private, like he's been caught in a moment of weakness he doesn't want to admit.

But when I open up the file, I find that he doesn't look like a demon at all.

He looks like a god.

～

I'M HARRIED and exhausted as I nervously supervise the couple of seniors hanging my photos. I don't know them, but they don't look too excited to be here at nine on a Saturday morning, so I try to make it easy for them.

The gym has been transformed for the showcase. There are two rows of slanted walls with a large aisle between them. They've been set up so that each display is as contained as possible. From my own designated wall, I can't see anyone else's photos. The special lights that have been installed shine a touch too brightly for my liking, so I make a mental note to bring something that tones that down.

Unlike some of the others, I don't have a big fancy display going on. I have an order and placement. Beyond that, I want the work to speak for itself.

A few of the others are milling around—I see a couple people have draped sheer fabric over their cubbies, battling the brightness issue—but everyone seems too distracted to talk much. Still too nervous to really stand back and look at my own, I take a moment to go scope out everyone's stuff.

Micha and Michaela are too young to have nabbed a spot in the showcase, but they're still represented. Near the back is a single wall, filled with pieces from the club. There are some pieces that are probably really nice, but because I haven't slept more than twenty minutes in two days, I barely process them.

Deciding to go back to my dorm for what's likely to become an eight-hour nap, I head back to my own cubicle to grab my bag.

I freeze at the shape of someone else occupying the space.

My heart slams into gear, vision going a little blurry at the edges. Sebastian is standing there, gym bag slung over his shoulder as he stares vacantly at the photos. If possible, he looks even more tired than I do. The bruising around his eyes has faded to a mottled, sickly-looking yellow. He's wearing a hooded sweatshirt with a smirking devil on the back, and his hair is more lifeless than usual, hanging limply around his face. His jaw is covered with thick stubble that I've watched grow from afar over the past week.

It should make me feel better, seeing him like this, knowing that he's a fucking mess.

It doesn't.

He's still gorgeous.

With a steeling breath, I gather up every ounce of courage I possess and walk softly to his side. From here, I can smell him—the lingering scents of old soap and cigarette smoke. I keep my eyes straight ahead on the photos, but I can still feel him stiffen beside me, going stock still.

"You're up early." It's a testament to my exhaustion that my voice emerges in a flat, but even tone.

There's a long beat of silence before his low voice responds. "Had to clean out my locker. Quit the team."

I look at him in confusion, but his eyes are still fixed to the photo, hooded and unblinking. "Why?" He doesn't answer, just moves his eyes to another of the photos—the one of the Devils. Inhaling, I look away. "So, I got my car back."

From my periphery, I can see his head turn, blue eyes finally landing on me. "*What*?" His voice, low and tight, sounds surprised. A little bit angry, too.

"Merle called me yesterday morning," I explain. "Told me it was ready, so I went and picked it up."

His hand flexes around the strap of the bag, an almost imperceptible movement, before he looks away again. "Right."

"It's amazing," I say, remembering the drive I'd taken after picking it up. I'd driven around Northridge, up to the hills, and then to that little spot overlooking the lake. I sat there for a long time, trying to reconcile the man who first brought me there and the one who so callously threw me away. "Well, 'amazing' doesn't actually do it justice. It's the..." My voice cracks, and fuck. *Fuck.* This is why I wanted to wait. I clear my throat, finishing, "It's the best thing anyone's ever done for me."

Sebastian is silent next to me, still rigid and motionless. "Merle does good work," he finally says. The words land tonelessly between us.

"Yeah." I nod to myself, muttering, "Sure, *Merle*." If possible, he goes even more rigid. He's clearly not ready to fess up, but he knows.

He knows *I know*.

I nod to the main portrait, seeing his eyes keep straying back to it, like a magnet. "It's from that night..."

He reads the text on the mat below it, "Hyperion."

"The titan of light and watchfulness," I say, letting my eyes roam around the photo. I've kept the fire saturated in color, but Sebastian, in the middle, is a harmony of steel and pewter grays. The fire is reflected in his eyes, giving them a sharp, dangerous glow. It's a contrast in dark and light. Hard and soft.

This, I decided while sitting in my car, overlooking the lake.

This is how I reconcile those two men.

"He's one of the twelve children of Earth and Sky." I shoot him a crooked, if limp, smirk. "Six male titans, six female titans. Seemed fitting."

He doesn't look impressed. "You shouldn't show these," he says, lips forming a tight line. "People will know that you—"

When he doesn't finish, I look at the photos, asking, "That I what? Attended a couple legally questionable gatherings? That I got my heart crushed by some asshole? That I loved him?" I turn my gaze on him. "That I know he loved me back?"

Sebastian remains still, tired eyes moving sluggishly back and forth between them. "You don't know anything."

"You're kind of right," I concede. "I don't know why you dumped me, and I sure as hell don't know why you did it like that. I don't know how you've watched me walk around here for the last week, knowing that you ripped my fucking heart out, and still sleep at night."

He finally looks at me then, blue eyes meeting my own. It's like an electric shock down my spine, even just this minor connection. Even though he's watching me with that same blank mask. Even though his eyes are heavy and bruised with a lack of...

Oh.

Right.

"Sebastian. *Bass*." My resolve to play this all cool and aloof completely crumbles. "Why?"

He looks away, emotionless, jerking his chin at Hyperion. "This isn't real. You should show something else." His throat bobs with a hard swallow. "You should show something honest."

Feeling defeated and too heavy for my own legs, I reach for my bag and walk away, leaving him with the reality of his own reflection.

"So should you."

～

I HAVE to hand it to Preston Prep. When they do something, they go all out.

Despite being held in the gym, the art exhibit feels professional, as fancy as the field trip I took in the tenth grade to the High Museum in downtown Atlanta. We're instructed to stand near our work so that we can talk about our pieces. That's the part I'm most uncomfortable with. It's one thing to have my work, my life and

423

feelings, displayed for everyone to see. It's another to have to talk about it.

When the waiter walks by with a glass of sparkling cider, I grab one, just to have something to do with my hands.

"Sugar!" Vandy cries, coming around the corner. "It looks so good!"

Aubrey stands beside her. I peer around in search of Georgia, but I don't see her red hair anywhere.

"Thank you." My fingers grip the glass like a lifeline. "And thanks for letting me keep the dress for a few more days."

Vandy waves this off, eyes wandering back to the photos. "This is one of my favorites," she says of the overpass from the first race.

I awkwardly shuffle my feet, knowing they're avoiding talking about the huge face—literally, the biggest piece in my showcase—staring back at the three of us. "It's making me paranoid, to be honest. Like I keep expecting someone to come detain me."

"I think the police are going to be too busy with other things tonight," Aubrey says with a small smirk on her lips.

"What are you talking about?" I glance around again. "Where's Georgia?" They exchange a guilty look and I press. "What's going on?"

"So, Sebastian is fighting tonight—" Vandy starts.

"V!" Aubrey hisses, jabbing her friend in the side. "We agreed!"

"No, *you* agreed! I don't like secrets." Vandy steps toward me, pitching her voice low. "Carlton got word this morning that Sebastian is supposed to fight tonight. Some awful thing his brother set up. Georgia tried to talk him out of it earlier, but he won't talk to her. He swears up and down that there's no way out of this."

"For me," I whisper, putting a voice to the suspicion that's been nagging at me since our meeting before. "I think he's fighting because of me."

Again, the girls share a look. "What are you talking about?"

"That day, after we..." I swallow, "After we had sex, but before everything went to hell, he and Heston were bickering in the kitchen. Heston mentioned something about this weekend and Bass said he wouldn't do it. I didn't connect the dots at the time, but then later... in the car, on the way home, he kept getting all these vague texts from Heston. Talk about a winter transfer. Someone's 'poor dad'. A scholarship, and how they can be 'fussy'. Someone's tits. And then..." God, I just feel so stupid for not realizing it all sooner. "Something about needing a fix for his sweet tooth, and tasting it for himself."

Vandy face screws up. "Because your name is Sugar."

"Yeah," I say, eyes rolling. "After that one, Bass completely shut down. I'm thinking... I'm guessing it was a threat."

Aubrey winces. "Fuck, no wonder he freaked out."

"But I don't understand," I say, shaking off the uneasy feeling. "What do Sebastian and Heston have to do with Georgia?"

Aubrey looks over her shoulder, checking that we're alone. Once she's sure we won't be overheard, she leans in, eyes serious as she explains, "She's going to the police to report him for that fucking video. And she's going to try to get Sydney to go with her."

I let this sink in slowly, rolling it around in my mind. I flash back to yesterday—her insistence that she could never do such a thing. I'd wonder what changed her mind, but there's no need.

Devils protect their own.

A waiter passes and I put my glass on his tray. "Let's go."

"What?" Vandy asks. "Where?"

"Georgia needs us right now," I say, gathering up my things. "Not just for support, either. We need to convince Sydney to do the right thing. If G's going to try to take down Heston Wilcox, then it's going to take more than the two of them to do it."

If Sebastian, the strongest, most protective man I know, is afraid of Heston, then it's going to take all of us to bring him down. And even then, it may be too late.

31

It's been a while since I've been down to Ormewood Park. It's a little different in the winter, all bare and bony, a grim skeleton of its warmer self. I sit in my car, blowing smoke out the window as I observe it. The last time I was here, I got my ass beat. There's just no sugar coating that shit. It was a dirty play, my brother riding my ass to stoke up the fight, making me talk all that shit to the guy, only to end up tossing him a goddamn bat. It was a dirty play for the guy to use it, too.

But it's all dirty around here.

My phone dings with a text and I don't even need to check the screen to know it's him.

Heston: Tick tock.

Your ass better be here.

I hear your girl has a little thing tonight.

Looks like there's a lot riding on that.

She'll probably be there late and leave alone.

Don't test me.

I shove the phone under the seat, knowing I can't take it in the ring with me. God, that fucking art exhibit. Just figures I'd go

426

through all this trouble to make sure it looked like we were nothing to each other, and she goes and shows them the exact opposite.

Because there's no mistaking what those pictures are.

They're a love letter.

At first, it seemed like a love letter from her, which was baffling as fuck. You don't get your heart stomped on the way she did and still...

But I was wrong. The longer I looked at them, the more I realized they were a love letter from me. Every look, every glance, every moment captured were just snapshots of how badly I wanted her. How much I loved having her. How intensely I didn't want to lose her.

If I thought I had half a chance of denying it, then realizing she knew about what I did to the Mustang squashed that right under its boot. It's just something else that's making my blood buzz with frustration. I should have fucking been there. I should have seen her face when she saw it for the first time. Her expression when she opened the door and saw inside. The way her face lit up when she cranked it and it started, easy as breathing. I should have been there beside her when she took it on the road and opened it up.

I should have done—and been—a lot of things.

None of that matters now.

Reluctantly, I resign myself to leaving the Shelby on the side of the road. It's a shitty part of town and the Ford is perfect for getting jacked. Nothing about this night is going the way I want it to, but the sooner it starts, the sooner it's over.

I activate Jasmine's alarm, pausing to look at her there under the glow of the streetlight, all battered and sad. Shoving my hands into my coat pockets, I head down the path that leads behind the overgrown baseball fields. The park has been abandoned for years, but a preservation group keeps the city from razing it entirely. Past the dugout, I take the old cement stairs down to the crumbling deck. In the distance, I can already see a crowd of kids huddled around a makeshift fire, 40 ounces in hand, weed wafting through the air. The sound of skateboards zipping back and forth bounces off the curved floor of the empty pool, spray paint covering the interior walls. That's where I'll fight tonight, down in the well of the deep end.

Seems fitting, says a voice in my head. It sounds a lot like Sugar's.

"Dude."

Turning, I see Emory. The rest of the Devils, minus the girls, aren't far behind him.

"Came to watch the show?" I take a final drag of my cigarette and toss it on the concrete, stabbing it out with my shoe. I tell Ben, "Make sure you get your bets in, because I've got plenty of shit to work out on whatever unlucky bastard fights me tonight."

"Bass, stop," Em says, eyes full of that patented Devil arrogance. "You're not going to do this. You don't *have* to do this."

"No? I'm pretty sure I do." It's me or Sugar. Heston has made that perfectly clear. Maybe this will buy me time to really sell that she doesn't mean anything to me. Maybe it won't. But I have to try. If I don't fight, he'll come after her, and I have no fucking idea what his depraved, twisted idea of payback will be. "So, you might as well get a good seat."

I claim an area by the edge of the pool and drop my bag, reaching for tape to wrap my knuckles with. I can already hear some of the whispers. People are realizing I'm actually here. That it's really going to happen. The buzz in the air grows to something frenetic, full of anticipation. I reach into my bag for my lucky shoes next, easing out of my current sneakers to put them on, face set as I pull the laces tight.

"Wilcox." Reyn appears suddenly at my side, his voice tight with annoyance. "He's right, you know. Whatever you're afraid of...it's over. Georgia and the rest of the girls went to the cops. They got Sydney to go, too. Vandy was there and everything."

I pause for a moment, looking over my shoulder to read their expressions. "Why would Georgia...?"

Only, now I'm realizing exactly what Georgia has to do with all this. I'm realizing why that video of Sydney seemed uncomfortably familiar. It's been years since I saw the video of Georgia, and even then, I'd only gotten halfway through it before closing it out.

"He's the one," I say, not even feeling surprised. "Of fucking course." I had been wondering. Heston making a threat toward Vandy, but not Georgia, hadn't made sense to me at the time. I understand now. He never needed to threaten Georgia. He's been tormenting her for years without even having to lift a fucking finger. "Well, that sucks, because all they did was expose themselves. When he finds out—which, he will—he'll tell everyone it's them in the videos. Their last shred of anonymity will be gone."

"I don't think you're picking up what I'm putting down," Emory stresses, expression strangely urgent. "Georgia said the cops believed them. They're pressing charges."

"Oh," I tug off my sweatshirt, hoping the chill in the air can energize me. "The cops believed them, huh?" I nod over their heads. "Then what the fuck is my brother doing here?"

Reyn looks back, jaw tightening at the sight of Heston. "Maybe they're still looking for him?"

"Or maybe," I rip off a piece of tape with my teeth and begin wrapping my hands, "my father already made this disappear." The grin I give them feels brittle and wrong. "There's no getting out of this, boys. But do me a favor?"

Emory grimaces. "What?"

"If things go badly and I end up in the hospital or something, make sure I get a hot nurse, okay?"

"Don't be such a fucking—" Carlton starts, but I've already jumped into the pool. That act brings a round of excited cheers from the kids sitting and standing on the deck. My opponent strolls down the shallow end steps, like he's Muhammad Ali. I half expect him to be wearing a goddamn cape. I search the crowd, looking for familiar faces, but only see the Devils down on the end, none looking too pleased. Heston stands by the bookie, arms crossed, like *he* should be the one wearing a cape. Why not? We're all just his fucking pawns. Me. This kid I'm about to pummel. The girls...

I look around one last time, but none of them are here. I don't think they've ever missed one of my fights. Not since we all became Devils. I want to get pissed that they're not supporting me, but I know that's not right. The last fight of mine they watched was a shit show. And it's not like I can expect Sugar to come here and watch me get my brains splattered on the concrete like I had that night. She's had enough violence for a lifetime.

Which is just one more reason we can't be together.

I hop on my feet, trying to get some blood pumping against the cold. The guy in the ring with me, for all his swagger, doesn't look so tough. But that can be deceiving. He's shorter than me by a couple inches at least, even if his arms are bigger. This is probably as fair a fight as I can expect from Heston.

I don't talk shit this time or hype up the crowd. This is a job. This is something I'm doing because I don't have a choice. Nothing about this is fun or exciting.

It's not like it used to be.

This becomes clear after I draw first blood, landing a whopper of a punch right in the guy's teeth. At this point, my blood would usually be pumping hard and fast. As it is, I feel sluggish and slow, completely unable to block the punch he answers with. It snaps my neck back, but I recover quickly, shaking off the ache.

It seems like everyone's screaming now, bodies looming along the rim of the pool like a fence, trapping us in. There's just no fucking excuse for the next hit I take, stumbling back a couple steps before regaining my footing and ducking the next swipe.

Fuck, I need to get my shit together.

Centering myself, I focus on the guy in front of me, following my tight, bouncing circles out of his reach. It's not hard to imagine he's Heston. I've gotten really good at that over the years. It gets me a couple more solid right hooks.

But there's just something about it.

Something isn't clicking.

Maybe it's the lack of sleep, or that I've been hitting the booze and weed a little too hard this week. Maybe, like with lacrosse, I've just been out of the game for too long, less capable of competing.

But even deep down, I know that's bullshit.

I could have kicked ass on the field—if I really wanted to. If I wasn't consumed with this bitter fucking resignation that Heston will always knock down the best parts of me.

The guy takes a shot at my jaw and it grazes me too high,

glancing off my cheek in a bad way. I feel the skin split, but it doesn't hurt. Nothing hurts. I try to dodge his next hit, only for my hair to be caught in his other fist, driving me down into his knee with a blow that makes my vision go momentarily white.

I shove him off and try to shake it off, using a wrist to wipe the blood from my mouth. He gives me a slick grin, clearly proud of himself. "Motherfucker," I spit, some of that hot fury finally coming to life inside my chest. I clutch onto it for dear fucking life, willing the ember to grow, to *burn*. I strike out, finally getting in a good round of blows. The crowd's shouts pitch higher when he stumbles to the side, running from my wild barrage of fists. It's sloppy, primitive bullshit. Not my finest work.

He comes back moments later, recharged and smarting from the energy of the crowd. There's a clear favorite here, and it's not him. His fist meets my temple, and goddamn. Cocky little fuck, but there's some power behind his hands. I edge away, willing my sight to steady out before he returns, and I can't pretend anymore. My heart's not in this.

Fuck, I don't even think my lungs are in this. All of my organs are firmly out of fucks to give. It doesn't make sense. All I wanted for months was to finally get in a ring with some motherfucker and go to town. Beating Doug's ass, for all the turmoil it caused, was the highlight of my whole fucking winter.

What changed?

Apparently, I'm spending too much time in my own head about this, because the guy gets a good one on me, right in the eye that just began healing from Doug. It's a real bitch of a hit, too. Nearly sends me right to my knees. I skirt around him for some distance, because that's apparently how I fight now. I run and wait.

Because there's nothing to fight for.

My fists drop, landing heavily against my thighs as I gasp in huge, sucking breaths of chilled air. I get this split-second thought that I should just lose. I should get my ass handed to me down here, let Heston think that I'm useless to him.

That's when I know I'm done.

The guy laughs when I climb the steps of the shallow end,

pushing past the throng of confused, disappointed people eager for their pound of flesh.

"Not gonna fucking be mine," I mutter, clumsily tapping out a cigarette as I idly watch Heston shove through the crowd.

"What the fuck are you doing!" he shouts, face gnarled with fury.

I take a long drag from my cigarette in reply. "Seems obvious, doesn't it?"

There's this vein in Heston's temple that gets all bulgy and gross when he's pissed off past the point of maintaining composure. It hardly ever makes an appearance, considering composure is his whole thing, but there it is. *Bulge bulge bulge.* "I have seven fucking grand riding on this fight. You get your ass in that pool and beat that motherfucker down, or—"

"Or what?" Reyn's voice comes from behind me. A bored glance over my shoulder reveals the other four Devils.

Heston gives them all a scathing look. "This is none of your fucking business." He thrusts a finger in my face. "You know exactly what I'll do, don't you? Remember that ragdoll you talked about last week?"

I scoff. "This shit again? I already told you I don't give a fuck about Sydney."

But Heston smiles, sharp and menacing. "Imagine she was someone else." He nods at the look on my face, voice pitched low when he leans in to hiss, "I will fuck her within an inch of her life."

Everything goes a little fuzzy then, because I do. I imagine him doing to Sugar what I saw him doing to Sydney.

Heston hits the ground so hard, I can practically hear all the air escaping his lungs. He tries to push me off, but I get a knee into the center of his chest, pull my fist back, and slam it forward. The crowd from before notices a new skirmish and quickly surrounds us, swallowing up the sounds of my knuckles meeting Heston's face. He tries to buck me off, that vein still bulging, but it barely moves me. He tries to turn his head away from the blows, but I don't mind hitting his fucking skull, so that's what I do.

I beat the shit out of him.

It's the easiest fight I've ever had.

He strikes out, of course. He lands a few clumsy, wayward hits. One to my throat, another to my already-swelling eye. That shit doesn't even slow me down. The longer I kneel there over him, finally—*fucking finally*—burying my fist into his face, the hotter the thing inside me burns. It's hungry and eager, exactly what was missing from the fight before. And every memory, every threat, every goddamn bit of hurt he's inflicted on the people I love is like a steady source of gasoline, feeding it.

I could hear Ben and Carl egging me on before, but now they're quiet, even as the crowd is losing their goddamn minds. I barely register how fucked-up Heston is looking—bloody and apoplectic —or how my knuckles have gone numb, or that I can barely see out of my right eye.

I don't stop hitting him.

Not until Emory pulls me off. "Cops, dude. We have to bail. It's done, Bass. It's done!" My fists are still swinging, even when he's yanking me back. It's not until Reyn takes my other arm and drags me away with him that I finally let go. I keep my eyes on him, writhing on the ground, turning to his side to spit blood on the ground below. A sick surge of satisfaction rises within me at the sight, which is new and interesting. I've fought a lot of guys in my time, but winning has always just been something that came to me like a bare fact. I never got off on it. It never made me feel good to know I'd hurt someone, even when they were dicks.

Now, I do.

I feel it as I shake Reyn and Emory off, and then some more as we run toward Em's truck, the crowd dispersing in much the same way. The park is filled with blue flashing lights so quickly that, for a moment, I begin worrying about another concussion. It's not, though.

It's just that two cruisers are that close, sirens blaring harshly in the silence of the park. We jump into the truck—closer than the Shelby—but even though Emory cranks the ignition, he doesn't put it into gear.

"Oh, shit," he says, leaning over the steering wheel. "Reyn, look."

From the back seat, I crane forward to see why the fuck we aren't peeling out of here. Four officers are surrounding Heston, probably because he's beat to shit and sitting there, too gassed to flee.

It takes me too long to wonder why they're putting him in cuffs, but no one else.

There are at least five other people dragging ass at running away. The cops don't even spare them a glance. It's almost like they didn't come to break up the party.

It's almost like...

"I told you," Em mutters. And then, louder, turning to me with a shit-eating grin, "I fucking told you our girls were handling that fucker!"

Reyn's razor-sharp smirk beams back at me. "Guess your dad didn't bail him out, this time."

I hope he can tell through my swollen eye that I'm looking at him like he's a moron. "Not yet. He probably doesn't even know about it." My father is home right now, probably sitting in his office, sipping some scotch, completely unaware that he's about to get a phone call.

The hurt still hasn't come, all that adrenaline still pumping through me like fuel. Maybe that's why Reyn's words come floating back to me from before.

Be better.

I'd be lying if I said I haven't been thinking of them for the last couple days. Wondering what that would even mean. What it might look like. What it would take to get my father to give up his prodigal son for the sad specimen sitting right here.

I've been wondering what kind of sacrifices that might entail and if they'd be better or worse than a life spent dodging Heston's bullshit.

I think I already know. "Em," I say, falling back into the seat, eyes fixed to the roof of the car. "Could I ask a favor?"

I see his eyes flick to mine in the rearview. "This isn't the hot nurse thing, is it? Are you concussed? Do you need to go to the ER? Goddamn it, Bass, I fucking told you—"

Breathing out a laugh, I shake my head. "Nah, I'm good. I feel fine." I meet the reflection of his eyes, voice feeling thick with exhaustion. "I'll take a ride to my house, though."

If I can get there before that phone call, maybe I won't have to wonder anymore.

32

─────────

Georgia finally falls asleep around two in the morning. She's been a mess since she got back from the station, two hours ago. Aubrey's in the bed with her, having passed out long before Georgia nodded off.

I'm lying in my own bed, watching the clock tick away. Since I'd slept all day, I'm completely fucking wired, although I suspect a part of it is because of what happened after leaving the exhibit tonight.

The whole thing was a tough sell to Sydney, who basically wanted fuck-all to do with anything that incriminated Heston. It kind of made me sick, knowing she was protecting him, even after all he's put everyone through. Even when we told her about the video—even when she looked surprised to find it existed—she still swore up and down that she didn't care. I'm not sure if the others could tell she was lying, but I sure as hell could.

I happen to know a thing or two about excusing abuse for the sake of keeping your shit cogent.

Eventually, Vandy got fed up with it all and pulled her outside the dorms. They talked for half an hour. I'm not sure what was said, or why Sydney returned with a blank, tear-streaked face, but she gave Georgia the nod and that was that.

Aubrey, Vandy, and I all sat in the car while the two of them disappeared behind the doors of the station. We listened to the radio for an hour, then sent Aubrey off to get us some burgers from across the street. We ate and waited. We talked and waited. We waited and then waited some more. They didn't get out until midnight, both returning to the car with tired eyes and grim faces. Their expressions said it all.

This wasn't the end of a fight.

It's the beginning of one.

I'm still doubtful it's a fight Sydney is willing to finish, but eventually the other girls will learn. You can't force someone into seeing themselves as a victim—as a survivor. It has to be something they realize themselves, and even then, the hunger for justice isn't a universally shared ache.

What Doug did to me was untenable, but the thought of trying to bring him down—legally, *officially*—makes me physically ill. Maybe that makes me the kind of person who doesn't stand up for herself. Or maybe that makes the kind of person who *does*—by acknowledging that it'll only hurt me more. Because the truth is, the thought of looking back at it makes me tired.

Sebastian was right that day in the garage.

I'm tired of fighting.

I'm still tangled in these thoughts when I hear a knock at the door. It's so gentle, so quiet, that I almost question if I heard it at all. But who knows? It could be one of the Devils, coming to check on their girls.

So I climb out of bed to open the door.

Sebastian's leaning against the far wall, head hanging low on his shoulders. His blond hair is messier than it was when I last saw him, a tangle of golden chaos. He's wearing a heavy jacket that's opened, revealing his bare chest, hands shoved into the pockets.

When he lifts his head to meet my gaze, it feels like the floor has fallen from beneath me.

"Jesus fucking Christ."

It was all for nothing.

It's a horrible, selfish, myopic sort of thought. The kind that I'll be kicking myself for later. Georgia needed to report Heston because he hurt her. In a way, so did Sydney. It was never really about stopping the fight—not at its core. It was about making sure that there was something on record. Proof that Heston Wilcox is dangerous. A predator.

But seeing Sebastian standing there, eye almost swollen over, face bloody and bruised and battered, I can't help but think that it isn't fair.

"Hey," he says in a rusty voice, slurred with something I'm hoping like hell is just the same exhaustion I saw before. "Should see the other guys."

Guys? "Plural?" I think he tries to smile. It ends up looking more like a painful twitch of his cheek. "What are you doing here, Sebastian?" It comes out plaintive and quiet, and not at all the way I intend it. What I mean to ask is why he isn't at the nearest urgent care center.

But he just rests his head back against the wall, staring down his nose at me with those tired eyes. "Showing you something honest."

The words make every cell in my body come instantly to life. Unwilling to let him see this, I prop a shoulder against the door jamb, ducking my head. "You honestly look like you're about to collapse in my hallway. Why aren't you in yours?"

His shrug is a loose, lazy thing. "I wouldn't be able to sleep," he says. Even his inhale sounds exasperated with it all. "Not until I told you that it was all bullshit. Every word of it."

Softly, I reply, "I know," but even though it's still nice to hear it like this—said aloud, to my face—it doesn't take it all away. It soothes the hurt, but deep down, the sting remains.

"I don't know exactly how to fix it." He pauses, shoulders sinking impossibly lower. "I just couldn't let another night go by with you thinking I don't love you. And I doubt I'm currently in the position to do shit like *think*, or make promises, or tell you that I'll do whatever it takes to get you back. Because I think I'm sort of a loser, and not worth it for you."

"That's what you think?" I ask, lifting my eyes to see his heavy nod. "Then you're right." I watch his face fall, shaking my head in response. "You're not in the position to think right now."

His eyes spark, head lifting from the wall in order to watch me closely. "I'm really fucking not."

I shuffle my feet, taking in his crazy hair and fucked-up face. "Wait here a second."

Leaving him in the hall, I throw on my coat, reaching under my bed for various supplies. I pause to look at Georgia and Aubrey in the bed, still sleeping soundly. Truthfully, it used to make me a little jealous, how close the twelve of them are. They're always calling each other their boys, or their girls. Maybe the Devils are some dumb, pretentious, over-the-top secret society, but they're also so much more. They love each other—sure, in their own weirdo, messed-up ways—but it's a kind of love, nonetheless.

That's why I leave a note, quickly scrawled on the back of someone's old Bio homework:

Off taking care of your boy.

~

He doesn't ask where we're going, even though it should be obvious. Instead, it's like he just follows me blindly down the stairs, out the door, across the space between the buildings, over to the boys' dorms. I put in the code myself, letting us inside.

When we get to the fourth floor, something clicks.

He stops in the middle of the hall, eyes cast to the side. "Uh..."

"What?" I whisper, looking nervously up and down the hall.

"It's a fucking mess in there."

Pausing, I slowly assure him, "That's okay," but when he meets my gaze, his are full of a strange sort of dread. When he pushes open the door, I see why. "...oh."

He sighs. "Yeah."

It looks like a bomb went off in here—if there were such things as takeout-beer-laundry bombs. I step carefully over a textbook, face down, pages all crumpled beneath the hard cover. His lacrosse equipment is strewn about the room, and even though the floor looks like a tornado ripped through, every flat surface is oddly clean. It takes me a moment to understand what this is.

I purse my lips at him. "Had a bit of a tantrum, huh?"

He reaches up to rub at the back of his neck. "A bit."

Nodding, I survey the room, but quickly decide to ignore it. This can't be fixed tonight. Instead, I nod my head toward the bathroom, waiting for him to follow me. At least in there, I'm relieved to discover, everything is still in its place.

"Sit," I demand, opening my bag to retrieve the first aid kit.

He doesn't sit on the toilet like I expect him to. He slides up on the counter, reaching over the sink to crack the window. I don't protest when he pulls a pack of rumpled cigarettes from his pocket, pinching one between his lips and lighting it.

"My mom's doc already looked me over," he says, eyes tracking the way I set out the antiseptic wipes, bandages, and ointment. "No concussion. No stitches. Just some bruises. Superficial bullshit."

I arch an eyebrow at him. "It's going to feel a lot less superficial in the morning. Take these." I hand him two pain relievers, watching as he swallows them down with a handful of water from the tap. "Now stay still."

The cut on his cheek isn't deep enough for stitches—the doctor was right about that—but it's still caked with dried blood and debris. I tear the package to the antiseptic wipes and rub one over the open wound.

"Son-of-a—" he winces back, brow furling. "Jesus, that always hurts."

I run the wipe over it again. "Then maybe you should stop always needing it."

We're silent after that. I check out his eye, wondering what the likelihood of him having ice in that kitchenette might be, before moving to his bloody knuckles. He hisses just as badly when I run the wipes over them. For someone who clearly gets some level of gratification from getting into fights, he sure is a big baby when it comes to the aftercare.

Once I've tended to his wounds to the best of my abilities, I put all the supplies away.

And then I start undressing.

He watches me shuck off my shirt, a deep crease forming between his eyebrows. "The fuck?"

"Take off your clothes," I tell him, nodding to his pants. "And where did your shirt even go?"

He obeys me like someone paying very little mind to why, fingers going to the button on his jeans as he watches me shimmy my pants and underwear off. "Couldn't find it fast enough. We had to bail." Even though his pants are undone, he's still sitting on the counter, looking at me with a baffled expression.

Naked, I stand there and nudge at his knee. "Come on, get down." He complies in a slow, stilted way, tossing his cigarette butt in the sink before sliding to his feet. There aren't any protests when I reach out toward his hips, tugging his pants and boxers down his legs.

I pause, staring at his erection in disbelief.

"You're the one who wanted to get naked," is his weak defense. "The whole bloody and beaten thing turn you on or something?"

"Yep," I answer tonelessly. "In fact, I'm about to get soaking wet for you."

Understanding dawns on his face when I reach in the shower, turning the knob with a jerk of my wrist.

"Come on," I say, dragging him under the spray of the shower.

It hasn't escaped my notice that he hasn't touched me.

Not once.

His eyes watch me the entire time I clean him, running a wet, soapy rag across his chest, over his throat, his neck. Even when he tilts his head back under the spray, letting me strain up against him to lather some shampoo into his hair, he still looks on, like he's in some weird, exhaustion-induced daze.

"You don't have to take care of me, you know."

"You don't have to take care of me, either." I make him turn so I can run the cloth over his broad, muscled back. "But I feel like maybe you do."

When he turns back, some of the ache constricting my chest begins to ease at the sight of him, bruised but whole. I sweep a palm down his chest, checking my work, finding it satisfactory. With the task completed, I feel adrift, wondering where I should go from here. I hadn't really been thinking beyond 'Sebastian' and 'hurt'.

When our eyes meet, I know what he's going to ask before he even does. It's there, in the way he looks cautious and lost.

"Can I touch you?"

I can't even remember the last time he asked me that. Probably not since that night in his backseat. Ever since, he's just done it, pretty much banking on the fact he could. It's all at once a relief and a jagged wound, seeing him transformed into this quiet, careful man who's disinclined to brush up against a boundary he might not be privy to.

It's simple to answer, "Yes."

He touches my cheek first, wet thumb brushing over the skin, soft as a whisper. He looks like maybe he's expecting me to flinch, but I don't. There's no fear here, involuntary or otherwise, just a sense of release. My eyes slide closed when his fingers thread into the hair behind my ear, palm cupping my cheek. It's not like I haven't been touched since that awful fucking day. The girls have been feeding me touches in small, measured doses for the last week.

But this is just different.

I hear him sigh, right before his palm moves to the back of my head. He effortlessly pulls me into him, arm coming around my shoulders to hold me close. The feel of our chests pressed together is like being wrapped in a large pulse of warmth. My shoulders hitch, knees trembling at the feel of him against me.

Fuck, he knows I like that.

Not fair.

His skin is clean-smelling, wet and warm against my cheek. I feel his nose nudge into my hair, lips moving against my temple when he speaks. "This mean you forgive me?"

"Sebastian," I warn, hands fisting against his back even as I melt into him. "You really fucked me up." I hate the way my voice breaks, eyes welling with tears.

"It wasn't true," he says urgently, arms crushing me closer. "Heston would have—"

It's not enough. "I know you didn't mean it, but that's not the point. You fight—you fight all the fucking time—but you didn't fight for me. You just threw me away. You gave up."

His chest sinks with a long exhale, breath damp against my temple. "It didn't feel like that. It felt like I was tearing myself in fucking half, just to keep you safe. I know it doesn't matter. You're right, I should have—I fought the wrong way. I get that now."

"Do you?" I wonder.

He pulls away, taking my face in his hands. If I hoped my tears might be lost in the water, then it's futile. His face falls when he looks at me, jaw going taut. "I talked to my dad tonight." Despite knowing he must be minutes from collapsing with fatigue, he's suddenly surging with energy. "I was there for hours, talking him out of bailing Heston's ass out of this." His eyes are beseeching. "I made a plan, okay? I'm going to go to college somewhere he approves of. I'm going to stop fighting. I'm going to get back on the team. I'm going to be the picture-perfect little robot he wants me to be, and he'll do it. He'll let my brother fall."

I look away, unable to hold the intensity of his stare. "You don't want to go to college."

"Doesn't fucking matter," he says, chasing my gaze. "This is how I'm fighting now."

"You already said, Sebastian. You want to travel. You won't be happy like that." I don't voice my real fear—that if he's doing this for me, he'll end up resenting me for it. That'll it be too much to live up to.

"You're wrong," he insists, voice strong and sure. "Wherever you go, I'll go to the closest school. That'll make me happy." He huffs at my expression. "Don't give me that look. Listen to me. I'll be nineteen in two months. I have plenty of time to travel. Plus, we can take a road trip this summer. Think about it," he asks, eyes full of excited fire. "You and me, the Shelby—or hell, the *Mustang*. We can just fuck off for three months. We can go anywhere we want. We can do it every summer. Every vacation. I don't fucking care, just as long as I do it with you."

I search his eyes, and the thing is, that sting is still there, like a scab on my heart. It's the reminder of his words, still stirring the nagging doubt that I'm not enough—not for him. That he's too fine to hold, like grains of sand running right through my fingers. That he'll get bored of me, distracted by something shinier.

But scabs can heal, and if I don't shine brightly enough, then maybe I'll just burn.

Sand can be made solid if it's hot enough.

The kiss I give him isn't anywhere as gentle as it should be. If it hurts the soft, bruised parts of him, then he doesn't show it. Instead, he pushes me back against the tiles, licking hotly—frantically—at the crease of my lips.

He tastes like warmth and blood, thumb digging almost painfully into my cheek as he deepens the kiss. With a level of coordination he shouldn't rightly possess, he reaches behind him to shut off the water, emptying the room of every sound that isn't our harsh breaths and sucking mouths.

"Sorry," he mutters gruffly into the kiss, and at first, I have no idea why. Even if I weren't distracted with the way his hard cock is driving into my hip, I still wouldn't make sense of it. Not until he adds, "Come to bed with me." He dips down to suck a kiss into my neck. "Please?"

I swallow, stomach twisting at the implication. "You want to fuck me," I guess.

He breathes out an eager, "Yeah," like I'm suggesting something that hadn't even occurred to him. "I could fuck you." He returns to my mouth, teeth tugging at my lip. "I could definitely fuck you."

I jab my thumb into his side, curving an eyebrow at his responding flinch. "You're a walking bruise, Bass."

"Shit." He blinks his wet eyelashes down at me, like he's remembering it all. "Well there's nothing wrong with my dick. Let the rest hurt. I don't give a shit." He slots his thumbs into the hollows of my hips, bumping the aforementioned uninjured dick against my belly.

He captures my mouth in another scorching kiss, but his hands are moving me, guiding me from the shower. It's not until I almost trip over a lacrosse stick that I realize he's walked me all the way into the living area of his suite.

"Shit." He steadies me with an arm around my waist, yanking me up against his broad body. Into my neck, he promises, "The bedroom is cleaner."

I let him guide me there.

Barely getting a look at the bed, I fall onto the mattress—a double, the spoiled jerk—and he's not far behind. He surges into me, hips slotting neatly between my legs as he mouths down my jaw, my neck, my collarbone.

He ducks his head to clamp his mouth around my breast, licking a wet path around a peaked nipple. I push my head back as he takes the other in a warm, damp palm, cupping it. The feel of it is nearly unbearable, something sharp and bright igniting across my nerves, in the pit of my core. I bite my lip on a moan when his hand wedges itself between us, long fingers finding my clit.

And then, he winces.

"Son of a *bitch*." It's only now that I'm noticing the fresh bloom of a bruise on his ribs, mottled shade of ominous purple. The momentary spike of pain makes it easier from me to roll him, settling over his hips. By the time I do, his grimace is already smoothed out and he's muttering, "Yeah, yeah," and grabbing a thick handful of my ass. "Like this."

His eyes are bright and impatient as I dig a condom from a box shoved haphazardly beneath his bed. I take so long ripping open the wrapper that he finally just snatches it from me, ripping it open with his teeth and rolling it over his thick, flushed cock. He holds it there for me, fist loose around the base, as I slowly lower myself onto it.

He peers down his body to watch, breathing out a low, "Holy fuck."

It's different from the last time, having the power here, making my own pace. *Control.* Sebastian is tense beneath me, but also contrastingly soft, pliable. His palms run slow, deliberate circuits over my hips, my tits, around to my ass for a massaging squeeze.

I feel so full of him when I finally settle, jarringly aware of his hot gaze on me. It glides over me in phases, those blue eyes taking in the way my chest contracts with an exhale. He grabs my dog tags in a loose fist, eyes meeting mine when he tugs me down for a long, languorous kiss. It's better like this, pinning him down, forcing him to let someone else do the fighting for once.

His body is a wide expanse of well-toned perfection, and I take a moment to appreciate it. His abs quiver when I give a shallow rock, disjointed breaths jerking his chest as he rubs two rough hands up my flesh. All the reluctance from before is gone now, replaced by this clutching, handsy mess of need I somehow find myself in commanding.

I roll my hips, and then rock back into him, wondering breathlessly, "Is this...?"

"Christ, yes." His eyebrows pinch together in pleasure. "I've been dying to get inside you since that night we—" His words bite off with a grunt, head thrown back when I try a slightly more ambitious roll of my hips.

It's easy once I do, finding what feels good here. A slow, punching rhythm that makes the friction against my clit send shivers rippling down my spine. Sebastian touches me everywhere, hands gliding across my sides, around my back. Every now and then, he'll grab a handful of something soft—my breast, my ass, a fistful of hair—and buck his hips up into me.

It gets hard being quiet when he does that, planting his feet on the bed and fucking up into me. He swallows my cry with a kiss when I can't anymore, curling a hand around my shoulder to take control, driving me down into his hard thrusts.

My orgasm approaches like a runaway train, making my toes curl with every crash of our hips. It's powerful enough to take my breath away, chest seizing on a gasp as I tighten around him, face buried in his neck. He spits a low, guttural curse, arms trapping me against his chest as he drives his dick into me, over and over.

It almost hurts when he comes.

He squeezes me, the raw power of his arms seeming barely contained as he jerks up into me. It's over too soon, and from the way he finally loosens his grip on me, only to slide a slow palm down to my ass, tells me he feels the same.

We don't part for a long moment, the two of us wound together, body to body, breath to breath. And when we do separate, it's only long enough to clean up and get back under the covers. The thought of being away from him, away from the feel of him is too much—something I truly never thought I'd say or feel. I tuck against him, back against his chest, his arm holding me close. Just before I close my eyes, I hear him mumble, "I love you, Sugar Voss."

I turn to tell him the same, but exhaustion has won over and I let it take me, too.

33

SEBASTIAN

As soon as I wake up, I wish I didn't.

The sunlight is stabbing right into my eyes and even the simple act of squinting them hurts like a bitch. My head feels fuzzy and a little slow, and it's fucking *cold*.

Groaning, I roll into the warmth beside me, seeking its heat, finding my arms full of a small, naked, soft body. My groan turns into an appreciative hum, because even though I'm one big throbbing mess of aches, Sugar's naked body sort of makes me forget them.

I take the chance to crack an eye, vision filling with the delicate curve of her bare shoulder. Unthinkingly, I press my lips to the skin there. I'm slotted up nicely behind her and my dick is into it, pressing insistently against her ass. A careful raise of my head reveals the sight her plump tits, all pressed together as she lays on her side.

Goddamn.

My head falls heavily back to my pillow.

I must have racked up some serious fucking karma in a past life.

That's the only way to explain how Sugar could be in my bed right now. Last night, when I went to her room, I was barely even expecting her to speak to me. It wouldn't have been any less than what I deserved. I meant it when I said that I just needed her to know the truth.

I think, as she was leading me back to my room, I was remembering how hard I'd worked to get her to trust me. A marathon. I was remembering how persistent I'd been, always begging her for more, like a rabid dog nipping at her ankles. I was wondering if I had what it took to start back at square one, and indulging in some pretty pathetic self-pity.

But she trusted me enough to let me touch her. To let me kiss her. To let me inside of her. To say that she loved me back.

Not that I didn't miss the shift in dynamic last night.

That was Sugar, being in control.

Taking what she wanted.

Somewhere beside me, my phone chimes with a text, and I stiffen. For a week now, Heston's been hounding me, a constant barrage of menacing, loaded messages. That chime is something I've already been conditioned to dread.

But because of the girl sleeping soundly in my arms, I can't afford to not know if he's on the loose again. I mournfully roll away from her, hand fumbling around beside the bed until it finds the phone. Squinting at the screen hurts even more than squinting at the window had, but at least it's not him.

It's my dad.

"Christ," I mutter, combing my fingers through my hair. Good little robot boys who wake up at a 'reasonable hour' are apparently part and parcel of being the next big shot Wilcox.

Fucking kill me now.

I rise from the bed in fits and starts, muscles screaming in protest, determined not to look back at her laying there, all soft and warm and comfortable. I know if I do, I'm just going to roll back into her. My mouth tastes like something died in it. That, plus the fact that I'm dehydrated, nicotine-deprived, and hurting in places I only ever suspected existed are the only things that drive me to get vertical. I let out an involuntary hiss when I bend to pull on a pair of boxers. I'm not even sure who's to credit for that. The guy in the pool? Heston? Reyn, when he jabbed me with his elbow as we stood outside my house, telling me to grow a pair?

One thing's for sure. I'm done being a punching bag for a while.

I find a pair of sweats in a heap on my floor, and then an LAX hoodie draped over the foot of my bed. Pulling that on hurts even worse than the bottoms had, and by the time my head pokes out the top, I'm already feeling a little surly about it all.

I'm halfway out the door when I hear Sugar's voice.

"Where are you going?" She's sitting up when I turn around, sheets gathered over her chest. Her eyes are still puffy with sleep, but there's no mistaking the spark of dread in them.

Of course, seeing her there makes every ounce of my getting-out-of-bed resolve completely disappear. "To take a piss," I say, wandering back to the bed, scratching my chest under the sweater. "Smoke a cigarette. Brush my teeth. Down a whole bottle of Advil."

Her eyes are still wide, too alert for someone who just woke up. "You were leaving."

I watch her, not understanding the way she's gone so still. "Just to the bathroom."

"You were leaving," she repeats, eyes holding mine. "*Again*."

I tilt my head at the way she's looking at me, something angry in the hunch of her eyebrows. "Hey," I say, crawling up the bed to her, settling easily into the vee of her legs. "I told you I wasn't—I'm not going to do that again. I said I'm fighting for you, and I meant it."

When I nose below her ear, pressing a kiss to that spot of skin where her neck meets her shoulder, some of that tension leaves. "I know that," she says. "I just meant..."

I pull back to give her a quizzical look. "What did you mean?"

"That morning." She looks away, cheeks blooming a soft pink. "After we... when I woke up. You were gone."

"Oh," I realize, sitting back on my heels to rub her sheet-covered knees. "I was just making you breakfast."

Her eyes flash angrily when they meet mine again. "You fucked me. I woke up alone, in a strange place, not knowing what—" Her jaw tightens. "And every moment after, right up until fucking *yesterday*, you treated me like... like someone you were done with. Like your old, *discarded lay*."

I blink back at her, mouth parted in a defense that I already know I don't deserve to make. "It wasn't like that."

"Well, it *felt* like that,' she bites out, and residing alongside the angry eyes and set jaw, there's the hunched, vulnerable curve of her shoulders. There's no mistaking the fissure of hurt in her eyes.

I scrub a hand over my face, so goddamn frustrated with myself, I don't even care that it hurts. "Fuck, I'm an idiot." She doesn't push me away when I reach for her, sending us both tumbling back into the bed. She lays there against my shoulder, shoulders still tight. "I'm a dick."

"Yep," is her terse reply. But she throws an arm around my middle, holding me down.

For the thousandth time, I offer, "Sorry," fingers threading in her hair. "I don't know if it's occurred to you yet, but I actually have no fucking idea what I'm doing. I've never had a girlfriend before." I push a kiss into her hair. "You might have to tell me when I'm messing up. It might be a lot."

Instantly, she says, "Trust me, I will."

Well.

That's something.

"So, no leaving the bed the morning after. Anything else I need to know?"

She sighs, the stiffness of her body leaving with her long exhale. "I don't really like pancakes."

I frown into her hair. "Oh."

"French toast, sure. Waffles are fine, too. I wouldn't say no to—" She shifts, tilting her head to look back at me, immediately wincing. "Shit, you actually really need that Advil, don't you?"

I guess I don't need to wonder how bad I look. "Nah," I lie, wrapping my arms around her shoulders.

She rolls her eyes, breaking away. "I think I remember hearing something about a cigarette and a toothbrush. Let me in on the ground floor of that and we're all good."

That's how we find ourselves back in my bathroom. I'm trying not to think about that mess in the main suite, or about how Sugar is looking really damn fine in one of my uniform button downs. That gets a little harder when she crowds me back against the counter, forehead creasing as her fingers run over my face.

"You're sure nothing's really bad here?" she asks, voice skeptical.

Now that my teeth are brushed, I'm free to answer with a kiss, arms winding around her waist. "Everything's perfect," I answer.

It's only a little bullshit. There's a lot of work to be done. Somehow, I have to convince the coach to let me back on the team. I have to start planning for school next year and getting used to my dad's constant presence over my shoulder.

That's confirmed when my phone rings from the other room.

Groaning, I break away, giving myself a moment to enjoy the way she's gazing up at me, all dazed and pink-cheeked. "Hold that thought. It's my dad."

Of course it is. Who else would legit fucking voice-call me at seven on a Sunday morning? I flop back on my bed as he yaps in my ear about making myself 'available' next weekend for a dinner with some boring old venture capitalist he's buddied up with this month. In truth, I probably got off lucky. My college applications are already in, so I don't even have to worry about his manic attempts at making me look like an 'attractive candidate'.

Yet.

I don't really tune in until he mentions that Liesel is loading the car for his flight to Tucson. I can hear my mom in the background —something about a boarding pass—and I can tell just from the way she sounds annoyed that she's having a good day.

When I hang up, I already have a plan brewing.

"Hey," Sugar says when I return to the bathroom, finishing up the end of her braid. "You never told me about the kittens. How are they doing?"

I wrap my arms around her from behind, chin resting on her

head as I hold her gaze in the reflection of the mirror. "How do you feel about going to see them?"

Her fingers suddenly stop moving. "You mean...at your house?" Her voice is full of something dark and cagey.

"Heston's gone," I assure her, knowing from the text earlier that he's still sitting somewhere in county. "And my dad's on his way to the airport as we speak. We can go see Abby and her babies, and you can finally meet my mom. It'll be chill."

"Your mom...?" Her eyes raise to mine, and even though that faint sheen of dread is still present in her eyes, I don't miss the hopeful tone in her voice.

"Yeah, you'll like her. She's really nice." Taking her by the hips, I spin her around to face me. Her hands fall when I pull the braid from them, making a clumsy attempt at finishing it myself. I fix my eyes to the task as I explain, "She has a lot of problems because she has a depressive disorder. It comes and goes. Sometimes she's really bad, but other times she's completely fine. A little reclusive, but really cool." I can't help the way my mouth lifts when I remember, "When I was a kid, she was the most fun adult I knew. She'd take us places when my dad was gone, like go-kart racing or laser tag, and she was never like the other parents who stood off to the side, you know? She really liked playing with us. Sometimes I think she must be really bummed that we grew up."

That's when it started getting worse—once Heston and I were too old to care about playing with toys and going on roller-coasters. Although, the more I think about it, the more I wonder if it wasn't just easier to hide back then. Like maybe it was always there, just under the surface, and there came a point where hiding it behind laughter and new, shiny games wasn't possible anymore, because we were old enough to know better.

Sugar's hands gently take the braid from me and I snort a laugh at it. The top half is perfect but the bottom is all lumpy and uneven.

She secures it with a hair tie anyway. "Okay."

∼

THE SIGHT of Sugar behind the wheel of the Mustang is seriously doing things to me. Not to toot my horn or anything, but it did turn out fucking amazing. The interior is sleek as fuck.

I've pushed the seat back so that I'm lounging out, just enjoying the feel of the engine. "Turn here," I direct, pointing to the next right.

She looks wary, teeth sinking into her bottom lip, but does it anyway. "We didn't go this way last time."

I watch the way she holds the wheel, comfortable and sure. "I'm taking you the scenic route so you can really open her up."

Her eyebrows raise. "Open her *up*?"

"Fuck yeah," I insist, running a palm over the dash. "You've gotta learn how to treat a lady like this, Sugar. Take her out somewhere special every now and then, give her a reason to look nice, hear the way she purrs, get her muffler vibrating..."

Sugar stops me with a look. "Do you need a minute alone with the car, Bass?"

I smirk at her. "And you think I can't do romance."

She looks vaguely disgusted, but I don't miss the way her lips purse with a restrained smile when my hand rests over hers on the gear shift. "Are you sure your mom won't mind?" she asks for the fifth fucking time.

"Positive." I'd given Liesel a call, just in case, to confirm that she was in a condition to receive visitors. "You seriously don't need to sweat it. She's going to like you."

She's sweating it. "I should have worn that dress." She shifts gears, a little divot appearing between her eyebrows. "Shouldn't I look nice?"

"You do look nice," I argue, pointing up ahead. "Take a left here."

"So, last time..." I can tell from the way she says just which 'last time' she's referring to. "You didn't introduce me to your mom because she was..." She shoots me a meaningful look.

I roll my head against the seat to look at her through my sunglasses. "She wasn't doing well then. I went to see her and it was...just not a good time. Trust me."

For some reason, she looks oddly relieved to hear this. "Oh."

"I wasn't, like, *hiding* her. Or you." Although, now that I think about it, I know that's probably how it seemed. "Maybe I should have told you before, it's just..."

"Private," she guesses. "I get it."

I direct her to turn onto the old service road, and when she does, I say, "Stop."

She looks at me, then back at the deserted road. "What?"

"Just stop, right here in the road." At her confused face, I explain, "No one comes down here, it's fine."

Finally, she listens, pressing the brake. "Why am I stopping in the middle of the road like a moron?"

I flash her a wide grin. "Because you're about to see what kind of power this sweet thing is packing."

"Oh no," she groans. "Bass, I'm not a fucking street racer."

I straighten in my seat. "Well, you're fucking a street racer, and he put a lot of work into these horsepower's, so humor him."

Rolling her eyes, she starts checking her seatbelt. "This is dangerous."

I give mine a firm yank too, grinning. "Yep."

"You look way too excited about this," she says, eyeing me disapprovingly. "If you make me hurt my newly very pretty car, I'm going to break my foot off in your ass."

I wave a hand. "Don't worry, the road is nice and straight. I bring Jasmine here all the time." I very purposefully do *not* tell her this is the road Vandy and Reyn had their accident on. In my defense, how many deer are crossing this road in the daytime, anyway? "Okay, get ready."

Truthfully, I am excited, but not quite for the reason she's thinking. Sure, barreling down a road in a roar of exhaust will always be a good time, but mostly I just want to see her feel it. The adrenaline. The grip. The feeling of absolute control in a moment of chaos.

I coach her through the right way to safely come up to speed. It's not quite as easy as just pushing the throttle. She listens intently, eyes tracking where I point, and she doesn't even look nervous about it.

She kind of looks excited too, actually.

When she finally gets going, both hands planted on the wheel until I direct her to shift up, an edge of a smile finally starts to break free. When she gets it up to sixty, it grows, back pressed against the seat as the scenery rushes by us. At seventy-five, I start really appreciating what I've done. It's a fucking growler of an engine, but almost as smooth as Jasmine, who I've easily put four times the work and money into.

At eighty, her breath starts coming in a little shallower, anxiety warring with that flash of thrill in her eyes.

"Holy shit," she says when it reaches ninety. It's almost too quiet to hear it over the engine, and I wish the road were longer so I could really get into the way she looks right now, mouth parted, cheeks flushed, eyes wide.

Lucky me, it's still there when she begins shifting down, the RPMs rapidly decreasing until she brings it to a smooth stop. She's breathing heavy, chest rising and falling. When she turns to me, the exhilarated smile on her face makes my heart hammer faster than going ninety-five just had.

I exhale, "Goddamn, I'm in love with you."

Her breath stutters for a moment, right before she meets me over the console in a searing, open-mouthed kiss. I grasp at the back of her head, grunting at the way she fists a hand in my shirt, dragging me closer.

It's sloppy and frantic and completely artless.

But it's ours.

~

Sugar still looks anxious when we finally arrive at my house, but the drive and ensuing make-out session seems to have leeched some of her nerves. Liesel meets us in the foyer, taking our jackets and directing me to the drawing room.

Mom's obviously been waiting for us. She entertains more often than she'd probably like, but she's never been super happy about it. Memories rush back to me of her doing the bare minimum as my dad followed behind her, happily lavishing everything up. It makes me feel a little guilty when we enter and I realize she's gone all out —tea, scones, doilies, and all.

She stands upon seeing us, instantly coming over. "Sebastian! Twice in one weekend. You're going to spoil me. Thankfully, you're not bloody this time." She presses a kiss to my cheek before leveling me with an exasperated look. "Who are you, Bono? Take those sunglasses off in the house." I reach up to remove them and she pauses, frowning at my shiner. "Never mind, put them back on."

Sugar snorts a laugh, drawing our attention.

"Mom," I say, reaching out to rest a hand on the small of Sugar's back. "This is Sugar Voss. My girlfriend." I have this split moment of vision-blurring panic, because is she? Yeah, we fucked and slept together, and maybe there were some declarations, but none of those had been—

Sugar gives my mom a small smile, greeting, "Pleasure to meet you, Mrs. Wilcox."

Mom presses her fingers to her mouth, a grin peeking out from between them. She shoots me a glance that says just how precious she thinks this all is. "Sugar, the pleasure is entirely mine." She extends a hand and I panic again, because I hadn't thought to tell her about the whole touch thing.

Sugar looks down at her hand, and after a beat that's barely even awkward, reaches out to take it. "Thanks for... having me."

Mom leads us over to the sitting area, letting us take the couch side by side. "I've heard so much about you! I have one of your pieces, you know."

Sugar looks briefly confused before she remembers. "Right, Abby. He said he wanted it for you."

"It's gorgeous!" Mom pours us each a cup of tea—gross—and nods to the scones. "I'm told you had a bit of a show yesterday. That must have been so exciting."

I pretend to drink the gross-ass tea as I watch them talk. Sugar still looks a little awkward, but her smiles come easy, especially when the talk comes around to Abby and her kittens.

"She's such a good mama," Mom says. "We moved the box and everything into my rooms, because I couldn't handle kneeling on that floor of his all day." When I'd come here last night, I realized that she's taken over watching Abby and the kittens. According to Liesel, it's been good for her mood. "I think she likes it there. I've noticed her roaming out more. This morning, I found her on my settee, laid back, just as comfy as you please. Needed a break. I know the feeling." She shoots me a fondly annoyed look, and I know she's still smarting from both the trouble with Heston and the way I burst in here last night. Come to think of it, it's probably a miracle that she's in such good shape today, all things considered.

"Sorry," I say, even though I've already apologized.

She turns back to Sugar. "Would you like to see them?"

"Oh, um..." Sugar sets down her full cup of tea, sliding her eyes to me. "Only if it's not any trouble, or—"

"Don't be silly," Mom says, already on her feet.

Her rooms are nice and tidy, curtains open to let in the sunlight. She has the box all nested up in the corner where an end table used to be. Abby's inside, head popping up over the edge at our approach, ears dipping low in nervousness.

Sugar coos, "It's okay, sweet girl," and instantly reaches into her bag for the treats. At the sound of the bag, Abby lumbers to her feet, disengaging the little army of eating kittens. "You remember, huh?" She gives one to Abby from her hand, and leaves another on the floor in front of the box. She looks surprised when Abby jumps right out to get it.

"She's warming up," I explain. "I think the new bougie life probably helps."

Sugar shoots me a smile, edging forward to get a look at the grumpy pile of kittens nosing into the warm spot Abby just vacated. "Oh my god," she gushes. "Look at them! This one looks just like her." She reaches in to run a gentle fingertip over its weird little bean-shaped head. "They're already so much bigger."

"I think their eyes will start opening soon." I poke at a little orange one. "This one is a fat little fucker."

She swats my hand. "It's just *hardy*. Doesn't it look kind of like Lucy?"

"Yeah, Abby's probably her mom, too." Come to think of it, "Probably Hades's as well."

Sugar pauses, processing this. "Ew."

"Yup."

Abby returns, clearly feeling a bit sketchy about all the hands currently occupying her nest. We back off a bit to watch her aggressively clean the fat little orange one, working through a few names.

"Bub, obviously," she says.

"Bub? That's obvious?"

"Beelzebub."

"Oh, right." I point to the smallest. "What about Lilith? If it's a girl."

She grins. "I like it. I think the last one, should be Morningstar—"

"Since he came late on that wintery night."

"Yep."

We toss out a few others, Loki, Hela, but Sugar's phone goes off. She pulls it from her pocket, thumb sliding over the screen. After a moment of reading, eyebrows furrowed, she says, "I guess everyone's taking Georgia out for breakfast. I'm supposed to ask you if..." She buries a chuckle into a fist, quoting, "...if you got your head out of your ass far enough to come be a Devil again."

I fight down a cringe, knowing that my mom and Sugar might have been the first stops on the Sebastian Wilcox Apology Tour, but are by no means the last. "What do you think? You down?"

Better to get it over with now.

Nodding, she shoots me a grin before putting her phone away. "Sure, I could do breakfast with my boyfriend and his weirdo secret society."

We say goodbye to Abby, and then my mom and Liesel, walking out into the cool March air. I still get a frission of satisfaction when

I see the Mustang sitting there in my driveway, all shiny and good again.

"You have to name her," I say, nodding to the car.

She narrows her eyes. "Who says it's a girl?"

"Come on," I say, lifting my hands toward it. "Curves like that? She's all woman."

She opens the door, sliding behind the wheel, and I follow suit. Even though she looks dubious about the tradition, she still mutters out a, "Well..."

I realize, "You *did* name her."

She cranks the ignition, cutting me a narrow-eyed look. "Maybe."

"So?" I prod, watching as she pulls down the drive, looking like she was born to be in that seat. "What is it?"

I think at first she won't answer, but once we get onto the highway leading to The Nerd, she finally cracks.

"Theia."

I look at her in surprise, wondering, "Theia?"

She nods, cheeks flushing. "She was a titan. The goddess of sight."

I hum, gears turning over in my mind. "Like photography."

"Kind of. I guess." She shrugs, eyes fixed to the road as she shifts. "She and Hyperion were also..."

Feeling my mouth curl into a slow smile, I take a guess, "Super-hot lovers?"

She rolls her eyes. "Fine. Yes."

I laugh, but can't deny the warmth that floods my chest. "It'll fit on a plate."

"No," she says, holding up a hand. "I'm not going to be one of those douchebags who gets their car's name on their license plate. Offense totally fucking intended."

"None taken," I respond, shrugging.

When we get to the Nerd, I find that most of the gang is already there. It's fucking ridiculous, four tables pushed together in the back, Emory arguing with Tyson over a menu while Ben and Reyn engage in a game of table hockey with someone's discarded bagel.

The girls all surround Georgia in the front, and they've left a chair open beside Vandy, who turns to see who's walking up.

She looks between me and Sugar, standing hand in hand, and lets out a loud, "Oh, thank god! You two were making all the drama between me and Reyn look downright *cute*."

The rest of them turn to see us, and it's all crazy then. Aubrey, Afton, and Elana all looking grossed out and worried about my bruised face, while the guys just point and laugh. I know I was a dick to them all, that a big part of letting Sugar go to protect her included doing the same for them. But they don't even look mad.

They clear me a seat right beside the one being saved for Sugar, like it's not even a question. I guess that's part of being a Devil now. It's not something you can shake away from when shit gets tough. I sling an arm over the back of her chair, thinking that it's a damn good thing.

Shit's never been easy for any of us.

I lean into Sugar's side, offering, "They have good waffles here." She turns to give me a smile and I can't help myself, tipping forward to press a kiss to her lips.

"Aw, this is fucking great," Carlton mutters. "All these gross couples now. I liked it better when you fuckers were single and emotionally stunted."

Afton flips her menu over. "They're still emotionally stunted, no worries."

Around me, life goes on.

It's not half bad.

EPILOGUE

Sugar

Spring at Preston is a lot warmer.

Everyone is gearing up for prom and some big swim meet going down next week. Finals loom in the air. The chatter around me regarding everyone's summer plans borders on unreal. Vacations to Spain, studies abroad, volunteer programs in South America, internships at Fortune 500 companies...

I shake my head as I make another circle on the map.

There's a knock on the door—two loud, quick raps—before Sebastian waltzes through it, tossing his bag on the floor.

I watch over my shoulder as he kicks off his shoes. "Someone could have been naked in here, you know."

He glances up at me, mouth slanted into a wry smirk. "Baby, I live in hope."

"Don't call me baby." I use my pen to point at the bed next to mine. "Georgia lives here, too."

"I just saw her in the quad." He shrugs, landing obnoxiously on the bed at my side, stomach-down, just like me. It makes the map crinkle and tear at the corner, and I shoot him a glare. He ignores it, inspecting the marks we've been making for the past week. "Huh. You added another one."

Defensively, I say, "Yes," and tug the map closer. He's always got something snarky to say about my itinerary choices.

"Are you for real?" he groans, realizing what I've circled. "Four Corners? That's the most touristy shit ever."

Hotly, I argue. "It's *neat*. Who doesn't want to stand in four places at once?"

He slides his eyes to me. "Are we taking fanny packs, too?"

"It's on the way to the Grand Canyon."

He flops onto his side, face pained. "I was really convinced you were cooler than this."

I jab him with an elbow. "Stuff it, or I'm putting the Sea Glass Museum back on the list."

"You're lucky you're cute."

I nod. "Ditto."

Despite all that, his hand comes out to rest on my lower back, sweeping beneath my shirt. "Got the last one today." I look at him, noticing now that he looks tired. "Brown."

I instantly sit up, stomach swooping. "Really?"

He rolls onto his back, pulling an envelope from seemingly out of nowhere. "Came this morning."

We made a deal to discard the email acceptances, dumping them the instant they hit. Instead, going old school so we could assess it all together. I take the envelope from him. Although I know letter thickness doesn't mean anything, I still weigh it in my hand. "So, I'm just waiting for Chicago now."

"Yep." His eyes follow as I stand to tuck the letter away in my drawer, next to my letter from Rhode Island. His Chicago pick—or maybe more accurately, his father's—is Northwestern. The envelope for that one is already right there, all snugged up between Emory and SCAD. Our two Yale letters are at the bottom. "We could just open them now."

I slam the drawer shut. "No!"

He thrusts out a hand. "Come on! We've got seven of eight."

"You're worse than a kid sniffing out Christmas presents," I snipe back, folding up the map and stowing it away beneath the bed. "It'll be better once they're all here. That way, we can make a choice."

He makes a low, frustrated sound, because he's an impatient fuck. "Maybe we can open two per day. It'll be here by then, won't it?"

But I stand firm, kneeing up onto the bed. "Patience is a virtue."

"Virtue can suck my dick."

"You're tired," I say as I snuggle up to his side. I've learned that Bass can get on a serious tear about some things, but that he's also easily distracted. "How'd your test go?"

He grunts, arms coming around my shoulders to press me close. "Fine, probably. I never have a bad test." I know he's not lying. He might have issues with behavior and actual, like, *attendance*. But school comes easier to Bass than it does to me.

I settle my cheek against his shoulder, suddenly feeling tired myself. "Nap."

He hums, sounding like he's already halfway there, his soft breaths warming the top of my head. This is probably my favorite place now—all alone with him, curled up against his body as his hand makes the little idle rubs against whatever part of me is closest. When he's tired like this, his movements will slow, falter, before starting back up in a random bout of renewed vigor, like he's fighting not to nod off.

When his hand finally goes still, breath evening out, I let my eyes close, wondering where we're going to be in four months.

"Oops!" Startled awake at the sound, I turn my head to see Georgia in the doorway. I can tell from the light in the room that it's almost dark outside now. She shifts her feet, eyes apologetic. "Need the room?"

I stretch my legs, yawning. "No, we just fell asleep for a bit. It's all good."

Looking relieved, she enters the room, closing the door behind her. "Thank god. I cannot handle anymore prom shit. The hourly texts from my mom about choosing a date are bad enough."

Bass, still sound asleep, lets out a little whuff when I roll over. "Still no candidates?"

She wrinkles her nose, head shaking. "You're lucky, snagging a Wilcox. My mom's convinced I'm doomed to utter destitution unless I lock down someone rich and popular within the next month." She rolls her eyes, flopping back into her bed. "George never has to deal with this crap."

My forehead wrinkles. "Who's George?"

She gives me a strange look. "Uh, my brother?"

I sit up, still feeling half asleep. "You have a brother?" I gawk at her. "Named *George*?"

"Duh." She points to a photo on her desk of her and some guy, standing with bland smiles in front of a decked-out fireplace. "Twin brother."

"Your *twin*?!" Sebastian stirs and I whirl around to him. He blinks up at me, looking momentarily confused. "Georgia has a twin brother named George?"

He chuffs a low laugh. "I know."

"Why didn't *I* know?"

"Because," he explains, pushing himself up. "It sounds so fucking ridiculous that you wouldn't have believed it, anyway."

Georgia rolls her eyes at him. "George is *George*. We don't really hang in the same circles. Or squares. Or rectangles."

Sebastian looks at me, translating, "He's a loser."

"Don't call my brother a loser!" Georgia cries, throwing her pillow at him. "Only *I'm* allowed to call him a loser." She looks at me, asserting. "He's a loser."

"Good to know."

Sebastian stands, pulling on his shoes. "I'm going to go grab something to eat. Any takers?"

Georgia waves him off. "I already made Carlton buy me pizza."

"I'm in," I say, reaching for my own shoes.

"You still need to give me that list," he suddenly says, still clearly blinking sleep from his eyes. "The film and shit?"

Ah, right. "I decided to just take a few rolls. I've got it covered."

It's a bit of a bummer, sure. A big part of the appeal of a huge summer road trip had been the ability to take a shit-ton of photos.

He pauses, throwing me a confused glance. "What? A few rolls isn't going to even get you out of the state."

Sighing, I explain, "I won't be here next year, and I don't know where I'll be next year. I won't have a way to develop them myself, so just..." I flick a hand dismissively. "I don't know. Maybe I'll save up for a digital—" My mouth clamps shut at the sudden spark in his eyes. "*No.*"

"Let me buy you one," he bursts, even though my head is already shaking. Fuck, big mistake. If there's one thing Bass loves, it's blowing truly absurd amounts of money. "Come on! I've been trying to get you into digital for weeks now."

"No!" I say, voice firm. "It's too much. I hate it when you buy me shit. You never just get me something sufficient, you always go over the fucking top!"

"One camera," he insists, pulling my hands into his chest. "Maybe some lenses or whatever fancy bullshit comes with it. It can be a graduation present."

"No."

"Please?"

"Hell no."

He pulls me closer like he thinks I don't know what he's doing, those blue eyes blazing back at me, lashes fluttering. "Please?"

"Just how pretty do you think you are?"

His answer is immediate and unapologetic. "Devastatingly."

Smoothly, I lie, "Not nearly."

He takes my face in his palms, thumbs sweeping over my cheeks, which are totally not feeling hot and flushed from his devastatingly pretty *anything*. "Sugar," he begins, eyes earnest. "I love your pictures. I love the thought of you being able to take them, without feeling like you have to ration resources. I love that you have a passion that will, most likely, earn you your own living some day, completely independent of anyone else. I love seeing shit through your eyes, because you always see it a little different from me, and that's neat as fuck. I love the idea that I can help you do that, and with something that just so happens to come easier for me." He presses a soft, slow kiss to my lips, finishing, "But most of all, I love *you*."

I feel a little dazed when he pulls back. "Oh." I blink heavy eyelids at him, tongue sneaking out to taste him on my lips.

Oh, *he's good.*

Georgia's voice snaps me from the trance. "For Christ's sake, let him buy you a damn camera! You two make me want to hurl." I throw her a hot glare, but she just rolls her eyes at me. *"Boo hoo, my super rich boyfriend, who is totally hot and completely adores me, wants to buy me expensive things."* She scoffs. "Your problems are the first worldiest ever."

Turning back to Sebastian, I release a defeated huff. Georgia has a point. "I'm only saying yes because I know if I don't, you're going to use that graduation present excuse to buy me something even more stupidly expensive."

He plants another kiss on my lips, looking satisfied.

Satisfied and devastatingly cute.

"WHERE ARE YOU?" I mutter angrily, pacing back and forth in front of his door. I loop my thumbs into the straps of my bag and squeeze. I'd sent him three texts, but they all went unanswered. He's been a lot less diligent about charging his phone since his dad began blowing it up regularly. Fucking inconvenient bullshit.

It's a half an hour before I finally hear steps ascending across the hall, Sebastian finally coming into view.

"Where have you been?" I hiss, grabbing a handful of his shirt and tugging him toward the door. "I've been waiting forever."

The question is unnecessary. Going off the way his hair is still wet, gym bag hanging from his hand, it's already obvious. "I was at practice. Same time every Wednesday. You know this."

Right.

"Well, come on, let me in," I say, flapping a hand at the knob.

He raises an eyebrow, cheeks still flushed from practice. "Need it that bad, huh? I'm a little wiped, but my stroke game is probably still on point." That cocky grin of his disappears the instant I hold up the bundle of letters. He swipes them from my hand flipping through, realizing. "Chicago came."

I confirm. "Chicago came."

He stares down at the stack, eyes jumping up to me. "So, we're going to do this?"

"We're going to do this."

"Are you going to just keep repeating everything I say?"

I push his shoulder. "Open the door!"

"Alright, geez. So much for patience being a virtue." Despite his grumbling, I can tell from the way he fumbles with his keys that he's just as anxious as I am.

We get into his suite, which is thankfully nice and tidy. I've discovered that the state of Sebastian's living space holds a direct correlation to his mood. I turn around in the room, watching him dump his things off, holding the letters carefully out of the way.

When he's done, he says, "Okay," and drops down on the couch. "Which first. SCAD, right?"

I frown at the way he says it, like it should be obvious. "Why SCAD?"

"Because," he explains, giving me a quick, guilty look. "Save the best ones for last, right? Not that SCAD isn't a good school, or that I don't want you to get in, or that I wouldn't—"

I drop into the space at his side, stopping him. "No, I get it. Three-hour drive between there and Emory." It was the closest school his dad approved of.

He hands me one envelope and plucks another from the stack. "You first."

I nod, taking a breath before jamming my nail between the—

"Fuck, wait," he says, jolting forward. "Hold on." I watch in confusion as he crosses the room, toeing his shoes off and kicking them aside. He bends to grab another, darting back to the couch to put them on.

Baffled, I ask, "What are you doing?"

He shoots me a glance as he tightens the laces, a lock of hair falling in his eyes. "They're my lucky shoes."

I blink. "I'm sorry, you have lucky *shoes*?"

"Laugh all you want, but these babies," He sinks back into the couch, kicking a foot up on the table, "have won me many fights."

"You know what? I'm not even going to comment on that." I rip open the envelope, stomach fluttering as I pull out the letter and unfold it. I scan it quickly, not feeling any less full of nerves when I realize, "I got in."

"Good," he says, like it was never even in question. He rips open the one from Emory, eyes sliding over the page. "Me, too."

We both pause, looking at each other.

"They're good schools."

He agrees, "Some of the best."

I nod, eyes straying to the other letters, "But I'm sure we got into others."

He tosses his letter aside. "I'm gonna be real here. Emory would never let me live it down if I went to Emory."

"That *would* get confusing." I'm not sure why anyone would name their kids after their alma maters, but that's the Halls.

I fold my legs beneath me to contain my bouncing knee. "Chicago next."

He raises an eyebrow. "Yeah? Not feeling the Chi-town, huh."

I hurry to add, "Not that Northwestern isn't an amazing school! Of course, I mean, obviously that's a fine option."

"Better than Emory and SCAD," he volleys back.

"Exactly." He hands me the envelope to Chicago and we tear into them at the same time, the room quiet as we read the letters. I exhale slowly. "I got in."

Sebastian frowns at his. "Waitlisted? The fuck?" He turns it over, like maybe he's expecting an explanation.

"It's not a rejection," I say, trying to sound excited.

But he just snatches the letter from my hand and throws them both aside. "Fuck Chicago."

Trying for a rueful smile, I reach for the next two. "Okay, Rhode Island and Brown!"

Easily distracted, he tears open the envelope while I rip into mine. "Well," he says, "Brown at least knows what's good." He turns the letter, showing me his acceptance.

My stomach sinks when I read mine. "Oh. I didn't get in."

"What?!" He rips the letter out of my hand. "That's bullshit!"

I shrug, trying to shake it off. "Come on, two out of four? That's really good, considering. And SCAD and Chicago are really good schools, so it's not like I don't have options."

He's still seething at my rejection letter. "Well if you're good enough for SCAD and Chicago, then you're good enough for Rhode fucking Island. What's so great about Rhode Island anyway? The world's largest bug?"

I reluctantly point out, "I actually still want to see that."

"Nah." He tosses both letters aside with the rest. "Fuck Rhode Island. We're not going there, we're boycotting. Let's open Yale." He hands me one of the last two envelopes, and he looks so casual about opening it that I don't have the heart to tell him that's it for me.

It was the only really big-league school I applied to, and even that was mostly a lark. I was already well aware it'd take a miracle, but if I couldn't get into Rhode Island, then I have absolutely no shot at a place like Yale.

Somehow oblivious to this very simple fact, Sebastian rips right into his, tongue peeking out to wet his lips as he reads. I know from the slow smile that curves his mouth that it's good news. His eyes rise to mine. "Got in." And then he turns to the discarded Northwestern letter, flipping it a middle finger. "Suck on that, bitches."

I roll my eyes, but inside, my chest aches. Yale is such an amazing school and now he's going to have to choose between it and me. "Bass..."

"Don't give me that look." He nudges the letter in my hand. "Open it before you admit defeat."

My face feels warm as I open it, knowing that I'm going to have to be rejected twice in front of him. And then he'll get mad. He'll say a bunch of bullshit about how it's their loss. He'll say he won't even want to go to Yale anymore, not if they don't want—

I shoot to my feet. "Oh my god, I got in!" I don't actually believe it, even after reading it three times, hand clutched to my chest. How the fuck does Cliff trash get into Yale motherfucking University? I look at Sebastian, eyes wide. "Did you have something to do with this?"

He's halfway up himself, expression caught somewhere between celebration and confusion. "What am I, the mob? I got waitlisted at fucking Northwestern. If I had that kind of pull, I think I could have gotten you into Rhode Island, don't you think?"

"So this is just..."

"Just you," he says, gently plucking the letter from my hand. He folds it carefully with his own, blue eyes shining back at me. "Because you're fucking awesome Sugar Voss."

Slowly, I realize, "Holy shit, we're going to Yale." He doesn't even stumble when I leap forward to hug his neck, squealing. He effortlessly lifts me, sweeping my feet off the floor and carrying me forward. I don't realize we're in the bedroom until we fall into the mattress in one excited, breathless heap.

In one month, it'll be just like he promised that day in his shower, when he decided to fight for me; just the two of us, and the open road. Three whole months of nothing but having him at my side.

And then four years of the same.

He leans down to kiss me, the warmth of his palm dragging deliciously up my shirt. It's almost hard to remember a time where I was afraid of this, the brushing heat of him against my skin. Sebastian Wilcox barreled into my life in a whirling dervish of fists and flame, and he rearranged me. Tossed me about. Settled me into someone tidy and sound. The kiss he gives me is all at once sweet and stinging, a lot like the trail of fire left by his fingertips.

That's just what it's like to be touched my Devil.

～

Pre-Order Book 4, Devil Incarnate Today!

AFTERWORD

GUYS!

Whew, things got tense for a minute, but if there's one thing about me and Samantha. We may rip everyone to shreds but we will do out best to patch everyone back up at the end.

Thank you for taking this journey with us. When we started Preston Prep it was a one shot with Hamilton and Gwen. The world exploded with the rest of the Devils insisting on telling their own stories.

Special thanks to the readers on our ARC team, Angel's Antics, Lisa for her patient Beta reading and VC Edits! Sam, as always killed it with the cover.

See you next book! Things are about to get rough.

Angel

Thanks so much for reading our self-indulgent angst porn! Big thanks to Angel for dealing with my constant overthinking and 3am manic emails that made almost no sense. And to my Discord nonnies for always being solid and listening to my arguments with myself. And Lisa, who is the best cheerleader. And to my husband, who stood behind me while I wrote the last chapter and acted as such a convincing cutman that I was able to crush it.

Sam

ABOUT THE AUTHORS

Want to keep up with new releases and what's happening with
Angel & Sam? Here's how!

Angels Antics Facebook Group
Samantha Rue's Mailing List

~

Have you read the other books in the Preston Prep Series? Each is a
standalone in a larger series.

Devil May Care
A Deal with the Devil

And don't miss out on book 4, Devil Incarnate, coming in 2020!
Read on for a sneak peek!

~

I look into the camera, testing a crooked smile before clicking
the button. I lower my phone to assess the picture, deciding that it's
garbage. I try another, this one with my cleavage in the shot. Oh,
yeah. That's definitely it.

I add a caption:

*Getting ready to crush these lame PhysEd credits. Should I do swim,
bball, or track?*

The bench in front of the gym is nice. It's a warm day for March —warm enough that I've abandoned my sweater in favor of undoing a few buttons on my uniform. I get a couple instant responses from people who don't even go here, so I'm scrolling down my ChattySnap when a group of people walk by.

I look up, realizing who it is.

It's *The Devils*, capital T, capital D.

They ignore me, of course. As they should. I'm just a freshman, and they're all juniors. Well, not just juniors. They're some of the most popular people in school. Athletic. Smart. Rich.

Just then, one of them makes eye contact with me. Heston Wilcox. *Oh, god.* He's so ridiculously handsome that my heart instantly starts pitter-pattering. It beats even harder when his steps falter, slowing.

"Hey, you're Georgia, right?" he asks.

I nod, holding back an inner, girlish, squeal at the fact he knows my name. *My* name! "Uh, yeah. Hi!" I feel a little cringe at the excitement in my voice, but he just walks back a step, facing me.

Heston's lips tilt into a wry smirk. "You busy tonight?"

I feel a hot blush creep up my cheeks. "Er... me?" A couple of his friends wait nearby, and my eyes dart over. They're all Devils. Hamilton Bates, Ansel Davenport, Emory Hall. There's a girl tucked under Hamilton's arm. Her name is Campbell, but I'm not sure if that's a first or last lame.

"Yes, you," he says with a little laugh, amusement dancing in this ocean blue eyes.

I push my shoulders back, trying to adopt a façade of perfect cool. "No, I'm not busy tonight."

He lifts his chin. "I'm having a party. You should come."

Holy shit! Heston Wilcox is inviting *me* to a party! I stammer out, "To your house?"

"Yep."

Blush deepening, I admit, "I don't have a ride."

He glances over at the guys, eyes zeroed in. "Campbell can give you a ride. Isn't that right, Cam?"

Campbell scowls, obviously not pleased at someone telling her what to do, but Hamilton leans down and whispers something into her ear. Whatever he says is enough to smooth her expression. She gives me a look and calls out, "Meet me by the parking lot at eight."

"S-sure," I stutter, trying to look casual as I cross my legs. "Yeah. Sounds great."

They walk off, just like that—as if Heston Wilcox hadn't just socially anointed me.

*

The ride with Campbell is awkward. I try to strike up a conversation three times, but it falls flat. She barely answers me. I give up, spending the rest of the drive staring at my phone, full of excited nerves. I've been to parties before, but nothing like one thrown by the Devils.

And definitely nowhere like the Wilcox Compound, which is what everyone jokingly tags it as on social media. This place is insane.

When we arrive, Campbell all but leaves me to scurry after her in my heels. About the only thing that makes me feel a little less like an out of place loser is the way Heston looks at me when his eyes find me.

He smiles. "Hey. You made it."

Breathlessly, I say, "Yeah. Hi."

His eyes have that little gloss to them, like maybe he's already a bit buzzed off something. I don't blink an eye when he hands me a beer, a hand landing on my lower back to lead me into a room with a billiard table.

We spend a long time like that, him leading me around the party, talking to people here and there—people I know *of*, but don't actually know. None of them really pay attention to me, but sometimes, Heston will bend down to say something into my ear, like, "You have nice legs," or, "See that guy over there? That's Carl. He can get you anything you want," or, "Want another drink?" Every time he does, I get a small shiver, and the hand on resting on the small of my back rubs a little, like he knows.

I wasn't totally expecting it, so it's surprising to find that I'm definitely the girl on his arm for the night. The other girls seem surprised at the way he keeps me at his side too, throwing me the occasional confused or jealous glance. Even when he starts up a game of pool with his boys, he still returns to me, leaning in to talk some whispered smack about Ansel's form.

Never one to be bashful about these things, when the game winds to a close, I play it up, straining to give him a kiss on his cheek for good luck.

When he sinks the eight ball, his eyes find mine, mouth slanting into a wicked grin.

It's such a thrill. Heston isn't just good looking and popular. He's a *Devil*. He's one of the Four Horsemen of the school. He and the other guys have reputations beyond being smart and athletic. The Devils have impossible standards. Each one is rumored to have a 'test' girlfriends are supposed to pass to even be with them. Passing a test, getting 'marked' by one of them, is the fastest way to the top of the social ladder.

But that's not why I'm here. I don't really care about status. I've had my eye on him for a while—there's something magnetizing about him. Dangerous. Sexy. I've heard the rumors about his cock and I'm positively dying to give it a spin.

Sometimes you see the big, life-altering events barreling like a freight train down the track. Other times it happens in a blink, no warning sound, no flashing light, no barricades keeping you off the tracks.

I should know this is one of them, but it's hard to think when his lips are so warm, tasting bitter-sweet like beer when he kisses me, right in front of everyone. It's impossible when he whispers in my ear, "You're so pretty. Want to go upstairs?" And I'm too far gone by the time I'm up in his room, taking in the *boyness* of everything; the scent of his body spray, the box of condoms on his dresser, the grinning Devil on the flag hanging over his messy, unmade, bed.

"Do you live out here by yourself?" I ask, chills running down my spine from the feel of his lips on my neck. "Not in the main house?"

"I like how it's quiet," he answers, voice deep and smooth. "Private."

It's not quiet now—well, not downstairs. Down there, the party is in full swing; alcohol, skinny dipping, loud music. The bass vibrates through the guest cottage walls, shaking the dresser mirror with every thump and thud. It's a crazy party, one made even crazier by the fact I was invited by Heston Wilcox himself.

He crosses the room and stops in front of his desk, fussing with a laptop. Music streams through the speakers, covering up the rowdy rap from downstairs. The curve of his shoulders, the way he moves—sure and masculine—makes something low in my belly spark.

I know how it is for guys. They have to flirt and put on a bunch of pretense to get into a girl's pants. I've seen the games.

I'm not here to play.

I know what I want and I know how to get it. No frills, no bull-shit. I want on Heston's dick, like ten minutes ago, and I'm not about to make him work for it.

I take off my sweater and take a quick glance in the mirror to adjust my purple lace bra. The bra makes my tits look fantastic, probably my best feature. Guys are super into them and I know it.

When Heston turns back to me, he blinks once, slow and long, as he takes me in.

My stomach flips at the intensity of his gaze. "It seems so grown-up to be out here alone. No parents, free to do whatever you want." I watch as his fingers tug at the zipper on his hoodie, and he shrugs it off, tossing it on the back of a chair. Next he removes his shirt and I'm treated to his lean and long body. The perfect swimmer's physique. "It's cool that you can have parties like this, even though you're only a junior in high school, and no one cares. My dad is pretty strict—"

His mouth is on mine, cutting me off, tongue pushing through my lips. His fingers move quickly, confidently, under my bra strap.

"Fuck, you're stacked," he says eyeing my tits hungrily. He's right. My tits *are* big. He circles my nipple with his fingers, sending a tremor between my legs. He pinches it and grins. "You like that?"

Electricity zings through my body. Pain and pleasure. I arch back against it. "I do."

"I heard you like it dirty," he says, biting on my earlobe.

I'm distracted by his upper body. The hard lines of his chest and abs. I parse his words and look up, feeling dazed. "What?"

"I heard you like it dirty and *hard*," he says, kissing me, lips rough against mine. One hand circles my waist, thumb digging into my flesh while the other squeezes my breast.

"Who told you that?" I ask, reaching for the button on his jeans. I unzip his pants and pull his cock out. I just about die when I get my hands on him, a slow heat building between my legs. He's long and thick. Big like the rumors. Warm and ready.

His hips buck forward, pushing it into my palm. He shrugs at my question and gives me a smirk. "Think you can take that?"

I open my mouth to answer, to tell him that I'm not a virgin and I'm ready to do this, but he kisses me again, harder this time, using his body to angle me to the bed. I try to keep up with his kisses, with his warm tongue, and when the back of my knees hit the mattress, I run my hands down his chest, hoping to slow him down. This isn't like Reilly from Spanish, or Trevor from The Nerd, or Lance from my parents' Christmas party. Being with a guy like Heston is something I want to savor.

"You're so sexy," I tell him, kissing along his shoulders.

He cups my face in his hands and grins down at me, a twinkle in his eye. In that moment, I feel like I'm the only girl he sees. The only one he wants. I feel special. His thumb runs down my cheek, and he bends to kiss me. Sparks ignite across my body, down my limbs, to my fingers and toes. His hand runs down to the hem of my skirt and then back up, fingers twisting tight in my panties. When the kiss breaks, I look at him once again.

"You want this, right?"

"Yes," I admit, but as I say it something feels... *off*. It's the change in his expression. It's the feel of my panties digging into my sides.

It's the dark glaze in his eye that tells me I'm not entirely sure what it is I'm agreeing to.

"Good." He moves faster than I can blink, using his size, power, and athleticism against me. He pushes me back on the bed and before I can bounce, he's on top of me, yanking my panties down my thighs in a sharp motion. His cock presses into me, hard and intimidating. He shifts and thrusts a finger inside, making me gasp. "Jesus you're tight. Sure you're not a virgin? Is Halloway a liar?"

I blink, trying to follow his words while he fucks me with his finger. *John Halloway*? We'd hooked up a few times over the summer. I'd gone down on him behind the tennis courts at the club and let him fuck me at the Fourth of July party. Did he say something to Heston?

"I'm not a virgin," I gasp out, trying to get into the rhythm. Heston moves fast, hard. It's a challenge to keep up. I sit up to meet him, to find his mouth. He withdraws his finger and plants a hand right into the middle of my chest, shoving me back down flat. He waits for a beat, glancing over to the laptop. From this angle, he's like a magnificent animal, muscle stretched tight, corded and perfected. I reach for his cock, stroking it with my fingers. He looks down on me, his expression shuttered, and falls forward, both hands cinched roughly around my wrists. I grimace but spread my legs, giving him access.

This isn't quite like Reilly, or Lance, or Trevor, or even Josh, who fucked me fast and hard in the coat closet. There's this spark in Heston's eye, a strange tightness at the corners of his jaw. He's just excited, I think—*by me*—but a dark shadow flickers across his face, and a chill settles in my belly. It intensifies when his grip grows tighter and I say, "Wait, can you—"

His hand loosens, but not to release me. It's just enough to gain leverage so that he can flip me on my stomach. The heavy weight of his hand presses on my lower back and I twist my head to the side. "Heston, I—" but the air stalls in my lungs, pushed out by the weight of his hand around my neck, curling around my throat. Over the music, I hear the tear of foil and the sound of him rolling the rubber down. My heartbeat is like thunder now, but I can't untangle the threads of fear and arousal long enough to decide which wins. I squirm against his hold, and the thing is, I've been with a few guys by now. I've been with the sweet ones and the rough ones. The clumsy ones and the experienced ones. Generally, I'm down to try every flavor.

Absolutely nothing has made me as wet as I am right this second.

A moment later, fingers dig into my hip, lifting me up, and he enters me fast and hard, the sound of our flesh coming together a deafening slap.

It strikes me then what that tight, dark shadow on his face reminds me of.

Like someone who wants to hurt me.

I close my eyes and let him.

Afterwards, when we're pulling our clothes, he looks different again. Relaxed, calm. Like everything is normal, totally casual. I try my best to mirror this, taking my cues from the way he moves languorously around his room, pulling on a clean shirt, even though there's a lump wedged in the back of my throat.

He says goodbye with a two-fingered wave, goes back to join the party, and barely looks at me again the rest of the night.

An hour later, I'm back in Campbell's car. It's quiet again. I don't try to make small talk this time, instead staring out the window at the passing streetlights, wondering what this knot is that's taken residence in my chest.

It was just sex.

Truthfully, I don't even really mind that he blew me off after. That's what guys do. If they want some more, then they'll start being nice again, paying me attention. I'm used to it. Probably better off anyway, because boyfriends are just drama and a long stretch of same-same boring.

It was just... not the kind of sex I'm used to. Hot, but also cold. It felt good, but also hurt. It was nice, but also mean. Savage. Scary. Heston's a strong guy—a lot stronger than me. Being at his mercy like that—being hurt like that—should have been repulsive and terrifying, and in some ways, it was.

Mostly, it was the best sex I've ever had.

My cheeks burn with shame, because I might be young, and maybe I've only slept with a few guys, but I'm pretty sure that's not what sex is supposed to be—even casual hookups at parties with older guys. I already hear whisper behind my back at school, that I'm easy. What would people say if they knew that I liked… that?

From beside me, Campbell lets out this long sigh. "Are you, like… okay, or whatever?"

I turn to her, blinking in surprise. "Yeah."

"Heston didn't do anything to you, did he?" Her gaze slides over to me. "Something you didn't want? You're not drunk or stoned?"

"I'm not drunk," I assure her. I had a beer, but it was gross and I ended up ditching it halfway through. "And Heston didn't…" I swallow, feeling a moment of panic that maybe she knows. Maybe she's looking at me like that because she's perfectly aware that I'm some kind of sexual freak. Meekly, I finish, "Everything's fine."

Everything's *fine*.

*

"Damn," Emory Hall says, leaning over Ansel's shoulder. They're sitting at their little lunch table, looking at Ansel's phone. I walk by, wedged between trying to catch Heston's eye and pretending like I don't care if he looks at me at all. It's been a month since the party, and although he hasn't outright rejected me, he also doesn't seem like he wants to come back for more.

In any case, I certainly never got an invite to sit at the table or any of the perks the Playthings get. I'd nearly talked myself into believing it'd been his 'test', but if it had been, then I must have passed.

I *must* have.

"God, he's just drilling her," Carlton says, holding up his own phone. Hamilton glances over and then away with a bored look. Xavier sits with his arm around Skylar Adams—*that's new*—who wrinkles her nose in distaste.

"Are those even real?" Ansel asks. "They're huge."

My eyes skim the room and see that almost everyone has their phone out. The reactions vary—wide-eyed, amused, impressed. I make my way over to a table with the other freshman girls that I know from soccer. Every one of them have their phones out, eyes glued to the screen.

"What's everyone looking at?" I ask, sliding into my seat and placing my tray on the table.

"You've got to see this," Amanda says.

Betsy frowns and puts her phone face down on the table. "This video that just went viral. It's... gross."

"Oh god, is it another video of some guy squirting milk from his nose?" I dig in my bag for my phone and see that I have a dozen notifications—maybe more. People are sharing the video like wildfire. I open up my phone, going to my ChattySnap account. The video is in the top ten spots. I click on one, and although it takes my brain a second to adjust to what I'm seeing, my body reacts differently, going fiery hot and ice cold, all at once. I know instantly, a ball of nausea building when I process what's happening on the screen.

It's a girl face down on the bed, a strong naked guy pounding into her while he holds her down. Neither of their faces are visible. Her hair covers her features, and he manages to stay just off screen. Bile runs up the back of my throat and I swallow it back.

The girl is me.

"Who—who is that?" I ask, pretending to narrow my eyes.

"No clue. Not even sure if it's from Preston. It just started popping up all over today." Amanda peers over at my phone. "Can you see anything identifiable? Like something that would tell whose room that is?"

I've spent all month trying to forget about hooking up with Heston. How off it was. How *bad* it felt afterward, when I was sore and spent, and wishing pathetically for one soft touch. How it was too hard, and too fast, and how despite all that, I've been alternately relieved and confusingly disappointed that he's not like those other guys who wanted to come back for more.

Looking at the video, small pieces click into place. The way he preened toward the laptop. How he kept me down and my face covered. How we didn't speak, how I *couldn't* speak with his fingers around my throat. How, when it was over, he wouldn't make eye contact. No, that's not right. His eyes were dark and emotionless. Cold.

Speculation flows around me, while all I can do is stare at the video, looking for anything that would identify it as me. Thank god my hair looks more brown than red. How long will it be before everyone finds out that it's me? That I let him do that to me? That I *liked* it? I finally shut it off, eyes stinging and every inch of my skin feeling the warm heat of guilt and humiliation. The rest of the table is still obsessed, eyes glued to their phones. I glance over at the table of Devils, and Heston's all grins, looking smug and proud.

For the first time in weeks, he meets my eyes.

And winks.